SEEKING OUR HUMANITY

PART II

OTHER BOOKS
Presented by Claudia Helt

Seeking Our Humanity
2020

The Answer in Action
2020

The Answer Illuminated
2019

The Answer
2018

The Time When Time No Longer Matters
...Continues...
2018

The Time When Time No Longer Matters
2016

The Book of Ages
2016

Messages From Within:
A Time for Hope
2011

Messages From The Light:
Inspirational Guidance for
Light Workers, Healers, and
Spiritual Seekers
2008

SEEKING OUR HUMANITY

PART II

CLAUDIA HELT

BALBOA.PRESS
A DIVISION OF HAY HOUSE

Balboa Press books may be ordered through booksellers or by contacting:

Balboa Press
A Division of Hay House
1663 Liberty Drive
Bloomington, IN 47403
www.balboapress.com
1 (877) 407-4847

Because of the dynamic nature of the Internet, any web addresses or links contained in this book may have changed since publication and may no longer be valid. The views expressed in this work are solely those of the author and do not necessarily reflect the views of the publisher, and the publisher hereby disclaims any responsibility for them.

The author of this book does not dispense medical advice or prescribe the use of any technique as a form of treatment for physical, emotional, or medical problems without the advice of a physician, either directly or indirectly. The intent of the author is only to offer information of a general nature to help you in your quest for emotional and spiritual well-being. In the event you use any of the information in this book for yourself, which is your constitutional right, the author and the publisher assume no responsibility for your actions.

Any people depicted in stock imagery provided by Getty Images are models, and such images are being used for illustrative purposes only. Certain stock imagery © Getty Images.

Print information available on the last page.

ISBN: 978-1-9822-4889-5 (sc)
ISBN: 978-1-9822-4890-1 (e)

Library of Congress Control Number: 2020910237

Balboa Press rev. date: 06/08/2020

INTRODUCTION

Greetings, Dear Reader! It is good to be in your presence once again. So gratifying it is to see that you have continued with your desire to assist the planet Earth. She awaits your help, and she is most grateful for those, like yourself, who are willing to assist her in a manner that may be new to your usual way of assisting another who is in need.

Although many people who live upon this remarkable Life Being are already familiar with the simple and profound techniques of sharing energy with another, many more are needed to assist a Being as large as this magnificent planet. She requires attention from the masses, not just a few. And her needs are urgent!

In *Seeking Our Humanity*, the truth about Earth's dilemma is spoken more forcefully than in *The Answer* series. Speaking the truth was necessary. Although the message is not easy to hear, the reality of Earth's declining health must be faced. There is no easy way to deliver such disturbing news, but living in denial is not an option. We have the means to restore Earth back to full health, and this is the part of the message we must focus upon. THERE IS REASON FOR HOPE! We cannot allow ourselves to fall into despair, which leads us to a state of hopelessness and paralysis. Action is needed and it is needed now.

Seeking Our Humanity offers a dual path that assists our wonderful planet and also facilitates the recovery of our humanity. As we learned in the first book of this trilogy, our negative energy, meaning yours and mine, and everyone else's on the planet, is the primary cause of the Earth's decline. We are already acutely aware of the impact of our wasteful ways—our pollution, our pillaging of her natural resources, our production of items created solely for our own convenience without regard for her health, and on and on. The list is lengthy. And now, we learn that all these careless, thoughtless deeds are not even the worst of her problems. We learn that our unkindness, our meanness and cruelty to self and others profoundly affect her health. She feels every insult, every abuse that we think or physically perpetrate because she is ever-present for every one of these mean-spirited actions. Our ill manners have been called out, Dear Reader. We each have a role in her decline, and we each have a responsibility to help her. And this can be done!

Every person on the planet regardless of age, sex, status, location, or presumed busyness can effectively aid in her recovery by offering her a few minutes of time every day. The solution is so easy, and yet so challenging. We need to become nicer, kinder, better people! Is that too much to ask of anyone? If your answer is slow in coming, then you might want to spend some time with yourself and ask why you wouldn't want to take steps to become a better person. This is in your best interest! And the ramifications of everyone participating in this self-improvement process will assist the Earth. If we change our ways, if we heal our ill behavior, our wounded hearts, then she will heal as well.

Dear Friend, we owe this to the Earth and to ourselves. The truth, spoken truthfully, is this: we do not have a choice. For the Earth to recover, we must change our ways!

WELCOME HOME!

As you can see, Dear Reader, we have taken the liberty to break tradition. Although this next step of introducing the sequel to *Seeking Our Humanity* will address numerous tasks, its most significant one is the act of welcoming you home. Oh, Dear Reader, Dear Friend, you have arrived at the right place at the right time, and now is the time to remember who you are.

Welcome to the reality that you are here now because you choose to be. You came into this lifetime with a purpose and numerous goals that you aspired to achieve. This is true for all the readers of this book; you are in very good company! Imagine this, please. At some time, in another setting, you and many others gathered together for the purpose of deliberation. You came with special interests in mind and heart, and you also came with an understanding that your next life experience would be one of service to you, to others, and to a Life Being who was in great need of assistance. This situation is actually not new to you or to the others who joined you in that discussion, because the truth is: all of you have participated in similar life experiences for many, many lifetimes. Of course, the times, the places, the roles, and the interactions with these other companions were different from your present experience; however, what is similar with all these experiences is the mutually shared effort by all participants to offer aid and assistance to a cherished member of the Universe. We speak, of course, of the Life Being Earth. Her current, precarious situation has not transpired over night. Other members of the Universe were aware of her decline far longer than those who reside upon the planet. Attempts were made to assist her throughout many generations of the human species, but alas, these efforts were not successful, and her health worsened as the population dramatically increased.

Our appeals for assistance on her behalf have thus far had little impact. So we now come forward to speak the truth truthfully, even though we are aware that doing so may create more disruption among the peoples of Earth. The issue of climate change is a relevant example of providing information to a populace who is not inclined to accept the truth even when scientific evidence is provided. The proof that so many demand to see is available, yet it is disregarded as if it is of no value. The truth, the facts that are provided, from which responsible actions could be made, seem to be perceived according to personal inclinations and preferences. Those who are open to factual evidence are inclined to take responsible and necessary action. Those who do not value substantiated evidence choose to cause delays and disruptions that result in the continued diminishment of Earth's fragile health. Dear Reader, this can no longer be an acceptable approach to the Earth's crisis. Those who refuse to help the Earth will make our efforts harder, but we must come to her aid regardless of our numbers. For every person that resists, another will persist, and as the Earth regains her vibrancy those who see the difference in her state of wellness will join the cause. Remember, Dear Friend, human behavior is the primary reason for the Earth's ill health. As we address our ill will, she will become healthier. As we become kinder and more compassionate with one another, she will be relieved of the stressful ramifications of our hostile and embittered behavior.

What we must understand and accept is the power of our goodness. So long have we dwelled in our own unwellness that we have forgotten how powerful we truly are. The joy that resides within us can change lives. Our goodness has the power to bring life to one who is depleted of hope and energy to live. We are gifted with the ability to help others in ways that we are yet to understand, but our truth lies within us. We need not look far to find that which will bring peace, good will, and health to the planet and to ourselves. We can save the Earth from her current crisis, and we can do so from the comfort of our own homes. Wherever you are, no matter what your situation is, you can help the Earth with the amazing powerful energy that resides within you. This is real, Dear Reader. Indeed, our story is presented in fictional format, but the premise of this series of books is not fiction. The Earth is in severe crisis. This is a truth that must be faced. And we have the means to heal her. That is also a truth and it must be accepted, because we are running out of time.

Dear Reader, regardless of your present situation, please offer a moment of your time every day to help the Earth. A thought, a word, an act of kindness, and/or a transfusion of energy are all within your means to offer her. So little is required of us, and yet, so much have we to give.

Please take the next step, now! Read *Seeking Out Humanity, Part II* and learn about your natural gifts and what you can achieve with these gifts. Turn the page, my Dear Old Friend! You are here for a reason! The time is now!

1

"Good Morning, Dear Friend! Have I called too early?" And the day began as usual. Early morning phone calls were the norm for these two old friends. They were both early risers, each with her own particular morning ritual that started the day in a fashion that was well suited for the lifestyle that each preferred. Their friendship, founded in shared interests and curiosity, created a level of trust between them that developed into a sense of family. They often referred to each other as Sisters, and over time came to regard each other as such. Barb, the younger of the two respected her older Sister for countless reasons and often reached out to her for comfort and for verification of her own thoughts and ideas. She believed wholeheartedly that her Sister was a person of wisdom, and was always amazed when this Sister of hers expressed similar sentiments toward her. Their relationship grew from an initial meeting where they immediately felt that they had known each other before, to a point of deep heartfelt trust that their first encounter did indeed happen for a reason. The bond between them is solid, supportive, and uplifting. And these early morning discussions serve as nourishment for the heart and soul as well as fuel for the day.

"You've called at precisely the right time and I am most delighted to hear your voice. Tell me everything!"

"No! You tell me everything! It is your time to go first!" Barb was determined, but she also knew that her Sister was an avid listener. It was definitely one of her callings in life. She was truly an exceptional listener; nonetheless, she wished her Sister would go first, just once.

"You called, Dear One, so there must be something on your mind. Out with it!" My voice was firm, but playful. I imagined Barbara shaking her head, as if once again she had lost the battle of who goes first. This playful bantering was as much a part of our relationship as was the tender care that we provided each other. We joked about the sibling rivalry that we often acted out, and agreed it was evidence of another lifetime.

"Well, you're right as always! I was the one that initiated the call, and yes, I do have something on my mind." She paused briefly and took a deep breath, which was her way to approach most topics that she felt strongly about. "Sister, when are we going to have another meeting? I know we just had one a few days ago, but it feels like it is time for another. Of course, this may just be me, but I doubt it. I suspect our friends are ready to convene as well." Her enthusiasm and her sincerity were evident. Barb was a force of nature: hardworking and eager, combined with a sense of urgency about completing whatever task she was currently addressing. Her latest project included our dearest friends, and it was an adventure that had all of us contemplating our respective purposes in this lifetime. I sensed that she was having doubts about her need for another meeting, so I jumped in to offer reassurance.

"Barb, I agree with you. And I appreciate you expressing your concerns about this. I too am ready for another meeting, but for many reasons, I have been reluctant to make the move. So, you see, Dear One, we are, once again, in alignment. Let's initiate another meeting with our friends, and at the meeting, we will bring this topic up for a bit of discussion. Again, I agree with you that our friends are probably having similar deliberations. For clarity's sake, it would be wise for all of us to discuss these urges and discern how we want to handle them for future gatherings." Barb offered to call everyone and extend the invitation. Long distance hugs were exchanged, and we each began the second phase of our day.

Since Barb's call had preempted my usual contemplative time, I returned to my favorite setting in the house, and of course, to the preferred chair. There, everything I needed for my morning meditation awaited me. The other favorite items that are dear to my heart rested nearby on the center table dividing the two matching chairs. The journal, the fountain pen, and the Tibetan bowl were all situated conveniently, just in case they were needed. And, of course, the Tibetan bell with its mysterious, welcoming sound was always needed. How I love the invitation offered through that elongated resonance of sound! A smile came to my face when a memory flitted through my mind. I can still remember hearing the deep transformational ringing of a magnificent gong that I discovered in an antique store many years before. At the time, I was just opening my heart to this anomaly called a spiritual journey, and in my lust to know everything, I felt compelled to acquire anything that might enhance and expedite my experience. The aged gong was large, and it was expensive, and oh, how I wanted it! I turned away from it numerous times as I tried to focus on other unneeded items in the store, but the gong continued to command my attention. In my eagerness to explore this mysterious journey that I had embarked upon, I felt certain that the beautiful instrument had crossed my path for a reason. Its sound was stellar! Never had I experienced such a glorious resonance. But it was very costly. Eventually, I left the store empty handed with the understanding that if I returned a week later, and if it was still there, then surely the gong and I were meant to be together.

I obsessed about the gong for days, reliving its magical reverberation in my head over and over again. I fantasized where it would be placed in my home and how it would echo throughout the entire house and reveled in the joy it would bring. I imagined hearing it from the kitchen, from my office, and from my sacred space, and in each setting, the invitation for connection and healing called to me. Fortunately, at some point during the week of longing, sanity returned. It occurred to me finally, that my entire week had been consumed by rumination over this wonderful, delightful, and intriguing instrument. I was lost in its beauty, and totally irrational.

"Ah, Dear Friend! You were charmed by the otherworldly sound of the ancient instrument!" The comment came from seemingly out of nowhere and was not accompanied with a visible form. What once was a shocking experience, now was one that was very comfortable, and welcomed.

"Hello, Dear Friend! I am so glad you are here. I've been missing your company!" Pointing to the matching chair, I invited my invisible friend to join me. Presuming that he had accepted the invitation, I proceeded to address the empty chair. "I assume you are here for a reason, but before you apprise me of your mission, will you please tell me how you are. Tell me everything, Old Friend." Part of me was shocked by my brazen manner, and another part of me was delighted to see how our relationship had grown. At some level, I trusted that the invisible friend would also find comfort in the exchange. My assumption was confirmed when he materialized with a huge smile on his face.

"I too am most pleased with our renewed friendship. Often have we had similar interactions and to see this developing in this present relationship is indeed gratifying. My Friend, your reminiscence regarding the much-wanted gong tickles me. Obviously, you did not choose to

bring the item of obsession into your home. What brought you to that conclusion?"

My thoughts took me back to the moment of clarity. I laughed out loud. Just as I had done at the time when good sense finally returned to me during that week of lusting and fantasizing. Embarrassment briefly overwhelmed me, but it was a sweet story that I was comfortable sharing. "Well, I finally realized how foolish I was being. In each fantasy I had about listening to the gong, I had envisioned myself in various rooms in the house: from this favorite chair, or at the dining room table, or on the living room sofa. As I imagined enjoying the beauty of its sound from these different locations, I realized that I would never actually be able to have these experiences unless I hired someone to attend the gong for me. I amused myself with silly thoughts about striking the gong and then rushing back to another room to listen to it, but that just didn't seem to be a peaceful beginning to a meditative moment. Fortunately, I let go of that idea, and now, I am deeply grateful for my small, but powerful Tibetan bowl. Its rich, deep resonance brings me great comfort and satisfaction. So that's my silly story, Old Friend. Now, you must tell me yours."

"I share your passion for the ancient instrument. Its history is complicated, but the sound still speaks to those who are willing to listen. My Friend, I come on a mission as you already detected. But I will begin by saying that those who accompany me are extremely hopeful. The peoples of Earth are beginning to awaken to the reality of their situation. This is very good news and we must continue to apprise them of the truth about the Earth's declining health so that they respond with haste.

We are pleased with your initiation of another meeting. We will, of course, be present with your permission, and if I may, I would like to facilitate the gathering. Does this meet with your approval?"

"Of course! Your presence is essential to the progress of these meetings, Old Friend. Is there anything I can do in preparation for the meeting? How may I be of assistance?"

"I require your presence as much as you believe you require mine. We are all essential to this project. We are here to assist the peoples of Earth; however, we can achieve nothing without your participation. My Friend, do not make me more than I am. Like you, I am one who has lived upon this planet many times before. Like you, I am one of the many Children of the Earth. And like you, I do not wish to see her in her present state of

ill health. She suffers, Dear Friend. This cannot continue! She needs our assistance now.

What I require of you, my Friend, is your willingness to serve. Because you take this situation seriously, others do as well. Because you speak out, others are opening their hearts to do the same, and because you are devoted to the Earth, others feel the fire within themselves. Your presence models for them what they are capable of doing. You do not realize the importance of your presence, but your commitment is affecting others, and this is what is needed. My Friend, we must all persevere in whatever ways that we can, and this you already do.

Fortunately, the assistance that the peoples of Earth can provide requires very little of them. The solution to Earth's problems lies within every person on the planet. It costs nothing. It requires a minimum amount of their time, and the power that resides with them is capable of restoring the Earth back to a state of full vibrancy. The acts of generosity are so easy to provide. Willingness and concern for another are the only qualities that are needed. This is not too much to ask of anyone.

So, my Friend, be present. Speak the truth. And persevere! This is what I need of you at our next meeting. You also have a unique quality, my Friend, that is essential to the work that lies ahead. You are Listener! You do not appreciate the importance of this skill, but listen to me. Few have the ability that you have. You listen with the ears of your heart. This ability connects you with the heart and soul of the one that you are listening to, and because of this you can reach people at their core level. This too will facilitate the next meeting and all events that follow.

We must reach out, heart to heart, in order to make our plea heard. This must be done. We cannot fail the Earth. The consequences of her demise are unimaginable." The Friend of Old fell into silence as we confronted the reality of what might come to pass. I could feel his pain, and it was so deeply unpleasant that I almost broke into tears.

"My Friend, I will help in whatever way that I can, and others will join us. You began our conversation with reassurances of hope. Remember, what you said. People are awakening to the Earth's needs. There is reason for hope." His response was immediate. How he managed to pull himself out of the depths of misery that he was in astounded me. But he did it! I noted the experience in the recesses of my mind for future conversations with this remarkable fellow. His ability to feel great pain, and then suddenly return to the present, was remarkable. It was a lesson to be learned.

"My Friend, I appreciate your assistance. You pulled me away from my heartfelt concerns for the planet Earth. I do not regret my moment of grief. I desire to feel all feelings fully, but I rarely allow myself to overstay in the company of misery. It is a place to visit not to dwell. Rather than focusing upon what you believe was a skillful act of removing myself from an unpleasant setting, instead, please understand and accept that reality is sometimes difficult to abide. Nevertheless, one must engage with such truths to fully appreciate the magnitude of their power. The memory of what was felt remains within me, but I choose to have this memory serve as a reason to strive harder on the Earth's behalf. I know the Earth can recover from her current health issues. I know this to be true and I choose to make this truth my reality. I choose to be hopeful. I choose to persevere. I choose to focus all my intentions upon healing the Earth. This is a deliberate process by which I choose to live. It has served me well, and it can also serve you well, my Friend."

Thoughts swirled about in my mind, as is often the case when you encounter a powerful message, but nothing needed to be immediately discussed. The Friend from parts unknown had spoken a truth that settled deeply within me. I nodded in agreement and hoped my mind had recorded every word that was spoken.

"Do not worry, my Friend. You will remember what is intended. I will take my leave of you now, and look forward to seeing you again at the gathering. In peace be, Dear Friend." I wished him safe travels as he disappeared before me. A deep breath was necessary.

I wonder if I will ever get accustomed to this! My unspoken thoughts did not expect a response but when none came, a smile crossed my face. *I know you're listening! In peace be, my Friend!*

Barbara sat quietly, while her thoughts went in many different directions. Topic after topic raced by attempting to grab her attention, but she wasn't interested. Underlying all the activty of her mind was a sense of urgency. She knew the Earth needed help, and she wanted to do something significant for her. She thought about an energy transfusion, but then questioned the validity of such an endeavor. *Does this really help the Earth? How can we know for sure?*

"*Old Friend, must you have proof before you will offer the Earth a particle of your Source energy?*" The arrival of the invisible Friend took her by surprise, and his question was even more surprising.

"Welcome, my Friend!" Barb was sitting at her coffee nook and offered him the seat across from her. They had never convened in this area of the house before. She naturally felt compelled to offer him a cup of coffee or tea or part of her pastry, but knew these usual acts of hospitality would be for naught. "Thank you for stopping by! Your timing is noteworthy. I apologize for my lapse into doubting behavior and I appreciate your challenge. It is a good reminder." Looking towards the empty chair, she wondered if he had seated himself. Presuming that he had, she playfully asked him to state his business. This brought about a quick response. He appeared, as was his way, and placed his elbows upon her table. Then he leaned forward, stared deeply into her eyes and declared, "*I am here for a reason!*"

They both burst into laughter at the same time. "Of course, you are! You wouldn't just materialize for nothing!" The giggles continued and then Barb turned serious. "Okay, my Friend, I appreciate the humor, but now, let's get down to business. You are here for a reason and I am here to say, 'Count me in!'" More chuckles were shared before the guest took the lead.

"*It is good to be in your presence once again, Friend Barbara. And yes, I am indeed here for a reason, and your assistance will be deeply appreciated. I have just visited with the one you refer to as Sister, and she is prepared to assist as well. My Friend, at our next meeting, all of you will be asked to take another step forward in assisting the Earth. Each will be required to seek within for greater awareness of the gifts that you will contribute to this long-term involvement with helping the Earth. This self-discovery experience will naturally bring forward other matters that will require our attention. Just as you were challenged by doubts just now, so too will others have issues that must be managed. You are one who is especially skillful at listening deeply and finding just the right words to offer support and encouragement. You are capable of enacting inspirational moments that lift others to greater heights. This is as it is, and it is a remarkable gift of which you must become more aware. You take this side of you for granted, because you are unaware of the power of your words, but now is the time that you must be more realistic about your influence upon others and you must use this gift masterfully. Old Friend, I acquaint you with this truth about yourself now so that you have time to contemplate your reality. Do not fear this truth for it is a truth founded in your lovely nature, and it is a gift that must be honored and monitored. Presently, you are stunned when you announce a message of importance, and you wonder where the words came from: the point being, that you are pleased with these moments, but you do not give them the credence they deserve. Old Friend, your gift is large and it must be used wisely. Ponder this, please, before our next gathering. You will find that acknowledgment of your gift will anchor it into your very being and you will then have more command over the inspirational moments that are yours to define. My Friend, your gift will assist you to assist others, including me, and I am most eager to bear witness to your evolutionary expansion."*

Barb tried to grasp everything that was being said, but she felt lost in the moment. Her guest waited quietly. He understood her apprehension, but also knew her strength, and he trusted she would achieve the task of incorporating her true self into her present self. She remained speechless for a moment longer and then finally responded.

"Thank you for your patience and your trust. At the moment I am not certain that I deserve your trust, but the fact that you have offered it pleases me. And it gives me confidence to move forward. I truly hope that I can find this true self that you're talking about." Barb's response to her Old Friend's unspoken thoughts was evidence of her true self shining through, but she wasn't aware of that yet. She was still stunned by their interaction, but also honored by it; and that she was able to address.

"My Friend, I am deeply grateful for your visit today, and I definitely will be available to assist you in whatever ways I can. You have given me much to think about, and you have totally distracted me from my doubts. So I have benefitted in many ways by this interaction. I look forward to seeing you at the gathering."

"And I, you, Dear Friend. Just remember, you are more than you appear to be. And with that thought, I bid you adieu. In peace be, Dear Friend." In typical fashion, he disappeared as quickly as he had appeared.

She remained silent as she stared at the remaining bite of her apple cinnamon pastry. Rarely was Barb stunned into silence, but on this occasion it was the appropriate response. With a deep sigh, she rose from her chair, and retreated into her designated Sacred Space. It was time to meditate.

"Old Friend, your assessment is accurate. These Children of the Earth are indeed prepared to assist us in our endeavors to rescue the Earth from her present precarious state. They are noteworthy in their commitments and sincere in their desires to be of assistance. We are very grateful for your work, Old Friend. The task has been accomplished."

"I have done very little, my Friends. These Children, our descendants, were ready to hear our message about the Earth's health issues, and they are now ready to take action. They are aware of the misinformation that has been provided by those who are not concerned about the planet's well being. And they also know that others are taking steps to improve their relationship with the Earth. The conflict of interest among those who wish to save the Earth and those who blatantly disregard her is mounting. The masses must make their wishes known. They cannot rely upon leaders whose personal interests lie in sabotaging efforts that are essential for her recovery.

These Old Friends will spread the truth to others, and the truth will spread across all lands. We have succeeded, my Friends, because our Children are ready to stand for their planet. And we have also been successful in reassuring them that they are not alone. Soon our efforts will unite all the residents of Earth, and as One, they will take the necessary steps to save the Earth."

2

"**B**arb, thank you for calling. I'm sure this will not come as a surprise to you, but Stephen and I were just talking about this topic earlier this morning. We are both eager about spending more time with all of you and were debating whether or not it was appropriate for us to initiate another meeting. So, your call takes that decision-making process off of our To Do List." Jill paused briefly and then posed the question for which she really wanted an answer. "Barb, would it have been okay if we had initiated another meeting? We know we are newcomers and we don't want to overstep any unknown boundaries, but for future reference, we would like to know more about group protocols."

"Actually, Jill, I'm not sure our group has any protocols. This morning I went through a similar deliberation before calling Sister about another meeting. She, of course, was in the same frame of mind, and we agreed that we should give some time to this topic at the next meeting. I think it's safe to presume that when one of us is ready for a meeting, the rest of us are probably having the same inclination. We definitely are psychically linked. None of us can really explain this unusual connection that we all have, but we're having fun with it and will hopefully gain more clarity about it at some point. I think you and Stephen fit in quite nicely, don't you?"

"Yes, we both felt very comfortable at the meeting. And yes, we embrace the mystery of unusual connections. We look forward to exploring that with the group as well." Goodbyes were exchanged before the call came to end. Jill immediately rose from her chair and went in search for her husband. She found him on the back porch, mulling over three separate stacks of papers.

"Excuse me, Stephen. May I join you for a minute?" Her appearance took him by surprise, but he was also delighted to see his adorable wife.

"Hey there! I didn't hear you coming. Ah! You are bare-footed! That explains the silent approach." They exchanged a tender good morning kiss before he invited Jill to sit down. This was not the first kiss of the day, but the Carsons were of a mind that kisses should be enjoyed at all times in all places. "So, what are you up to, dear?" he asked as she situated herself in the chair nearest his.

"Well, I'm sure you will enjoy hearing this, since we both so adore coincidences." As she smiled in his direction, his right eyebrow reached upward towards his hairline.

"Coincidence?" he responded.

"Yes, dear! Barb just called to invite us to another meeting! I thought you might be amused by that!" The couple giggled with delight.

"Well, I guess we know how to handle our desires with this group in the future. If we want another meeting, all we have to do is think about it. And they will pick up the message! Amazing!

These people really are telepathically inclined. This is great! When are we meeting?"

"Tonight!" she answered expectantly. "You are available, aren't you?" Her face expressed disappointment when he responded hesitantly.

"Jill, I have a phone call scheduled. But let me give this fellow a ring and see if we can reschedule. I definitely want to attend the meeting." Her spirits lifted when she heard that her husband would try to clear his slate. He quickly texted his client, and within an instant, the appointment was rearranged.

"Yay!" she exclaimed. The two best friends exchanged a high five and then giggled about the so-called coincidence that had brought this gathering together. "This coincidence is about as valid as our first meeting." The thought was mutually relived and more giggles were enjoyed.

"What a story that is!" declared Stephen. "We literally ran into one another, while bicycling across campus." Each was rushing to get to the next class, and in one of those rare moments, they both looked in opposite directions at the same time, and crash. The next moment found them lying on the ground entangled with their respective bikes. At first, each was indignant about the incident and then their eyes met. The aggrieved disposition quickly disappeared and the rest is history. The class was skipped, the afternoon was spent in deep conversation, and the two were fast friends from that moment forward. Neither one believed the collision was a coincidence when it happened and they don't to this day. Life changed when they met each other, and for that particular coincidence, they have been forever grateful.

"Isn't it wonderful how our lives have been guided by coincidences?" mused Jill. Stephen nodded in agreement.

"Me thinks we're off on another grand adventure, dear!" His Scottish accent was lacking, but enjoyed nonetheless.

"I cannot wait to see where this takes us!" Jill's response was filled with anticipation.

As Ron and Carolyn Barkley ended their last lap around the small community lake, they were determined to take action. Their conversation around the lake targeted numerous items on their To Do List, but the one most focused upon was their desire to have another meeting with the group that they joined just the week before. Little did they know that other members of the group were having similar ideas. The couple, as always, had purposefully left their cellphones in the car, because they didn't want their quality time to be disturbed. Their morning walks were dear to them, and years before, they decided to make them a private affair.

"Ron, as soon as we get back to the car, I will give Annie a call and see how she feels about us broaching the topic of another meeting. I seem to remember someone mentioning that they were gathering regularly. Hopefully, we won't appear pushy or forward by our actions."

"I suspect they will be delighted, Carolyn. These folks are on a mission! I think they will be very excited about our interest in another meeting." Once they were in the car with seatbelts buckled, Carolyn captured the phone from underneath her seat.

"Oh, this is interesting," she declared. "There's a message from Barb. Let me put it on speakerphone so we can both hear it." Needless to say Barb's message was happily received. She quickly responded and accepted the invitation.

"Do you believe that?" Her question required no answer, but Ron's excitement could not be curtailed.

"Of course, I believe it, and so do you! These people are energized and they are committed to helping the Earth. This is exactly what we've been looking for, Carolyn. We've found a group of folks who are of like mind and who are ready to take action. No coincidence, Dear Heart!"

The two old friends chattered a bit before leaving the lakeside, and then each went silent on the drive home.

The Barkleys were nature lovers. In their younger years, their travels were all about hiking and camping. Even now, they still needed to be outdoors as much as possible. Their walks were shorter and less strenuous now, and they avoided rugged terrain, but the lust to be with Mother Nature was still as strong as it ever was.

Carolyn and Ron's first so-called mutual coincidence brought them together over fifty years ago. After graduating from colleges that were based on opposite sides of the country, they each signed up for a hiking adventure, through different agencies, that just happened to be centered at the same campsite at the same time. As you may have already guessed, the pair literally crossed paths on the trails, fell in love, and truly lived happily ever after.

Over the years, the couple became increasingly troubled by the lack of respect afforded this wonderful planet. At first no one seemed to share their concerns, but later, more and more folks began to speak out about the blatant mistreatment of the Earth. But the complaints didn't seem to effect any change, and in truth, the situation worsened. Decades of more abuse and neglect were witnessed and still little interest could be generated on Earth's behalf. In the last decade, the Barkleys' concern turned to fear. They believed the Earth's survival was in jeopardy. Evidence of her declining health was everywhere. The media were filled with scientific reports verifying what they had been worrying about for years. And still, people ignored the issue. Then misinformation became predominant. Truths were distorted. Scientific evidence was scoffed at, and people who were trying to bring the truth forward were shamed and humiliated for their efforts.

Like many others, Carolyn and Ron felt hopeless and helpless about the Earth's situation. They wanted to help, but did not know where to turn. While they were comfortable in their retirement, they were not wealthy by any means, and they simply didn't know how to effectively help the planet. They managed their waste products according to official guidelines, and created more of their own. They turned off lights that were unnecessary, used their car limitedly, refrained from buying products in plastics containers, and they planted trees. They wished they could do without a car, but for safety's sake, they were afraid to let go of it. They walked as much as they could, buying groceries, doing errands, but sometimes, the car seemed like a necessity. And they hoped some day to have solar panels on their house, but the chances that they could ever afford that were unlikely. The truth is: the Barkleys, like so many others, simply didn't know how else to help Mother Earth.

"Carolyn, I think these folks are on to something really important. I was so impressed with them last week. Obviously, I didn't understand everything that they were talking about, but I am optimistic. I want more information. There has to be something more that we can do for the Earth, and I think these folks are going to show us the way. I'm really excited about this evening's gathering."

"Me too, Ron! Meeting these people wasn't a coincidence. We were all brought together for a reason, and I am so grateful we were on the guest list. We're going to save the Earth, Ron!"

3

"Jim, Annie, please come in. So good to see you again." Mark graciously welcomed their friends into their home. The three dear friends exchanged hugs before proceeding down the hallway to the combined kitchen, dining, and living room. There at the stove, they found Faye attending a quiche. Sunlight filled the large open space.

"Oh my goodness!" declared Annie. "This room always takes my breath away."

"It's just like being outdoors," Faye remarked as she turned to greet her guests. "We love sharing this space with our friends, and we are so happy to see you. Thank you for coming, even though our reason for gathering was overridden by Barb's phone call."

"Isn't that a stitch? We should have known that everyone would be thinking the same thing at the same time." Annie's comment created a stir. Jim expressed his amazement about the synchronicity of the communication, while Mark marveled about the increased regularity of these telepathic communiques.

"You don't think this is just a coincidence, do you, Mark?" Jim's questions started another round of comments, beginning with Annie.

"Now, Jimmy, you know we do not believe in coincidences!"

"Yes, Dear, I do know that, but this is one of those times when circumstances beg one to wonder. We are all very committed to this project, and it makes sense that we would want to come together to talk about things." Before Annie could add another thought, Faye shared her thoughts.

"I wonder about this as well, Jim, but I still believe that we are unwittingly connecting with one another. Even though we do not have scientific proof about this, we certainly are witnessing increased frequency in these unusual experiences. Perhaps we should be more diligent in pursuing proof, but how would we go about that? Obviously, this morning we were all in our respective homes when Barb's call came through. We had no way of knowing what another was thinking. We were not in close proximity. I guess we could say it was just dumb luck, but that seems disrespectful of our burgeoning abilities." Mark remained quiet while others voiced their opinions. He shared the same doubts as his friends, and just like his friends, he didn't believe in coincidences. Finally, Annie turned in Mark's direction and urged him to express his opinion.

"Well, Annie, I'm relatively certain you already know what I'm thinking. That intuitive spirit of yours is a primary reason that we all believe in existential communication. To say nothing of the fact that we have an Existential Being in our lives who also validates our belief in this form of communication. So, I'm here to remind all of you that our doubts naturally come to the surface occasionally, but the truth is, none of us believes in coincidences."

"Well said!" declared Annie and Jim simultaneously. This brought about a few chuckles, which were interrupted by the oven alarm.

"Ah, lunch is ready!" declared Faye. "Mark, lead our friends to the table as I fetch the quiche from the oven. We can continue our talk over lunch." Everyone followed directions and soon the four friends were comfortably seated about the table. The Moores always arranged the table in such a way that everyone had a view of the back yard. It was a serene setting that invited intimate conversations.

Faye began with a short blessing that honored their lengthy friendships and also celebrated the Earth. It was a sweet, but powerful prayer. With just a few sentences, she successfully acknowledged the Earth for her care of and devotion to all the beings who resided upon and within her. Hands tightened around the table before everyone concluded with a robust Amen.

Then the focus turned to the exceptional lunch. Aromas were inhaled, yummy sounds were made, and plates were filled almost instantaneously. One moment the plates were empty; the next moment, they were filled. And then the first bite was taken!

"Oh my goodness! This is delicious," declared Annie. Jim agreed and added his own account of the culinary experience.

"Great combo, Faye! Quiche, asparagus, and fruit salad. You did good, girl!"

Mark gently laid his hand on Faye's and gave her a quick wink. "This is delicious, Dear. Thank you for clearing out the refrigerator!" His comment caught the Andersons' attention.

"Oh, don't mind him. He's just revealing my secret to making a good quiche. Every so often, leftovers accumulate in the fridge and the best way to make use of them is to toss them into a bowl of eggs and a quiche is birthed. One can never repeat the recipe, because it is always changing. But so far, the results have always been worth the effort." Small talk and food related commentary continued for a few minutes before Mark led the conversation to a more relevant topic.

"My Friends, I have a question for all of you. Apparently, everyone in our group was ready for another group meeting. And it seems that the energy created by our desire to reunite resulted in action being taken. That in itself is a significant event, but my focus lies elsewhere. What was going on for each of you, when you realized that you were ready for another gathering? Are you aware of what you were feeling and thinking at the time?" Mark's question brought a pause to the table. Eyes gazed out toward the back yard as if they were looking for an answer, but Mark's question led his friends inward.

"Those are good questions, Mark. I assume you've been working on this already." Jim smiled at his friend, while he continued to sort through his thoughts. "I must admit my thoughts are a bit muddled, but if memory serves me, I felt a sense of urgency. I wanted to do something for the Earth right then, in the moment. And for some reason, which I still don't understand, I felt it needed to happen with the group. As I talk about this, it seems strange to me that I didn't rely upon my own abilities to help her. And maybe, that is exactly what I'm supposed to learn from this, Mark. I didn't trust myself to be able to help her on my own. I felt like the group had to gather or my efforts really wouldn't be adequate, or good enough.

Geez! This is an important point to realize about myself. Until now, I don't think I was aware of these thoughts of inadequacy. I really believe what our invisible Friend has shared with us, and I trust him. He told us that we all have the ability to help the Earth. He has repeatedly said this to us. And I bought the message! I believed it! And I still believe it! But at some level, there must be a part of me that really doubts my ability to be successful at this task. Friends, this is difficult for me to hear, and it's more difficult to admit it to all of you. Wow! I really feel as if I've flunked this 'Save the Earth' class.

Guys, I'm okay, but I need some time to think about this. I need to be quiet now. Please continue. I promise I'll pay attention."

Annie leaned over to touch her beloved's hand. She whispered softly, "Good work, Jimmy! You've led us down an important path." He acknowledged her support with a gentle nod.

"Jim, I really must thank you for your comments," Faye sighed. "You took me to the place I need to be. When Mark and I started talking about initiating another meeting, I was uncertain about my own needs. I felt antsy, but couldn't really identify the cause of my unrest. I wondered if I was feeling lonely, but that didn't resonate. I carry all of you in my heart, so I am not inclined to loneliness. Mother Earth was certainly on my mind. I wanted to help, but I didn't pause to send her energy. I think I wanted to meet with everyone because I didn't feel comfortable initiating connection with the Earth on my own. This is so strange! Like you, Jim, I believe in this process. I believe we have the innate ability as we've been told, and I believe that each of us is capable of assisting her by ourselves. In fact, I believe it is necessary. And still, I've been remiss. Yes," Faye announced adamantly, "I wanted to rejoin with the group so that we would do something for her. This is really shocking. My reluctance to reach out to the Earth by myself stuns me.

Jim, thank you! This is very important information that has surfaced, and because of you, I am here in the middle of it, and I can't run away from it. You've saved me hours, if not days of work. Thank you so much."

"Well, Jim, I want to thank you too. My questions were selfish. I was searching for an answer and you brought it home," Mark's comment caught Jim's attention.

"I thought you had the answer," Jim responded. "Your questions grabbed me and took me to this deep place of sorrow. Sorrow for the Earth, sorrow for myself, and now sorrow for all of us. What is wrong with us? We are powerful people. More than that, we are Beings with healing powers. As our Friend has repeatedly told us, we have the ability to heal the Earth, so why aren't we stepping up? What is holding us back?"

"We are holding us back, Dear. We are powerful Beings, and we are also humans who are just adjusting to our newfound abilities. It is only natural that we would experiences doubts about ourselves and about these remarkable abilities. Fortunately, we also have each other! Look how quickly we discerned what is going on with us. We know that we are being remiss in attending the Earth. We know that we are prone to have doubts about our abilities. And we know we must rely upon each other to maintain our strength of character and to fulfill our commitments to the Earth. We were holding ourselves back. But that is no longer an option for us. We now know more about ourselves, and our needs. We have the ability to heal the Earth, and we need the support of friends to carry this mission forward. I think it is fair to say that we had an important reason for gathering today."

"I agree with you, Annie. You know, we could have cancelled this lunch after we heard from Barbara, but we didn't. For some reason, we all felt the need to come together, and now, we know why." Mark took a deep breath, before continuing, and his friends joined him. "This lesson was an important one, and we must share it with the group. We also must bolster one another to carry out our commitments to the Earth. Friends, we've just learned that we all have been remiss in giving time and energy to the Earth. We committed to do this! And we must follow through. I encourage all of us to think about this before tonight's meeting. We need a plan, because our present one isn't working."

"Well done, Mark!" Faye's compliment came with a request. "Dear, will you lead us in an energy session? Your comments were so energized and inspirational that it makes me believe you are prepared to lead us in an energy infusion." Mark observed himself. And he witnessed the twinge of fear rising upon within, and then, he made a choice.

"My Friends, for a brief moment, fear attempted to squelch me. I recognized the old feeling that has silenced me countless times before. But I will not allow that to happen this time. It may sneak up on me again at another time, but not now. My Friends, we must stand together, or better said for this moment, we must sit together. Here in this lovely setting, let us hold hands, and take several deep breaths. Each of us knows how best to achieve this calming, relaxing change of pace. We do this for ourselves, and we do it for the Earth. Take several more deep breaths, my Friends, and align yourself with the pulse of the Earth. It will naturally transpire. Your breath will merge with hers and together we will become One.

Dear Mother as we prepare ourselves to send you energy, we ask your permission to do so. We assume you will allow us to offer you the gift of Source Energy from our hearts to your heart.

Within each of us resides the powerful healing energy with which all are gifted. We are grateful for this remarkable gift and we ask for assistance in sharing this powerful healing energy with the Life Being

Earth. Friends, feel the energy welling up within you and see this energy exiting from your heart space and joining in the center of this table. And now, witness our combined energies moving out to our back yard. It hovers there briefly and then the energy releases into the Earth. Please accept this energy, Old Friend, and know that it is accompanied with our love. We are so deeply grateful for everything you do for all of us. And we commit to you that we will hold you in our hearts and offer you energy every day until you no longer are in need. Thank you, Dear Friend, and in peace be!" Deep breaths were heard around the table as everyone accepted that the gift was delivered. Time passed as everyone recovered from the energy transfusion. The task was done, and the unrest that was felt before the meeting began was at peace.

"My, oh my! Mark, that was a wonderful experience. Thank you for accepting and commanding that leadership role." Annie's compliments soothed his soul.

4

"**B**arb, you're here! Thank you so much for coming early. I am running a bit behind."

"Not to worry, Sister. We are taskmasters!" Her reply didn't surprise me. We quickly exchanged hugs and then headed in different directions. I returned to the kitchen to put the finishing touches on several trays of goodies, while Barb tackled the living room. Within minutes, she had rearranged the furniture to accommodate our guests and was scurrying down the hallway to help me in the kitchen.

"Wow! Great job, Sister! The trays are abundant and beautifully arranged. Can I place them on the table for you?" Although, Barb's comments were appreciated, the trays were not complete.

"Actually, I need a bit more time with the trays. Can you fill the water pitcher instead? The glasses are already on the table." Barb was a wonderful friend. She had the energy of a teenager and was always eager to lend a helping hand. As she managed the beverages, I added a few necessary sprigs of parsley to each tray. Parsley was an obsession of mine. I was convinced that a food tray wasn't complete until it was adorned with the aromatic herb. For one who had very limited interest in the culinary arts, I found myself ridiculously adamant about the role of fresh parsley when entertaining. Once the revered sprigs were perfectly placed on the trays, I was done with my kitchen obligations. As Barbara delivered the trays to the dining room, I quickly spruced up the countertops and made a quick tour of the house to reassure myself it was ready for guests.

"Not to worry, Sister, the house looks great." I shook my head in amazement.

"Barb, are you aware how often you are responding to my unspoken thoughts?" My question caught her by surprise.

"Geez! Did I just do it again?"

"Yes, you did." Barb's look was one of disbelief. "Dear One, I'm not scolding you. Please don't misunderstand me. I'm really astonished by your abilities, and I suspect you don't realize how often you are actually responding to people's thoughts. You certainly do it with me on a regular basis now, and you also do it in the group. Are you aware of this?"

"No! I'm not. It seems my exceptional hearing is becoming more exceptional. Sister, you're bringing this up for a reason. I can tell you are worried about me. Please tell me what your concerns are?" Before I could answer her question, the doorbell rang. Our guests had arrived. Before opening the door, I reassured my friend that my concerns were not of a negative nature. We agreed to finish the conversation at another time.

"Welcome, everyone! Please come in!" Hugs were already underway on the front porch and continued as each person entered the house. This lovely gesture of connection held great meaning for our group. I marveled at our blessings. How fortunate we were to have one another!

As we all moved towards the circle of chairs, Annie grabbed me by the arm and whispered in my ear. "You're right, dear! We truly are blessed to have one another. Someone must be watching over us." Her comment was so sweet and endearing that I almost didn't notice what had happened. Like my Dear Friend, Barbara, Annie had just responded to my unspoken thoughts. I wondered how many times this subtle, yet unusual act was happening without my notice.

Chatter continued about the room as we situated ourselves into our favorite chairs. It was obvious that everyone was delighted to be together again. As we settled in for the evening, I realized that no agenda had been made for the meeting. When our special guest requested to facilitate the meeting, I let go of that responsibility. Now, I wondered if I had been remiss, but before my mind had a chance to start worrying, our guest arrived.

"*May I join you, my Friends?*" As always, his arrival was a sight to behold. First, the gasps were heard, followed by joyful amazement. "*Peace and blessings to you all! I am most grateful to be in your presence once again. Thank you for coming!*

My Friends, there is much for us to discuss this evening, and with your permission, I will take the lead. Today is a day of new beginnings. It is a day of renewed commitments and expansion of our intentions." His words electrified his audience. Each heard his message in his or her uniquely personal way, and each understood that once again, they had been called to service.

"*Today, each one of you faced a reality that was a shock to your sense of self. You experienced what we have experienced for millennia. The commitments all of you made to assist the Earth were made with sincerity. The need to help her pulsates within you. The desire to take action calls to you and causes great unrest. You know that you are intended to assist her, and still, you are compromised by an annoying, inexplicable reluctance to act. My Friends, the Earth needs help now. She cannot wait while you stumble through your personal doubts. Please, Dear Friends, you must confront your uncertainties and conquer your fears, and we must do this tonight."*

As one might imagine, all of us remained perfectly still as our guest from unknown origins called us to task. His demeanor was that of a revered teacher. He spoke a truth that none of us could deny, and he did so in a manner that was calm, yet compelling. Our challenge was to listen to the message without allowing our judging nature to twist his intentions. As our teacher sat quietly, our minds, each in their own way, raced about attempting to manage this call to action.

"My Friend, once again you have brought a truth to our attention that must indeed be addressed. Personally, my mind is working very hard trying to take charge of what it perceives as a 'situation' that must be managed, and I do not want that to happen. I prefer my heart to be the leader of this self-exploration expedition. That is what you are asking us to do, is it not? You want us to explore the underlying motives for our inaction."

Our teacher, nodding his head in agreement gently replied, *"Yes, you have summarized my intentions accurately. And you have a suggestion to offer, do you not?"*

"Yes, I do." Pausing briefly to collect my thoughts, I found myself instinctively taking a deep breath. "My dear friends, how wonderful it is to be together again. As usual, our Friend here has challenged us to improve ourselves. He's good about that! I think we have all come to expect this from him. With his help, we have grown, and he is presenting us with another opportunity tonight to do so again." I looked around the room trying to make eye contact with each of my friends. "As he said, I do have a suggestion to make, but now as I broach this topic, I realize that my suggestion is actually a request for a favor. Dear Ones, as our teacher challenged us to explore our commitments more fully, I realized that my mind immediately felt the need to take command, and truthfully, I do not want to enter into this exploration process under its leadership. I want to move forward from my tender heart—that's where my strength lies, and I believe that is true for all of you as well. So, I wish to ask a favor of you, Dear Friends. Let's begin this self-improvement project from our strongest and best position. Let's begin by participating in an act of kindness that will inspire us to reach for our greatest good. Will you join me in an energy session for the Earth?" The idea delighted my friends and our teacher. Everyone immediately responded by repositioning themselves in their chairs. Their reaction inspired me to open my heart to this opportunity. *Dear Friends of Old, please provide me with the words and the wisdom to facilitate this session to the best of my ability.* Sweetly and lovingly, numerous 'Amens' were voiced in response to my silent prayer. The gesture soothed my heart and emboldened my spirits.

"Make yourselves ready, my Friends. Take the necessary deep breaths that aid you in your process of centering. Seek the deep, quiet space that invites you into the mysteries of our existence. Travel safely my Friends, and know that you are not alone." Pauses came automatically without my attention, and each group member benefitted from the silence. More deep breaths were taken as the company of friends moved deeper and deeper into their personal sacred sanctuary.

"Mother Earth, we come on your behalf. And we request permission to send particles of our Source energy to you. We gather now and prepare ourselves for the transfer of energy. Please, accept our Gift." More deep breaths were taken. The anticipation of assisting this wonderful Life Being energized us. Such a privilege it is to meld our energies with hers. The gift of giving benefits all involved.

"My Friends, intensify your efforts. With each deep breath that you take, feel the power of your Source energy rising within you. Experience this expansion within you and know that it is real. This is not an imaginary action. It is an act of Divine Kindness flowing through you to the Beloved Mother Earth. Prepare yourselves, my Friends. With our next deep breath, allow your healing energy to exit your body, just one tiny particle of your Source energy is all that is required. Allow that powerful particle to flow from you to the center of our circle and allow our energies to merge together. There, these particles of healing energies become even more powerful. Let them blend for a moment, and as they do, let us express gratitude for the opportunity to be of service. We are most fortunate." Another pause was appropriately provided.

"And now, my Friends, let us envision our combined energies rising above us and exiting though the ceiling of this house, and let us propel this mass of energy forward to the school yard located just a few blocks away. See the ball of energy hovering above the playground. And with our next deep breath, bear witness to the energy merging with Mother Earth. Feel her gratitude as the Source energy enters into her body. Feel her gratitude, and share yours with her." Time passed as we experienced this exchange of energy. No explanations were needed. All who participated understood that the process was real and that the act of kindness was gratefully received.

"Dear Ones, when you are ready, please return to our Circle of Friends. Return to your respective bodies and rest, knowing that you have assisted the Life Being Earth in her recovery process. Breathe deeply, Dear Friends, and be in peace."

At some point, people began to stir. Limbs were stretched, deep breaths were enjoyed, and new positions were taken.

"That was lovely," sighed Faye. "I am in a completely different place now, and I'm ready to tackle our self-improvement project." Numerous comments confirmed Faye's position. The act of generosity had served many purposes. The Earth was infused with healing energy, and the group members were also energized, centered, and strengthened to face the task that their teacher had proposed.

"Sister, that was a brilliant suggestion and such a tender energy session," Barb spoke softly. "My anxiety was rising before, and similar to you, my mind, without my permission, was responding to our Friend's challenge by taking control of the alleged situation. So quickly it reacts to what it perceives as an affront. And even though I didn't agree with my mind's assessment of the so-called affront, the mind is a force of nature with which to deal. Sister, your suggestion to do the energy session quickly brought me back into focus. I am now in a great place to proceed with our task. Thank you so much!"

"Indeed, Old Friend, your leadership is founded in wisdom. By focusing everyone's attention upon an act of kindness, the mind's protective instinct was abated. You served well, my Friend, as did all of you. I hope you were able to sense the Earth's gratefulness. She was humbled by your generosity and sustained by your efforts. Your goodness takes you to new places. My Friends, you are most impressive."

"Thank you for your kind words, Old Friend. Thanks to you all. May I take another moment for a teaching opportunity?" My friends reacted positively, so I continued. "As I said earlier, my suggestion to do an energy session was actually a request. I needed to get away from the antics of my mind, and I also needed to feel helpful. The Earth has been on my mind and in my heart for days. I ache to be of assistance, and yet, the ache doesn't lead me to action. And, Dear Friend, when you challenged us about our reluctance to help her, I felt myself slipping into a place I did not want to visit. So, I decided to reach out to all of you via the energy session. The minute I thought of doing this, doubts rushed forward. I chastised myself for presuming that you were having similar feelings. I questioned my motives. Was I trying to distract myself from revisiting the commitments that I had made to the Earth? Did I really believe that we had the ability to heal?

Was this invisible man, whom we consider to be a revered teacher really real? And on, an on, and on! But then, a truth flashed before me that I could not doubt! I remembered our relationships! And I trusted that you would stand with me regardless of my moments of insanity. That reality strengthened me to move forward with the energy session.

I want all of you to know about my process so that you may benefit from it and/or provide me with feedback for future reference. And please be truthful with me. I'm so grateful for your companionship in this endeavor to save the Earth, and I trust all of you with my unsightly vulnerabilities." Our teacher listened quietly. I assumed my participation was in alignment with his desires for the meeting, and then, as my mind so often does, it questioned my assumption. I chose not to be bothered by its behavior.

"I must commend you, Dear," stated Sally Moore. "Your openheartedness serves as a guide for all of us. Sharing one's vulnerabilities is not easy, but you meet the challenge with grace and dignity. I'm grateful you are willing to speak so candidly about your doubting mind. This helps me to understand my own process, which can be tedious at times. I also wish to make a suggestion, Dear. Trust your assumptions! I suspect what you are identifying as assumptions are actually intuitions." She paused purposefully to allow me a moment to ponder the message. You are remarkably gifted! I think you are already aware of that, but I'm not sure you understand the breadth of your intuitive capabilities. I strongly urge you to open your heart to your full potential. You are so much more than you presently allow yourself to believe. You are a Gift, and I am pleased to be in your company." Sally's message was breathtaking. To say that you could have heard a pin drop would be an accurate description of the moment. Everyone in the room recognized a special moment had just transpired, and each person was captured by the mesmerizing incident.

Tears welled up in my eyes. I was overwhelmed by Sally's acknowledgement and grateful for her act of kindness. Her willingness to deliver this powerful message was another example of role modeling. There are times in one's life when you know, without knowing how you know it, that you witnessed an act that was greater than the ones involved. I knew the message was a Divine Gift. It was humbling to receive such a message. A whisper of gratitude was all that I could manage.

Dave Moore quietly entered the conversation. "Take a big breath, Sister! And allow that message to really sink in." Then he turned to the other members of the group, and spoke from his heart. "Sally and I are very grateful to be part of your group. When you called this morning, Barb, we were both so relieved. We were sitting on the steps of our deck when you called, trying to decide if it was appropriate to initiate a meeting." His smile embraced everyone. "We didn't want to be pushy, but we really felt compelled to be with all of you. I can see now that we were all operating from the same intuitive inclination. We needed to come together and I am so glad we did. We've only been together for short amount of time and look what has already happened. We've sent energy to the Earth. We're facing our issues. And we just witnessed an unusual, but potent message being delivered by one member of the group to another member of the group. I can't wait to see where the evening takes us.

Sister, thank you for opening your lovely home to us, and also for leading us in that energy session. You do that really well. Your guided imagery takes one to another place without interfering with the individual's process. Practicing this in the group inspires me to do it on my own. So thank you for that and also for sharing your struggles with your doubting mind. And most importantly, thank you for trusting us." Dave's gentleness was refreshing...calming. He and Sally were wonderful contributors to the group.

"Your comment regarding the group's intuitive inclination towards another session was accurate, Dave. Indeed, all of you felt pulled to come together for a variety of reasons. At the time, you presumed it was an individual reaction, but now you realize that the feeling was a mutually

shared desire. My Friends, you are here for a mutually shared purpose, and the desire that burns within one, also burns within all of you. Long ago commitments were made to assist the Life Being Earth. Even though you do not remember that initial commitment, the essence of it still resides within you, and it is accurate to say that it calls to you. From deep within, the awareness that you are here for a reason reaches out to you, reminding you of a task that you desperately wish to fulfill. This occurs, Dear Friends, and your recent experience demonstrates that reality for you. This wish, this desire, this need to fulfill a mission of intention made long ago becomes the ache that compels you to seek your reason for being.

My Friends, you are not unique in having this unusual, yet natural experience, but you are unique in that all of you have come to the realization of your mission's purpose at a similar point in time. This is not a coincidence, but it is a delight to awaken to an awareness and know that you are accompanied in the task that lies before you. So often this does not come to fruition. We must count our blessings for this remarkable convergence of energy. Because you are here together in union, you know that you are not alone in your mission to save the Earth. Because I am here with you, I know that I am not alone in my efforts to aid this wonderful Life Being. And hopefully, because of my presence, you also know that your company of assistants is far more expansive than you previously imagined. We are not alone, my Dear Friends. Let us be grateful for this precious awareness, and let us strive to remind others, so they may enjoy the truth of this reality as well.

My Friends, we are here together for a reason of extreme importance. The Life Being Earth must also be reminded that she is not alone. Each time we offer her assistance, she recognizes that she is loved, and this is remarkably important for her healing process. She requires healing energy, and she requires the loving care of other members of her Existential Family. You are the nearest Family members she has, and as such, your role is paramount in her recovery. Just as you would visit an ailing friend or family member while he or she is hospitalized, you must also attend the Earth in like manner. To know that one is loved is a most soothing awareness that can sustain one during a prolonged crisis situation. The Earth is made of the same essence as all others, and she, like all others, needs to know that someone cares about her. My Friends, you have no idea how helpful your presence is to her. Please let her know how much you care. Please do not hesitate. Do not wait for the company of your Dear Friends.

Take action frequently, daily, and then, in those glorious moments when you are together, combine your energies and extend that mass of healing energy to her." Our Friend paused and breathed heavily. His love of the Earth overwhelmed him. We were all able to feel his sorrow and the experience was informative. So connected was he to this marvelous Life Being! Images of events and places over countless life times filled our cognitive pathways. The connection was intense, intimate, and divinely beautiful. Such love he shared with Mother Earth; such sweet beauty! She was, is, and always will be a Friend of Old. His heart was full, and because we bore witness to his experiences, our hearts knew more than they had known before. The moment was exquisite.

"Dear Friend, you honor us with your memories, and teach us through your own experiences. We are so grateful for your presence, for your wisdom, and your generosity." Faye's words came from the heart and expressed what we all felt. "You are not alone, Dear Friend. And thank you for reminding us that we are not alone either. You have confirmed for us that we are in the Company of many others." Faye reached for the sky when she made this comment. "Even though we cannot see those Companions, or remember them, they do exist. That is so comforting. I've always believed there was More, but I didn't know how to describe that sense of knowing. But now, I feel comfortable not having to explain it. I don't need to. I simply know there is More.

My goodness, you have changed my life!" Faye's voice weakened and she responded with a deep breath. "I am so grateful that you came to us. Please help us to grow, and show us how to help you with this mission to save the Earth."

Our teacher, our Dear Friend, appeared to be revitalized by Faye's comments. His resilience was remarkable. He felt emotions deeply and he was able to recover from those experiences very quickly, or at least it seemed that way for those of us who had very little time with him.

"Old Friend, how do you manage to return so quickly from your emotional voyages?" Barb's question was more than mere curiosity. She admired his ability to feel fully and recover rapidly. It was a skill that she wanted to learn.

"Your question is one of merit and it has numerous facets. The first entails a choice that was made long ago. I chose to trust myself." Our teacher looked about the room to see our reactions before continuing. *"Like you, my Friends, I have lived many lifetimes and many of those*

experiences were restricted by my fears. Unfortunately few people recognize how fearful they actually are. Nor do they understand how limiting life is when fear is their guide.

Eventually, I realized most of my fears were based in misunderstandings. The lesson was not learned easily or quickly. Because of my fears, I avoided situations that actually held the answer to my erroneous ideas. Because I believed I could not handle intense emotions, I avoided them. Because I feared that I could not handle relationships, those too were avoided. No matter what the fear was, I avoided any opportunities that might prove my fears were accurate. Sadly, in my efforts to avoid what I believed was the truth, I actually delayed the opportunity to discover the real truth—the truth that is relevant to all. Dear Ones, we are all capable of experiencing our emotions. And when we do so, we discover that our emotions are not something that should be feared, but in truth, they are our strength and that which assists us in living life fully. When I finally came to realize this, I decided to trust myself. My decision was not perfectly executed, but over time, I learned that trusting myself was one of the most important decisions ever made throughout all of my lifetimes."

"Goodness!" whispered Annie Anderson.

"Indeed!" responded her husband, Jim.

"My Friend, you are an extraordinary teacher!" My compliment was heartfelt and sincere, and other group members offered similar sentiments as well. Our teacher was moved by the responses. When the comments drew to an end, I continued with my thoughts. "Because you generously shared your experiences with us, we now know more about you, and about eternal life, and about our own current vulnerabilities. Obviously, I have many questions, but now is not the time. Your story brings us back to the topic of our reluctance to individually reach out to assist the Earth. We are actually talking about our fears, aren't we? We've used 'safe words' to discuss our behaviors. We described ourselves as being 'reluctant' to take action, and being 'hesitant' to act on our own. Those are words that skirt the real issue, aren't they? In truth, we are 'afraid' to take action on her behalf."

"Yes, my Friend! Your assessment is accurate. Perhaps, it is time, Dear Friends, for you to address your commitments to assist the Earth from this newly gained perspective." His invitation brought about an immediate reaction.

"I find this absolutely fascinating," initiated Mark Goodman. "It never occurred to me that fear was the reason behind my resistance to connecting with the Earth. This gives me pause. My mind is racing about creating all kinds of suppositions and what ifs about this idea. Obviously, I don't enjoy thinking about the Earth's declining health. It's deeply painful, and sad, and depressing. And those emotions are not ones that I'm inclined to embrace. This is such a surprise to me! All kinds of emotions are surfacing as we speak about this. I'm really going to need to do a lot of soul searching about this. Sorry if I'm rambling, but it's hard for me to articulate everything that's going on inside of me." Mark turned to face our teacher, "And I want you to know that I'm grateful you sneaked this lesson into our conversation. I had no idea how successfully I've avoided my fears throughout my life. This is a life-changing experience for me. Thank you!"

"I agree," added Stephen and Jill simultaneously. Jill pointed to her husband and encouraged him to continue. He accepted the invitation.

"This is a revelation for me, and that is not a word I use lightly. I am stunned how our culture...no, I do not want to talk in generalities. I am stunned by this new awareness. I had no idea how much I personally avoid my fears, by articulating my thoughts with words that disguise the truth from myself. What an incredible cover up! I've been deceiving myself for decades." Stephen's look of disbelief was appreciated. Jill quickly tagged on to her husband's comments.

"Stephen, you're right, this truly is a revelation that we must study carefully. This is a remarkable growth opportunity, and one of the things that we all must remember is to approach this new information carefully and lovingly. From this point forward, we must practice having compassion for ourselves. We've just learned something new. So, good for us! We recognize that we have something new to assimilate into the libraries of our minds, and we are not going to scold ourselves for not having learned this in the past. Agreed?" Her question demanded a response and she immediately received one.

"Agreed!" declared the Circle of Friends.

"Wonderful advice, Jill," declared Annie. "I must admit this is indeed a new perspective for me to wrestle with, but it's exciting. I wonder how often avoidance vernacular is used when addressing other emotions. We are an interesting species," she mused. "How, where, and when did these fears originate?"

"Indeed, you are a wonderful species! A species with great potential that is intended to continue. My friends, fears have interfered with the evolutionary development of the human species, but this does not have to be the way of your future. Openheartedness and trust are the guides that you seek, not fear and misconceptions from the past. You have a choice, Dear Ones. Because you have come to an important realization this evening, you have a choice to change your future. You can choose to continue as you now live, in awareness that fear is an underlying force in your interaction with the world, and more information about this approach to life would be gained. However, in your brief introduction to the idea of being led by your fears, each of you has learned that this is a life pattern that is very limiting. Please ask yourself, why would you choose to continue a path that impedes your evolutionary progress?

My Dear Friends, this is question that each of you must discern. No one can make this decision for you. Having expressed that reality to you, I am also going to express another reality that must be taken under consideration. The present course that humans are pursuing is not in their best interests. As you have learned this evening, your desire to assist the Earth has not culminated in the dedicated action that is necessary to save her. Inaction will not result in the miraculous cure of her declining health. For the Earth to recover, she requires assistance now from those who reside upon her and also from those who have loved and cherished her for all eternity. Her needs are great!

The people, who call this planet Home, are the ones who have to respond to her crisis. The human species is responsible for her ill health and they are the ones who must rectify this error. As all of you now know, the ability to heal the Earth lies within you. You have the means and the power to save this remarkable Life Being. This is a truth that each of you knows and believes. And still, fears and doubts successfully derail your good intentions. My Friends, there no longer is time for more delays. Action must be taken on her behalf, and it must be done now, and tomorrow, and every day that follows until she reaches a point of complete recovery.

This is the reality that you must face.

I cannot believe, my Dear Old Friends, that you will choose to walk the path that your predecessors walked. You are wiser and more fully informed than they were. Please, my Friends, choose to face your fears, and take the next step. Rise early every day with the Earth in your heart, and send her energy before any other thought or task distracts you from this essential act of kindness. You are aware of the importance of this act of generosity. Why would you not make it a priority? For the sake of the Earth, for the sake of your own kind, please make this simple task the first priority of your day. So easy is this to do. So little time does it require." The revered teacher paused and inhaled a large breath. His emotions were prevalent, but he did not falter. A pause and a deep breath was enough to refresh him, and then he continued.

"Trust yourselves, my Friends. Such wonderful people you are— loving, tender souls. You are so much more than you allow yourselves to believe. Please access the riches that lie within you and utilize this power to save the Earth. Without her, your species will not survive. This is a reality that must be accepted.

My Friends, I come to you this evening to beg for your assistance. Move forward! Face your fears and move forward. In essence, you have done this all your life. You were not conscious of your actions, and your steps were more tedious than they needed to be, but you progressed forward anyway. Now, you are consciously aware that you have been impeded by your fears. That is helpful information! Because you are now equipped with this profound awareness of your vulnerabilities, you can move ahead more easily and more rapidly.

Accept your fears; do not deny them. Once fears are accepted, they lose their power. Just because you have a moment of doubt, does not mean that you have to succumb to it. When such moments surface, recognize them for what they are, and then take the necessary action anyway. Oh, my Dear Friends, do not delay. Your future existence is dependent upon your willingness to trust yourself. Each of you is ready for this. Each of you is stronger than you imagine, and in truth, each of you is an incredible Being with powers that you are yet to master. Trust yourself! And in so doing, the Earth will continue, and so will the human species." Our teacher's form began to fade. His energy reserves were depleted.

"Old Friend, please take care of yourself. And as you do that, we will send you a particle of our Source energy." I turned to my friends who were already situating themselves into their preferred meditative position. "Dear Ones, we know what to do. Please ready yourselves for another energy transfusion. Remember, only one tiny particle is needed. Our friend has weakened himself on our behalf. His inspirational speech energized us, but it depleted his own resources. Take the necessary deep breaths, Dear Friends, and when you are ready, release your particle of divine energy to our beloved teacher. We are together and we are ready to serve, but allow yourselves to act upon your own guidance. The energy will reach him and restore his own energy back to full vibrancy. My Friends, take the next step. Take action of behalf of our Dear Old Friend." And with that, I joined my friends in silence. With several deep breaths, I prepared by myself to release the powerful particle of Source energy. I did not need to understand the truth about this Source energy. I simply needed to take action and to trust the truth that all in existence is created from this same Source energy. It is what it is. And I chose to trust this truth and to trust my ability to assist this Dear Friend.

Time passed as it always does during these unusual sessions, and as always, closure was detected by the subtle sounds of movement that took place after a successful meditative experience.

"Welcome back, my Friends! I am sufficiently revitalized. Thank you for your assistance."

"You're looking well!" exclaimed Carolyn. "What a transformation!" Applause circled around the room. Everyone was pleased to see this beloved Friend and teacher in typical form. Barb began to laugh when she realized that his unusual form was now commonplace for all of them.

"We've come a long ways since our first visit with you. I remember how weird it was to be talking with someone who wasn't embodied. And now, here we are totally at ease. I'm so glad the energy infusion was helpful."

"Thank you my Friends. I am most grateful for your quick response to my situation. And as you can see, your efforts were successful. What you just witnessed is the impact of your remarkable healing energy. Compound this example by seven billion people and you begin to understand the potential for the Earth's recovery. Please remember what happened here, for it is the proof that your doubting minds wish to have.

My Friends, your immediate response to my failing energy showed no fear, no reluctance, no hesitation. You simply saw someone in need and you took action. Perhaps the Earth's present appearance confuses you. In many ways, she still remains beautiful and vibrant. In your present location, you may not notice the destruction that she incurs or the suffering she endures. You have grown so accustomed to her lands being consumed by industrialization that the changes are no longer exceptional to you. This is indeed a problem. Those who continue to believe that she is doing fine are ill informed. Those who refuse to listen to the truth about her situation are aiding and abetting those who continue to misuse and abuse her natural resources. Proof of her declining health is available. Whether one is living in an area where physical evidence is visibly noticeable or not, does not change the truth about the Earth's decline.

My Friends, the time is now. Face the truth about the Earth's failing health, and take action. Just as you immediately reacted to my situation, you must do the same for the Earth. Make a plan, my Friends, and implement it!

I thank each of you for coming tonight, and I look forward to meeting with you again.

In peace be, Dear Friends." With that said, our friend faded away. His departure seemed abrupt, but his instructions were adamant.

"Whew! What an exit!" Barb's response aroused a few nods and gasps for air. "He certainly is a man with a mission!"

"He's a man with a message, who is becoming more and more desperate." Jill's comment raised eyebrows. "His love for the Earth is undeniable, and his concern for her is so passionate that it is impossible to ignore the appeal. I believe everything he is telling us. And I understand his frustration. The information about the Earth's serious crisis is available, and we still plod along as if it is a hoax." She paused shaking her head in disbelief. "Stephen and I have been tracking the news about the Earth's decline and it is blatantly obvious. We believe this gentleman is speaking the truth, and we are onboard with his request." She turned to husband for reassurance.

"Yes, Dear, we are in agreement," Stephen reinforced his wife's comment. "And his, our teacher's, impassioned plea for help reaches into my core. I'm definitely on board. No more reluctance, no more hesitation. No more allowing doubts to be my guide!"

"Our assignment is clear, folks." I looked about the room to be sure we were all on the same page. "We have been lovingly challenged this evening. We received wonderful compliments for our efforts and we also were informed that our efforts are lacking. I think we all agree with this assessment. We know it is true, and we know it is unacceptable. Our Friend's message was clear!

We must make a plan and implement it!" A deep breath engulfed me and provided time for my friends to also indulge in a similar moment.

"Okay, we know what we need to do. When do we want to meet again to discuss our individual and group plans?"

"Tomorrow!" The simultaneous reply delighted everyone.

"Great! Same time, same place!" I announced. The group seemed energized and determined. As everyone began to pack up and exchange goodbyes, Annie interrupted the process with another announcement.

"Folks, before we leave, I want to address a couple of items. First, tomorrow is a new day and a new beginning. Each of us must individually attend the Earth. Are we in agreement about that?" Again, another simultaneous response echoed through the room. "Awesome! That's the kind of teamwork we want to have going into this new phase of helping the Earth. I suggest that we hold ourselves accountable by making some type of notation regarding the activity. Time, location, and description of the action taken: just a note, Friends, not a chapter. And of course, try to work in a conjoint session, and make a notation of it as well.

"That's a great idea, Annie! That will help us turn these activities into a daily routine." Annie's orderly fashion for addressing tasks was similar to mine, so I really appreciated her suggestion.

"Now, my second thought is in regard to the generosity of our dear co-hosts. What can we do to help you two?" Barb and I exchanged glances. She took the lead.

"I have a thought! It would be wonderful if the gentlemen of our group would accept responsibility for arranging the furniture before and after our meetings. And beyond that, I would suggest that each household take a turn at providing the goodies. By the way, our meeting has come and gone tonight without a break, so why don't we refrigerate tonight's yummies and serve them tomorrow." Everyone agreed again and the meeting was just about to come to an end, when Sally Moore asked for a closing prayer.

"Sally, that's wonderful idea. Would you like to lead us, dear?"

"I would love to. Let's form a circle and join hands, please. Oh, Dear Friends, how fortunate we are to have each other. Our time together is expansive, passionate, and loving. We can ask for no more than this. Let us be thankful for these blessings! And, Mother Earth, please know that we love you, and we will hold you in our hearts every day from this day forward. In peace be, my Friends." The friends exchanged hugs before tackling the closing chores. Within minutes the house was back to its normal arrangement. I watched my friends as they walked down the street, waving goodbye when they went out of sight. It was another stellar evening.

Although the night was still young, I retreated to my Sacred Space. I needed alone time with my journal.

5

A passage from
Speaking The Truth
(Chapter One)

"And the adventure begins! Now is the moment of relevance! Imagine if you will, suddenly awakening from a very deep sleep and finding yourself in a setting that is unknown to you. Perhaps this setting seems vaguely familiar; perhaps it does not. Perhaps you are shocked by your circumstances; perhaps you are not. Or perhaps, you are one of the many who awakens completely unaware that anything unusual transpired during your unremembered slumber. If the latter situation is your moment of relevance, just sit quietly with it, for you are in very good company."

I sat quietly with my journal turned face down on my lap. Appearances can be deceiving. Externally, I was indeed quiet, but internally, my mind was fitful. There was no discernable reason for my unrest. The meeting had gone well, as always. There was no cause for concern, yet I felt unsettled. I remembered what our wonderful teacher had revealed during the meeting. He said that he had chosen to trust himself. *What a concept! Is this one of those times when I should trust myself? There is no reason for me to feel so out of sorts, and yet, it appears that I am. What is going on?* The question asked within seemed important for me to pursue. It was interesting to observe myself. Part of me was ready to take action and another part of me was reluctant. *This is fascinating. I'm watching myself behave in the manner that was discussed in the meeting.* "I don't know what is happening here," I announced to my empty room, "but it seems important for me to explore this. If I truly want to better myself, then I must trust myself to investigate this odd scenario." For a moment, I wondered if our invisible friend was present, and embarrassment rushed through me. "Oh, for goodness sake. If you're here, I just want you to know that I talk to myself on a regular basis. And," I said elongating the three-letter word as much as possible, "I trust this behavior is not a sign of insanity." Voicing my intentions to trust myself invoked no response from another realm, so I was forced to continue my self-exploratory process on my own. I amusingly noted to myself that part of me was relieved that no one was hovering about; and another part of me was disappointed and striving not to feel rejected.

Turning my journal over, I chose to focus my attention to the matter at hand. At the top of the page, I entered the date and time as usual, and then in large block letters, I printed, "I CHOOSE TO TRUST MYSELF!" And then, the great pause came. *What now?* Eventually, I closed my eyes and hoped for the best. For an unknown amount out of time, I sat quietly, focusing upon my breathing.

The muffled sound of my phone awakened me. I was surprised to see sunlight filling the room. Undoubtedly, I had fallen asleep in my chair, because that was where I found myself. The phone continued to ring. I delved deep into the crack of the chair and found the device. It was Barb, of course. I caught her just in time. "Don't hang up!" My words were spoken with greater volume than intended. "Oh, sorry about that, Barb! You caught me asleep in my chair. I'm bit discombobulated."

"Geez, I'm sorry that I awakened you. This is becoming a habit, friend. What's going on with this new 'sleeping in' routine?"

"Good question, Barb, but I don't know what the answer is. I wanted to do some journaling last night after the meeting, but I wasn't able to settle down. Undoubtedly, I fell asleep at some point. But this is boring; tell me why you're calling. What's up?"

"I just wanted to let you know that I'll be working late this afternoon, so I won't be able to help you set things up for the meeting."

"Not to worry, dear. Everything is ready, remember?" Barb was so accustomed to helping with the meetings that she had forgotten the conversation the night before. She too acknowledged that her night had been restless. We both agreed that we needed to move forward with the day and each promised to check in if it was necessary. I glanced over at the clock and noticed it was unplugged. "Hmm! Guess my sleep was assisted last night."

"Indeed, I took the liberty to extend your time of rest."

"You're up early, old friend. How may I be of service?"

"It is I who come to be of service. My Friend, do you feel refreshed this morning?" His question gave me pause. I had no idea how to answer his simple question. My guest undoubtedly sensed my discomfort and elaborated upon his question. *"You worked late into the night, my Friend. You only had a few hours of rest, which is why I took the liberty of unplugging your alarm clock.*

"I'm surprised!" My response came quickly. His comment was confusing; it made no sense to me. I did not recall working at all. "Obviously, my memory escapes me. All I remember about last night was my frustration with myself. My restless mind interrupted my plans. Fill me in, Friend. What transpired last night?"

"Actually, Old Friend, your desire to engage with your journal last night was fulfilled, and your self-exploration was extensive." Before he could say another word, I grabbed my journal. He was right! Pages and pages were filled, none of which I remembered writing.

How can this be? My thoughts unspoken were heard by my companion.

"Do not concern yourself with this momentary loss of memory, my Friend. You have entered a phase of great expansion, which will enhance more awareness of self and others and more. What is happening is happening for a reason, and you will find this a very exciting and intense time of life. Because of this, you will expend more energy than usual, and this means that you will need more rest to accommodate your period of self-exploration. Old Friend, you are one who attends many matters throughout the day. This is your preferred way of being. You live a full life each day, and now you will be extending an already full day. I ask you to manage this need for additional rest with care. It will require a modification in your present routine, but once adjusted, you will feel more energized than before. This is a wonderful phase, Old Friend. Enjoy it fully!"

"I will definitely try to do so. Your description of what is coming does sound fascinating. And I am excited about the possibilities. However, I am a bit confused about the process. Obviously, last night was very busy, but I do not remember any of it. I hope this isn't the way of the future. How can I benefit from this learning experience, if I do not remember it?"

"*Do not fear, my Friend. When you read your journal entry, the memories will return, and the knowingness that you desire will remain for all times to come. Often you have heard the words, 'Seek within.' Today, I urge you to seek within your journal, and the answers that you desire will be found. My Friend, I must take my leave of you. Live this day and all days to the fullest. In peace be, my Friend.*"

"In peace be. Thank you for coming." Left alone, I sat quietly staring at the journal. My thoughts wandered, then returned to the journal. *What secrets does it hold? When did my life become so odd?*

A passage from
Speaking The Truth
(Chapter One)

"*The time is now! Once again access your imagination… visualize awakening from the previously suggested long deep sleep to find that you remember everything. In this scenario, you rise in awareness of your recent respite, including your travels during the apparent sleep state and the encounters, engagements, and interactions you had. Perhaps your awareness is extensive, facilitating detailed memories of your transitional experiences; or you may be one whose memories of the events seem quite distant, even though your knowing of the transitional journey remains remarkably sound and heartfelt. Although each experience is and always will be uniquely individual, the truth about such experiences remains the truth. Each who comes into existence remains in existence and each who seemingly exits existence remains in existence.*

Having just revealed the first of many truths that will be shared throughout this small literary presentation, we apprise you of yet another truth…the messages that come forward through these pages have been revealed countless times before and will, because of necessity, continue to be shared with all who are in need whenever and wherever the need arises. Consequently, we alert you to another truth already exposed during our brief commentary. The time is now! Now is the moment of relevance."

At first, I scanned the pages trying to convince myself that it was the best way of acquainting myself with these writings, which supposedly were my own. Perhaps there was an element of truth to that notion, or perhaps it was my way avoiding the true essence of the materials. I honestly don't know what my motivation was. But based upon the conversations from the night before, I presumed some presently unknown fear was guiding my actions. So, I took a deep breath and returned to the first page of my last entry. There was the date and the large block letters defining my intentions—I CHOOSE TO TRUST MYSELF! *Okay! I remember doing that!* My words were not spoken aloud. The conversation between me and myself came from within. *But that's all I remember! After that my mind took over, and all I remember was the frustration that was felt with what seemed to be a futile attempt at journaling. But look at this!*

'Each who comes into existence remains in existence and each who seemingly exits existence remains in existence.' I read the beautiful words, clearly written by my hand, and was stunned. And there was more!

A passage from
Speaking The Truth
(Chapter One)

"Throughout all existence, even before time came into existence, the present and all it entails is the moment of relevance."

Pages and pages of what appeared to be ancient wisdom filled my journal. *How can this be? There are no explanations for this amazing experience. I can pose questions about this forever, and probably will, but*

what I am bearing witness to is beyond comprehension. My mind raced about, trying to find answers to this confounding mystery. Its antics were not helpful. Instead I took another deep breath and returned to my headline—I CHOOSE TO TRUST MYSELF!

I spoke aloud, feeling certain that my Companion would hear me. "Old Friend, I cannot pretend to understand how or why this is happening, but I presume it is directly related to the expansion phase that you referred to earlier. You know as well as I do, these beautiful words of wisdom are not my words, but the handwriting is definitely mine. As you can imagine, my questions are abundant, but I believe at this moment in time my purpose is to trust what is happening. The evidence of what is happening lies before me. My journal speaks the truth. Even though my mind wishes to contest this reality, I choose to accept the truth that rests in my hands.

I choose to trust myself! What appears to be odd is also amazingly beautiful, and I will learn to be comfortable with this unusual and remarkably wonderful experience.

Obviously, what has poured through these pages demands considerable attention. It is too much for one sitting. I promise to return to these materials daily. I know they were presented for a reason, and I accept responsibility for their care.

But now, I need to focus upon the Earth. Her health is the moment of relevance. Old Friend, you are welcome to join me if you have a moment to spare."

I took a deep breath, which is my entryway into the meditative state. In my mind's eye, I envisioned our honored teacher and my circle of friends each in their own location joining me in this energy session. I invited all who were within listening ear to participate as well. I spoke as if they were all in my presence, which I believe is true. "My Friends, near and far, our Beloved Friend, the Life Being Earth, is in need of assistance. Be with her now, and offer one of your particles of the original essence of life that exists within all. Just one particle is enough to effect great change. As you prepare yourself for this event, call out to others who are within your range of connection and invite them to participate as well. We invite all who are available to join us at this precious moment to participate in this healing session for our Dear Old Friend. Breathe deeply my Friends, and access the healing energy within you and activate its power. Embolden this powerful energy to assist the Earth. And when you are ready, send your particle of healing energy to the Earth. You choose the location of distribution. Infuse her with your energy and express gratitude for all that she has done. Remind her that she is a Beloved Friend who is cherished by all in Existence." Silence ensued. I felt good about the session and grateful for the opportunity to aid the Earth. I thanked everyone who participated and wished them a beautiful day.

6

A passage from
The Time is Now
(Chapter One)

"When the time had come for All who have been,
to assist All that are,
the people of the Earth will at long last know
who you really are.
We, the residents of the Universe,
have watched over you since your time of beginning,
and still, we watch
with caring eyes and concerned Hearts."

"**G**ood morning, Dear! How is your morning going?" Sally turned around to face her beloved husband when she heard his voice. She had arrived earlier and was already perched on the top step of the stairs that led from the deck down into their back yard sanctuary. They had agreed in the wee hours of the morning to attend to their personal tasks before joining for a mid-morning snack and conversation.

"I'm doing fine," her reply was accompanied by the smile that captured Dave's heart long ago when he first laid eyes on Sally. He fell in love with her immediately. The welcoming smile, along with those sparkly eyes, was all the information he needed to make his decision about their future.

"I've been in deep thought, Dave," she stated casually. "And I also did a lot of writing. You know that always helps me to sort through things." Her husband nodded in agreement. He was aware that writing was Sally's primary means of seeking her soul's companionship. That was a concept that escaped him for many years, but with age and a modicum of maturity, he began to appreciate her process. He still wondered about it at times, and did not pretend to fully understand the depth of its meaning for his dear, sweet wife, but he respected the extraordinary impact it had on her growth process. For Sally, writing was her way of going inward, as she referred to it. She found the exercise both therapeutic and healing.

"Well, tell me more, Dear. What wondrous things have your discovered about yourself?" She almost accepted his invitation, but then pulled back and encouraged Dave to go first.

"I always go first, Dave, and I take up way too much time and then you rarely have enough time to share your activities. So," she declared with presumed authority. "You go first, and then I will follow your lead!" Dave started to reply, but then became hesitant. He felt the feeling washing over him, and instead, chose to stop the downward spiral.

"Well, that's interesting. Our Friend's talk last night has opened my eyes to behaviors that are not serving me. My goodness! Why am I just now learning about this? How long have I been avoiding opportunities because some unknown fear pops up and effectively shuts me down? Sally, why would I be hesitant to accept your invitation to speak first? It doesn't make sense! Do you have any insights about this, Dear?" His best friend took a long deep breath, which caused a reflex action in him. He was glad for the fresh gasp of air. Maybe, it would clear out his fears and help him to understand himself better.

"Dave, I have several thoughts, but they're just that. I don't know how relevant they are." He encouraged her to continue.

"Sweetie, anything you can offer is more than what I'm coming up with, so please share your thoughts."

Sally paused to gather her thoughts and inhaled another long breath. This one was for courage. "Dave, my first thought may not ring true for you, but let me throw it out as a possibility anyway." He nodded his approval. "Your reaction seems similar to people who have performance anxiety. And I'm thinking of a wide range of examples, including experiences when someone is performing in front of a large crowd or giving a presentation to small audience. And it can even happen when someone is sharing a story or a thought with a beloved partner. I think there are times, Dave, when you really want to participate, but your fears surface. They may be fears of failure, or of not being good enough or smart enough. Whatever they are, the fears rise up from within you and basically paralyze you." Sally paused to give Dave time to think about her ideas. He seemed intrigued, but urged her to continue.

"Okay, there is another thought that I had, which may or may not be on target, but here we go. Your reactions are also indicative of someone who may have been teased, or scolded, or shamed when they attempted to speak out in their younger years. Incidents such as these can have long lasting effects. I know this is still an issue for me at times, even though I've done tons of work about it. And," she continued, "I just had another thought. Dave, you are a shy person. Few people know that, because you hide it well. But you were a shy kid, and you're a shy adult. Shy folks often have trouble speaking out. Does any of this ring true, Dave?"

He stared out into the backyard trying to escape the question, but he was determined not to fall victim to his fears again. "I'm just too old for this!" he said disgustedly. "Bear with me, Hon! I'm not going to victimize myself with a lot of negative self-talk, but I do have to admit that I'm frustrated with myself. Dear Heart, everything you suggested rings true. I am a shy guy, and it's been an issue all my life. And, I do not like being the center of attention, and all the examples you provided come from that. My tendency is to freeze up when I'm in situations that put me front and center, so in order to protect myself from the possibility of having an incident, I strategize dozens of ways to alleviate the possibility, which serves only to intensify my anxiety. Sal, I've been filled with fear for decades and never identified it as such." He shook his head in disbelief, and then chose to take action.

"Sally, thank you for those suggestions. They were very helpful. They give me a lot to think about, and I'm up for it. I am not willing to continue being silenced by my own fears. So, first I want to promise you that I intend to continue to work on these issues. I know they are long-term patterns that will demand attention before they finally subside. But in this moment, I want to accept your earlier offer. I know we've been working on my stuff for some time now, but I haven't been leading the conversation. So thank you for getting me to a point where I feel able to take the lead." Sally softly clapped her hands. The small gesture empowered her husband. He began with huge deep breath.

"I am so grateful to you, Dear, and to our wonderful teacher, for awakening me to this vulnerable part of me. I was intrigued last night by the ingenious ways that we developed over time to deceive ourselves about the truth of who we really are. It never occurred to me that I was a fearful person, and now, just look at what I've discovered. This fear began at a very young age. And here I am now, an old codger, who finally realizes his truth! The truth is: knowing this is a lot easier than living in the dark about it. Sal, this feels great! I can actually do something about this now. Before, I was clueless; and it is hard to make changes when you don't know what needs to be changed. Well, I know now. And I'm not going to allow fears to be my guide any longer."

"Yay! We must celebrate your new resolve, Dave! I am so happy for you and very proud, as well. This is good work! Congratulations!" Her husband blushed from the compliments, but also reveled in them.

"How shall we celebrate? What exactly do you have in mind?" Dave's eyes sparkled as brightly as did his beloved's.

A passage from
Speaking The Truth
(Chapter One)

"The time is now! This curious pronouncement is one that has been repeated throughout all ages by more authors than are remembered, and yet; these four words remain as timely and significant to our present moment as when originally articulated.

The time is now! Is it a statement of urgency or simply a declaration of truth, reminding each recipient of the message that the present is the moment of relevance? How you choose to perceive the message is yours to discern. It may indeed be a simple reminder for you to focus upon the present; and if so, it is certainly a message of extreme importance, for many are in need of assistance with this not-so-simple task.

What if this message is simply as suggested—a reminder to focus upon the present? And what if we presume that the present now being referred to is the present directly before you as you read these very words? What if these four words are truly here for a reason and what if these purposeful words were just delivered to you at this point in time so that you might choose to focus your attention upon the significance of the message? The time is now!"

The two old friends decided they would celebrate with a decadent treat...one that included a walk, which was a completely different, but equally enjoyable treat. They paraded to their favorite nearby bakery, selected their favorite pastries, and then headed for their favorite bench situated under their favorite gigantic beech tree. It was a morning of "favorites," as it should be, when one is celebrating a personal achievement. With the first bite taken, they giggled like children who were being secretly naughty. Their yummy sounds echoing through the canopy of the ancient beech attracted the attention of several favorite pigeons. These feathered friends, long acquainted with this lovely couple, joined the celebration. Of course, an additional pastry had been purchased in anticipation of their company. As Dave carefully separated the croissant into small pieces, he returned to their earlier conversation on the deck. "Sally, tell me about your soul-searching this morning. Where did your deep thoughts and your writings take you in the early morning hours?" Her first response was a deep breath, which made her chuckle.

"What would we do without this instinctive reaction? First, it nourishes us with a fresh breath of air, and then, it provides us with a moment to gather our thoughts. Thank goodness for that, because nowadays it seems I need more than just a moment to recall previous thoughts and insights." Sally paused to enjoy another bite of her preferred pastry. Dave waited patiently. He appreciated his wife's reflective approach to conversations. She was not one who spoke hastily.

"I was deeply touched by last night's meeting. It is amazing to be in the presence of someone who is so capable of speaking from the heart. He is a remarkable teacher. Makes one wonder about other lives we've shared together." She turned to Dave, "Do you also have thoughts about past experiences with him? Do you feel as if you have known him forever?"

"Yes, I do. Although, there are no clear memories," he spoke tentatively, "what I experience is a sense of knowing. I know, without knowing how it is known, that we have been friends for a very long time. Let's face it. We just recently encountered this guy, and yet we feel completely comfortable in his presence, as unusual as it is. That kind of heartfelt reaction speaks for itself. I don't understand it, can't explain it, and still, I trust my gut and I trust the present relationship we have with him."

Sally patted her husband's thigh, "Well said, Dear! And I am in agreement with you." Sally paused before returning to the topic. "So, last night, his words about the frailty of the Earth reached in and grabbed me. I was struck by the realization of this awful truth. We've heard it before. His words confirmed what we already believe, but last night, for some reason, I got it! I felt his despair for the Earth, and his fear for the future of humankind. His sincerity cannot be denied. This fellow is here on a mission to the save the Earth. And he is here to save us as well. His understanding of the severity of Earth's situation is far greater than we can comprehend.

Perhaps we are unable to fully grasp the truth, because it is too frightening. I can be with the reality for a moment, but then my mind deflects in another direction. I'm finally coming to understand the denial process that is playing out among our peoples. The reality of Earth's demise is so overwhelming that we cannot remain present with the thought, which renders us incapable of taking action on her behalf.

This essentially is a cognitive malfunction that is operating globally. It explains part of the malaise that our civilization is experiencing. And it correctable! Dave, we do not have to abide by this malfunctioning thought process. And when I speak of we, I'm referring to everyone. The peoples of Earth are bright individuals and we are people of goodness. Our inaction regarding Earth's failing health has not made sense to me, but now I get it. Our fears are disabling us! We are so frightened by the devastating news that we are not capable of hearing the reality that we can help her. So many practical and sustainable ideas are already being incorporated into our daily living habits. We are doing something! But we forget this, because we are repeatedly overwhelmed by the enormity of the situation. The public must be educated to the truth, so they can participate and recognize that their participation matters.

We now know that there is a way of assisting the Earth that takes us to another level of providing aid. Even though some people may find the idea of healing her energetically is questionable, they must be informed about the reality of this approach. The idea of healing through energy assistance is not new to this civilization. People have been practicing these techniques around the world for millennia. Our people need to be informed about these ancient techniques and they need to understand that we are all naturally endowed with the ability to participate in healing activities. People need to have hope!

I honestly believe if people understand that fear is compromising their ability to take action, most people will confront their fears and reclaim their action-oriented ways. We are not a species that is typically stymied by outside interference. We are problem solvers. We are proactive. We are people who take action. Our inaction regarding climate change, our unwillingness to accept scientific evidence, and our willingness to continue executing harmful acts that are clearly detrimental to the Earth's health make no sense. This is so oppositional to who we are as a species. Obviously, there are those who are functioning from their own misguided greed and corruption, who are sabotaging efforts to help the Earth. But those of us who have felt helpless and hopeless have abetted those who are defiling her by doing nothing.

I finally get it, Dave. I understand that we have all been diminished by our fears. This must stop! We are more than a cognitive malfunction. We are more than our fears. We are more than those who lie about the truth of the Earth's condition, while they continue compromising her health. We must take our humanity back. We can save this beautiful planet, and we have the means to do so.

Dave, last night our Friend said that we must choose to trust ourselves. And he's right! We must all face the truth about the Earth, and we must trust that we can help her. That is the answer to her tragic situation. We must trust ourselves to save her."

A passage from
Speaking The Truth
(Chapter One)

"What if you pause just for a moment and actually contemplate the possibility that now is the moment of relevance? Please consider doing this now. If you find that you are resisting this opportunity, ask why?"

"Sally, you take my breath away! Now, don't roll those gorgeous eyes at me. I'm serious, Sal. I just wish our friends were present to hear your inspirational message. Your point is exceptional. It's simple, easily understood, and it will make people want to change. No one is going to be content with being led by a malfunctioning thought process. We are proud people, and we simply won't tolerate it. And as you said, this is correctable, and it will empower folks. Sally, this will motivate folks to change!"

"I think you're right, Dave!" they both took deep breaths and sat in silence for a while. It was a beautiful day with spring colors popping out everywhere. A sight to behold! The pigeons, having enjoyed their goodies, moved on and resumed their roosting positions above, hidden by the branches of the magnificent beech tree. Everything seemed right with the world. But it wasn't. The Earth, in all her spring glory, masked the truth about her pain. Appearances can be deceptive. In this particular area, at this particular time, the Earth showed no signs of ill health. She is a very brave Life Being.

"She's beautiful, isn't she, Sal?" His wife, his best friend, nodded in agreement. "We've got to help her!"

"Yes, we do!" The couple rose from the bench with their napkins, cups, and bag in hand. Dave made sure that no remains were left. Goodbyes were expressed to the favorite tree and to the feathered friends. When they reached the small park's entryway, Sally turned around for another glance of this special setting provided by Mother Earth. "So good to be in your company. See you soon!"

7

A passage from
Speaking The Truth
(Chapter Two)

"The time is now. Once again, this timely message summons us into the present. No matter where one is or when, the invitation to participate in the moment is delivered through these four small words.

And you, Dear Reader, where are you at this present moment? Obviously, you are here reading these words and hopefully you may actually be present as you do this, but are you? Are you really present or are you merely physically present? Many of you will readily understand this question, if you are consciously here when you read it; however, if you are not consciously present then you are not really here and the question has passed you by. So let's try again!

Where are you at this present moment? Are you really consciously present as you strive to read these pages or are you merely physically here and only partially participating?

Assuming that you are really here, let us continue. Are you now presently focused upon this inquiry or is your mind meandering about its selected pathways addressing matters of its own preference?

If your mind is gallivanting about, please ask it to join you. Perhaps this is a silly remark; however, those of you in possession of a marvelous mind that embraces travelling will appreciate the comment. Although it has many favorite ports of call, please ask your adventurous mind to return home and join with you, for we have work to do."

The knock at the door was so quiet that Stephen barely noticed. He rolled his chair away from the desk and moved towards the door. In the brief few steps taken, his mood changed. The paper he was working on was no longer his focus of attention. Instead, all his energy was placed on the lovely lady on the other side of door. "Who's that knocking at my door?" Stephen's attempt to sound big and gruff did not merit an award, but his beloved wife was inspired to play along.

"Tis I, fine sir! Might I have a word, oh Great One?" Laughter, emerging from the playful couple, continued as the door flung open. A joyous, good morning embrace quieted the playfulness for the moment. Stephen invited Jill into his office, but she suggested meeting on the back porch. He agreed that would be a much better choice. Before heading downstairs, he quickly turned off his computer and grabbed his empty coffee cup.

In anticipation that Stephen would be open to a break from his work, Jill had prepared a light snack and their favorite raspberry zinger tea. "This is great, Dear. Exactly what is needed! How did you know I was thinking about raspberry zinger?" She rolled her eyes in the most exaggerated way possible.

"Well, we could pretend that this is another coincidence. But we both know it isn't. I started receiving the message about twenty minutes ago, and I know for certain it wasn't my imagination." Stephen was ecstatic!

Checking his watch, he became even more excited. "Twenty minutes ago? You're certain it was twenty minutes?" Jill nodded with equal excitement. "Yes," he declared enthusiastically! "I started focusing upon raspberry zinger twenty minutes ago. I checked the time before I started the experiment...and it worked! You got the message!" They reached for their respective glasses of tea and toasted their accomplishment.

"I'm so glad we are tracking these events," stated Jill. "Even though we both know and trust what is happening between us, I think it is wise for us to take notes on our progress. Obviously, someone could say that this was just a coincidence, because we both love this particular type of tea, but it wasn't a coincidence. I was planning on making a fresh pot of hazelnut crème coffee, which is also a favorite, but then your message came through loud and clear.

Intentionally tracking these incidents validates what we already know about our telepathic tendencies and it also informs us that practice enhances our skills."

"I agree, Jill. When we first started noticing these the so-called coincidences, we didn't give them much credence. You were the one who first broached the topic, and because you did, we finally realized that we had both been aware of these peculiar exchanges transpiring between us. But we didn't acknowledge them! Isn't that fascinating? Why did we just let those curious coincidences happen without even a moment of conversation?" Stephen shook his head in disbelief.

"I wonder how many other people are having similar experiences? Wouldn't it be interesting to know the answer to that? It would be fascinating to bring this topic out of the closet. I suspect the human species is on the verge of a transformational shift, and these incidents are indicative of an increased ability to communicate telepathically. But we're in the dark about the possibility, because no one gives these so-called coincidences any credence."

"Stephen, why don't you write an article about this! Bring this topic out into the open and see what kind of a response you get?" His wife's question brought the conversation to a halt. Jill noticed the change in her husband's demeanor and knew exactly what was happening. She took action.

"Stephen, please look at me." His gaze rose from the table and met Jill's eyes. "I don't know where you just went, but come back, please. Remember what we talked about at the meeting. We must trust ourselves! Your idea regarding the prevalence of telepathic behaviors in our society is worthy of an article, and you are capable of writing such an article. Trust yourself! Whatever inner voice just shut you down, release it now!" Jill's voice was firm and loving. A deep, elongated breath was his immediate response.

"Good grief! How quickly that nonsense can happen!" His frustration was obvious. "I can write an article on this topic, and I've actually already given this a great deal of thought. But talk about being blindsided by an incident from the past." Stephen closed his eyes and took another long deep breath. "You know what? I'm not taking this detour into the past. There is no reason to revisit that situation, but there is reason for me to take a stance, and I'm going to do that right now. I understand what happened long ago was a mistake. My Dad had no intentions of hurting me, but I misunderstood what was said, and my misinterpretation has caused me a lot of pain for a long time. I know my Dad loved me, and still does, and I also know he never meant to hurt me. Dad, you don't have to worry about me. What happened was just a silly misunderstanding, and it's over. I'm okay, Dad. I'm going to write this article because I can. I trust myself and I know this article is a project that I should pursue." A tear trickled down his cheek and he inhaled another deep breath. Turning to his dear wife, Stephen thanked her for her assistance.

"You were great, Jill! You got me out of that dark place so quickly that no damage was done. Thank you for rescuing me." She accepted his expression of gratitude and also applauded him for the strong stance that he had taken.

"I'm so glad we have found this new group of people to engage with, Stephen. I think good things are going to come from this." He agreed and mentioned that their new friends might serve as a resource for his article.

"Good idea! As far as I can tell, everyone in the group has telepathic abilities. I suspect they will be very open to discussing the topic."

A passage from
Speaking The Truth
(Chapter Two)

"Functioning from the assumption that you are truly present, both you and your mind, let us proceed with a question. Since the present is before us at this very moment, what shall we do with it? We might, if you are amenable to the idea, consider the title of this book... Speaking The Truth. It is a title that entices the mind to wonder and to wander. According to the introduction, Speaking The Truth is an opportunity for each reader to expand his or her present outlook on the world about them.

Speaking The Truth! Is this not a curious message that beckons you to give it consideration? Where does your beautiful mind go when it assimilates this message of just three words? Does the mind wonder if it is being asked to speak the truth? Or does it ponder if it is actually already speaking the truth? What does your mind do with this message...and more importantly what do you want to do with this message?"

"Jill, I appreciate your help, but now it's your turn. Please tell me where you are with the assignment that we were given at the last meeting. Was that just last night?" Stephen questioned his sense of time. "Time is really odd nowadays," he mused.

"So, tell me. Have you had time to think about the assignment or have you been busy with clients?" Jill indicated that her morning had been busy with a couple of clients, but she had also managed to spend some time with her journal.

"Well, I began the morning with an energy session for the Earth. And it went really well." Jill's excitement about the session showed. She was beaming. "At first, it seemed a bit weird. I think's it fair to say that I was tentative at best, but once I got into it, I really enjoyed the experience. Stephen, it felt like a sacred experience. I was in prayer, and I was in the company of the Earth. Don't really know how to explain this, dear, but I truly felt like there was a deep connection between the two of us, and it was astounding. I can't wait to do it again." Tears welled up in Jill's eyes as she tried to describe her experience. Stephen reassured her that he believed everything she was saying. "Did you spend some time with her this morning?" Her question was difficult to answer. He finally admitted that his attention had gone in other directions.

"Geez! I'm so sorry. Once again, I've neglected her." Now, it was Jill's time to reassure her husband.

"Stephen, the day is young. You have plenty of time to address her. Old habits are hard to change. You are one who has always preferred to work in the early hours of the day, so it makes sense that you got up this morning and did what you are accustomed to. Just remember, she needs help around the clock, so it doesn't matter when it happens. You'll make it work, dear. I trust you!" He nodded and then pointed to her to continue with her morning escapades.

"I must admit the time spent with the Earth was so exhilarating that I was able to easily move into the 'trust' assignment. They piggybacked nicely. By the time the energy session was over, I felt strong and confident, which was a great way to enter into my inner work. And as a result, the exploration into my vulnerabilities went very rapidly. I faced my fears unscathed and empowered to move forward. Stephen, it was remarkably easy and I think it was all related to my experience with Mother Earth. While I was attempting to heal her, I think she healed me. I am at peace, and it's a remarkable place to be." Her husband looked on in disbelief, but Jill knew he believed every word she was saying.

"Sweetie, I'm sorry my ability to articulate what transpired is so sparse. It's difficult, and yet, the experience itself was not difficult. I felt embraced in loving arms as I reviewed my fears. I did not enter the experience in fear, nor did I feel any fear during the experience, I simply reviewed various scenarios, understood the complexities of what had transpired, and released the pain that was still associated with the events. And then, it was done. I felt strong and empowered to engage with any situation, including the Earth's declining health. I can assist her! We can assist her! At this point in time, I don't have any doubts about our abilities to help her. Perhaps, there will be more moments of vulnerability, but isn't that just part of life? Sometimes, we meet challenges that are a surprise to us, but given a moment, and a deep breath, we can handle the situation.

Stephen, I'm so grateful we are together. Our years of happiness have prepared me for this new level of being. I am happier in this moment than I have ever been...in this lifetime. And because of the happiness you brought into our lives, I can wholeheartedly accept this blessing. We deserve this state of being. We are intended to live this way. And also, Stephen, we are intended to save the Earth. Aren't we lucky? We have the privilege of saving Mother Earth." Jill reached out and grabbed her husband's big paws. "We are so fortunate. There isn't any other place I want to be, dear. I am so glad we are here on this wonderful planet at this particular time and in this particular place. We are here for a reason. Isn't that a glorious thing to know?"

Tears streamed down their faces; tears of happiness, not sadness. The Carsons knew they were exactly where they were intended to be.

8

A passage from
The Time is Now
(Chapter One)

*"For many ages we have assisted species such as yours
throughout many galaxies and many neighboring communities.
With each evolving species, we assist when needed
with intentions of promoting goodwill
among the many members of the Universal Family.
Our purpose throughout the ages has been to assist All That Is
in caring for the children of the Universe.
We have entered many life experiences
in our attempts to guide and assist the various species
throughout the many galaxies
and in all our attempts to provide assistance,
our intentions have always remained the same.
Our primary reason for coming is to serve All That Is
and the children of All That Is, who are the priority of All That Is.
No other purpose is of more meaningfulness than
the tending of the children and their needs."*

"**W**hoa! That was a lovely experience! Carolyn, I don't think I've ever had a more effective guided imagery. If fact, it was so powerful that I wonder if I actually had an out of body experience. Is that possible, Hon? Do those really happen?" Her husband's reaction to their shared energy session piqued her curiosity. Carolyn encouraged him to elaborate upon his experience. He closed his eyes, attempting to gather and sort through his thoughts, but they remained jumbled. His frustration was obvious.

"Just take a few deep breaths, Dear. That might help you to recall what happened." Ron took her suggestion but still seemed agitated.

"Trust yourself, Ron! Remember that is our challenge for today. We both vowed to work on trusting ourselves. So, tell me what it was like to feel as if you were out of your body?" Her question ignited his recovery of the recently experienced unusual event.

"As we stood beside the sea, I seemed to be One with her. I could feel the swell of her waves and the pull of her undercurrents. It was amazing, Carolyn. But I wanted more, and she provided me with more. While you continued to facilitate the session, your voice became very distant. I knew I was sitting here in this chair, but I also felt like we, you and I, were still standing on the beach holding hands. I was in both places at the same time and it felt absolutely real to me. And the most incredible thing happened, I was given the gift of flight. I saw myself rise out of my body, and for a brief moment, I was directly above you, but that didn't last long. I was taken away by the wind and found myself flying over miles and miles of beaches and open waters. At times, I was high in the sky looking over the endless views of the ocean and then I found myself swooping downward and gliding just above the water. Carolyn, I could feel the splashes of water on my face when a wave surprised me. I swear it was the most amazing thing! And it didn't feel like a dream; it felt real." Ron opened his eyes and looked down at his shirtsleeves. The edges were damp! He looked to his beloved for validation, and she smiled, hoping that would be enough to allow him to trust his experience.

"Carolyn, I believe the Earth was showing me who she really is. She is so much more than our limited sight can see. I witnessed her expansive nature and felt her strength. The undercurrents were shockingly forceful. Although I felt no danger, it was blatantly clear that the power of the Earth is far greater than we can fathom. She is a remarkable creature. It was such a privilege to be so close to her. I feel I am more now than I was before.

This must sound crazy to you, but it's my story. I wasn't expecting anything like this to happen, but it did, and quite frankly, I'm not creative enough to make this up. Thank you, Carolyn, that was the experience of a lifetime." Ron took a deep breath and relaxed back into his chair. Carolyn was both pleased and amazed. She had no doubts about her husband's experience. He was not one to tell tall tales. She was very happy for the time he had shared with the Earth.

"What about you Carolyn? Were you able to have a good experience, even though you accepted the responsibility of leading our session?" It was her turn to take the life-giving breath.

"I had a very enjoyable time. My experience wasn't as extensive as yours, but it was most satisfying. I felt deeply connected with the Mother. And privileged to be in her presence. It is odd, but I intuited that she carries a deep sense of responsibility for being hospitable to us when we reach out to her. Perhaps we need to make ourselves clear that we expect nothing of her during these sessions. We must encourage her to simply receive. I suspect that may be difficult for her, because she is so accustomed to being the one who is taking care of others—many others." Carolyn appeared to be pondering what she had just shared. Ron assumed she was trying to evaluate her interpretations.

"Trust yourself, Carolyn. Your intuition is rarely mistaken. I think you've discovered something that is critically important to share with our friends. The Earth has been taking care of all of her residents for ages. And she is still trying to take care of us now, even when her health is failing. Seems only natural that she would try to extend herself to those who are trying to help her. This is an important insight, dear." Carolyn agreed.

"Yes, you're right. This must be shared with our friends and with everyone we encounter in the future. Thank you, Ron, for reminding me to trust myself."

A passage from
Speaking The Truth
(Chapter Three)

"Breathe deeply Dear Readers, for it is time for each
one of you to confront the meaning of your existence.
Breathe again, please. Focus upon this natural instinct
of Life and make it the center of your attention.

Breathing in, you accept the breath of Life.
Breathing out, you extend Life to every other existence in existence.

It is just this easy...this simple... to unite in Oneness with all others in this glorious existence we call Life. Thus you are invited to merge into Oneness now by breathing in and breathing out with the hope-filled intention of uniting with all that exist in All That Is."

9

"*O*ld Friend, may we interrupt you? We require a moment of your time."

"Indeed, my Friends, I am most grateful to be in your presence. How may I be of service?"

"We come to commend you, Old Friend, for the work that you are overseeing. These Old Friends learn quickly. They readily accept the commitments made long ago, but as is true for many in human form, they struggle with fears. This incessant problem continues to be an issue. We encourage you to discuss this issue with them again, Old Friend. Impress upon them the ramifications of their fears. They must gain greater understanding of this issue so that it does not continue to interfere with the Earth's recovery.

"Yes, your concerns are heard and understood. I will indeed revisit this issue this evening and encourage them to challenge the resilient nature of their fears. As you say, the more they understand about the tenacious characteristics of this diminishing behavioral trait, the more capable they will be in ending its influence.

Old Friends, few have we encountered who are as committed as this group. The agreements of old ring loudly within them. They feel the call to save the Earth. And they accept the truth about their healing abilities. They are a remarkable group of people. The goodness within them reminds us that goodness is still alive in the Children of Earth."

"Your assessment of these Children strengthens our hope. We are most grateful for all that you are doing on behalf of the Life Being called Earth. In peace be, Old Friend."

"And to you, Dear Friends."

10

A passage from
Speaking The Truth
(Chapter Three)

"...imagine joining with others through the mere activity of breathing. Visualize a loved one—your beloved spouse, a blessed child, a wonderful friend. Visualize someone who is remarkably dear to you and breathe this individual within you to the very depths of your innermost being. Do this now please, and experience the sweet beauty of this natural means of connection. Practice this again, now and throughout your day, because this natural ability to reach out and gain connection is intended to be of assistance to you.

If you are truly present while you experiment with this visualization, it is highly probable that you will be calmed by the experience. You may also wish to practice with other visualizations that include nature, pets, favorite places and settings that hold great meaning for you. The purpose of this activity is to enhance your sense of connection, which typically spawns a warm, serene, and heartfelt reaction that brings an extreme sense of peace to your present state.

Similar to other natural abilities, the ability to seek and create connection exists in everyone whether one is aware of it or not; and with attention, i.e., practice, the ability strengthens and becomes more easily accessible and readily beneficial. The need for connection with another exists everywhere in existence at every level of existence.

Is it any wonder that you are now reminded of another existential truth...one that will become increasingly more

evident as you pursue your reason for being? Simply and
truthfully, the truth is presented, 'You are not alone!'"

The doorbell rang before my guests were expected. I assumed someone in the group decided to arrive early to help with set up. Since I was running a bit late, I was glad for the yet to be seen Angel of Mercy. I opened the door, and of course, found Barb, who was looking a bit winded. "Come in, Girl! You look worn out!" We exchanged hugs, as she reassured me that she was fine.

"It's very windy out, so I'm not looking by best."

"You're looking great, but you also look tired. Have you had one of those days that was filled with surprises and complexities?"

"How did you know?" she asked as we both headed for the kitchen.

"Lucky guess!" came my response. I started grabbing trays from the refrigerator and setting them on the table. "Can you manage the trays, Dear? I'll keep unloading everything if you don't mind relocating them to the dining room." Kitchen duties were quickly addressed, enabling us time to focus on the living room. Fortunately, we were saved by the doorbell! Our guests were punctual as usual. The fellows entered first, offered quick hellos and hugs, and then went directly into the living room to rearrange the furniture.

"Hey! I knew these guys could be useful!" Barb playfully teased our friends. "Joking aside. Thank you a bunch! We were running late this evening and your muscles are greatly appreciated."

"By the way, folks," I announced, "if any of you want to bring a plate filled with goodies into the living room, please do so. Our meetings have been so full of late that we haven't had time for refreshments, so please just make yourself at home and do whatever you need to do to make the evening more comfortable for you." The men in the group immediately headed back towards the dining room, which made the women shake their heads and chuckle.

"Oh, well!" declared Annie. "We can't let them eat alone!" So plates were filled, beverages were selected and everyone settled in for the evening.

"Any idea if our beloved teacher is here or not?" David stated aloud what everyone was thinking. I looked at Barb and she returned my look and we both shrugged our shoulders.

"Your guess is as good as ours, but perhaps, we might ask." Before the question could be spoken, the Dear Friend from places unknown, materialized in his specially, reserved chair. As always, his arrival created a stir. Of course, it would. How often does one witness an invisible man acquiring visibility right before your eyes. It is indeed a sight to behold.

"Good evening, my Dear Friends, it is most agreeable to be in your presence once again. Please continue to indulge yourselves; the nourishment will sustain your energy for the energy transfusion that we will participate in shortly."

"Dear One, is there anything I can offer you that would be amenable in your present state?" Our guest chuckled heartily.

"Your offer is most kind, but in my present form, I am unable to indulge in such luxuries." Barb quickly responded with a question of interest. "Do you miss being in human form? I would imagine there are aspects of being embodied that one must long for." Our Friend sighed deeply.

"Indeed there is much about the human condition that is desirable, but what makes the heart ache the most is our invisibility. Just as you ache to see a beloved loved one who has passed, so too do we ache to be seen. At times it is most heart breaking." Our Friend's mood changed as a memory came to mind. *"Of course,"* he chuckled, *"there are times when I long for a good glass of wine and the homemade bread that my mother made so long ago. Yes, there are things that are missed, but when one is in this form, one remembers what is missed and the memories can be most consoling, unlike those who are in embodied form and ache for that which they cannot remember."*

"Well said!" declared Faye. "I must admit my mind takes me on great adventures when I think about what it is like to be in your present form. And of course, I have many questions." Pausing briefly, she mustered up the courage to propose one of the questions that really fascinated her. "So, may I ask just one question?" Their teacher nodded his approval. Faye was ecstatic. "Great! So, I would like to know if it is really possible for you to be in more than one place at the same time."

"Yes, one is capable of multi-locating when in this form; however, it is a skill that must be remembered after you return to this realm

of existence. It requires a great deal of energy, so it is done limitedly; however, those of ancient beginnings find the experience easily managed." Our teacher paused briefly before continuing. Aware that many others questions were rising within the group, he chose to redirect attention to the purpose of the evening's meeting.

"Dear Friends, I know you are fascinated by what appears to be mysterious, but we must focus our attention and our intentions now, for there is much to be achieved this evening. Please join me now for an energy session for the Earth. Although this will be a quick session, it will not be any less powerful than those that have transpired before. Our purpose is to transfer healthy energy to the one who is suffering. This, as you have previously experienced, transpires in a brief instant. However, our preparations in the past have been intended for you to experience the fullness of the event through an elongated learning introduction. Tonight let us begin with a new exercise, one that allows you to participate in an energy transfusion, which is brief in its implementation. One must know how to facilitate such an event and also trust that this exercise is as powerful as the one that demands more of your time.

We have noticed that the peoples of Earth are selfish about their time. Thus, we must adjust our methods to accommodate those who are in misunderstanding of the relevance of time. So, my Friends, I invite you to prepare yourselves now for this energy transfusion in the manner that best suits you. Rest assured, my Friends, we will achieve the same potency, as we have before, but we will accomplish this task in a shorter period of time.

So, please take your deep breaths now as you have done before in the past. Enter into the sacred space that you know so well and reunite with the healing energy that exists within you. Our goal is to infuse the Earth with our healing energy. Reach deeply within, my Friends, and ignite the power within you. With each deep breath, feel your healing energy amassing, and when you are ready, release your powerful energy to the Earth. Do this in a manner that pleases you and know that she will gladly receive your gift of restorative energy. Send your energy to her and wish her well. Express your gratitude for all that she has done, and bid her adieu.

Return home, Dear Friends, and trust that your efforts were successful."

Time passed before the usual movements were heard as people repositioned themselves in their chairs.

"That is a brilliant idea," exclaimed Stephen. "I'm embarrassed to admit this, but there are times when I've backed away from doing one of the energy sessions, because I felt like it would take up too much of my time. Do you believe that?" Looking directly at their teacher, Stephen continued, "I so appreciate what you said regarding our selfishness about time. I'm living proof of that. This has challenged my selfishness and my false sense of importance. Who am I? What is going on in my life that is more important than spending time helping the Earth? This exercise was very informative, my Friend. I'm grateful. Geez! Do I have deep work to do?" Several other group members echoed Stephen's reaction.

"Me too!" signed Mark Goodman. "My attitude about this is frightful. Once again, I am shocked at my behavior. But I'm also grateful that this is being brought to my attention. Although, it is uncomfortable, I'm learning a lot about myself."

"My Friends, the human mind so enjoys visiting the negative. May I urge you to let go of your embarrassment, your shame; and instead, focus upon your experience of assisting the Earth? Were you able to move beyond your mind's negativity and focus upon the Earth? And did you find our brief exercise to be one that you can incorporate into your daily routines?"

"Yes!" a chorus of voices responded positively and then Jill elaborated upon her experience. "Well, I too must admit this was an eye-opener. I am selfish about my time. I see that now, but I was clueless about it before this exercise came up. Thank you for this new breakthrough. What was inspiring though, was my ability to override my mind's distraction. I chose not to follow its lead and I turned my attention back towards the Earth. And I agree with Stephen! This is a brilliant example of how quickly we can assist the planet and still have ample time to address the activities for which we feel responsible. I love our lengthy, more meditative exercises. They are delightful and so grounding, but there are times when this shorter exercise is simply more convenient. I actually feel like my toolbox for helping the Earth is filling up. A variety of tools is necessary for any project, and this new tool is going to prove very helpful." Jill's comment brought some levity to the group, and opened the floor to more positive comments about the experience. Faye also felt the shorter exercise would entice more people to participate in the healing exercise.

"I think it is a human trait to want to be helpful, but our attention spans are limited. So many of us want to jump in, take care of business, and then move on to the next task. I think this is primarily based in our desire to be productive. We are so intent on meeting our goals, as quickly as possible, that we truly are not conscious of the selfish nature of our lifestyles. This learning experience will be very useful when we start engaging with other folks. As Jill said, this is a tool that is going to be very useful."

"May I take a moment?" inquired Ron. "First I want to acknowledge that I'm in agreement with everything just said. From the comments regarding selfishness to the toolbox scenario, I'm on board, but I want to bring up something that came up today during an energy session that Carolyn and I did this morning. It seems really important and may be another tool to add to the First Aid Kit for the Earth." Ron encouraged his spouse to share her story with their new friends.

"Yes, I would love to do that. This morning we did a conjoint energy session, which turned out to be rather exceptional and informative. Ron enjoyed an expansive journey. I know he will share it with you at another time. I also had a fascinating experience, which provided me with some insights about our wonderful, dear planet. As we were engaging with her, I became acutely aware that the Earth was trying very hard to be hospitable to me. This was the first time that I had sensed this. It was so loving, and also shocking. Even in her time of great distress, she is still trying to take care of us when we offer her these energy infusions. So, needless to say, I felt compelled to share this with all of you. Perhaps our teacher will speak more eloquently about this, but from my limited perspective, it seems vitally important that we impress upon her to simply receive our gifts. She's given so much for so long that I'm not sure she even knows how to be the recipient." Carolyn's news was startling to her friends and also to the beloved teacher. He seemed to retreat to another realm while his students looked on. Eventually, his attention returned to the group.

"I apologize, my Friends, but this news demanded my attention. Carolyn, I am most grateful for your insight. The information has been relayed to others like yourselves who are attempting to assist her. You are correct, Old Friend. This situation must be addressed immediately. We will communicate with this remarkable Life Being and implore her to accept our gifts of energy. Her generosity is embedded within her genetic

makeup, and she responds instinctively as a caregiver. We will, as you suggested, impress upon her that in this moment in time, she must, for the sake of all her inhabitants, be a gracious recipient. This will not sit well with her, but under the circumstances, she will understand and accept what must be done. She is a being of service, and will, above all else, do what is best of the good of all."

A passage from
Speaking The Truth
(Chapter Three)

"Throughout this reading adventure, you will find avenues of exploration that offer you greater understanding of your meaning in existence. At each juncture, you will decide how to continue. Although Speaking The Truth is intended to lovingly nudge you forward and hopefully ease your passage, you are ultimately the possessor of free will and you will discern and define how you proceed.

We began this journey by reminding you of the universal truth regarding time by firmly and repeatedly asserting, 'The time is now!' This truth was emphatically accentuated with another declaration claiming, 'Now is the moment of relevance.' Accompanying this insistent statement regarding relevance came an equally significant announcement emphasizing the necessity that one must be consciously present to actually participate in and experience the moment of relevance.

These reminders are purposeful. You are here for a reason, Dear Reader, and you are being called to pursue your meaning in existence. You are encouraged to begin now...the time is now! Now is the moment of relevance! And you are lovingly, gently...and boldly reminded, 'You are not alone!' Ultimately, the journey is yours and all decisions regarding the journey are yours to discern; however, before you make your decisions, there are a few more reminders that must now be expressed.

You are here for a reason!
You are needed!
You are necessary!"

"Old Friends, I must take a moment of your time to impress upon you the truth of your participation in this project to save the Earth. You are here for reason! You are needed! You are necessary! This evening's gathering brings this reality to the surface for all of you to face and to comprehend. You have learned from your own experiences that the Earth is benefitting from the energy sessions in which you are participating. You have learned this from your individual experiences, your conjoint efforts, and from our group sessions. Please accept that your actions are important and your continued efforts are essential for the Earth's recovery process.

I urge you to remember how much you have grown in recent weeks. You have faced your fears, and gained greater understanding about the influence of this behavioral issue. And you have learned how insidious this problem truly is. The resilience of fear is shocking. Even when one has learned about its pervasive nature, fear still has the potential for interrupting your intentions and impeding your progress. Each lesson that has been learned and shared with one another has diminished its potency, and still we must be vigilant. My friends, I must impress upon you to face your fears daily. With this protocol, you will become so aware of fear's presence that you will render it impotent. Imagine what life would be like without fear's influence. Imagine what your life would be like without fear, and then compound that thought by the seven plus billion people who experience fear on a daily basis. How would life on this planet be if it were not misdirected by fear? Think of this, my Friends, and then remember the important role you have chosen to live. You are here for a reason. You are needed. You are necessary" His words filled their hearts. Tears were shed. The Mission to save the Earth was real. And each group member realized that his or her participation mattered.

11

A passage from
The Time is Now
(Chapter One)

"As many times before, in many other places,
we came to your planet to assist you
in your process of developing intellectual abilities.
Our purpose when assisting species of reasoning capabilities is one
that shares our gifts of awareness
from many ages of developmental transformative experiences
with those of little awareness and few experiences.
Through many ages and many experiences,
our species has evolved from a simple cell of no awareness
to a complex multi-dimensional organism of great awareness."

I woke early the morning after our gathering and my thoughts immediately went to the night before. I had forgotten that Barb and I never had a chance to talk about her day. She was burdened by something. I made a mental note to myself to call when the hour was appropriate. Then my mind turned to the meeting itself. I wondered if our Dear Friend was okay. His reaction to Carolyn's news was interesting. He appeared to be jolted by the revelation that the Earth was not fully receiving our energy infusions. His reaction was impressive. Once he grasped what was transpiring, he immediately took action.

I wondered if I could react so forthrightly or if my fears would have disrupted my ability to react clearly and quickly.

"Old Friend, do not fear your fears. It is a serendipitous way for fears to reinstate themselves in your mind."

"Forgive me, my Friend, but I am still in bed. Let me gather myself and we can relocate to the sitting area."

"It is unnecessary, my Friend. I apologize for this early morning intrusion, but I overheard your expression of concern for me and I wanted to reassure you that I am indeed in good spirits.

Our group progresses rapidly and All are most pleased by this. The information intuited by Carolyn was indeed noteworthy. I acknowledge my initial reaction was one of embarrassment. It seemed impossible that we would have not recognized such an obvious response. The Earth is a Being of such incredible generosity that her natural inclination is to assist others. This simply is who she is. We were remiss by not recognizing that she would lean in this direction even during her moment of great need. Our concerns have been communicated to her. She has agreed to open her heart fully to the energy transfusions. With great intentions and compassion, she was sharing the healing energy with others that were also in need. We convinced her that her recovery was paramount to the continuation of other species upon her. The logic of the situation came to her and she is in agreement to receive graciously until the time when she is strong enough to assist others. Her commitment to those who reside upon and within her is humbling. No greater love have I ever witnessed before. She is an exceptional Being!"

"As are you, my Friend. You have changed our lives, and because of your presence, we are now aware of our purposes. You have served well, and now, we will do the same. I am most grateful for our time together."

"As am I, Dear One. Please live this day to the fullest and know that you are loved and cherished by the Residents of the Greater Existence. In peace be, my Friend!"

"And to you, Old Friend!"

A passage from
Speaking The Truth
(Chapter Four)

"In days ahead, many of you will feel an ache rising within you that may create confusion. For some, it will be experienced and described as an 'awakening' and your

excitement will soar with hopeful anticipation. Others may find the experience disruptive, cumbersome, and annoyingly disorienting. And some of you, probably most of you, may experience all of the above and more. Please try not to be worried, bothered, or distraught about any of your reactions, for you are exquisitely normal."

"Good Morning, Barbara, have I called too early?"

"Sister, I am so glad to hear your voice. And no! This is not too early. Please tell me everything!" Her insistent tone made me giggle.

"I'm calling because we never had a chance to discuss your day last night. We were rushing about so much, and then the meeting itself really took the wind out of me. I went straight to bed after everyone left and didn't have another thought until I awoke a while ago. You were the first thought that came to me, but the hour was ridiculously early, so I tried to control my impulse to immediately pick up the phone and call you. So, that's why I'm calling now. What happened yesterday? And tell me everything!"

"Geez! Yesterday seems like a lifetime ago. Hmm! Let me think for a moment." I heard her moving about and assumed she was trying to find her journal. I was right! After a deep breath was heard, I knew she was ready to share her story.

"Sister, I can't believe this slipped my mind, but as you know, our lives of late have been somewhat unusual." We chuckled about that understatement and then, she began again. "Well, I've been very dedicated in my efforts to journal everyday, and I must admit it is both invigorating and challenging. I'm learning a great deal about myself, but I'm not quite sure what to do with this information. And perhaps, nothing needs to be done. But at the same time, Sister, some of the 'stuff' that I'm receiving is rather incredible, and it doesn't seem right to keep it to myself." She paused briefly and I took advantage of the moment.

"May I ask a question or will that distract you?" She urged me to take the lead. "Well, I'm just curious, Barb. Are you receiving information, as well as doing your own self-exploration?"

"You have no idea how poignant that question is, Sister! And the truth is, it varies. Typically, I try to write about the things we are doing and learning in our group work. That often stirs up a lot for me, and it seems that everything that's been stored in my heart and soul just comes pouring out on the pages. It's important work. As I said, I'm learning a lot about myself. Some of this work has been long in the making, but it seems like I'm processing things more deeply this time around. Hopefully, that's a sign of maturity." In my mind's eye, I could see Barb rolling her eyes in reaction to that last comment.

"And then, my work seems to be taken over by another kind of work that is so far beyond my comprehension that it just takes my breath away. There's a blending of the present, the past, and the future, which is mystifying and intriguing all at the same time. At times, I feel like I need a seatbelt to hold me into the chair. The words are coming so rapidly that I can barely keep up, and in the moment everything seems comprehensible, but when it ends, I don't understand anything, or at most very little.

Sister, I am stunned by what's happening. And I don't want it to stop! Whatever is going on is important, and I am absolutely certain that I am supposed to be doing this. It's exhausting and exhilarating! I am confused, excited, up, down, and living the most fascinating time that anyone could possibly imagine. Life is so rich. Our work with Earth is incredible and it makes me feel as if we are really doing something important and necessary. And this work that's going on between me and whoever is extraordinary. I'm happier than I've ever been!" The line appeared to go dead, but I knew that wasn't the case. I waited patiently, aware that she had just released a huge amount of Self. She needed time to recover.

"Well, Sister! So what's your verdict? Am I crazy or what?"

"Barb, crazy is not a descriptor that would ever enter my mind in regards to you. Oh, Dear Friend, you are having an incredible spiritual experience. And I am so happy for you! I only have one cautionary thought to share with you. So listen up!

This is an extraordinary time, Barb, and you must take very good care of yourself. Remember to eat healthy foods, to sleep as much as is needed, and continue to exercise even though you don't think you have time for it. This type of work expends a great deal of energy and you must take extra care so that you do not deplete yourself. Dear Heart, this is a joyous time! Do not fear what is going on, do not judge what is going on, and do not worry about your sanity. You are having an exceptional experience that is enviable! I am so, so happy for you. May I be so bold as to ask a favor of you?"

"Of course, Sister! What is it?"

"Will you please check in with me on a regular basis. I don't mean to insinuate myself into the intimate experience that is unfolding, but I do want to know that you are taking care of yourself. Will you do that for me?"

"Absolutely! And I appreciate everything you've said. It was very affirming. I really don't think that I'm crazy, but some folks might think that, so I'm going to be very selective with whom I share this information. Your advice about caring of myself is genius. Thank you for the reminder! I must admit the days are going by so quickly that I am not paying attention to practical matters. But you're right! I will definitely be vigilant about self-care issues. Thank you for being the best Sister in the world!"

"Well thank you for that, but we both know that's nonsense. Just take good care of you. You are a very important presence in my life, and I want you to be at your best while engaging with these incredible experiences."

"Me too!" she whispered. "Sister, I'm learning so much, and I cannot wait to learn more. There is so much More, Sister! More than we ever imagined!"

A passage from
The Time is Now
(Chapter One)

"The process of our evolution was of natural circumstance
with profound results.
As we grew in awareness,
our desire to know more of our surroundings also grew
and our need to know
became our ongoing, never-ending process.
The time of which we speak is far older
than any can imagine or remember,
but throughout this ongoing process,
we continued to grow in most delightful and unbelievable ways.
This process is so known and understood by our kind

*that we forget how unusual these usual circumstances are
for those unlike ourselves.
Our forgetfulness at times has created difficulties
for those we have tried to serve,
for misunderstandings have arisen from situations common to us,
but uncommon to those we were attempting to assist."*

12

"Jimmy, Dear, how are you this morning?" The couple exchanged their daily good morning hug, which was as genuine today as it was decades ago when they committed to this gesture of love. Jim Anderson grew up with this model of tenderness. Every morning, he witnessed his parents sharing a hug, even during those times when they were not particularly pleased with one another. Those times were rare for his parents, but when it happened, they would reassure the children that it was just a normal part of life. *"Sometimes, we get out of sorts with one another, but not to worry. We still love each other!"*

And life went on. It was wonderful role modeling for the children and Jim learned the lesson well.

"I'm feeling exceptionally well, Dear. And you?"

"The same!" she announced. "But my mind seems to be in a quandary this morning. Last night, we truly learned the importance of these energy transfusions. And particularly, I realized how important it is for us to be consistent about this. My tendency is to wait for us to do a conjoint session on the Earth's behalf, but I'm now wondering if that is a wise approach. And the phrase that keeps racing through my mind is 'Time's a wasting!' Do you have any thoughts about this, Dear?" Jim admitted to having similar thoughts.

"Annie, I think we've grown so accustomed to working as a team that we feel obligated to include the other in whatever tasks we are pursuing at the moment. Let's face it, Dear! We've had a team approach to life for a very long time, so it is only natural that we would expect that now with this new project. But the project is so big, Annie, that it demands more of us. We have to think more expansively, which means we need to do more. I suggest that we commit to two conjoint sessions a day and that we make this a ritual. And then throughout the day, we each give time to the Earth as the situation arises." Jim took a moment to view the morning light and softly thanked the large red maple for her years of service. "I love that tree! Every year, she fills the backyard with the most incredible colors. She has brought such joy to our lives. Thank you, Sweet Beauty!"

"So what I'm suggesting, Annie, is that we participate in our conjoint efforts and also do the individual work that must be done. I think the little gestures are as important as the big ones. You know, I think about the influence Mom and Dad had on us kids; that gesture of connection every morning. It was important! We witnessed their love and their commitment to one another through that small act of tenderness. We need to demonstrate our love and commitment to the Earth on a regular basis as well. She needs it! And so do we!"

"Yes, Dear, I agree with you. Thanks for speaking so articulately about the importance of acts of kindness. That was an important reminder. Hearing you speak so lovingly to our maple tree makes me realize the importance of being present and acknowledging all the beauty that is around us. We have a tendency to take things for granted, including all the glorious beauty that this wonderful planet provides us. And also, thank you for reminding me of the special qualities of relationships. We are a team and we also have our own identities. We've nurtured that in each other, and I'm glad. We both have our own lives as well as this remarkable life that we've shared together. We are so blessed, Jim. I am so very grateful for you."

A passage from
Speaking The Truth
(Chapter Four)

"Speaking The Truth is a timely message, for it addresses the present, the past, and all that is yet to be. Speaking The Truth relates to the moment; and yes, once again you are prodded to be in the moment...to recognize that now is the moment of relevance! Since we are declaring and reiterating the importance of being in the present, let us do so now as we open discussion about a situation that is transpiring among the peoples of Earth at this very moment.

Have you noticed how often you are elsewhere? Perhaps this seems an odd question, but it has merit. Take a deep breath, for it is time for a heartfelt, honest evaluation of your present ability to be in the present.

Only you can make this assessment, for you are the only one privileged to have access to your beautiful mind."

Jim grabbed his wife's hand and encouraged her to lead them in their morning worship with the Earth. "Shall we go out on the deck and spend some quality time with Mother Earth?" The two old friends did just that. They landed in their preferred wicker rockers and glanced about the yard that provided them with so much pleasure. It was indeed a privilege to live on this amazing planet. Annie initiated the session with a deep breath, and Jim followed. They relaxed into the moment. Reveling in the songs of their family of birds, they each merged with the rhythm of the Earth. "Oh, Dear Friend, how sweet it is to be in your presence. We come in gratitude for all that you have done for so long. We apologize for having taken you for granted. You deserve so much more from us. Please allow us to make amends. Old Friend, please allow us to share a particle of the Source energy that resides within All. As are you comprised of this powerful energy, so too are we. Please receive our gift fully, and accept this energy for your own healing process. We understand and respect your love of assisting others. But for this brief moment in time, please accept this gift for your own needs." The words poured through Annie and filled the hearts of all who were present. Jim heard the words and was soothed by them, as were the others who joined them during this session with the Earth. In Annie's mind, she saw the energy from within leaving her body and moving to the center of the backyard. She shared this with Jim and his energy followed hers and merged together. There, the combined energies intensified and grew even more powerful. And then, the two old friends witnessed the ramifications of their efforts. Their energies traveled all about the area, showering the trees, bushes, grasses, and flowering plants with this healing substance. The vibrancy of the plant life intensified from the infusion of energy and the healing powers continued. Somehow, the couple was gifted with images of the healing energy moving into the Earth and spreading among the roots, one plant to another. It seemed magical, and yet, they knew they were witnessing a truth. They were given the privilege of seeing the results of their efforts. It was not a dream. It was not make believe. They saw the truth and they felt the Mother's gratitude.

In time, Jim and Annie returned to their own bodies, and felt renewed. The sense of having assisted another was tender within them. The day had just begun, and it was already a very good day.

A passage from
Speaking The Truth
(Chapter Four)

"This is a time for you to take excellent care of you by learning everything you can learn about your magnificent mind and its daily activities. Before you begin your research, may we offer a suggestion? Assuming you have agreed to our request, we boldly and emphatically say, "Avoid comparisons!" This self-discovery process is not about competition, comparisons, or any other activities that may result in the diminishment of your self-perception or place you in a position of concern about another rather than your Self! Please listen to this with the ears of your heart. You are not here to compare yourself to another or to engage in competition with another. You are here to examine and evaluate your own way of being so that you can personally assist your Self in ways that are uniquely designed to enhance your growth and evolution. If you choose to participate in comparisons and competition, then essentially you are not in the moment, but you are in someone else's moment. Please remember this when your spirited mind begins to reveal its true self."

13

"**O**ld Friend, are you available?" I immediately regretted having reached out to our beloved teacher. It seemed presumptuous. *Who am I to request his presence? I'm sure he has many other commitments that he must attend.* My inner conversation was burdensome. A simple request was made. Either he would or would not respond. My mind was tedious and diminishing. I wondered why my mind resorted to these tactics. "Oh my goodness! This is about fear!" The idea astounded me. At some deep level, fear was the instigator of this inner conflict. A part of me who wanted consultation reached out for assistance. And another part of me was undoubtedly so afraid of being rejected that it scolded me for my efforts towards connection. *This is befuddling and sad. I am so sorry for frightening you, whoever you are. That was not my intention.*

"I simply wanted to talk with our Friend of Old. And even if he is busy, I trust that he will appreciate and respect my desire to talk with him. He is not one who will cause us harm." I hoped the part of me that reacted in fear might be consoled by my words, but this was unknown territory for me. I just knew that the reaction seemed youthful; the response of a small child who had been disappointed and/or wounded before and didn't want to experience a similar incident. This rationale made sense to me, but whatever the incident was, it was not relevant to my present situation.

"The past is often erroneously deemed irrelevant, when in truth, its reappearance may be indicative of a situation that requires assistance and resolution. Old Friend, I am most delighted that you requested my presence. I assure you that your request brings me great pleasure. I hope this truth will console the fear that surfaced as a result of your request for consultation.

As you discerned, the fear is very old. Older than you imagine! For this is a fear that lingers from another time and place. So deeply wounded was this young energy that it continues to seek assistance even in this time and place of which it has no awareness. The pain so deeply experienced by this young one exists in a memory that continues to survive throughout numerous life experiences. Because you presume it is not relevant, it continues to reach out to you for help. Ease the young one's pain, Old Friend. Comfort this one from the past as if it were a Friend in the present. Reassure this one that all is well. Have compassion for the pain that still aches for relief.

No greater act of kindness can be offered than to aid one who believes it has been forgotten. Help this Old Friend release the pain that impedes passage to peace of mind and heart. As will this one be served, so too will you."

"Oh, my goodness. You're insinuating that someone from the past remains secluded in a memory of pain from which he or she cannot escape. That this energy or essence, or whatever is the appropriate descriptor is essentially stuck and cannot find a means of moving on. Am I understanding this correctly?"

"Your understanding is limited. Sometimes, pain is so profoundly experienced that the holder of this pain cannot readily secure a means of release. Great information regarding the influence of pain is learned during these intensive experiences; however, there are times when one must seek assistance in removing oneself from the difficult situation. The bearer of the pain must discern when the experience must come to an end, and once that decision is made, assistance is made available. In this situation, Old Friend, you and the one who is suffering made an agreement long ago to assist one another in your respective lifetimes. The pain experienced by the Other has influenced your way of being in this lifetime, and much more will you learn of this shortly. However, at this time, it is your privilege to assist the Other in moving forward. It is time for this one to be released from the confines of the painful experience.

Old Friend, will you join me in assisting this Dear One with the passage that has long been awaited. Your presence is needed, Old Friend." My mind was in a whirl, but I didn't care about my confusion. I knew I was intended to be in this particular place at this particular time, and I wanted to help.

"My Friend, I want to help this Friend of Old. How may I assist?"

"Be with me, my Friend. Breathe deeply and allow our energies to merge into One. So privileged are we! At last we are able to welcome our Old Friend Home. Feel this one within us. We are One, as we have always been, and now the memory of unity restores this one to full vibrancy once again. Pain no longer burdens this Old Friend. The loneliness that

engulfed this Dear Friend is gone. Home is in sight now, and Friends from countless lifetimes celebrate the return of this Beloved Friend. Peace fills the heart and soul of the One who has come Home again. My Friend, feel the fullness of this moment. Know this reunion is real. Remember what awaits you. And remember the Gift of assisting another in their passage Home. No greater Gift can one give! Breathe this experience in, My Friend, and remember!"

I did as was directed. A huge, elongated breath was consumed, and I prayed that every moment of this experience would be remembered. Gratitude filled my being. Time passed. I had no idea how long this experience had taken or how long I had been in silence. And it didn't matter. What had happened, happened, and I was so grateful for the opportunity to be present and to be helpful.

"Old Friend, may I interrupt your thoughts?"

"Of course, I am grateful for this time together. Is it time for you to be off?"

"Soon!" he replied. *"But there remains time if you still desire a consultation. How may I serve you, Old Friend?"* His generosity warmed my heart. I tried to remember why I had reached out to him, but had no recall of the reason for doing so.

"I think you have already served me well, Dear Friend. Words fail! Today's experience was unreal, and it was the truth. I have no doubts about what transpired. It was real! And as you said, such a privilege! Thank you for everything."

"My Friend, our coming together today was no coincidence. We gathered for a reason, and you were the one that initiated the reunion. Because you felt the ache of old, you reached out to me, and together we came to Your rescue. It was a privilege to assist you in fulfilling your commitment to You. I am so happy for the You of Old who now resides at Home. And I am happy for the You of today who is happy here knowing that you have been of service to One you have known since you came into existence.

Ponder what has been said, Old Friend, and know that I am speaking the truth. In peace be, my Friend."

A passage from
Speaking The Truth
(Chapter Four)

"So, shall we delve into the inner recesses of your mind and discover its marvelous mannerisms? Rest assured this remarkable tool is intended to be an asset to you throughout this journey called life; however, many of you are so unfamiliar with your mind's daily operational patterns that you may be quite surprised by how unremarkably it functions at times. Hopefully, this unproven statement about your beautiful mind stirs you to action. Hopefully, you will pursue a self-examination process of your own choosing and prove to yourself that your mind is functioning at peak performance at all times. Hopefully, this will be your truth! You will never know unless you willingly accept responsibility for the well being of your mind. After making this decision of self-care, you will then be in a position of assessing your fine mind's functional capabilities. The privilege is yours!"

After the Friend from unknown parts departed, I remained seated in my favorite chair. I was still reeling from the experience. My mind seemed to be operating of its own accord, while I sat trying to grasp my situation. *When did my life become so odd?* The question was lost to the other thoughts and suppositions colliding with one another on the racecourse of my mind. The activity was more than I could manage. I was not in control of this mind of mine. A deep sigh was released as I tried to compose myself.

"Did this really happen?" I spoke the question aloud so that I could feel some sense of connection with my surroundings. "This is my sacred space," I declared in hopes that I could regain some sense of control. My pronouncement didn't seem to improve the discord I was feeling. "This is my space, and I want peace of mind!" I closed my eyes and took a deep breath, and then another. The chaos of my mind diminished slightly.

I asked for assistance. *"Dear Friends, I know that you are here. Please help me! I need to regain my peace of mind. So much is transpiring in this moment that I cannot grasp what is happening. Please help me to meld with the process so that the purpose of this experience is not lost to me. I wish to be of service, but the experience is unfolding too rapidly. I need your assistance."* My appeal was made internally; I did not have the energy to vocalize the words. Another deep breath was inhaled, and with this breath, I felt the Companionship that was desired. Another breath was taken and another and finally my racing thoughts and heartbeat began to slow. I knew my Friends were at my side and this provided me great comfort. *I am not alone! Thank you, my Dear Friends, for coming to my aid. What is wrong with me? Am I having a panic attack?"*

"Relax, Old Friend, you are not in jeopardy! Just relax and know that you are safe. Your Companions are indeed with you, and they will assist you through this experience of discovery and resolution." Many more questions surfaced, but my need for immediate answers waned. Whatever was going on was happening for a reason. I decided to trust myself.

"Trusting yourself is a wise decision, Old Friend, for you are one who is most trustworthy. My Friend, perhaps you might choose to open your eyes now, so that you can see for yourself that you are not in harm's way." The voice was one heard many times before. I did not hesitate. I opened my eyes but could not believe what lay before me. Never had I seen such beauty before. It was indescribable, and yet, there was a sense of familiarity. "Where am I?"

"Old Friend, you are indeed familiar with this setting. You are where the beginning begins and where one returns when the ending is completed. This is Home, Old Friend. And you are correct; this setting is indescribably beautiful. Awareness of this location remains within All, and when one aches for that which is unknown, this is the origination of the ache. This is where new beginnings are discerned and plans are implemented. The special connection that one often feels within is related to the close ties that are created in this setting. Old Friend, this is where the heart begins to beat and the first breath is inhaled. This is the Home of the heart that calls to All who embark upon the journey that broadens and expands the individual's evolutionary development. From this place, adventures are launched, and to this place, All return. Old Friend, you are here at a

special request. Be assured, your journey has not ended. Your reason for being still demands your attention.

May I accompany you, my Friend, to those who wish to fulfill a commitment made to you long ago?"

"Your company is deeply appreciated. I must admit, my Friend, a fear or two is lurking within me. A part of me desires to know if I am in trouble. Have I committed a grave error? Is that why I have been summoned here?" My fears were embarrassing me. I turned silent, not wanting to reveal any more of my insecurities.

A deep sigh was heard from my companion. *"The mind betrays you. It creates concerns that are founded in fears, not reality. My Old Friend, you are more than your mind. Trust me, Old Friend; you are not in trouble. Do not fear your fears or scold yourself for having these moments of insecurity. The human form incubates these tales, and sometimes one can be confused by these untruths, but not this time, Old Friend. Your fears are here to remind you of a time when you were confused by your fears, and this time, you will have the opportunity to release those fears so that they will never interfere with you again. For this reason, your presence has been requested. Many Old Friends wish to stand by you while you relive the memory of old. In the company of Old Friends, you will find the strength and the courage to dispatch this old painful experience."*

My body instinctively inhaled a long deep breath. "This sounds like an opportunity of many lifetimes."

"Indeed, it is! It is a privilege to be assisted in this way. You are deeply loved, Old Friend."

"Yes, I sense that. I'm no longer afraid. I feel a bit jittery, but that seems like an appropriate response for such an occasion. Will you take the lead, my Friend, and may I walk by your side? I would like to take the next step together."

A passage from
The Time is Now
(Chapter One)

"Misunderstandings created by our forgetfulness

have led to many more misunderstandings,
which when passed onto younger generations
became more misunderstood
and further still from the original Truths
that were misunderstood.
Regarding these many misunderstandings
and misinterpretations of messages
delivered in the distant past,
our kind wish to correct the mistakes made long ago.
With the assistance of our Old Friend Claudia,
we will attempt to clarify and correct the
mistakes of our previous coming.
It is our sincere hope and most heartfelt desire
that the good people of the planet Earth will hear our call to you.
On behalf of my people,
I will speak of many messages and ideas delivered to you so long ago,
which have created great misunderstandings among your people.
For these misunderstandings,
our kind are deeply sorry and most regretful."

"We've been here before, my Friend. The path was different, as is the landscape, but we were here before and it was not long ago."

"Yes, that is true. Do you remember what transpired during that visit?"

"No, I do not. I'm sorry! The experience is recorded in my journal, but the specifics escape me at this time." My mind feigned indignation, but I chose to ignore its attempts to belittle me. "I assume this visit concerns another matter that I am supposedly ready to address. I trust these Old Friends know what they are doing, so I will take the next step." With that statement a memory of a wall with a huge, ancient door returned. I remembered preparing myself to push the heavy door open and instead it moved as if it were as light as a feather. I wondered if the door would be encountered again. The gathering on the other side of the door also came to mind. It was a most pleasant experience. The warmth of those companions filled me again. I looked forward to being in their presence once more.

My Friend and I approached the edge of what seemed to be an endless canyon. The view was as expansive as it was beautiful. No words could do it justice. No cameras would ever capture the beauty that lay before me. Gratitude filled me. *I do not know why I am so blessed to experience this, but I am forever grateful. How may I be of service?*

"Old Friend, our next step is a leap of faith. Will you join me, as we step into the canyon?"

I did not hesitate. No fear attempted to stop me. I simply knew that the next step was nothing to fear. So together, my Old Friend and I stepped off the edge of the canyon, and continued our stroll. We were walking on air. It was a fascinating experience. I wondered what else we were capable of doing, which stirred a chuckle from my companion. His response reminded me of an earlier remark he had made regarding my limited understanding about a particular topic. Although no additional commentary followed his quiet chuckle, I was certain my lack of understanding was blatantly obvious. Eventually, we began a gentle descent from the heights overlooking the canyon and safely landed into a setting most dear to my heart and soul. How we traversed from the canyon ledge to this new setting was a mystery, but our final stop landed us upon a beach adorned with sparkling white sand that stretched beyond sight. My heart immediately aligned with the rhythm of the ocean. My arms extended as if they were capable of embracing the familiar waters. I belonged there. With all that I am, I knew this place was my beginning. From these waters, I came into existence. My heart throbbed with awareness; the connection felt was undeniable. I was Home. Tears streamed down my face. The return, that so many write about, paled to the actual experience. I could not bear the separation between us. I moved toward the water's edge, my breath was short. *How long has it been since we were together?* No answer came to mind, and none was really necessary. The moment of relevance was before me. *The time is now!* The words of old called to me and I moved forward to meet the oceanic waters. Gently and lovingly I stepped into the waters of my birth. How sweet it was! The swirls of the waves tickled by toes and wrapped about my ankles, an embrace by the Mother of a Child long ago released into the world. My heart was full. No greater moment could I remember. My breaths were large and each one reveled in the moment. I was at peace!

A passage from
The Time is Now
(Chapter One)

*"We ask your consideration in hearing our story
through this Book of Clarification.
The Time is Now
for the people of Earth to know the Truth of
Who You Are."*

I remained ankle deep in the waters of my beginning for what seemed like eternity. Memories of heartfelt connections filled me. Visits with Old Friends, one after another nourished my soul. And the sorrows of times past left me; they were no more. Comforted by awareness and understanding of truths from the past freed me to live fully in the present. Old wounds were healed with the knowledge that all interactions were for a reason, even those that were not appreciated at the time of their occurrence. There were no coincidences. All was intended, and All were served. In that brilliant moment of understanding All That Was, All That Is became gratefully cherished. I was relieved to know my injuries to others were healed and the consequences were beneficial for those who had incurred them, as were the injuries I had received from others. My time in the waters of my beginning rejuvenated me. Words of gratitude were exchanged, new commitments were made, and farewells were lovingly shared. And then, my Friends of Old exited the beach, giving me a private moment to express my goodbyes to the Mother of my existence.

Now, I understand my compulsion to be near oceanic waters. Thank you for bringing me into existence. Thank you, for reaching out to me all those times when I've been in need. I didn't know it was you who consoled me, but now I do, and the reality that you are here, wherever here is, fills me with joy. The waters of the Mother gently caressed my ankles again. How sweet her touch was.

"Old Friend, are you ready to return to your present home?" The tender voice of my companion brought me back to another reality. I stepped away from the water, which had receded with the tide, and turned towards my Friend. Instantly, he was before me.

"A good day, you have had!" I nodded in agreement.

"Shall we take the next step together?" And this we did.

In late afternoon, I found myself asleep in my favorite chair. The favorite pen and journal were in my lap. The last entry was this: "The Gift of this awareness is inconceivable. My heart was full then, and remains so to this moment. Life will never be the same."

14

A passage from
Speaking The Truth
(Chapter Five)

"Dear Reader, we have work to do so let us begin with an open mind and gentle heart. As you open your 'mind' to investigating your 'mind,' your 'mind' may have thoughts, ideas, opinions, and/or reactions about this scrutinizing action. If possible, quiet your mind by activating your heart. Let your heart take the lead at this point, and allow this gentle leader to instigate actions of kindness, reassurance, and acceptance. You are here to assist your mind, not to judge it. Remember please, change transpires much more rapidly with loving-kindness than with thoughtless commentary. Shall we begin?

Allow yourself to engage with your mind. Invite your mind to participate in this self-expansion process. Remind your beautiful mind that it is essential to the success of this endeavor.

In order to assess your mind, you must have access to it, thus you must gain its attention. This is our first task. Call your mind to order, please.

Were you successful with that task? Did your mind respond quickly? Has your mind responded, or is it attending other matters? Notice everything your mind is doing, for it is necessary to understand your mind's present style of functioning before any decisions can be made regarding its operational status. Perhaps your mind is reliving a conversation from an earlier encounter, or maybe it is exploring the future, attempting to ascertain and/or control what has not yet transpired. Or maybe your beautiful mind is simply lounging in inactivity, willfully selecting to ignore your request for its attention.

Review your mind's activities for the last few minutes while reading (or attempting to read) the previous few paragraphs. Do this now please, and attempt to remain on task as you do so.

What have you discovered about your multi-functioning mind? Isn't it a marvel? You may find it prudent to journal about this process, for your mind with all its wonderful qualities has the most remarkable ability to distract from tasks that are not its preference. Although you may think your mind is actively participating in this self-expansion project you may be surprised what you actually discover. Because you are essentially pursuing the possibility that your mind may indeed need some type of corrective improvement, it may be wise to consider that your mind may not agree with this endeavor and may choose instead to address its own favored activities.

Perhaps, some of you may be puzzled by the subtle insinuation that the mind and 'you' are separate entities, which of course is not the case; however, others of you may resonate to the notion that the mind at times truly appears to have a mind of its own. Is this just a silly notion or is it a notion worthy of your consideration? For those of you who are uncertain as to how to respond to this question, please be advised...careful and diligent deliberation is in your best interest.

Suffice it to say, each individual holds unique answers to the conundrum regarding the operational efficiency of the human mind; however, few are even aware that this is an issue of concern. As you continue examining your wonderful mind, you may find that it is in great need of your attention. Please do not be offended by this suggestion; it is not intended to be a comment of diminishment, but in truth is meant to be an opportunity for expansion."

Carolyn and Ron sat side by side on their favorite bench in the backyard. Although their yard was not large, they had managed to arrange it such a way that it had secrets. And the bench, which could not be seen from the house, was one of its best-kept secrets. "How was your day, Dear?" inquired Ron. He purposefully initiated the question first, so that his wonderful wife would actually focus her attention upon herself. Her usual mode of operation was to facilitate others to speak their truth while she patiently waited for her turn, which often times never circled back to her.

"I know you did that on purpose, Ron. You think I'm not taking care of myself, but I am. When I need to talk, I definitely will seek you out, Dear. You are a wonderful listener, even though you do not give yourself credit for that. And not only do you listen well, but you also give good feedback." Ron took the compliments in, and appreciated them, but he was still determined for his beloved to speak about her concerns.

"Concerns? What concerns are you referring to, dear?" Ron rolled his eyes.

"You're doing it again, Carolyn!"

"Doing what?" she asked innocently. "Oh! Did I just respond to your thoughts again? Geez! That's happening a lot, isn't it? Well, excuse my poor manners."

"Sweetie, you do not have to apologize for your remarkable skills. Such a gift you have! But, I want to know what's going on with you. You've been inside yourself all day today."

"Ah, it's my quiet self that's bothering you?"

"You're not bothering me, Carolyn, but something is going on. You may be quiet on the outside, but you're stirring about on the inside, so talk to me. What's up with you?"

His wife sat quietly, not knowing how to reply to her husband. He was right of course. She had been, as he said, stirring about all day. Her mind was flitting from one topic to another, reliving conversations, and questioning everything that she was doing or saying. How can the mind manage so many things at the same time? Sometimes, she wondered if her mind was a friend or an enemy. Finally, after battling with her mind, she was able to speak. "I feel stuck, Ron! We both agree that we are here to help the Earth, but what exactly is that going to entail? We're both committed to participating in energy sessions, and I have done that three times today, but my mind is telling me that this simply isn't enough. I felt so good after my first individual session. My connection with the Earth was strong, and I truly believe that the session was a success, and then the doubts came flooding in. One after another! My moment of satisfaction and joy was devastated by these insinuations that my actions weren't good enough. So the next two sessions were more difficult. Each one felt like a challenge rather than a privilege. And during the entire session I felt as if my participation was being judged. This mind of mine is a piece of work!

Truthfully, sometimes my mind hinders my ability to function.

I feel very strongly that I am here for a reason—that we are here for a reason, individually and conjointly. But sometimes, like today, I just feel defeated and clueless."

A passage from
Speaking The Truth
(Chapter Six)

"The time is now! At this point in time...in this present moment...let us discuss your reason for being. Many of you are acutely aware that you are here for a reason, yet you wander aimlessly as if this awareness is insignificant. Dear Reader, let us speak bluntly and truthfully. YOU ARE HERE FOR A REASON! MOVE FORWARD!

As this chapter is being received, Speaking The Truth comes forward in its quest to fulfill its reason for being. There are no coincidences. This book is being presented for a reason. The one called Claudia, the receiver of Speaking The Truth, received it for a reason. You, the Reader, are presently reading Speaking The Truth for a reason. Each who is touched by Speaking The Truth is touched by these intended messages for a reason.

In case you have not sufficiently grasped this scenario, let us remind you another time. You are here for a reason.

Please sit quietly with this information just for a moment. Allow the message of truth to settle within you while you adjust your attitude to this incredible, yet simple truth. Dear Reader, you are here for a reason. Quiet your mind's discourse and simply be with the truth."

"Dear Heart, I'm sorry you were having one of those frustrating days. I thought that might be what was going on, but I wasn't sure, so it didn't seem right to intrude upon you. I want your permission to intervene if I think that's what is going on. Would that be okay, Carolyn? Will you let me reach out to you, if I notice that it is happening again?"

"Actually, Ron, I would really appreciate it if you did. When this happens, I seem to have a really hard time pulling myself out of that disparaging place. It's a lousy place to be and the longer you dwell in it, the worse it gets. Leaves you feeling out of sorts and disgruntled."

"Yes, and that's my clue! You aren't someone who lingers in a solemn place, and rarely do I find you grumpy. Carolyn, you are definitely here for a reason. Your intuitive skills are improving daily, as was proven by your awareness of the Earth's caregiving tendencies. You know that was an incredible insight. There's a reason all of this is happening, Sweetie! You cannot allow yourself to fall victim to your mind's nonsense. We need to find a way to help each other with our recalcitrant minds. Our lives are too full and rich to be derailed by negative thoughts. Agreed?"

"Agreed! And thank you! Thank you for paying attention to my mood, and thank you for offering to help. I feel so much better. Shall we take advantage of the moment to send some energy to the Earth?"

"I think this is the perfect time and the perfect place. May I do the facilitation this time?" Carolyn urged her husband to do so.

"Wonderful!" he replied. "Let's begin by asking our minds to cooperate with us. Beautiful minds, we need your help. It is time for us to focus our intentions upon the Earth. In order for us to do this, we need your assistance. Please participate in this action of kindness by focusing your attention upon our intentions. We are grateful for your assistance. And now, let us take several deep breaths as we rest quietly in this wonderful secret space that we've created.

Here together, we release the distractions of the day, and we focus only upon joining with the Earth. Breathing in, we move closer into alignment with her. Breathing out, we release our distractions and our frustrations. With each deep breath, we become closer in union with this remarkable Life Being. Here in our garden, our feet merge with the soil of this Being, and we are filled with gratitude. So much you have done for us, and so little have we done in return. But that is changing, my Friend. We are awakening to our foolishness. Our behaviors of neglect and unkindness no longer will be tolerated. We are here to assist. As we align ourselves with your rhythm, we ask permission to send you particles of our Source energy, the energy that exists within all in existence. Our energies are One and we desire to share ours with you." More deep breaths were taken and the moment was upon them. "Dear Friends who are in listening range, join us if you can. We are preparing to send energy to the Earth; she is amenable to our request. With another deep breath, ignite your powerful healing energy and offer a particle of this energy to the Earth at any location that you prefer. We will release ours to the garden in which we are seated. My friends, far and near, inhale again. And with the exhale that follows, release the particle of healing energy and share it with the Earth. Old Friend, so grateful are we for your presence and your participation in our lives. We are forever grateful, and we will continue sending you energy as long as it is necessary. In peace be, Dear Friend."

Silence filled the garden. Not even a bird could be heard. All were quiet for the sake of the gentle giant. Time passed. The favorite goldfinch was the first to make herself noticeable. Her whispers, soft and sweet, could barely be heard. Although, she was not as flashy as her handsome spouse, she was equally beautiful. Soon all the voices of the garden returned, including theirs.

"That was lovely, Ron, really well done. And this was the perfect setting for an energy transfusion. Did you notice how our garden friends participated? Not a peep out of anyone until the session was over."

"Yes, it seems everyone was participating in helping the Earth...even our minds!"

15

A passage from
Speaking The Truth
(Chapter Seven)

"In days ahead, the challenge of the wayward mind will come and go, as is its way; however, the directionless mind is best aided when it is attended by a loving heart.

For those of you who struggle with the mind's restlessness, you will come to appreciate your heart and its able ways, for this magnificent gift is so much more than a mere organ. Rest the mind now, Dear Reader, and bring your heart to the forefront of your awareness. There, resting quietly within you, is the instrument of universal consciousness in which lie peace, serenity, and wisdom.

Accessing and joining with the Sacred Space within you, your precious Heart Space, requires nothing more than intention. Truly, intention is all that is necessary. Breathe that truth in and luxuriate in the idea that you are but a breath away from your Sacred Space.

Shall we practice? As you know, practice refines and enhances the innate abilities that we possess, awakening the possibilities of our natural gifts to their unlimited potential. Rest comfortably, knowing that you are in possession of your very own Heart Space.

Breathe deeply...settling into a pace that is comfortable for you...

Breathe deeply...gently descending into the core of your existence...

Breathe deeply...nesting into your Sacred Space... your Heart Space...

Breathe deeply...simply be in the moment...rest in your Heart Space...

Breathe deeply...simply exist in your Heart Space... simply be...

Nothing more is required than this simple practice. Your wonderful gift is already perfection; however, with your loving attention, your Heart Space will serve you even more completely because you will be consciously aware of your delightful gift of inner connection.

The benefits of this connection will fill you with wonderment, awe, and gratitude. No words will ever adequately express the reality of this remarkable experience of connection, for each one is deeply and uniquely personal; however, each effort made is rich and worthy of the attempt.

Practice joining with your Heart Space regularly, daily, and frequently.

Your 'practice' will soon be as commonplace as breathing. It will not feel like an obligatory exercise of diligence and commitment, but a gesture of endearment and heartfelt preference. Practice, Dear Friend, and receive the gifts that reside within you."

"**F**aye, are you upstairs?" Mark called out to his spouse. No answer came. He had already checked the usual hiding places. He called again, a bit louder than before. "Faye, dear! Are you upstairs?" Again, no answer was heard. Then a flash of genius came to mind. "She's in the garden!" Mark filled two coffee cups before heading out the back door. He spotted her in the distant corner of the south side of the yard. She was a fashion statement in her faded jeans, big yellow gloves, and one of his old white shirts with the sleeves rolled up to the elbows. She was bustling about, which was her normal operating speed. He questioned his desire to interrupt her. *Perhaps this isn't a good time. Or maybe she is ready for a*

break. He decided to proceed with his initial idea. He placed the coffee cups on the table and headed in her direction.

"Hey there! What's going on out here?" Faye responded to his call with a wave and big smile.

"I'm tending Mother Earth, Dear! And I truly think she is enjoying my company and my good work. Although she needs no improvements, I thought she might appreciate a little grooming here and there. I gave her a few supplements as well." Faye always referred to plant food as supplements. She believed everyone needed an occasional boost now and again, and figured that was true for Mother Nature as well. Although she had no scientific proof to back her theory, she was convinced the Earth would favor vitamins on a regular basis.

"How are you this morning?" she asked as she reached up for the morning kiss. "Hope I didn't wake you when I decamped this morning."

"Not at all! Didn't hear a thing until the alarm clock went off."

"Oh goodness, the clock caught you in bed! It must have been so satisfied! So rarely does it get to serve its true purpose!" They both chuckled about the neglected clock that was specifically bought thirty plus years ago for its alarm feature. They often wondered how many times it had actually awakened them.

"So, have you been out here since you got up? Everything is looking beautiful by the way."

"Thank you. As I said, there wasn't much to do, but a little freshening up." She glanced up and down the flowerbeds with a great deal of satisfaction, and then returned to the conversation. Actually, I did some writing first, and then felt drawn to come out here. It's been lovely. I've enjoyed the quiet and the connection with the Earth, and I also sent her some energy. And that also felt great. I'm really trying to make her a substantial part of my daily living. And today's experience has really gone well. Is that coffee, I smell?"

"Yes, at the table waiting for us!" Faye took her gloves off, gave the garden another quick look and then headed for the caffeine. Even though she had brewed the coffee earlier, she had not yet had the first sumptuous indulgence of the day.

"It's unusual for you to sleep in, Mark. Are you feeling, okay?" He leaned back into the wrought iron deck chair and gave her question careful consideration. "In general, the answer to that question is yes. I am feeling fine; however, I am also feeling torn." His answer surprised

Faye. She fiddled with her cup for a moment to see if he was going to continue, but when he didn't she responded.

"Torn? About what, Mark? Please tell me. I'm interested and concerned."

"Well, there's no need for concern, Faye. Please don't be worried about this, but ideas are beginning to form in my head, and I want your input of course." Faye urged her husband to continue. "I'll begin by saying that I am very happy with our life. It is so good to be in close connection with our friends again, and also to share this incredible project with people that we love to be with. This is such a blessing that one sometimes loses sight of the reality that we have united over this tragic situation. My point is: I am totally content with our lives presently. Obviously, I'm not content with the Earth's crisis, but I am very pleased with the role we are playing in this rescue project." Faye was pleased to hear these positive remarks, but was still waiting to learn more about Mark's comment about feeling torn.

"I know you are getting restless, Dear, so let me move into what feels like the other side of the coin." A deep breath preceded the second part of his story.

"Faye, I think our group needs to expand. Obviously, there are options for how that might happen, but it seems inevitable to me that we must split up and create new group circles. Don't get me wrong, I don't particularly like this idea, because I really enjoy our Circle of Friends, but all of us are capable of facilitating these group meetings. Logic tells me that we should pursue starting six new groups. Think of the expanded outreach.

Hopefully, our present group would continue to meet regularly but less often, because our initial group would be the hub for the expansion process. I think this is the next step that must be taken and I feel compelled to bring this forward to the group. Do you think my idea sounds reasonable, or am I off the mark?"

"I think it's the direction we're moving towards, but it does take my breath away. Are we moving too rapidly? That's really a question, not an insinuation that we aren't ready for this. I agree with you Mark, we are all able facilitators and this certainly seems like the next step, but... let me phrase that differently. This seems like the next step, AND it seems lacking. If we really are going to apprise the populace of this information then we need to move a lot faster. We really need to strategize about this.

I suspect that beautiful mind of yours already has a list of possibilities that we might pursue." Mark nodded his head in agreement and indicated that he had many ideas on his list.

"Well, Mark, this sounds exciting and I want to help with the next step, but before we end this conversation, tell me about the other part of this story that you haven't revealed yet."

A passage from
The Time is Now
(Chapter Two)

"When the time came
for the decisions to be made regarding the ailing planet
and its residing populace, All were in concerned deliberation.
Such a task as this was never before attempted,
for never before had such an unfortunate event occurred.
All in the deliberating process
weighed heavily the alternatives available to those of the dying planet
and All took these deliberations very seriously."

A loud sigh was heard from across the table. "You probably already know what I'm thinking and feeling about this, Faye. This project is huge! And we're just a few folks with limited funds, varying technological skills, and not a lot of contacts that we can reach out to. So how do we move this project forward from a household of people into the houses of everyone across the globe? This is what takes my breath away, Faye. This is a massive project! How are we going to make this happen?" Mark and Faye both took long, deep breaths and then dipped into the confines of their own minds. Faye quickly retreated from that location with an announcement.

"Mark, are we in agreement that you are going to bring this up at the next meeting?" He confirmed her question with a quick nod. "Okay, then let's change the subject, or we are both going to end up in the whirlwinds of our respective minds. We are not alone, Mark. There are others in our group with whom we must consult, and there are others around the world who are also tackling these ideas." Remember what we were assigned to practice. We must trust ourselves. Just because this project is beyond imagination doesn't mean we have to let our imaginations fester in fear. There are answers to our questions, and we will find them. I trust you, Mark. And I trust our Friends. The next step that we each must address is the hardest trust issue of all. We must trust ourselves. Let that be our focus today!"

16

"Sally, look ahead! I believe those are familiar faces." Dave's farsightedness was always helpful, but it was exceptionally convenient on an occasion such as this.

"Inform me, dear. My vision just doesn't measure up to yours."

"It's the Goodmans, dear. Ah! They've recognized us as well, and they are now waving at us." The couple returned the gesture and hastened their pace.

"How wonderful it is to see you!" declared Faye. "Isn't this a lovely day for a walk?" The four friends exchange greetings and hugs, and then immediately turned the conversation to their recent adventures within the group. Dave suggested that they move off the trail to a natural sitting area, courtesy of two large fallen yellow pines. The trees provided ample seating space.

"Well, isn't this a wonderful gathering place?" commented Sally. Everyone seemed to find the perfect spot to accommodate his or her needs. Large ferns and spindly trees grew around the downed trees forming a room-like setting that welcomed passersby to a respite from their journey. Sally imagined many intimate conversations had occurred in this setting. "Tell us, Dear Ones, what are you two up to? I sense a great deal of activity racing about in those beautiful minds of yours." Faye and Mark started laughing while Dave blushed and rolled his eyes.

"I'm sorry, folks! She's doing it again."

"Sally Moore, you are a marvel! How do you manage to know so much?"

Sally leaned over and pointed her finger at her friend, "The same way you do!" Laughter filled the wooded area. Dave noticed that the forest seemed to perk up. Perhaps it was just his imagination, but it seemed that the forest was very pleased by their company. He discreetly patted the fallen tree that he was resting upon and thanked it for all its years of service. Even now the tree continued to nourish its companions and would for many years to come. *Such dedication! What a remarkable being you are.* Dave returned to the conversation just in time to hear the Goodmans validating Sally's supposition.

"Yes, you are absolutely right, Sally!" acknowledged Mark. "Our conversations have been long and our thoughts have been many, and still there is more cogitation before us."

"Well, that sounds intriguing," inserted Dave. "Tell us more!" And they did! Words poured from their hearts about their concerns for the Earth and their ideas about the rescue project. They shared everything they had been thinking about, and the Moores listened enthusiastically to every word.

In closing, Mark added one more comment. "So, Sally, you were absolutely right when you intuited that our beautiful minds were in overdrive today. They certainly have been. And," he said somewhat sheepishly, "if truth be told, it is questionable just how beautiful our minds really are. At times, their behaviors do not merit applause."

A passage from
Speaking The Truth
(Chapter Eight)

"Perhaps it is time for greater understanding regarding the title of this book. Speaking The Truth is a book with a purpose. It is intended to assist the reader in gaining greater clarity of the 'truth' that lies within and, additionally, actually coming forward and speaking the truth once the truth is ascertained and fully understood.

And how will this be done? How will this small book achieve such a lofty purpose? How can a book help you to discover the 'truth' that lies within you? How, indeed?

Within each of you reside the answers to all your heartfelt questions. There is no mystery to this...it simply is. Many of you already know this; however, if you are reading this book now, then there remains something that is still missing, something that you continue to long for... something that continues to call to you, to beckon you, to summon you. Dear Reader, you seek within these pages that which resides within you.

Thus we must make the absolute most of this purposeful book so that you will learn from its pages where you are to seek. Within, Dear Friend, seek within. No greater guidance will you ever receive than these two words...seek within!"

Dave felt great empathy for his friends. He felt the sincerity in their hearts, and the fear they shared about successfully completing such an enormous project. Their concerns were legitimate; the project seemed insurmountable. "You two deserve a pat on the back, and a big thank you! What a day you've had!" His deep breath seemed to echo through the umbrella of trees. He was stalling, trying to find the right words without much success.

"Mark, Faye, I truly want to thank you for everything you did today. I know you're too wrapped up in the process right now to realize how much you've achieved, but listen to me, please. You two have made a great contribution to the future of this rescue mission. I'm sure your minds are going to wrangle with this repeatedly, and that's okay, because it will bring clarity to your thoughts. Don't let frustration get in the way of your deliberating and resting and deliberating some more. You two are both brilliant, and you're going to come up with an avenue for success. There will not be a singular answer to all these thoughts and ideas you're having. There will be many steps that lead you, and all of us with you, to a place of determination and a plan for implementation.

Along the way, I want you to do something for me, for the Earth. Every day, many times a day, seek within for some guidance. Your beautiful minds will take you in one direction; but in here," Dave thumped his heart, "you'll find additional and essential information. Trust yourselves! And trust the information you receive from seeking within."

Sally listened with the ears of her heart. And so too did Faye and Mark. They got it! They each had heard a truth spoken. One never knows when a messenger will come along and speak the truth that was needed at a particular time for a particular reason. But this time, the message was so blatantly obvious it could not be denied.

17

A passage from
Speaking The Truth
(Chapter Eight)

"Seek within. No matter where you are, where you have been, or where you are going, the ever-present guidance for all seekers of the truth is the same. Seek within.

The sweet beauty of self-illumination is that it lies within, waiting to be ignited by the interested pursuer of the truth. Quietly, patiently waiting for the curious seeker to come forward, the truth hides from no one. Although many paths have been and will continue to be followed in the ongoing, never-ending search for the truth, there remains one simple realization that every journeyer comes to recognize...all paths lead to the same destination...and the destination lies within."

Barbara sat quietly at her desk, which belied the activity that was underway in the recesses of her mind. Her day had been successful, and there were more tasks that required her attention; however, the mind that has a mind of its own clearly usurped her intentions and was leading her in directions not of her own accord. *This is so frustrating. Stop this immediately! I do not want to linger in this story that you have created without my permission or my desire. So stop it! I'm serious. I do not want to spend even a minute more engaging in your worriment. And rest assured, mind of mine, this is your story, your worriment, your problem! I choose not to participate.*

Barb pushed her chair away from the desk, left the room closing the door behind her. *Enough already!* She had learned over the years that there were times when "the mind" simply took charge as if it had the right to do so. Although she had greatly benefitted from her meditative practice, there were still times when the mind could commandeer her preferences. Over time, she learned that these unwanted interruptions usually held some type of valuable information that she needed. Barb wished her mind would find a better means of delivery; these elongated, agitated meanderings of the mind were too annoying to endure. She decided that a walk would be helpful. Donning a light jacket and a scarf, she took off for an encounter with peace of mind. Fresh air was often the antidote for the wayward mind.

"Oh, my word! Mother Earth, you are gorgeous!" Everywhere Barb looked was another sight to behold. The forsythia hedge across the street from her house was truly borrowed landscape. The bright yellows filled the block with joy. She was so grateful for the Smiths' loving attention to their yard. The entire neighborhood benefitted from their hard work. Barb headed south so that she could enjoy the row of blossoming pear trees just a block away. Her eyes absorbed one beautiful view after another. "Isn't this wonderful?" she remarked aloud. This neighborhood is an example of collaborative work between the Earth and all the gardeners who love assisting her. "We have done some things right!"

"Indeed, you have!" The familiar voice was a delight to hear. No form accompanied the voice, which of course was necessitated by the circumstances. She paused for a moment to address the formless voice, but then realized how odd that might look to a passerby. Barb laughed out loud and then continued her walk, realizing it was in everyone's best interest if she communicated through her inner voice.

Old Friend, I am so happy that you have joined me. Your company is always appreciated. To what do I owe this unexpected surprise?

"May we just enjoy the scenery for a moment?" One could not deny that request.

Of course, came Barb's reply. *The Earth is in her glory period!* Her comment puzzled her. She wondered if it were true.

"Old Friend, you are allowed to have preferences. Some prefer the Spring, while others are enamored by Autumn. Regardless of the season most enjoyed, each preference is acceptable to the Life Being Earth. It

pleases her when another is impressed with her bounty. She also enjoyed your acknowledgement of the combined efforts that are evident in this particular neighborhood. As the people of Earth awaken to the wrongs that they have done to her, they must also remember all the good they have done. Many on the Earth have devoted their lives to her well being. These contributions cannot be lost to the collective memories of the Earth's development. She is a magnificent being with remarkable abilities, and still, she welcomes the creative energies of others. Much of what has happened began in innocent intentions, but with growth came avarice, and ill-informed decisions followed. More information is now known about proper care of the Earth, and from this new information, wiser decisions must be made on her behalf. What is in her best interest is also the best interest of those who co-exist with her.

She is indeed a most beautiful Life Being!" As they neared the park, Barb pointed to a path that was one of her favorites. It was a selfish act. With her invisible friend, Barb followed the meandering passageway until they reached a secluded bench encircled by a wall of rhododendrons. *"Ah, this is indeed a wonderful setting. A perfect place for a tender conversation."*

"Is that the purpose of your visit? Are we going to have a tender conversation?" Barb's companion materialized on the bench beside her. He looked around, continuing to enjoy the secret hideaway before answering her questions.

"I am here to assist you with the part of you that is frustrated with the mind that seemingly has a mind of its own." Shifting positions was Barb's way of expressing her dissatisfaction with the idea of reengaging with her ornery mind.

"Well, good luck with that, Friend. To say that we, my mind and I, are presently at odds with each other would be an understatement. Sometimes, the mind can ruin one's day. That almost happened today, but I chose to stop its nonsense. I'm not in the mood for one of its detours into areas that do not need to be explored." Her manner was firm. The Old Friend wondered if this was a good time for this conversation. He took another long look at the beauty that surrounded them, and smiled.

"Now is the moment of relevance, my Friend. What better time or place could we have than here and now in this peaceful setting to discuss a matter that interferes with who you really are?"

A passage from
Speaking The Truth
(Chapter Nine)

"Speaking the truth means standing up and showing up. It means looking deeply within to see who you really are and facing the truths you may not wish to see. In truth we are all Children of the Light, and as such, we are perfection and unconditionally accepted; however, were we not given free will to access and use wisely? Is it not wise to carefully scrutinize the self that you see in the mirror and ask the difficult questions? Are you who you are truly intended to be? Speaking the truth challenges you to do just this. Look into the depths of your being and see what you find. Are you in alignment with what you find? Are you pleased with what you find?

Too many do not face the task of seeking within, for they fear what may be found, but these fears are for naught. If the Source that all seek already accepts you as you presently are, then who are you to deny who you are?"

Although Barb felt resistant to her Friend's gentle challenge, she knew he was right. "Oh, dear!" she whined pathetically. And then in typical Barb form, she perked up, and announced that she was ready to tackle the situation. Her resilience was just one of her many admirable traits.

"I knew you could not resist an opportunity to learn, Old Friend. It is the driving force within you, which is why you must face your fears."

"Fears! What does fear have to do with my obstinate mind? I don't think you have any idea how tenacious it can be. I often wonder who is really in control? Me or this mind that has a mind of its own?"

"Yes, I can understand why you wonder that. Your mind is indeed willful and it does act out in the most inopportune times. Do you know why that happens, Old Friend? Have you noticed a pattern?" Barb carefully considered the questions. Realizing the merit of this exploration, she

decided to delve into the process. What better time than now and with this remarkable teacher?

"Well, believe it or not, my mind is much more manageable now that it once was. My Sister of Choice has been so helpful. She's the one who encouraged me to do meditation on a regular basis. It was really hard in the beginning, but over the years, it has become easier, and it is absolutely a Godsend. I have the ability to create peace of mind for myself with just a few deep breaths, and often that leads to many other opportunities, as you well know. So having shared that bit of history with you, perhaps you can understand why I get so frustrated now, when it sometimes seems as if I am back at square one with practice and with my 'journey' in general.

I'm so happy with everything that's going on in my life, so this resurgence of my unruly mind is particularly unsettling. In the old days, my mind would act out when I was worried about something or if I felt overly pressured by my work. But that isn't relevant now. I'm more confident and optimistic than I've ever been before, so this old behavior is very puzzling. And I know this may sound crazy to you, but it seems as if my mind has become more clever than it was before. It can distract me in an instant with one of its tricks, and then we're off and running down some ridiculous path of irrelevant nonsense. Sorry, Old Friend, I'm getting riled again just because we're having this conversation. Don't mean to burden you with the nonsense of my mind."

"I do not feel burdened, Old Friend. I am honored to be part of this healing process, and grateful that you allowed me to be part of your evolutionary development." Once again, Barb was taken aback by her Friend's comments. His perspective often surprised her. Her mind was filled with questions, but she managed to restrain herself.

"Why do you choose to restrict your desire to ask questions? This is one of your finest methods of self-study. Please feel free to be yourself, Old Friend!"

A passage from
Speaking The Truth
(Chapter Nine)

"We were gifted life with a mandate to evolve and the freedom to actively participate in our evolutionary process. What a tragedy it would be to allow fear to disrupt and paralyze our expansion process. Face your deepest fears. Seek within and discover your truths.

You were also gifted with wonderful skills and abilities to finesse your evolution. Access these gifts, utilize everything you have been provided so that you can actively participate in your creative development. You were gifted with life, what will you do with this wondrous gift?"

His words brought tears to Barb's eyes. She attempted to hide them from her Friend, but he knew immediately that her heart was breaking. He could feel the pain of the incident that had wounded her so deeply that it continued to this day. *Oh, such agony!* He wished to bring the learning experience to a halt, to release the memory of old, but knew to do so would be a disservice to his Friend. Only she could make the decision to free herself. His role was to be the Listener until she was ready to make her decision. He focused his intentions upon a speedy recovery to the renewed injury.

"I'm sorry, my Friend. It seems I've been visited by a memory that I thought was long ago forgotten." The image of Barb's father in an alcoholic rage came into the invisible Friend's mind. It was excruciating to witness. No wonder she strived so diligently to discover who she really was. The need to know who she was, and who she was to be came long before the humiliating incident with her father, but his disgrace had impeded her developmental process since that crucial moment. To recover from the diminishing experience, she immersed herself into a lifelong quest to prove that she was not what her father had labeled her.

The incident and the label were long driven from her mind, but the pain, the heartache remained within and continued to impede her self-discovery process until this very moment in time.

"Old Friend, you are more than you appear to be!" Tears streamed down Barb's cheeks. The part of her that remembered what transpired so many years before could not hear what the Friend was saying. That part of Barbara was hearing the shaming words of the father than damned her to years of fear that was so unbearable that the memory lived in the unconscious part of her mind. Resting there in the darkness of her mind, the cruelty simmered quietly waiting for opportunities when it could surface and do more harm. The pain, which came seemingly from out of nowhere, would be deeply experienced, but the source of the pain would remain anonymous. Then the drive to understand who she really was would propel her forward again. Through these agonizing periods, she grew into a woman of great character. She became more as she strived to be more and the process continues to today.

"Barbara, Old Friend, will you please listen to me?" His words went unnoticed, as her tears continued to flow. He spoke again, *"Old Friend, I am in need of your attention. Please pull yourself away from the time of old and return to the present. Now is the moment of relevance."* Barb had to shake the past away from her. She literally swept the pain from her body to free herself from its entanglement. And deep breaths were repeated taken until the deed was done. Her breathing became normal, the tears stopped, and she was able to look her Friend in the eye once again. *"Thank you for coming back, my Friend. I am most pleased to be in your presence once again."*

"Thank you for helping me. I am not what my father said I was. I hope you know that is not my truth." Her fear of being misconstrued was palpable. The damage done was heartbreaking.

"Old Friend, I have always known who you really are, as do all your companions who watch over you. Never have we doubted your goodness. So very sorry are we that the father was so burdened by his own pain that he could not rise above it."

"He wasn't a bad person," Barb quickly proclaimed. "He just couldn't figure out how to manage life. He was so unhappy and miserable that the drinking overtook him. I'm sure his suffering was why he committed suicide. I'm sorry that mental health services were so limited back then. No one knew how to help him. I hope he knows that I love him and that I don't blame him for anything. He had a hard life. I just hope he is okay now."

"You are a remarkable individual, Old Friend. Rest assured your father's pain was released when he chose to exit his life experience. He worried about you and regretted his words and actions. And he continues to watch over you. He is deeply relieved by your words and wants you to hear his. He wishes you to know that he is very proud of you. His unkindness was never intended and he wants you to know that you are moving in the right direction. He says that you are already who you are intended to be, and you are becoming more. He urges you to trust yourself, because you are someone who can be trusted. You are One who will inspire others to trust themselves as well.

Barbara, Dear Friend, the words of the father speak the truth of who you really are and of who you are becoming. You live an exemplary life and your presence touches the hearts of many. This is a truth that you must hold onto.

The fear of the past no longer has any hold on you, Dear Friend. You know who you really are and this is the truth that now guides you. The energy of that old memory is released from you and from the father. No longer can you be wounded by it.

I hope this brings you peace of mind, my Dear Friend."

"Indeed, it does. Thank you for facilitating this healing session. I feel much better and I sense that my Dad does as well. You're a good friend, Old Friend!"

"As are you, Old Friend!"

18

A passage from
The Time is Now
(Chapter Two)

*"The fate of the children of the planet destined to destruction
lay in the hands of the forbears of the Universe.
The magnitude of this responsibility
was far larger than any experienced before,
and with many unknowns not experienced before;
but this commitment, All accepted,
for no other conscientious alternative was there to pursue.
As each deliberator pondered the options,
each came to the same decision.
To do nothing would be an act of unconscionable consequences,
yet to take action was an act of conscionable intent,
with unknown consequences."*

The need for another gathering kept coming to mind. I thought about connecting with our Old Friend, but it didn't seem necessary. I knew it was time and I was confident that everyone else felt the same way. So, I made the phone calls, and as I suspected, the gang was relieved.

"Thank goodness!" declared Faye, "Mark will be so happy to hear this. He was talking about calling you today. Maybe you picked up on his intentions." I agreed that his messages were probably received along with numerous other ones.

"You know, I was just sitting here, Faye, and it became evident to me that everyone is ready to get together again. So, let's do it!"

"Sounds great! And by the way, don't worry about refreshments. I'll take care of managing that." My appreciation was expressed and we wished each other well.

"Good evening, everyone! Please come in and make yourselves at home." As always, hugs and greetings had begun on the front porch. The Moores and the Goodmans entered first with their enticing trays of goodies. I was trying to get my own share of hugs amongst the bustling of this well-trained crew. Faye and Sally encouraged everyone to grab their treats before settling in for the evening and everyone joyfully obliged. Within minutes we were all situated in our favorite chairs and ready to begin the meeting.

As the hostess, I felt compelled to say something, but I was at a loss. As is so often true in this group of friends, someone took a deep breath on my behalf, and everyone followed. This warmed my heart, and I knew it did for my friends as well.

"My Friends, it is such a pleasure to be with you again. Like you, I find time particularly unusual nowadays. Even though we were just together, it feels as if years have transpired. You have been missed even though you are only blocks away. Thanks for being here! And thank you for being in my life!" Similar sentiments were also expressed by other members of the group. It was a lovely way to begin our time together.

"I'm curious. How many of you were ready to call another meeting?" All hands went up! This created a stir. Mark Goodman admitted that he had felt a sense of urgency for another meeting and the Andersons concurred.

"I felt a sense of need," acknowledged Barb. "There is so much going on currently that I feel the need to be in connection. As Sister just said, even though we are seeing each other frequently, I really miss you in between the times we are together. I've come to a much greater understanding how important you all are to me. You are my family and I am so grateful for each and every one of you." Her sentiments touched everyone.

"Isn't this a lovely way to begin our meeting?" inserted Annie. "We are a family, aren't we? Actually, we have been for a long time, but these recent events have tightened our relationships. I'm very pleased about this. We've always known over the years that we were there for one another, but our lives became busy and I think we just took our relationships for granted, which in many ways is a compliment. It's a sign of trust, but relationships need nourishment, and that's what is happening now. We are enriching each other's lives by sharing our experiences and our hearts with one another, and as a result of our connections we are becoming more involved with our concerns about our world, and about Mother Earth. Which brings us full circle, doesn't it?

We are here this evening because of the Earth. So why don't we start our meeting with a healing session for her. Who wants to facilitate the session?"

"May I have the privilege of leading the energy session?" The voice was followed by the materialization of their Old Friend. His arrival brought great joy to the group.

"I am most pleased to be in your presence once again. With your permission, all who are in listening range will also participate in this evening's healing experience. We are most eager to be of assistance." The session began as usual. Deep breaths were accessed to quiet our minds and to regulate our intentions. Our beloved teacher was a wonderful guide. Through his leadership, our intentions of healing the Earth became an inward journey from which we all benefited.

"Friends, far and near, we come on behalf of the Life Being Earth. So much she has done for so many, and for all her sacrifices, we are humbly grateful. No greater service can any provide than the tender loving care of another. This she has done for millennia. She has provided homes for the homeless, food for the hungry, water for the thirsty, and space from which life could expand freely in its own magnificent ways. She has been the ultimate provider and caregiver, and now she requires our help.

Thus, we gather on her behalf. Our numbers are large and we are grateful for everyone who is participating. Thank you for standing for the Earth. Thank you for sharing a part of your own Source energy with this Dear Old Friend. And thank you for continuing to assist her as the days ahead unfold. Breathe deeply, Dear Friends. Ignite the powerful healing energy within you. With each deep inhale, feel the strength of your healing energy growing stronger. As you prepare yourselves, I will approach the Mother with a request.

Old Friend, we come in peace, and we ask another favor of you. So many requests have you already satisfied, but another must now be made.

Dear Old Friend, you are One who is so accustomed to helping others that you have forgotten how to receive. We come forward at this time to remind you that in your present circumstances, it is essential that you allow yourself to receive the energy that will be transferred to you. We do this because we desire to assist you and we do this because we are presently healthy and able to do this with no detriment to ourselves. Please accept our desire to be of service. Please allow yourself to freely accept this energy transfer so that it reaches maximum efficiency.

My Friends, from many locations, let us begin the transfer. With another deep breath capture the Source energy particle within and visualize it exiting from your form. Propel your energy to the desired location and release it into the Mother now. Know that your provision of healing energy is well received and it will have powerful consequences. Each energy transfusion aids her. New vibrant energy has restorative capabilities. Rest in knowing that you have assisted the Earth in her recovery to full health.

Rest now, Dear Friends, and return to your respective homes. Gratitude abounds! In peace be."

A passage from
The Time is Now
(Chapter Two)

"All were in agreement and All were of committed intentions.
The situation occurring on the most recently developed planet
in the distant galaxy
was of dire circumstances,
and the members of the Universal Family
would not neglect their duties as guardians of all in the Family.
Unknown it was to the recent newborns
that they belonged to a family,
but the Family knew.
And the Universal Family considered the care of all newborns
its most important responsibility.
No other responsibility equaled that of caring for the children.

With the highest regard for the children of the newly evolved planet,
the members of the Universal Family chose to intercede
on behalf of these children destined to doom."

"What a wonderful session!" "Thank you," Annie said sincerely, "for facilitating that healing experience. And thanks to everyone, everywhere for joining with us. I hope the Earth is receiving freely now. I know it's against her principles, but she must take care of herself."

"I believe the wisdom of our request has been understood. However, it will be wise for us to remind her of this frequently, because her maternal instinct drives her to do otherwise. Fortunately, the insight that came from this Circle of Friends is now reaching others near and far. Another reason to be in gratitude and to be hopeful. We have witnessed the importance of sharing information. Because of Friend Carolyn and her highly intuitive abilities, we learned valuable information about the Earth's inclination, and now that knowledge has been spread to others. All who desire to participate in her healing process must be aware of her proclivity to put others' needs before her own.

Since our last meeting, much growth has transpired and new ideas have arisen. Who wishes to share their valuable thoughts first?"

Mark did not hesitate. He respectfully asked for permission to address the group and his friends were pleased by his initiative. With thumbs up from Faye and a deep breath, he introduced his idea regarding outreach. Everyone listened carefully. When he finished what seemed like a presentation to him, he was relieved, until he saw the glazed over eyes of his friends. He turned to Faye for support and she gave him an almost unnoticeable nod. Only one of their friends caught the subtle gesture. She waited to see what Mark would do, but was ready to intervene if necessary. He continued his silence, as did the beloved teacher, and everyone else.

Eventually, I made an effort to assert myself, but then thought better of it. *Or did I?* I turned in Faye's direction, and realized that it was her strong telepathic abilities that had reached out to me. I could see in her eyes that she did not want me to interfere with Mark's process. Although, I didn't understand her reasoning, I trusted Faye's awareness of what was best for her husband. And then the deep breath was heard.

"Okay, Friends, I'm needing some feedback here. My mind is beside itself right now, and I need to let all of you know that your silence is bringing up issues for me. Of course, I'm embarrassed about that, but it is what it is. So before I go off into my mind's arena of fear, I need to check in with you. Tell me what's going on with you. I hope my ideas haven't offended anyone."

"Not at all," replied Dave. "Please, forgive my slow reaction time, Mark. Your ideas are great and I think you're right on target! But, I got lost in my own sadness about this group breaking up." Other group members nodded and made similar remarks. "I heard everything that you suggested and was definitely relieved that this group would continue to be the hub for other future groups, but my mind couldn't let go of the idea of not seeing everyone as frequently as we've enjoyed in the last weeks. I'm sorry we left you hanging, Mark. That must have been very uncomfortable. I know it would have been for me. So again, I'm sorry. And I agree with your ideas. It's the next step that we need to take."

"Mark, I had a similar reaction to the idea of separating our group," added Jim, "but I too agree that it's the right thing to do. Your ideas seem congruent with where we're heading, but it defines a timeline. Rather than thinking about it as happening sometime in the future, you're suggesting that it must happen now. We need to strategize our plan and implement it. I agree. My heart is heavy, and I'm not really facing the loss of contact with all of you, but I know this is the right thing to do." Mark was breathing easier. Hearing his friends' affirmations was releasing the tension that had built up so rapidly during the brief moment of silence that occurred after he finished telling the group about his ideas. For him the time felt like an eternity; for his friends the time was incomprehensible. They were lost in their thoughts about being separated from one another, so time had no meaning to them.

"I would like to add onto the feedback you've already received, Mark." I quickly glanced in Faye's direction and saw the barely noticeable nod giving the okay to do so. First, thank you for going first, Mark. I don't really understand why that is so difficult, but it is, and I always appreciate it when someone takes the initiative. So thank you for that. And secondly, I want to acknowledge your courage. Bringing this idea forward wasn't easy, but you did it, and you did it well. That took a lot of courage, and I was even more impressed with your ability to speak your truth when your anxiety and fears were rising up. That was great role modeling,

Mark." I was grateful to see Mark relaxing into his chair. He was taking in the compliments.

"You know, we've all been so fortunate to enter into this topic of saving the Earth in the company of wonderful friends. Even though the subject is difficult, we've had each other to get through these weeks of exploration. We've truly been blessed. I hope when we expand our work with folks who are not known to us that we have similar experiences as we had with the Carsons and the Barkleys. You guys just blended in as if you had always been a part of us. Hopefully, we will all have similar experiences as we expand our outreach. But in the meantime as we are solidifying our plans, we may have moments of doubts. And we may have to face a few more fears, but we can do it. Mark just provided us with a wonderful demonstration of being straightforward, sincere, and truthful. He did it, and so can we!"

A passage from
Speaking The Truth
(Chapter Ten)

"Speaking The Truth is a framework, a guide, from which to progress in our daily living. We must join together as members of a greater community and find a common ground for each who exists within and beyond our sight to freely exist from a truth-filled place.

What exactly does this mean?

Although we prefer to think that we speak the truth at all times in all places to all others that we encounter, we are now ready to review this belief about ourselves and truly assess where we stand with this presumed truth. Do we really speak our truth at all times?

Do you? Do you really speak your truth at all times?

We are ready, Dear Friends, to explore this aspect of our human nature. Perhaps this statement is too boldly asserted, or perhaps it really is our truth. Each of us will have to discern this next step. You are encouraged to delve deeply within to determine your readiness. Can you face the truth about your ability to speak the truth? Are you ready to understand the full meaning of this simple, yet profound idea?

As with all topics of great significance, time and deliberation are necessary. Will you take the time to examine this vitally important aspect of your evolutionary development? Only you can answer this question...ponder it with a clear mind and open heart."

"My Friends, your words are most gratifying to those who watch over you from afar. Indeed, the next step demands that you leave the comfort of this safe place for the purpose of creating other safe places where the truth about the Earth's situation can be presented. Your willingness to take the next step pleases all. We are most grateful.

As was already stated, it will take courage to proceed. However, a simple reminder is offered to ease your concerns. The strength that is needed already resides within you. The energy that you so generously share with the Life Being Earth is the same energy needed to combat one's fears. Seek within, Dear Friends, and the courage needed for this next step in the project to save the Earth will be found. Your efforts on behalf of the planet have shown your abilities to access and effectively use the powerful energy that resides within. So too will you utilize this energy in the days to come.

Each of you has faced uncertainties that have arisen since entering into this mission of rescue, and you have done so with grace and dignity. You know the vulnerabilities that you experienced and that others will face as well. Your compassionate hearts will be your guide, my Friends. You will speak the truth to all you encounter and they will grow from your honest and humble ways.

Because you trust each other, the tasks ahead will be easier. You have learned so much from one another, and you will still have each other to consult with when you encounter situations that puzzle you. Remember this, Dear Friends, for it is an essential element for all your work to come. Trust each other! Speak the truth to each other at all times, and if and when you falter, openly acknowledge that you are in need of assistance. Do not diminish yourselves for a moment of fear that rises from within you. Simply accept such an experience as a reminder that you are not alone. Always, we will need the assistance of another and always must we be available *to offer assistance to another. This simply is the way when one exists in human form. In truth, it is a means for connection from which all involved can benefit. View fear in this way, and you will never need to fear it again.*

Old Friends, please trust yourselves as we trust you. Because of you, we have hope that the Beloved Earth will continue. The people of Earth have the ability to save her, and we trust that you will do so.

I suggest we meet again in seventy-two hours to discuss the plan that you have devised. Are you in agreement with this time frame?" Everyone agreed. I personally wondered if we should discuss the grief that we all were experiencing, but decided not to bring it up at this time. But as is often the case, another was already attending the idea.

"My Friends, I have another suggestion, before I take my leave of you. Your hearts are heavy, Dear Ones, because you anticipate the loss of connection that is coming. I urge you to discuss this before you depart each other's company this evening. Your sadness is real, but it is founded in misunderstanding. Please remember, you are not losing each other. You are merely readjusting your visitation schedules. Never will you lose the support of one another. Friendships endure the test of time, and eternity lasts forever. In peace be, My Friends!"

A passage from
Speaking The Truth
(Chapter Ten)

"We will proceed with hopeful anticipation that you choose to join us.

Breathe deeply. Join with your Sacred Breath as you begin one of the greatest adventures of this lifetime. You are not alone in this self-discovery process, even though it appears to be a solo-journey. Your travels are yours to discern, yours to experience, and yours to blossom from, as each new bud of awareness opens into full consciousness. Your growth, your evolutionary expansion is yours to command and this will be respected and honored at all times, for this is your Divine Privilege...your Gift of Free Will... that allows you to be in complete authority as you move forward in your journey to discover the truth of your True Self.

Rest assured your journey is and always will be accompanied, even though at times you will wonder if this is true. Fortunately, Dear Friend, this is a universal truth. Unfortunately, it is a truth that is sometimes forgotten, during which one often wanders about in doubt, uncertainty, and aloneness; but even during these times of confusion, the truth remains the truth. You are never alone. This truth is best remembered when joining with your Sacred Breath. Do so now, as you embark upon your newest excursion."

Silence gripped the room after the departure of the beloved teacher. I wondered who would take the initiative to speak this time. The answer came suddenly when our dear friend, Barbara started to cry. She could not hide the tears, and hers invited others to join the tearful party. And as is often said, the tears were healing. Eventually, Barb was able to articulate her love for her friends. "You are such an important part of my life. I am really going to miss these wonderful meetings and the great conversations that we've shared. This has been a remarkable time. I'm feeling very testy about this, even though I know it is absolutely the right thing for us to do. Please tell me that we will not lose touch with one another." Reassurances were abundant. No one was happy with this aspect of the outreach program, and yet, outreach was paramount to the success of rescuing the Earth.

"Well, I have a suggestion," announced Annie. "It requires that we begin our conversation about creating a plan for outreach. So, my suggestion is that we decide right now to continue meeting twice a month after our other groups have started. And this suggestion isn't just about my selfish need to have contact with all of you, which I openly admit is part of the reason for continuing to meet. However, we really will need time for consultation about our new groups. I expect that the groups will go well, but it is only natural that we will experience circumstances that we have not addressed before, and we need each other as a sounding board. So meeting will be utilitarian as well as socially satisfying. For my own sense of security, I want an agreement that we will continue to meet twice a month." Annie's last sentence was asserted firmly. Jim chuckled, as he remembered Annie's father describing his daughter. *She's just a little bit, but she's mighty!* Truer words were never spoken. As always, Jim was very proud of his dear, sweet, tiny wife.

Everyone immediately replied positively to Annie's suggestion. Satisfied, she was able to sit back into her chair and relax.

"Well, I'm totally in agreement with the idea that we continue to have our own meetings, because I think they are going to be necessary. My Friends, I think we may have some challenges ahead of us and I want to be able to access the wisdom that exists within this group.

I'm not speaking from a fearful place. I truly believe that we are all capable of facilitating these meetings, but we are a good team. We work really well together and that makes our group meetings easy to manage. Until we find that type of rhythm with our new groups, I think it is important that we have close contact for consultation and brainstorming. Plus, I suspect we will be experiencing new adventures that we will need to share with one another. As you all well know, we've known each other for so long that we can predict what each other is going to say or think. Who knows what we will encounter with folks who are new to us? The possibilities that face us are actually very exciting, when you allow yourself to think openly and positively about it. But it is also a bit worrisome. And I want to know that we can reach out to one another if the need arises."

"Amen!" responded Sally. "And this brings up another thought for me," she continued. "What about our invisible Friend? Is he still going to be available? Is he going to assist us with the new groups, and is he still going to be available to us as he as been so far? I have to be honest. The idea of losing his companionship takes me to another layer of grief. I'm not sure that I'm able to face that at this moment. Have any of you started thinking about this yet?" Sally's question brought on another round of silence.

A passage from
The Time is Now
(Chapter Three)

*"Unknown to these children evolving on this distant planet
was the fate of their circumstances,
for unaware were they that a perilous situation had evolved
on their beautiful planet.
So busy were they living their experiences
that they did not see the path of destruction,
which lay before them.
These newborns, innocent and of no understanding,
evolved in ways that perpetuated their path
to an ever increasing point of no return."*

Jill was startled by the entire conversation. Even though she knew the goal of this group was to spread truthful information about the Earth's situation, she hadn't anticipated the group splitting up so soon. Having just joined the group, she was not ready to let go of these wonderful people that she and her husband had just met. And now, the conversation had turned to the revered teacher. Her heart was sinking! She did not want to lose these people or this incredible connection with someone who was from another realm of existence. Being invited to this group was the gift of a lifetime. She did not want to think about this adventure coming to an end. Her heart was racing and her body naturally responded with a loud deep breath. It caught everyone's attention.

"Jill, Dear, are you okay?" My question surprised her. She turned to her husband, Stephen, before responding. He reached over and placed his hand upon hers. No words were spoken; they were unnecessary. The gesture communicated his support.

She sighed freely before speaking her truth. "Honestly, I'm not sure how to answer your questions. In general, I'm fine, but my heart is definitely unsettled at the moment. We are so grateful to be part of this group. We were just talking about this earlier today." She glanced at Stephen and he affirmed her statement. "Our lives are so much richer since we joined your wonderful gatherings. We feel like we've finally found our tribe.

Please, don't misunderstand. Stephen and I are in agreement with the need to extend our outreach. It's absolutely necessary or this important message will never have the impact it is intended to create. So, we are totally on board with this next step, and..." Jill was struggling to complete her thoughts. "And we do not want to lose the connection that we've found with all of you. The best I can say is that we are here to help save the Earth, and we are... Oh, excuse me, even though I am certain that Stephen feels the same way, I will let him speak for himself. Personally, I am grieving the idea of less contact, but I can deal with it. I will deal with it! But, just be on notice, you may find me reaching out for some quality time occasionally. Hope that we can leave that opportunity open." The Circle of Friends reacted instantly and positively, which raised Jill and Stephen's spirits. The other newcomers to the group, the Barkleys, were relieved by Jill's suggestion. They too were feeling antsy about the group splitting up.

"Jill, thank you for sharing your concerns," asserted Carolyn. "I feel the same way. Obviously, we will all experience some growing pains with this new situation, but we will adapt. And we will meet the challenges as they arise. We have to! I think each of us will have to find a balance between grieving the changes that confront us while remembering our commitment to the Earth. In essence that's the reality we've already been facing.

Earth is changing right before our eyes, and it's been wonderful facing this agonizing issue in the company of special friends. And we will continue to be a support for one another. That's what we are learning through this conversation. What I'm hearing is the making of another commitment. We are committed to saving the Earth, and we are committed to maintaining these powerful relationships. That works for me!"

The group collectively agreed with Carolyn's suggestions. The conversation seemed to be at a place of rest, but before ending the meeting, everyone agreed that a moment of silence on behalf of the Earth was needed. Each member reached deeply into their hearts and embraced the moment of connection with this magnificent Life Being. So tender was her heart. So blessed were they to be aware of her presence. With gratitude for all present, the meeting came to an end.

Those from afar watched the proceedings with great interest. *"What was hopefully anticipated is coming to fruition. The heartfelt connection created among this group has cemented itself and will not be lost due to the changes that will be coming."*

"Indeed, they speak from their hearts, and the truth solidifies their relationships. This is most encouraging."

A passage from
Speaking The Truth
(Chapter Eleven)

"Let us begin old friend. The time is now. In what ways do you presently speak the truth? Think expansively while you ponder this, for it is a question that is more far reaching than you may initially imagine. Once again, you are encouraged to merge with your Sacred Breath as you step into the realm of Speaking The Truth.

Do you presently speak the truth?

Do you presently speak the truth to your Self?

Do you presently speak the truth to others?

As you can readily see, these are not easy questions. At first glance one might quickly respond positively to each of these inquiries, but by all means give these questions another moment of your attention. To answer truthfully, one must speak the truth, but to speak the truth, one must know the truth. Let us look more deeply into these questions. Do you presently speak the truth?

Before you answer, allow a moment to reflect upon your reactions. How is your mind reacting to reading this question? How is your body reacting and where in your body is the reaction occurring? What new questions are arising as a result of your introspection and what are the corresponding reactions? Pursue each question in a heartfelt manner, for each answer brings you more information about your truth of speaking the truth.

You may find it beneficial to ponder these questions with pen in hand. Each answer will build upon the other and each deserves your time and consideration.

As you investigate these questions, your sense of self may come into question. You may feel insulted by these questions...or challenged...or threatened...or merely curious. We strongly urge you to be optimistically curious. Hopefully, you will find this exploratory process one that awakens your senses to your True Self and brightens your awareness of the goodness within you. The questions are not intended to diminish you, but are in truth your pathway to freedom. What you may learn has the potential of freeing you from misunderstandings about self and others, as well as your understanding of your True Self.

Please do not be shy or reticent about these provocative questions. Each is a stepping-stone to new beginnings, to new awarenesses, and to a new and fuller acceptance of your True Self. Breathe deeply, Dear Friend, and find comfort and courage from the Breath that sustains you."

19

Sleep did not come easily. My mind continued to process the meeting ad nauseam. *Oh, dear mind of mine, what are you so bothered about? The discussion was lovely. Heartfelt commitments were made and the reassurances exchanged were sincere and supportive. All is well. Will you stop insisting upon reliving every conversation as if they are not yet done?* The mind persisted. Instead of listening helplessly to the ongoing tribulations of the insatiable mind, I got out of the bed. "Enough!" I announced to the empty room. Glancing towards the journal, I quickly dismissed it as an option to my frustration. Although that probably wasn't the best decision in the moment, it was the action taken nonetheless. As I stood at the side of my bed not knowing what action to take, a view of the full moon came to mind. *Oh goodie! That will make me excessively happy!* Grabbing my robe, I followed the mind's suggestion and went out to the front porch to take a peek. "Breathtaking! What sweet mysteries do you hold?" I spoke as if the moon could hear me, and as if I had the privilege to address her.

"*She does! And you do!*" came the familiar voice.

"Goodness, Old Friend, I wasn't expecting your company, but I am delighted to see you." I pointed to the porch swing and suggested that we sit there. My suggestion was accepted. "So, were you just hanging around out here or are you here for a reason?" My question tickled my Friend. His laughter made me laugh as well.

"*I am here, my Friend, because you are in need. But before we address your circumstances, I wish to impress upon you that the moon heard your comments, and She was most pleased. You are aware that She too is a Life Being, similar to but different from the Earth. And like the Earth, she too delights in being noticed and admired. All in existence share the need to be loved and respected. So difficult this is for humans to understand. They live in misunderstanding about their place in the Universe, and unfortunately, assume that only they are deserving of such sentiments. How sad this is! Not only for the human species but also for all those with whom they coexist. Mutual acceptance of All is the preference of all others in existence."*

"What happened to us, Old Friend? Why have we evolved with such cynicism and distrust of everyone that is different from what we presume ourselves to be?" Before my Friend could answer, I answered the question myself. "It's fear, isn't it? Fear has distorted our views of self and others, and we've become lost in the distortions that we've created."

"Yes! Fear has limited the potential of the human species. So very sad this is, but not all is lost. The potential still remains in each of you. And because of this, hope abounds!"

"Your optimism in us gives me hope! I hope we deserve your faith in us, Dear Friend."

"Indeed, you do. No one blames the Children of Earth for their misunderstandings. All are deeply concerned and wish only the best for those who are the future of humankind. Remember, Dear Friend, many came before you who contributed to your present circumstances, and many more will follow who will improve upon the advances that have already been made. All are involved with this tragedy and all are responsible for mending it."

"How do we do that? No! Let me rephrase that. How do I help? Sometimes, my Friend, I feel helpless and impotent. How can I help solve this huge crisis? Can we really save the Earth? And can we humans really learn to love, respect, and accept one another?" Tears streamed down my face. "Sorry Friend, don't know where all this is coming from. Please forgive me."

"Your concerns are coming from your tender heart! The conversations experienced earlier caused you to move into rumination. The mind misconstrued your tender feelings as a weakness and then attempted to help by reliving the experiences in hopes that you would choose another response. The mind does not grasp the importance of the heart's role and often creates issues when there are none. So sweet were the reactions among the Circle of Friends and so profoundly helpful. Grieving was achieved, new ideas blossomed, and new commitments were made. The tender, loving atmosphere produced great results. The mind simply misunderstood the dynamics of the intimate relational experiences.

Once confused, the energy of the mind can cause discomfort and even increase the concerns that were previously at rest. Thus, your worries about assisting the Earth and your people surfaced again. Your questions are most relevant, Old Friend, and there are many answers that you and others will continue to discover. In the meantime, the most salient answer I can propose is this. Trust yourself, Old Friend, and at all times, speak the truth. You are one to whom people listen. With this comes responsibility; therefore, you must speak carefully, truthfully, and with hopefulness as your guide. If you are unable to sustain the energy for such a conversation then it is best for you to be silent. What I say to you is important, for you are one who is here to spread the truth to the peoples of the planet Earth. There will be times when you feel weary, and when those times befall you, then you must graciously decline to make comments.

And when there are times when you must speak of your own frailties, there will be those who are available to assist you. Do not fear this responsibility, Old Friend. You have lived it many times before, and once again, you will serve well. In so doing, you will be providing the assistance that you so dearly wish to achieve. My Friend, I am most grateful to be working with you again, and I offer to be a listening ear, whenever you are in need."

"Old Friend, you take my breath away! As always, I am feeling better. You have the most amazing effect, my Friend. Thank you for joining me. I believe sleep will come easily now. In peace be, My Friend!"

"And to you, Old Friend!"

Before I went to bed, I did something I hadn't done since childhood. I got down on my knees with elbows leaning on the side of the bed, and I prayed. I prayed for the Life Being Earth, and I prayed for all the people on Earth who were facing great changes. I prayed for my Family, my Family of Dear Friends, and I prayed for the invisible Friend, who so carefully watched over me and guided me. I also prayed for those who had gone before. We were all in this together. I prayed for all of us. And then the time for slumber came.

A passage from
Speaking The Truth
(Chapter Twelve)

"Let us return to the question before us. Do you presently speak the truth?

In what ways do you speak your truth? Where? When? How? With whom? Will you honor yourself today by witnessing your truthful acts? Be alert throughout the day and notice all the various ways in which you practice speaking the truth. This simple act of bearing witness will greatly expand your awareness of your truthful ways and validate the goodness that exists within you. Please understand the purpose of this exercise is not trickery, but illumination. Many of you are afraid to confront your fears about your truthfulness, yet within each and every one of you, there is an abundance of goodness waiting to be recognized, acknowledged and accepted. As you approach the topic of speaking the truth, remember this truth about you...you are a beautiful work in progress. You are a masterpiece in motion, constantly refining and redefining your Self as you progress towards never-ending completion. You are...you become...and you continue.

Everything you learn about speaking the truth will simply perfect perfection. Rest your fears, Dear Friend, and open your heart to new beginnings.

During this particular refinement period, you are encouraged to learn everything there is to know about your manner regarding the art of speaking truthfully. Some of you may come to realize that your skills are already exquisitely developed and only require fine-tuning, while others may recognize the need for additional skill building. Regardless of your personal level of development, examination of your present abilities will augment your future capabilities, as well as expand your perspective concerning this vitally important characteristic of the human condition.

Open your heart to this inner exploration, for the heart is your ultimate guide to transformation, and learning to speak the truth truthfully is a pathway with unlimited potential.

Shall we proceed with a plan? For the next week, from this day forward, will you accept an opportunity for self-growth? Will you choose to be the witness of your truthful behavior? Will you notice when you speak the truth, how you speak the truth, and where this transpires and, if applicable, with whom you speak the truth? Also notice the topics of exchange with each encounter of these truthful events.

Will you accept the challenge and the opportunity to explore your truthful ways? Take another deep breath before you fully commit to this adventure, for it is indeed a quest of a lifetime...and maybe more. Suffice it to say, you will learn much about yourself. Your potential for transformation is tantamount to the effort you exert in this escapade of self-discovery. This work is best done with the company of a journal...whether you prefer the pen or the computer is yours to discern, but documenting your findings is a wise decision.

One week! Just one week is so little to ask of you!"

20

Seventy-two hours came and went like the blink of an eye. I wondered how the meeting would unfold tonight. Hosting a gathering with no agenda in mind just didn't seem right, but the previous events didn't have agendas either and those meetings certainly unfolded nicely. *Just relax! This group facilitates itself. There's nothing to worry about!*

Once again, I was saved by the doorbell. It was early, so I assumed Barb would be on the other side of the door.

"Who's that knocking at my door?" I yelled with my deepest, gruffest voice.

"It's me, you rascal! Open the door! My hands are full!" And indeed they were. Hands and arms were filled up to her chin.

"What are you up to, Barb? Get in here and how can I help?"

"Just help me set these on the table before I drop them." We accomplished that and then exchanged hugs. "How are you, Sister?" I told her that all was well with me and asked the same of my wonderful friend.

"Oh, I'm doing fine, too. But the last few days have been busy, which I'm sure is true for you as well. And these," she said pointing both hands towards the table, "were the solution to my anxiety. I simply could not stop thinking about all of our friends, so every time I took a break, I made a present for the team."

"You are amazing!"

"Hardly! Between devising a plan for our outreach program, as well as revising my own personal program, I've been a bit wonky. And let's not forget the reality of our splitting up the group! That too has heightened my anxiety level. So I engaged my creative juices to help me through the last seventy-two hours."

"Well, as I said, you are amazing! Can I see my gift?"

"NO! Absolutely not! And you mustn't peek, Sister! I forbid it!" We laughed like children, which often happened with the two of us.

"Come sit down, Dear. We have a few minutes before the rest of the group arrives." Barb followed me into the living room and we instinctively went to our usual chairs, which were on opposite sides of the room. "Oh goodness, this won't do!" I moved next to my friend.

"You already rearranged the furniture," she mentioned.

"Yes, I managed that during my lunch break. Guess it was my way of addressing my own internal unrest." Barb acknowledged that it was comforting to know that she wasn't the only one struggling with the upcoming changes.

"So, how are you feeling about our progress, Sister? Do you think we are ready to move forward with the outreach program?" Remembering the conversation with our beloved teacher, I thought carefully about what I was about to say. I wanted to speak the truth, and I wanted to be certain that the words were of a positive nature.

"Barb, I fully trust that each one of us is ready to facilitate conversations regarding the Earth's situation. I think it's important that we remember what our purpose is. We are here to express our concerns about the Earth's declining health and we are also here to open the space for safe and healthy conversations about how we can help her during this precarious time of need.

All of us are capable of doing this. Let's not forget how frightened we were when the Carsons and the Barkleys joined us for the first time. We could not have imagined a better outcome! So, Dear Friend, we already have a good track record and there's no reason to think that our future encounters won't have similar results.

We just need to trust ourselves, Barb. We will learn how to pace our conversations, and soon the new group meetings will feel as comfortable as our old group meetings. We can do this, Barb!

We will do this!" My Friend took a deep breath, nodded in agreement, and then burst out with a question.

"We are going to be co-facilitators, aren't we?" Her request surprised me. I had just taken it for granted that we would be working together.

"Of course, Barb! It never occurred to me that it would be otherwise. I assumed, for convenience's sake, that each couple would create their own groups, and that you and I would do the same. Dear One, has this been a concern for you?" She admitted it had been a major heartache for her.

"Goodness, Dear, I'm adamant about this. We are a team, and our friends will agree with us. I'm so sorry that this was a worry for you. Why didn't you call?" She quickly confessed that she did not want to appear foolish. "If necessary, I know we would both volunteer to do whatever is needed, but at this point in time, I really want us to work together. I think it's important, Sister. I can't explain it, but we've been brought together for a reason, and I firmly believe this is intended."

"Well, that doesn't sound foolish to me. I trust you, Barb. And I want you to trust yourself as much as I trust you!" And with that said, the doorbell announced the arrival of our guests.

A passage from
Speaking The Truth
(Chapter Thirteen)

"Everything matters. At this point in time, let us discuss a truth that arouses mixed reactions. The truth is this...everything matters. While some believe this often-debated concept, others do not, and while some are undecided about this thought provoking topic, others are simply uninterested. No matter where you fall on the continuum of believing or not believing this simple, but profound truth, rest assured: everything matters.

Perhaps some of you are taken aback by the assertive manner in which this is stated and wonder why it is necessary. The answer is simple...because it matters!

Speaking The Truth is a book presented for a reason. Some readers will resonate to this truth while others will not, and some will never even know of its existence, but the simple truth is this. Speaking The Truth is a book that matters. Speaking the truth matters and understanding the reasons underlying this truth matters.

Hopefully, those of you reading Speaking The Truth will understand the significance of speaking the truth. Hopefully, you will be curiously interested in learning more about this uniquely human characteristic, which has no territorial boundaries or limits. Pervasive and insidious, humankind's confusion about speaking the truth is noteworthy and warrants consideration by everyone who defines him or her self as human.

Hopefully, you will be one who chooses to actively participate in revealing the truth about speaking the truth. Remember, you are not alone in this self-discovery process; in fact, you are in very good company. You are here to make a difference and will do so by examining and assessing your present skills, and you will then determine what steps you wish to take to better your Self. This self-improvement project is not about comparisons or competition; there is no room for such pettiness in a mission of this importance.

Speaking The Truth is intended to create camaraderie and community as participants strive for self and global betterment. Hopefully, by speaking the truth about speaking the truth, union will come about rather than continued separation and dissension. Speaking The Truth is intended to manifest hopeful optimism among all peoples, but for this to happen, it must begin with you and me, and all others...one person at a time joining the effort until the movement spans the globe. Each person who reads Speaking The Truth and chooses to participate in the meaningful work it offers can directly influence the future that awaits humankind.

Many of you are keenly aware that changes are already in motion. You feel it; you know it, and even if you cannot adequately describe what is happening, you are aware that a transformation is in progress. So why not be an active participant in the process? Rather than waiting for changes to transpire as if you have no power or authority to participate, why not purposefully and intentionally become involved in the transformation process that so many are talking about? You can do this. You do not need an invitation, although you are being extended one now as we speak the truth about this situation. You can choose to participate in changing the course of humanity by accepting responsibility for changing your Self.

No other person has the right or privilege to change you...but you do. It is a private matter...and it matters that you consider this vitally important opportunity to alter the course of humankind's future. Your input matters. You matter.

Think of this just for a moment...or more. You matter. Please accept this remarkable truth about you. You matter."

"Welcome, Dear Friends! So good to see you again." The presents in open view quickly captured everyone's attention, and Barb confessed she had a surprise for everyone. As hugs were exchanged and small talk was made, guesses began to fly. Faye was certain the surprise entailed food. Jim disagreed, but he hoped that Faye was right. He was longing for a chocolate chip cookie. Barb giggled, but revealed nothing. Our guests filled their plates with the goodies brought by the Carsons and the Andersons and promptly relocated to the living room. Barb and I followed with the small packages and placed one in front of each quest. More giggles and guesses circled the group.

"Barb, what is your preference? Should the gifts be opened before the food or after we have thoroughly indulged ourselves with these wonderful treats."

"Easy question!" she replied. "Let's eat, folks!" The first essential task of the evening was accomplished quickly. I wondered if we were all famished because of the time of day or if it was because of the topic of tonight's meeting.

"Okay, Barb! I think you're up next! Drum roll, everyone!" My Friend began to blush. I realized her enthusiasm had been struck by shyness. I chose to intervene. "Dear One, I personally cannot wait a minute longer. When do we get to open the presents?"

"Immediately!" she responded. "Please do so now, and then I will explain the purpose behind these gifts." Everyone carefully unwrapped the gifts and found beautiful blue globes of the Earth accompanied by a cobalt blue glass candleholder and the necessary votive candle, of course.

"Barb, this is so thoughtful," whispered Faye. "This is for an altar, isn't it?"

"Yes, it is. I've been thinking about all of you the last few days, and about the reason that brought us all together. I wanted to find some way to honor the Earth and also to honor our relationships, so this idea came to mind. Sister, may I use your globe to demonstrate its potential? What I've been doing at home is placing the globe in my Sacred Space with the votive candle in front on it. I light the candle during my meditations and I find it very comforting." Barb, ever efficient, had brought matches with her. She handed the match to her Sister and invited her to do the honors. I was happy to do so. The effect was lovely. The cobalt blue candleholder against the blue globe was spectacular. "So, my Friends, every time I light my candle, I will be thinking of all of you and of the Earth, as well."

"This is a sweet idea, Barb," spoke Annie, whose mind was racing with other ideas. "You know we should always have one of these with us when we hold our meetings. I think this is another way of spreading the word about saving the Earth. People can be encouraged to make their own altars for the Earth. This is a great idea, Barb!"

"Thank you, I'm glad you feel that way and I hope all of you will enjoy using the globes in whatever ways you imagine. Truthfully, I had mine burning all day today. It felt very sacred. Every time I glanced at it, I felt aligned with the Earth."

"Well, Dear One, you just said the magic words. Shall we align ourselves with the Earth now? Who would like to take the lead tonight?"

"I would like to facilitate this session, if I may?" Carolyn's voice was soft, but determined. She knew she needed to practice and wanted to take advantage of this opportunity. The group welcomed her offer.

"Dear Friends, please prepare yourself for the wonderful opportunity that awaits us. Enjoy the deep breaths that are necessary to take you to the sweet place that you know so well. With each breath taken, trust that the efforts we make together this evening will be successful.

Breathing in, we unite with the energy within us; breathing out, we express our wishes to the Mother for whom we come to serve. Breathe deeply my Friends, for our task is one of great privilege and great responsibility. Our Dear Friend, our Provider since our kind came into existence, is in need. And we are here together, existing in the same energy, as does she. We are One, and our energy can assist her energy to revitalize itself.

Breathe deeply again, Dear Friends, and prepare yourself to release a particle of your healing energy into the center of our circle. Do so now, please. Let us each send our powerful energy particle to the center of the room so that they can all merge together. Envision this in your mind's eye and see the particles of healing energy empowering one another. They grow in strength and potency. And now let us propel our energy through the ceiling and up into the sky above this neighborhood. Send the ball of energy into the sky and witness it as it bursts into millions of particles that spread across this area. Each particle reaches out to the Earth, enriching her with the Source energy that exists within all. The energy assists her! She pulsates with this new restorative energy. So grateful are we to be a part of her healing process.

Old Friend, please rest assured that we are committed to sending you energy every day. We are most pleased to do so. Please rest now as we return to our respective bodies. In peace be, Mother Earth!"

As is always the case, a few minutes were required for the participants to settle back into their present circumstances. The sounds of movement were the cues that led me to check in with everyone. "Well, that was a delightful session. Well done, Carolyn, and thank you!" After several similar comments were made, I posed a question.

"Carolyn, may I take a moment to learn from you?" The way I posed the question surprised her.

"Goodness, I'm not sure what you can learn from me," replied Carolyn, "but if you wish to pick my brain, please do so."

"Actually Carolyn, I believe we are all teachers and we are all students in this group, and I believe we can learn a lot from one another."

"Well stated, Sister! I've already learned so much from all of you that my life has changed considerably. And my hope is to share the things we've learn together with the new folks that we encounter, and I'm confident that we will learn from them as well, just as we have with the four of you. Your presence has expanded our breadth of knowledge."

"Exactly!" I tagged onto my team partner, as we unwittingly practiced being co-facilitators. "Your immediate response to facilitate the group made me wonder if you had prepared for this session in anticipation of having such an experience. Or did you just jump at the chance when the opportunity arose?" Carolyn's response was not quick this time. She considered her answer carefully before responding.

"Actually, I think it was a little of both. Ron and I have been practicing on our own, and of course, we feel very comfortable facilitating when it just the two of us. But we haven't had much opportunity to practice in front of people. So, I really wanted to experience this tonight. Practice increases your familiarity with the process, and not only do you reach a level of comfort with the presentation of the energy session, but you also gain confidence. You learn to trust yourself.

I feel good about how the session unfolded, but I would appreciate any feedback that any one might wish to offer."

Her husband Ron was the first to speak up. "I'm glad to hear that you feel good about your facilitation skills, Sweetie, because you did a good job. Your delivery was smooth and rhythmic, allowing us, or at least me, to be with the words without being led by the words. I think that is a very important part of guided imagery. You must invite someone to enter into the process, without dictating the process for the participant. I heard your invitation and that engaged me, but at some point my own authority took over my connection with the Earth. I participated in the deep breathing with you and the others, but the experience was primarily an individual connection between the Earth and myself. For me, it was very satisfying and successful. I think you did a great job. Thank you!"

Carolyn and Ron exchanged a special look. She appreciated his support. "Well, folks, as you might imagine Ron's feedback was nice to hear. It really was, Dear! But naturally, there's a part of me that's diminishing his beautiful feedback, because he's my husband." She accented her words by physically denoting the quotation marks. "The truth is I'm not diminishing Ron, but I am diminishing myself by not fully accepting his kindness. Another truth that must be stated is that I need to hear feedback from others besides my beloved."

"You did just the speak the truth! And thank you for doing so," exclaimed Sally. "I don't know why we do this, but we do, and because we do, all of us need to remember the complexities of our own vulnerabilities when working with our new group members. We want and need support from our spouses, AND we also need feedback from others until we reach a place where we can fully accept the support of our spouses. Fascinating! What odd creatures we are!

Now, my Dear, let me provide you with necessary and truthful feedback. So listen up!" Carolyn sat straight up in her chair to receive Sally's feedback. "Carolyn, Dear, you did a lovely job. Your voice is perfect for this work: soft, quiet, but loud enough to be heard, without the participants feeling as if they have been intruded upon.

You also accurately assessed your audience, and allowed us to follow our own lead. This is an important piece of information, my Friends. When we start working with a new group, we cannot presume they are skilled meditators, nor can we presume that they are not; so we will need to seek information and ask for feedback to get a good sense of our new

Friends. And we must remember that we are talking about new Friends. So if we treat them the way we treat each other, we will be on the right track.

Carolyn, I think your determination to acquire practice is also noteworthy, and something that we must be diligent about. That was a good reminder for all of us. Thank you Carolyn, for a wonderful session. Oh, one more point! Trust Ron's feedback; it was accurate!"

A passage from
Speaking The Truth
(Chapter Fourteen)

"Let us continue our conversation regarding your significance to existence. Your truth bears repeating. You matter.

Speaking The Truth is intended to assist you in assessing and articulating many truths that may come forward as you proceed with your journey to discover all you really are. Shall we practice now as we discuss the truth about your existence? You matter! Your existence is for a reason and your presence in existence matters.

For those of you who learn by repetition, let us review this truth again. You matter. Your existence matters. Your reason for being matters. You matter.

For those of you who loathe repetition, this is an opportunity for you to practice acceptance of another's learning preference, as we once again remind every one... YOU MATTER!

There is a saying among many people of Earth that is fitting at this particular time. The adage assertively pronounces 'Practice makes perfect.' Dear Reader, this is a time for practice. Although each of you is already regarded as perfection, your acceptance of your significance is indeed in need of improvement, thus you are strongly encouraged to practice, daily and frequently, some form of exercise that emphasizes, 'I matter!'

Whether you boldly announce your self worth or mumble it under your breath is for you to decide, but create an activity that transforms your awareness and belief about your true worth and begin now, please. You are worth it...you matter...your existence matters.

Breathe this in please, and allow this truth to settle into your very core...you matter. You are here for a reason and your existence matters.

This truth is yours to accept; everything else is already in place. You exist. Your existence matters. You matter. What remains to transpire is your acceptance of this truth. Your acceptance matters.

Will you accept that your existence matters?"

"My Dear Friends, may I join you? I so desire to be in your company." The arrival of the beloved teacher brought great joy to the group. Warm greetings were exchanged and he was noticeably touched by the reception. As I observed the interactions exchanged among my Friends and our exceptional guest, I could not help but wonder how much longer he would be available to us. My heart sank with the thought, so I put it aside as best was possible. *How could he possibly oversee all the groups that soon would be forming across the globe?* My thoughts impressed me. *Groups all across the globe?*

"Indeed!" he replied to my unspoken thoughts. His reaction surprised me, as well as my Friends. *"Do you wish to share your thoughts with the group?"* My reaction to having my thoughts responded to still amazed me.

"Will I ever become accustomed to having my unspoken thoughts heard by another? As often as it happens around here, you would think that this was the norm, but it still takes me aback." As my friends looked on, I apprised them of the workings of mind which our beloved teacher tuned into. The topic of his availability was on everyone's mind. Although we had been assured about this before, the time had come for another discussion about his feared departure.

"I'm glad this is going to be discussed," expressed Jill. "I personally have been concerned about the upcoming changes, and the truth about your travel plans would be greatly appreciated." Others in the group raised their hands indicating that they too wanted clarification. Annie admitted that she was aware the topic had been discussed before, but that she needed a recap and some reassurance.

Our beloved teacher sat quietly; his eyes turned downward. The time had come. *"My Beloved Friends, so dear you are to me, and so happy have I been spending time with you. Indeed, our circumstances are changing. We will, of course, still be working on behalf of the Earth; however, we may encounter periods of separation. Please remember those times are an illusion. We are always connected through our hearts, and because my travels are unlimited, I am available even when I am not near.*

Your work this evening demonstrates that you are prepared to proceed on your own. Each of you is capable of facilitating a session, and you have the privilege of working in the company of your partner of choice. Obviously, you are well suited to serve with your spouses and also with your Dear Friends. Be open to all situations. As circumstances change, your needs will change. Most often you will serve with the selected companion, but times will necessitate flexibility. At times, you may desire the company of a Friend to enhance the influence of a particular topic. And you must be prepared to offer your own expertise as well. My Friends, your Circle of Friends affords you options. Discern the most convenient means of facilitation in the beginning of your endeavors and then improvise when it is necessary. So able are you! Be at peace, my Friends!" His praise was heartwarming, but the prolonged pause caused everyone to hold their breath. The topic of his own presence still needed clarification. Actually, the prolonged pause wasn't nearly as long as it was presumed. He felt their anxiety rising, and invited everyone to take a deep breath with him. And this they did!

"My Dear Old Friends, so wonderful it has been to be in your presence during these recent weeks. We have achieved more than was anticipated. Your progress does not surprise your Friends of Old. Always, you are Ones who fulfill your commitments and offer more when the day's work is done. Dear Ones, you give us great hope. The Earth is depending upon you and others like you. Without your assistance, she will not survive, and without her presence, you will not survive. The circumstances are unbelievable and they are real.

Though you do not remember the commitments that were made long ago, you are fulfilling them as if you do. And we must ask you to do more. Each day that goes by without change, the Earth's health weakens. She cannot continue to live in the present conditions that she now exists in.

Although no one wishes to accept this; it is her truth. Presently, she is dying from the pollution that is forced upon her by human waste. Her natural resources that are necessary for her well being are being stripped from her, and the atmosphere that provides her light and life has become so disrupted by manmade pollution that she can no longer sustain stability for those who reside upon her. Her problems are not self-made; they are directly related to the disgraceful maltreatment perpetrated by her inhabitants.

As you well know, my Friends, change is necessary. You are a primary part of the change that is in process, and which will continue in the days ahead. Because of the work that you are willing to participate in, the Earth's potential for survival has increased. To say that your role in this situation is important is the understatement of all time. What you have committed to do, my Friends, is an act of generosity that may actually save the Earth.

Because you are willing to change and to grow, so too will others. Because you will speak the truth about the Earth's crisis, others will listen, and they too will spread the truth to others. This is why you are here, and this is what must be done. One person speaking the truth and taking appropriate action will inspire another to do the same, and in this way, the Earth will be saved from her present course of decline.

My Friends, you are needed. Each of you will play a role in changing the energy of the Earth. Presently, the energy is defiled by the unkindness that spreads about the globe in a disease-like fashion. This is not who the people of Earth are. This is not intended to be. The Children of Earth are people of goodness, and it is their goodness that will save the Earth. So little change is necessary. Simply be the people of goodness that you are created to be. Treat all others as you prefer to be treated. Act in love and kindness towards everyone you encounter. Accept that every other being on this planet is made of the same pure energy that you presume you are created from, and know and accept that you are no more than any other, and no other is greater than you.

All on this magnificent Life Being are equal, and all deserve to be and must be treated equally, lovingly, and respectfully. Until all are regarded equally, balance and safety will not return to the Earth. She cannot continue to live under these inharmonious conditions.

The solution is simple. Treat each other as you would have another treat you. Accept all others as you desire to be accepted. And above all, do no harm to anyone. No act of meanness perpetrated upon another is acceptable. There is no conceivable reason that justifies doing harm to another.

My Friends, you are people of goodness, and with your assistance, others residing upon the Life Being Earth will remember this truth about themselves." Our beloved teacher fell silent, as did we. Time passed, as we all attempted to absorb the information just received.

A passage from
The Time is Now
(Chapter Four)

"On the planet of eventful circumstances, the illness was growing and creating the circumstances of which we need to speak. These circumstances were not the blame of those in participation, for what occurred was unknown to them, but the impact of the circumstances contaminated the innocent ones and from then on they too were involved in the evolutionary malfunction. This malfunction, which began of natural circumstances, grew so rapidly and in such odd ways that in crises these children were before the Family was in awareness of their situation. Soon the children, evolving naturally and rapidly, were all in contamination and so subtle was this illness that none was in awareness that the epidemic of destruction had begun."

"My Friends, the truth has been spoken, and you each know this. You hear the words of old, spoken long ago, and they resonate with you now as they did so long ago. This is who you really are. You are beings of exquisite goodness. You came from goodness. You remain in goodness. You are of goodness. As are you, so too is everyone existing on this planet and throughout the Greater Existence. You are beings of goodness who are here in this place at this moment in time for a reason. You are here

to save the Life Being Earth, and you will do this by changing your ways and by assisting others to change their ways.

Old Friends, soon our time together will become less frequent, for the pace of our work will profoundly intensify. Each of you will go forward to assist others, and then those will do the same. The movement will progress rapidly and the days will be long. And at day's end, we will light the candle at our Earth altar, and we will remember our Friends of Old.

Please do not fear our reduced frequency of connection. Always, we will be together through the heart, and if ever you are in need, I am but a breath away.

Dear Ones, do not focus upon the illusion of separation, for there remain more gatherings that demand our undivided attention. Hold my image in your hearts, as I do yours, and know that we will be Old Friends forever. In peace be, my Friends!

Please continue your meeting and I will join you when you meet again."

A passage from
Speaking The Truth
(Chapter Fifteen)

"How is your practice coming along? Hopefully, you are moving forward and steadily gaining greater acceptance of the remarkable being you truly are. How wonderful it is to grasp the significance of your truth...to know that you are more than you appear to be...and to accept that your presence matters.

If you doubt this for one moment then keep practicing, for it is essential that you and I and all others gain clarity of this simple yet profound existential truth. Your presence matters, as does mine, and as does every being's in existence. Imagine this just for a moment. We are all significant...we all matter. Sweet beauty!

As you sit in the moment of this overwhelming awareness, please simply allow the serenity of this knowing to fill your very essence. Breathe this truth inward to the very depths of your existence, awaken your entire being to

*the memory of old, and revel in your regained awareness
that you are a being of extreme significance...a being of
importance...a being who matters.*

*Be with this moment. Please do not rush through this
precious experience...be with it...extend this moment for
all eternity. You are a being of exquisite composition and
your existence matters. You are all that is, all that was,
and all that will ever be...and you are more.*

*Please end your reading at this time. Simply be with
the reality of your newly remembered truth and immerse
your Self in awareness that you are truly here for a reason
and your existence matters.*

We will begin anew tomorrow.

In peace be!"

"Whew!" sighed Faye. "Please tell me I am not the only one feeling overwhelmed by the enormity of that message." Mark placed his hand on Faye's. His touch was very reassuring, but she needed to hear his voice. "Are you okay, Dear?"

"Yes, I am, and yes, his message was overwhelming. And to be perfectly honest, it brings up every insecurity I could possibly imagine. I'm trying very hard to avoid slipping into one of these abysses, because that is not what we are intended to do. Our Friend was emphasizing the significance of our work so that we would accept its importance and continue. His pep talk was inspiring and humbling. And a bit frightening as well, if we choose to go down that path, but we mustn't.

Numerous thoughts rose up from within me as he spoke, and at the time, I believed each one was a distraction not to follow; however, it might be helpful to note their potential influence. His insistence regarding the importance of the work made me wonder if one might begin to feel full of oneself. And the point is, we must be alert to that. Just because the work is important doesn't mean that 'we' are important. We are here to help and to help others learn how to help. I feel really good about participating in an act of generosity that inspires more acts of the same.

And then, at another point, I began to hear all the questions of diminishment. Can I really do this? Who do we think we are to pursue such an activity? What are strangers going to think when we tell them that we have the power of healing the Earth? And on, and on, and on.

Folks, we really are here for a reason, and we can speak our truth about healing the Earth with the same humility as we've done with one another. Like he said, we are good people. And there are lots of other good people out there who will share our desire to help with this project. We are not alone! We really must remember that! And when one of us forgets, the rest of us need to stand up and remind that person of the reality of our companionship. We have each other! And we have More.

And by the way…Earth needs to be reminded of that as well. Sometimes, she must feel so lonely. After all these years of neglect and abuse, she must sometimes fall into despair. Let's accept responsibility for reminding her every day that she is not alone. I think that will matter! She needs to know that she matters to us.

So, Faye, I was overwhelmed by our Friend's message, but we came here for a reason, and we have to fulfill our commitments." Faye reached over and hugged her husband.

"That was inspirational, Dear. Thank you for being the love of my life. I'm ready to walk this path with you!"

Friend Barbara sat pensively debating whether she was ready to insert herself into the conversation. She was deeply moved by Mark's uplifting message, but also intimidated by it. She wondered if she had the courage he did. When that thought raced through her mind, she raised her hand. "Friends, I would like to speak my truth regarding our so-called reason for being. There are times when I wish none of this had happened. I wish the strange invisible fellow had not entered my life and I wish I could just run away from all this intense sense of duty. It can weigh heavily at times. And then, when I get over myself, my attitude totally shifts." Her smile lit up the room.

"Life is so much richer now. And to be perfectly honest, life was really good before. I am so grateful to be part of this 'reason for being.' I think the reason people refer to a life event as a 'reason for being' is because it is. We all know this is happening for a reason, and no matter how many times doubts may surface, we know from someplace deep within us that what's transpiring is happening for a reason. I'm glad to be a part of this, and so grateful we are doing this adventure together. Whoever planned it did a great job. I cannot imagine embarking upon this journey with anyone other than you guys. And what's very interesting is that I am absolutely certain that everyone we encounter will also feel like a Dear Old Friend that we are intentionally supposed to meet. That idea excites me!

I know we are here for a reason. I believe it and accept it. And I'm looking forward to the work that lies ahead."

A passage from
The Time is Now
(Chapter Five)

"When the time came
for the decision to be acted upon,
All were in puzzlement.
This dilemma of such large proportion
required a plan of monumental strategy,
for to assist the ones in need
without their awareness of being assisted
was a challenge most difficult."

The Andersons sat hand in hand as they listened to their Friends speak their truths. They too had a truth to speak but were waiting for the right moment. When Barb completed her thoughts, they took advantage of the moment. Jim cleared his throat and asked the group's permission to go next. He was, of course, welcomed to do so.

He turned to Annie, and her nod encouraged him to speak on their behalf. "Well, folks, we are here for a special reason tonight. We have come to express our thanks to all of you for this incredible time together. We've always enjoyed these friendships, but in recent weeks, our hearts have been full with the close connection that we've shared, and we feel that it's important for us to acknowledge that to all of you. You all know that we don't have any remaining family members in our lives, and we were never blessed with children, so it's just the two of us. Sometimes, we worry about that, but not anymore. You see, we have come to think of you as our Family, and we are very grateful for your presence in our lives.

So, Dear Friends, we want to make an announcement this evening. We are officially notifying you that we are adopting all of you as our Family. We hope you will accept this invitation." And with that, Annie pulled out a small stack of papers that were elaborately designed. "Declaration of Adoption" was the headline of the document created by these two Dear Friends. Annie was beaming while Jim was blushing with embarrassment.

"This is one of the most lovely gestures I've ever witnessed. And it is an honor to be a member of the Anderson Family." My smile was almost as bright as Annie's, but not quite. No one could match her beautiful glow. Their gesture truly touched everyone in the room. A few tears were shared and grateful sentiments were expressed.

"We truly are grateful that all of you are in our lives and appreciate your acceptance of our small gesture of gratitude. Before we pass the baton to another, I think Jim has something else to say."

"Yes, I do, we do! Although we're unsettled by this idea of splitting up the group, we've come to grips with it. And we made a list of folks that we feel are good candidates for a new group. So while we continue to develop our game plan here, we will also gather more information about these possible newcomers and determine if they seem like a good fit.

Bottom line, we intend to keep in close connection with all of you, and we're ready to take the next step."

A passage from
Speaking The Truth
(Chapter Sixteen)

"Dear Reader, welcome to a new awareness of old truths. You are indeed a being of exquisite lineage and your time here in this present moment is no coincidence.

You are here for a reason. Many of you already know this. You can feel the burning ache within you and these repetitive messages of purposefulness are merely confirmation of what is already brewing inside of you and serve as encouragement to continue.

Others of you are just awakening...or better stated, just remembering, and for you these messages may be confusing, annoying, mysterious, and more; but rest assured the messages are for a reason...and each one is necessary. If you feel aggravated by the repetitious manner in which these messages are presented, ask why?

Why would anyone continue to repeat a message over and over again, unless it was purposeful, necessary, and needed?"

"Goodness," declared Sally. "That's some incredibly powerful role modeling. You two are amazing." Sally shook her head in admiration. Before continuing, she turned to her husband Dave and asked if he was ready. With a deep breath and a nod, he affirmed that he was. "Well, before I pass this over, I just want to thank Annie and Jim for adopting us into their Family. This is a first for us. And I'm just delighted!"

"Yes, thank you both," added Dave. "That was a very thoughtful gesture. We've always felt like Family, but I like the formality of your announcement." Dave glanced around the room before he turned to the topic of the evening. "Truth is folks, Sally and I are still struggling with this breakup idea. We know it's the right thing to do, but we've really been enjoying these gatherings. They've been refreshing and enlightening, and we don't want to lose the exhilarating energy that is shared in our meetings. So, that's our truth. We thought we should be honest about that.

We've also been thinking about potential invitees for another group and have several names on the list. And of course, we've also been strategizing where to host our gatherings. We have several options in mind and will probably rotate depending upon the weather. We've talked some about the first meeting and how we would like to welcome our guests. We thought it might be nice if we all reflected upon how this group actually came about, and then also have the Carsons and the Barkleys provide us with feedback and suggestions regarding their experiences when they joined the group.

Now the invitation list may need to be a collaborative effort. Because we share numerous mutual friends and acquaintances, we may want to discuss how we divvy up the list, but we can talk about that at a later time. I think that about does it for us." Dave started to relax back into his chair, and then had another thought. "Oh, there's one more thing. I am really going to miss our teacher. It was comforting to hear that he will still be available if we need him, but that doesn't ease the sense of loss. He's been an incredible asset to our development and honestly, I just don't know what it will be like without him. I'm really concerned about that. Hopefully with time, I'll have a better attitude about it. Okay, I guess that's it for me."

"Well," added Sally, "Dave's comments brought up my grief about our teacher as well. I hope we have more opportunity for closure with him. There are things I want to say to him. He's been a powerful mentor and I really need to honor this relationship in some appropriate way." Tears welled up in Sally's eyes. She didn't apologize; she knew it wasn't necessary.

Jill empathized with Sally. Though her own experience with the beloved teacher was limited, she felt great disappointment about having less contact with him. She had hoped for more opportunities to learn from him. "Sally, I share your sadness. It is very disheartening to think about this and it makes me question myself." Jill paused for a moment as she tried to sort through her thoughts. "So many of you this evening have specifically and purposefully expressed a need to speak the truth, and I wish to follow your lead. I must speak my truth about this unusual experience that we share with our beloved teacher. It is confounding! Who is he? Do we actually know who this individual is? And does it even matter?

As you can probably tell, I am conflicted about this. Part of me is completely satisfied with indulging in this mysterious relationship without having any additional information about this invisible man. Let's face it! What we are learning from him is beyond imagination! I've never been so enraptured by an experience before in my life. It is exhilarating to be in his presence.

And I'm not happy about this! At times I feel like a petulant child who wants answers to my dissatisfaction. Why is he leaving us? Why must he go? Clearly, he is vey pleased with our progress, and yes, he believes that we are capable of proceeding on our own. I get all that. But what about our relationships! I feel like he is abandoning us." Jill turned away to hide her tears. She was embarrassed by her outburst. *Speak the truth!* Whether the words were spoken to her or if they were her own thoughts, she was unsure, but the truth of the words was obvious.

"Oh, my Dear Friends, I am sorry for my outburst. But this is my truth: I do not want him to leave us. I understand his commitments take him elsewhere, but I don't want him to leave." Her sadness was palpable. Stephen leaned over and wrapped his arms around her, and the rest of us honored her sorrow in silence. The truth she spoke was true for all of us. She simply had the courage to express it.

A passage from
The Time is Now
(Chapter Five)

"For this challenge, the Ones most ancient were called upon,
for no other could be entrusted with such a difficult task.
Their knowingness, greater than any other's, would be relied upon
to determine a strategy of greatest care.
And for these Ancient Ones, older than any others,
and of more knowingness than all others,
this would be their most difficult challenge ever pondered.
Within they turned,
for nowhere else could such answers be gained,
but from the Source of All Knowingness.
The answers to this dilemma did not come easily,
for to correct a problem of such large magnitude
could not be solved with easy deliberations.
And so the Ones of Ancient Age
pondered and focused with great intentions
until a plan was devised
to rescue the children of the dying planet,
lost in the distant galaxy far away from others of similar kind.
So alone and so ill were these newborns that
All wept for their predicament."

Finally, a deep breath was heard, and others followed suit. Stephen had relaxed back into his chair and Jill was once again ready to continue. "Thank you for allowing me to express my sorrow with all of you. I hope none of you was burdened by my tears."

"Not at all," said Faye. "In fact, your honesty assisted me to release some of my own grief about our Friend's departure. Please do not concern yourself, Jill. Your willingness to share this part of you helped us all. I'm grateful." Several other comments of encouragement and gratitude followed Faye's remarks.

"Thank you all for your support. We are so fortunate to have this safe space to speak our truths. Folks, this is another reason for fostering more groups. Just look at what you created here! And then you had the courage to welcome others into your safe place, and the group blossomed even more. There's a reason this is happening, my Friends!" Jill's look of gratitude filled the room. She had returned to her peaceful, serene state. The encounter with intense sorrow had not worn her down, but instead relieved her pain, freeing her to a renewed state of being. She turned to Stephen and encouraged him to speak.

"Thank you, Jill! I too have been concerned about our Friend's departure, but his words today were reassuring. Don't get me wrong, I'm not happy about his leaving anymore than the rest of you are, but he really is assuring us that he will be available if we need him. Let's don't allow our sadness to overwhelm that truth. He's told us this several times now, and we need to remember it. This is another opportunity for us to stand firm in helping each other remember a truth, i.e., his promise. And I do believe it was a promise." Stephen's recognition that our Friend's reassurance was actually a promise added another layer of comfort to our grieving hearts.

"Now, let me provide an update on our thoughts about the future. Again, we share the same mixed feelings as the rest of you, AND we understand the necessity of pursuing the next step. We too have made a list of potential candidates, and I agree with you, Dave. We are going to need to collaborate about that, but I also had another idea about our lists. When we were gathering names for our upcoming group, we were choosing people that we already feel comfortable with, and of course, that makes sense; however, our lists could be much more expansive if we added folks who are only acquaintances at this point. Let's face it! The idea is to get this information out, which means we need to stretch beyond our comfort zones. Acquaintances are friends in the making!

And Jill liked the idea of creating some type of handbook for developing these groups. If these groups take off, which is the point of this endeavor, then we need to be able to find ways to assist new group members to move forward. Some people may be inclined to move out on their own before others are ready, and we need to be able to accommodate that. So this is an idea in the making, but we wanted you to know what we were thinking." He turned to Jill to see if she wanted to add anything, but she declined. "Okay, I think that's it for us."

A passage from
Speaking The Truth
(Chapter Sixteen)

"As you wonder why these purposeful reminders continue with such regularity, do you also wonder about these passages that continue to be presented as well? The passages speak of times past, yet seem vaguely familiar...not unlike the messages of purposefulness that also seem to come forward from the past, yet resonate in the present. Is it possible that the passages and the purposeful messages are related? Is it possible that this is happening for a reason, or is it a mere coincidence?

Seek within for your answer and gain confirmation about that which you already know."

The meeting appeared to be coming to an end, and still so much more remained to be done. We needed an assignment. "My Friends, usually our Old Friend is the one who charges us with an assignment, but it seems this is another responsibility that we must accept. My inclination is to take charge, but that doesn't seem appropriate, so may I make a suggestion?" The group was amenable to that request.

"I have two thoughts! First, if anyone has an idea for an assignment, please voice it. And second, when do you want to gather again?" The answer to the second question came quickly. For a variety of reason, the group decided to meet in forty-eight hours so that more time could be spent formulating ideas for the outreach program.

"Any assignment idea?" I asked.

"Stephen," asserted Sally, "I think your idea about expanding our guest list is exceptional. I suggest that we all work on that and bring our results back in two days. I also want to suggest thinking way outside of the box. I'm not exactly clear about my thoughts at this point, but I want to encourage all of you to think about inviting someone who may be willing to open their hearts to the energy transfusion method, and who may also be someone who has greater potential for spreading the word about this healing process than we do."

"That's an intriguing idea!" exclaimed Annie. "Do you have anyone specifically in mind, Sal?"

"Not exactly, but I'm mulling over it. For instance, our efforts complement the works of folks involved in climate change activism. Perhaps, we could collaborate with them and maybe create a conjoint effort. And what about getting children involved! What if we invited some teachers to one of our meetings and apprised them of what we are doing? They could give us feedback about including children in this healing process. I think it's a way of reaching more people through the means of the school classroom."

"Sally, that's a great idea!" My own excitement was aroused by the ideas coming forward. "And I think we could also reach more folks by giving some informational lectures at community libraries."

"What about hosting some workshops? We could target various groups and see what happens." Barb's suggestion triggered more curiosity. In response to questions about what types of groups she had in mind, she replied, "Energy workers, healing touch practitioners, climate change activists, peace activists, educators at all levels, nature lovers, and Earth lovers. Those are just a few that immediately come to mind, but our options are endless. That could be another assignment!" Barb paused briefly and came back with an adamant affirmation. "Yes! I think this is an assignment to add to our To Do List. Let's each do our own brainstorming and make a list of folks that we might seek out!"

The excitement of the group seemed to expend itself to the point of fatigue, and for what seemed a lengthy amount of time, the group remained quiet. Part of me wondered what was going on with my Friends. Should I be worried? *Why would you leap to worriment? Perhaps they are just thinking about the assignment that was just given. Why does my mind prefer to leap to a topic of distress rather than to topic of delight?* As I listened to my thoughts, I chose to change my way of thinking.

"Dear Friends, I am curious about our silence. What wonderful thoughts are you thinking?" Jim started to chuckle, and then Dave followed suit.

"Goodness, Dear, can't you tell what's going on with those two?" Annie teased. I truthfully admitted that I was clueless. "Are you going to fess up, or shall I reveal your secret?" The two old friends were giggling so much that everyone else joined them, including me. It was a great relief. Finally, the giggles came to an end, and Jim sheepishly announced that his wonderful thoughts were solely focused upon the chocolate cake in the next room.

"Amen!" added Dave. "It's time for a treat, and I invite all of you to join us." When the cake was sliced and served, we all retreated back to our preferred chairs. Yummy sounds circled the room, and for a brief moment, no one thought about anything other than the delightful, scrumptious treat in front of them. Each bite resulted in another sensual experience that demanded additional yummy expressions.

"Oh, I so wish I could record all these sounds of praise and approval," giggled Annie. "I believe it is fair to say that the cake passed the taste test!"

"Indeed, it has!" agreed Jim. "And you deserve a standing ovation, Dear, but I still have several more bites to enjoy, so the applause will just have to wait." The distraction was good for everyone. Laughter revitalized us. I made a mental note to myself. *Laughter is essential to our health. We must incorporate laughter into our meetings. It releases built up tension and brings us back to center.*

"Indeed, it does!" Sally quietly affirmed my thoughts. Soon, the forks were carefully placed on their dessert plates. Jim and Dave collected the dishes and carried them to the table and then resumed their seats. Big sighs were released about the room.

"My Friends, have we come to an ending point of this meeting?" The question hovered in the air before an answer was provided.

"Actually, I would like to lead us in a closing prayer for the Earth, if I may?" Jill's offer was appreciated and accepted by everyone. She began with the traditional deep breath and invited the rest of us to join her. Eyes closed, the inhalation of long breaths resounded, and the silence engulfed us. Moments passed before Jill issued the words so deeply meaningful to all of us.

"In peace be, Dear Friends. We gather on behalf of our beloved planet, the Life Being Earth. So grateful are we for everything that she has done for us and for all Those Who Came Before Us. No words will ever adequately express our gratitude for her hospitality, her tender care, and for her remarkable presence. Old Friend, you have lived your life more fully than any other Life Being could ever hope to achieve. So many have lived wonderful lifetimes because of your generosity. Without you, our lives would not be.

We have erred, Old Friend. Our careless ways have caused you great harm, and only now do we fully understand the ramifications of our misbehaviors. So deeply sorry are we for our selfishness. Please forgive us, but more important, please hold on. We now know that we have the ability to assist you, and this we will do. We will find a way to incite the masses so that enough energy can be generated to heal you. We will restore you back to full vibrancy.

Please allow us to send you an infusion of energy now before we retire for the evening. My Friends and I are ready to do so. With the next deep breath that we inhale, we will release the energy to you. Please use our energy in whatever manner is best for you. Now, Dear Friends, send your particle of pure Source energy through the floor of this house into the soil of the Mother. Let her consume our energy and disperse it as she sees fit.

Thank you, my Friends, and thank you, Dear Old Friend, for receiving our gift of renewal.

In peace be, and rest well this evening." As always, the energy transfusion soothed the hearts of the participants. The Circle of Twelve was at peace, as was the Earth.

The meeting came to a close. I watched my Friends as they walked down the lane to the street corner, where one by one they turned to wave goodnight. It was another special evening.

21

A passage from
Speaking The Truth
(Chapter Seventeen)

"Speaking The Truth is a title intended to spark your thoughts and engage your heart. Many of you, probably most of you, regard yourselves as people who speak the truth. You may even pride yourself on doing this and wonder why such a topic need be addressed. In actuality there is merit in your self-perception and you will discover many reasons that verify and confirm your understanding of yourself as you explore your personal relationship with speaking the truth. Validation of your present skills is just one of the many positive outcomes of pursuing more information about this often overlooked topic; however, you may also learn more about you than anticipated, and as you learn more about Self, you will naturally learn more about others as well. Humans are indeed an intricately related species, thus gaining information about any 'one' brings more knowledge about the whole. As a whole, humankind is a species of remarkable potential and the more understanding that is gained about each 'one' within the whole is in the best interest of all.

Now, is it in your best interest to explore this topic? Does it deserve your attention, time, and consideration? The simple answer to these questions is yes; however, each of you must discern this for yourself, for these are questions for you and about you. Is learning more about the process of speaking the truth important to you, and if so, what might be gained by doing so?

Speaking the truth about your thoughts regarding this exploration possibility is an opportunity to begin your personal research. How do you really feel about examining the topic of speaking the truth? Do you truly want to do this, and if so, why? And if this is something you really do not want to do, again, ask why.

Everything you need to answer these questions lies within you. You are complete. You need no additional education, training, or status...you are enough. Simply stated, you are all you to need to be to take this next giant step in your personal and evolutionary development.

Now is the perfect time to seek within and discover more about your beautiful self. Trust in you. You are more than you appear to be and you are ready to learn the truth about your wonderful existence."

Reentering the house, I paused and viewed my home returned to its usual state. "Thank you, Dear Friends, for bringing order back to my space. What kind and generous people you are!" I proceeded to the bedroom. It had been a long evening and I was tired, but my journal awaited me and I knew a moment must be spent with it. I opened to the last entry, and entered the date and time for tonight's addition. "Dear Old Friend, I know you are listening. Just wanted to let you know that I am so grateful you remained and listened to the rest of the meeting. I hope you were pleased. We are going to be fine. I hope you will continue to be a breath away, as you said, but just know that we will be okay. I'm so grateful for our time together. In peace be, Dear Friend."

Barbara was not inclined to return to her home after the wonderful meeting. She wondered if she would ever experience a time of disillusionment after their gatherings. She doubted this would be possible. Their meetings aroused many emotions, but never had she felt disillusionment. When it came time for her to turn right on the block to her street, she decided it was in her best interest to expend some more energy before returning to the house. Her neighborhood was a good walking area regardless of the time of day. Yards were blank canvases that their owners accessed to demonstrate their creative abilities, and they were skilled artists. The color arrays were tastefully achieved in the most delightful ways. One was never disappointed when walking the blocks of this section of their small community.

And she particularly loved walking at night. The moon was so hospitable, lighting the sidewalks along the way. The quiet was an exceptional companion. At night the only sounds heard were your own footsteps and the occasional owl hooting to another feathered friend. It was the perfect time for a walk when one was in need of alone time.

She strolled aimlessly. There was no reason for the walk other than to wind down from the intensity of their conversations. She was so grateful to have such good friends with whom she could feel safe to share anything. *What a blessing this is!*

"Indeed, you are blessed with exceptional Friends! You are most fortunate, Friend Barbara."

Barb turned about to acknowledge her companion, but he was nowhere to be seen.

"Thank you for your company. I am surprised, but delighted. I trust you were satisfied with the meeting tonight."

"Yes! Your Friends are good people! And the determination within them inspires all who witness these gatherings." His presence, even when invisible, was extremely comforting. She enjoyed walking with him.

"I assume you are here for a reason, but may I ask a few questions before you reveal your mission?" He indicated that he had time to walk and talk and invited her inquiries.

"Will we ever meet the Others that you refer to? I wonder about them, you know. Of course, you know that I think about them often. Are they your companions, as are you to us? Or are they your bosses, your superiors, or whatever is the appropriate title? Or are they members of a group with which you are associated, and are we, our local group, the recipients of your outreach efforts?"

"You have many thoughts and many questions, all of which are relevant and accurate. Indeed, there are many of us who are reaching out to people like you in our efforts to save the Earth. What we attempt to achieve with you is what we are encouraging you to do with others. We have attempted for many, many centuries to warn your peoples of the situation that was transpiring upon the planet, but our efforts were not successful. We do not, nor have we ever desired to impose our preferences

upon others, but your situation is now critical. The Life Being Earth is in grave jeopardy; your peoples are on the verge of extinction. The situation is so severe that we have no other option but to blatantly intervene. So yes, my Dear Friend, you and your Dear Friends are a strategic part of our humanitarian efforts. We desire to help the peoples of Earth." The invisible companion paused for moment. It was not easy for him to speak so bluntly, but he knew it was necessary, and he also knew that Barb could handle this level of truth.

"I am most sorry to deliver such difficult news, Old Friend, but your participation in this galactic effort is essential to its success. Regarding my Companions, your interpretation is accurate. Some are members of a group of associates with whom I work, and there are others who are of much greater understanding than am I. Our existence is very old, my Friend. And the Ancient Ones are far wiser than those of my time. These Ancient Ones guide us and we are most grateful for their assistance, but I personally have never seen them. As do you and your kind wish to see what More exists in existence, so too do I, and others of my time.

We all have great appreciation of the Life Being Earth. As she serves you, so too did she serve us. We are indebted to her for all that she did for us and for all that she has done for our descendants. Her significance in the Greater Existence is beyond your present scope of understanding. Old Friend, suffice it to say, she must continue."

They walked in silence for nearly a block. He held her in his heart and she did the same for him, each appreciating the contributions that the other was making.

"My Friend, you speak the truth, and I am grateful. May I pose another question?" He invited her to do so. "Do you ever doubt yourself, my Friend? Do you ever fear that you will not make the right decision at the right time? Do you ever ache for guidance so that you will know for certain what is the next step to take?" Her questions received no answer for another block. She regretted asking the questions and wondered why she had done it.

"Old Friend, please do not diminish yourself. You simply want to know if we share similar vulnerabilities. Is that not common among the human species? I am pleased that you have asked these difficult questions, because you will need to address this with others in the near future.

I wish that I could say to you that I never have doubts or fears, but to do so would be untruthful. I wish that I could say to you that I am always confident and that I do not need guidance, but those responses would also not be true. My Friend, like you, I have great concerns about the success of our mission to save the Earth. But I have the privilege of witnessing so many actions of kindness and goodness that I experience more hopefulness than you do.

Your news media report so little that brings hope and optimism to the people. They focus on that which is dreadful, for the culture is addicted to these types of stories. So long has this been the truth that the people no longer have awareness of this problem; thus they live their lives under the influence of misinformation and of terrible truths that are better not sensationalized.

How splendid it would be if the industries of news distribution would agree to seek out and publicize all the acts of kindness and generosity that are happening globally. This would profoundly alter the outlook of your people and your energy as well. With uplifted spirits and hopefulness, the Earth would recover more quickly.

My Friend, there is reason for hope! The fact that your group welcomed an invisible being into your midst brings us hope. The reality that you accepted the gift of your healing powers so quickly and that you actually practice sharing your healing energy with the Earth brings us tremendous hope. We also are aware of the many beings in the Universe who are gathering to assist the Earth and her inhabitants. This naturally brings us reason for great optimism. So much is transpiring, Old Friend, that brings hope to the forefront. We must trust this, and in those moments when our courage wanes, we must remember what the truth is. If we resort to seeing only the negative that is transpiring, then our mood and our attitude will lean in that direction. But if we choose to focus on the positive that is happening, even if it is not visible in the moment, then our attitude will continue to be positive and it will inspire the same in others. Old Friend, remember the truth about hope; and speak truthfully of it to others."

"You are a person of wisdom, my Friend."

"As are you, my Friend."

"Have you delivered the message that was your purpose in coming this evening, or have we strayed from the path?" Barb's intuition was indicating that the invisible Friend had more information to convey.

"Your intuition is correct, Friend Barbara; however, what remains to be said is in alignment with our conversation. Old Friend, you are One who brings great joy to those you encounter. You brighten the space that you enter, and as a result of this, you lighten the energies of those around you.

This is a Gift that you have been granted. Your Companions of Old wish to awaken you to the reality of this Divine Gift so that you can be consciously aware of the Divine privilege that accompanies your Gift. Old Friend, your delightful way of being influences the wellness of others. With your uplifting mannerisms, you make others feel better about themselves and about others. You do this with such ease and grace that you do not even know when you are participating in this process, but you are Dear Friend, and with this new awareness, you have the ability to be even more influential.

In essence, my Friend, we are inviting you to be more of who you already are. As you are, you are a wonderful inspirational leader. And you are much more than you now allow yourself to be. Ponder this, Dear Friend. The Gift lies within. Simply know that it is there and access it, as is your divine privilege to do so."

"As you know, your message is more than I can grasp, but I will ponder it as you suggested, and hopefully, I will be able to live into this Gift that you say I possess. You are a wonder, my Friend."

"As are you, my Old Friend! In peace be!"

Her companion departed just as their walk ended in front of her home. Without her awareness he had walked her home.

A passage from
The Time is Now
(Chapter Six)

"As the Ones of Ancient Age deliberated and devised a plan of rescue,
many came forth and volunteered their services
to assist the children of innocence.
As is the way of the Ones of Ancient Age,
service to All That Is is their purpose.
No other purpose do they serve,
for no higher good could they serve.
In deciding the fate of the children of innocence,
the Ones of Ancient Age considered no other purpose of higher regard,
and with determined commitment
they devoted their purpose to the children's rescue."

22

A passage from
Speaking The Truth
(Chapter Seventeen)

"Once again, you are reminded that you are one who is truly ready to continue your exploration of self. Although it may seem as if you are just beginning this assignment, in actuality, you have been participating in your Self-Discovery Mission since the beginning of your existence, and now you enter a new phase of the process which includes remembering and speaking the truth."

"Jimmy, I do not think another piece of chocolate cake is in your best interest tonight."

"Is this one of those times when you're speaking the truth, Dear?"

"Yes, Dear, I think it is," she answered maternally. "Actually, Jimmy, I would like to think that I always speak the truth, but the repeated emphasis regarding this topic in our meetings makes me wonder if my perception of myself is accurate. What do you think about that, Dear?"

Her husband was still deliberating his choices about the cake. A small slice, a bite, or none? His mind was in a whirl about this very important and immediate life decision.

"Oh, for goodness sake, Jimmy, just give yourself a tiny slice and be done with it. What harm can it do other than keeping you up all night?" Her response was not the invitation that he had hoped it would be. He gave the cake another moment and the decision was made. He would take the risk, and if it turned out to be a poor choice, he would not whine about it.

As he placed the sliver of cake on a small desert plate, Annie posed the question again.

"Okay, Jim, on a scale of one to ten, do you think I am a person that speaks the truth?" Her husband sat down beside her, carefully placed his plate on his lap, and then raised both hands, wiggling all ten fingers.

"I think you are one of the most honest people I've ever known, Annie, so I'm giving you a ten. However, I think there is more to this notion of speaking the truth than we are currently taking into consideration." His response surprised his beloved, and her curious nature was aroused.

"Hmm!" she replied. "This is intriguing. Tell me more, please!"

"I'm not sure there is more for me to tell, but I can share with you some of my discomfort with the topic. Every time this topic is raised, it causes me irritation. For some reason, my first response is guilt, followed by a sense of indignation. It's befuddling, Annie.

But I think it is significant.

Like you, I regard myself as an honest person, but my responses, which of course are internal reactions, make me wonder about myself. If I'm really an honest person, then why am I feeling guilty, and exactly what am I feeling guilty about? And then this righteous indignation rises up. What is that about? I find it all very puzzling, and I'm trying to sit with it. Something is going on here that seems important, so I'm trying to prepare myself for whatever is going to reveal itself.

And, if I were to speak the truth truthfully at this very moment, a confession would be necessary. I hope and pray, Annie, that I'm not the only one having these reactions." Jim's candor was delightful. He truly spoke the truth truthfully.

"That was really helpful, Jim. And let me reassure you that you are not alone with the internal reactions and thoughts that you are experiencing, but until you spoke so articulately about your inner responses, I was not cognizant of my own.

Jim, why are we reacting this way? What secrets are we hiding from that are causing these guilty reactions? I actually feel as if I'm am being exposed each time the topic comes up, but I don't know what the reason is for this response." Jim took a moment to enjoy one small bite of his dessert before responding, and then he began to giggle.

"I suppose I should feel guilty about indulging in another piece of this wonderful cake. But I don't! Not in the least! But like you, Annie, I'm not sure what's hiding in the closet. We are old, Dear. Perhaps there are things from the past that have been locked away for so long that we just don't remember them."

"Well, that's certainly a possibility! I've wondered if there are things from childhood that we still have a knee jerk reaction to. I think as children we sometimes felt extreme guilt about things that in actuality were really inconsequential. But to a child, in the moment, it was a huge offense that he or she might still be ashamed of to this day." Annie mulled over what she had just said and added, "I don't know, Jim. I'm just not sure what this is about, but I appreciate your strategy. We should just be open to whatever reveals itself."

Jim nodded in agreement as he enjoyed the last bite of the cake. "There's another component of this, Annie. Since this topic came up, I've been very vigilant about speaking the truth and also trying to speak it in a way that folks can hear it. Often times, people have a hard time hearing the truth. At least that's my perception. Perhaps my fears are misleading me to think that someone may not be able to hear the truth. I'm not sure about any of this at this point, but my confusion is telling me that it is important."

A passage from
Speaking The Truth
(Chapter Eighteen)

"Speaking The Truth is intended to assist you in remembering the truths that lie within you. It is intended to awaken the truths buried so deeply that you have been unaware of their presence. Actually many of you have experienced fleeting moments of awareness revealing the stunning gifts that live within you, but you may not have understood the extent of knowing that which is in your possession. Suffice it to say, you are the keeper...the holder...of much more information than you presently believe...or can even imagine.

Those of you already awakening to the truths of old can attest to the joyous exhilaration experienced when these wonderful awarenesses come forward. Because of your familiarity with these initial awakening experiences, you will be a normalizing force for those who are just entering this phase of development. As many of you can verify, the beginning stages of remembering can be, shall we say, curious? Choose an emotion, any emotion, and you will most likely experience it at some point during the process. Anticipate the highest elevations of jubilation, the lowest depths of heartfelt sadness, and every emotion possibly imagined in between...and proceed without fear.

Do not let fear be your guide as you enter this remarkable phase of your development. It is simply unnecessary, as those who journeyed before you can affirm. The highs and lows of your awakening moments are priceless, as are the in-between experiences. At times you will ache for more such moments, and other times, you will long for rest. Cherish every moment, the times of exquisite activity and the times of well deserved rest, for each one is essential to your remembering process, as well as your developing ability to speak the truth truthfully. Perhaps, you wonder how these two seemingly separate activities are related. Rest assured, as you awaken to the truths that lie within, you will most definitely desire to speak the truth about these wondrous memories. So much resides within you, patiently waiting to be remembered, to be discovered anew, as if for the first time, and yet, once the memory merges into consciousness, it will be as if known forever...which it was, is, and always will be."

23

"**D**avid, are you still awake?" Her husband turned over to face her.

"I assume sleep is escaping you too." Sally inferred that his comment meant he was available for conversation.

"I'm confused. And we both know how that routine plays out. When something confuses us, we mull over it, over and over again, until we find a proper place to file the presumed answer. Well, Dear, I'm not having any success at wrapping my mind around this conundrum."

"Are you trying to figure out why we are being implored to speak the truth?"

"Yes! How did you know that? Have you been reading my mind again?"

"No, no, wouldn't even consider that feat, Dear. But your thoughts are very loud." His response brought Sally to an abrupt stop. Dave started to chuckle. "I'm just teasing you, Hon. Truth is, I'm mulling over the same topic, and it makes sense that we are. The message has been repeating itself incessantly lately."

"Yes, that's true. But you just said something that really gives me another perspective to consider. You stated that we are being 'implored' to speak the truth. That's very different from my interpretation of the message. I have felt as if we were being directed, charged, commanded to tell the truth. Isn't that interesting? I received the messages as harsh, which also confuses me, because I've never felt that from our beloved teacher before. Even though the words were not spoken harshly, I received them as such. Well, this is fascinating. Are you feeling reprimanded when you hear the message to speak the truth?"

Dave gave the question careful consideration. "Well, I don't think so, Sal. The message has given me pause at times, and made me wonder if there are times when I haven't spoken the truth. And I have wondered how other folks are responding to this repeated and insistent message. So obviously, it has focused my attention on the topic of speaking truthfully. Sometimes, I've caught myself wondering if I were speaking the whole truth. Does that make sense? There are times when I know I am speaking the truth, but more could be said, but I was hesitant to do so. So maybe I need to explore this subject more thoroughly. In fact, before you nudged me, I was wondering about the reasoning behind this message. It seems to me that the repetition of this message indicates that it is urgent."

"Ah! That's another good point, and that might be part of what I'm sensing when I feel like the message is ordering me to speak the truth. My reactions are curious, and I expect they relate to old stuff, but I'm up for whatever comes to the surface. Let's face it! If I'm upset about the idea of speaking the truth, then something is amiss within me.

Thank you, Dave, our conversation has quieted my need to have a solution before falling asleep tonight. This is a project in motion. And it will be waiting for me when I awake in the morning."

A passage from
The Time is Now
(Chapter Seven)

"On that day so long ago
when the Ones of Ancient Age determined
what was next to come,
All were in agreement that the time was now
for the plan to begin.
In quiet resolution, the Mission of Mercy
to rescue the innocent children of the ailing planet commenced."

"Yes, our talk really was helpful, Sal. You know one never really knows what someone else is thinking or feeling, yet so often we presume that we do. Lots of heartaches are caused by these presumptions. I'm glad we don't lean in that direction, Sally. There's enough pain in the world without adding to it with this kind of miscommunication."

"I agree, Dave. We were both raised to speak the truth. We just take it for granted that we are both speaking the truth to each other. But what I'm learning is that not everyone hears the same truth that was spoken. For a variety of reasons, we, meaning everyone, hear things differently, so it is vitally important that we monitor our communication to be certain that we are all hearing and interpreting the same intention that is being spoken."

"Goodness, Sal, there is more to mull over. I'm so glad we're in this together. Wouldn't want to be dealing with this on my own. Good night, Dear."

A passage from
Speaking The Truth
(Chapter Eighteen)

"Speaking The Truth is here for a reason. It is intended to assist you with your awakening to old truths remembered anew. You are here for a reason and it is indeed time for you to awaken. You are not alone. Many are here to assist you with this journey of awakening, remembering, assimilating, and speaking the truth.

You are not alone."

～ 24 ～

"**M**ark, I'm so glad we came out here before going in for the night. Our deck is such a lovely place to be. Thank you for designing this beautiful retreat for us."

"You're very welcome, Dear, but I really think of our deck as a team effort. You had so many wonderful ideas about creating a special place for us, and look what came from your ideas. I'm just grateful we were able to talk our way through the project. The truth is, we've talked our way through many projects and issues, and I know we will continue to do so in the future. We're a good team."

"We are!" Faye agreed wholeheartedly. "We are so blessed, Mark. We've witnessed so many failed relationships that could have succeeded if only the folks involved had talked through their issues respectfully and kindly. It's so sad." The couple drew closer together, each appreciating the healthy relationship that they shared.

"What are your thoughts about our beloved teacher's repeated emphasis upon speaking the truth? I know he's doing it for a reason, but I suspect the reason is more far reaching than it currently appears." Mark's answer was vague.

"Everything that guy does is for a reason!"

"Would you care to elaborate upon that?" prodded Faye. "I think you're holding something back."

"Hmm! I don't mean to be." Mark struggled to wrap his mind around this particular topic, which rarely happened to him, but when it did, he had a difficult time expressing himself. "Well, to speak truthfully," he stated, "I don't know what to make of this, Faye. Most of the time when he brings this topic up, it feels like an appeal, an urgent appeal for us to speak the truth. And at other times, I have a sense that he is apologizing for times when his kind or his contemporaries did not speak the truth. I realize that this sounds ridiculous, but as I said, I don't know what to make of it.

My instinct tells me he is a man of goodness who can be trusted. Every interaction we've had with him indicates that this is the truth, but the emphasis placed upon this issue makes me wonder where he is coming from and where is he trying to lead us.

I also believe that he holds us in high regard, and that he truly trusts us. Again, all of our interactions with him suggest this. And still, one must wonder why he keeps returning to the issue of speaking the truth. Is he concerned that we are lacking in this area? I could certainly understand if there were concerns about this. Globally, we demonstrate so little trust in one another that any passerby would wonder about us. Our ill will and disrespectful behaviors are undeniable. Having just acknowledged that out loud, it makes total sense that he would be bringing up this issue. All of us should be reviewing our manners of speech and our unruly behaviors.

Faye, every time he brings the issue up, I question myself. Am I really speaking the truth? And particularly when he says we must speak the truth truthfully, then I really get confused."

"Mark, I've never known you not to speak truthfully. Why is this affecting you in this way?"

"That's the point, Faye! I don't really understand it. Let me give you an example. There are times when I am speaking the truth that I become very concerned about hurting someone's feelings, so I am very careful about how I express my thoughts. And as a result, I fear that the significance of the truth that I was trying to convey was diminished. So if that was the end result of my effort to speak the truth, did I really speak the truth? This is very confusing!

And sometimes, I wonder if our Old Friend's kindness and his gentle ways are interfering with preparing us for what is coming. His mild manner definitely enables me to hear the disheartening truths about the planet. I personally prefer his style of presenting difficult information, but I wonder if the people of Earth have grown so accustomed to sensationalism that his calm manner may not gain their attention. I'm afraid his ability to deliver unpleasant news in a gentle, methodical way may not impress the public. In truth, they may not give his information about the Earth any credence at all. It seems that speaking the truth isn't as admired and respected as it once was.

Faye, please don't misunderstand me. I am certainly not advocating that we stop speaking the truth. But the truth is, a lot of folks aren't speaking the truth nowadays, and it seems this misbehavior is gaining momentum."

"Goodness, Mark! Your point is well taken. The truth about the Earth's situation must be spoken truthfully. But there is so much misinformation being distributed that people don't know what to believe. We don't know who can be trusted; and as a result, we're having more and more difficulty having straightforward, productive conversations with one another. This is serious, Mark."

"Yes, it is! And there is only one way to deal with this situation. We must speak the truth!"

"You're right, Dear. Thank you for having this confusing conversation with me. It was worth it. I feel like we're working like a team again. If we can do this, so can others. We just need to be patient and remember that we are all One."

A passage from
Speaking The Truth
(Chapter Nineteen)

"Speaking The Truth is an invitation waiting to be accepted. Each of you now reading these pages knows that your encounter with this book is not a coincidence. You know this experience is for a reason, just as you know 'other' experiences transpiring about you are for a reason as well. You know 'more' than you presently understand and the need to know even more calls to you. Many of you, probably most of you, ache to know more, even though you do not know what the more is that you are seeking. You simply know that there is more to your existence than the ordinary, mundane way of being that you presently experience. You live life, yet you wonder if this is all there is. You proceed with necessary activities and perceived purposefulness, but at the end of the day, you ask, "Is there nothing more?"

You wish for more, you hope for more, you long for more, and in those most private heartfelt moments of aloneness, you beg for more. From the depths of your being, you know that there is more, and yet you cannot explain the intensity with which you feel this certainty. You cannot prove your knowingness to any other...you simply know your knowingness is real. You simply know it is true.

Dear Friend, you know that there is more, because you know there is more. This is your truth...accept it. Although your heart may ache to connect with others so that you may share your wonderment, you need not prove your heartfelt knowing to anyone. In actuality you cannot, for each must discover this inner truth in his or her own unique way.

Every being in existence possesses the Gift of Knowing, yet few are aware of it at any given time. Perhaps it surprises you to hear this, but it is true nonetheless. You are a wonderful example of this truth. At times you awaken and you know more than you knew before and that priceless moment is one of ecstasy as the new awareness overwhelms your essence, reminding you of that which you already knew, but had momentarily forgotten. The moment materializes, showering you with delightful wonderment that disappears just as quickly as it appeared, leaving you with but an afterglow... sweet, precious realizations that too hastily fade into the elusive passageways of consciousness. Although the Gift of Knowing seems evanescent...fleeting, temporary, and brief, nothing could be further from the truth, for your Gift is permanently lodged within you and will inevitably be visited again. Rest assured, Dear Reader, it is not the Gift of Knowing that is elusive; it is your consciousness that is the wanderer.

And this brings us full circle. We began this chapter by reminding you that Speaking The Truth is an invitation, which is now extended. You are invited to accept your Gift of Knowing."

25

"**B**eloved Friends, are you available? I require a moment of your time."

"Indeed, we are always available, Old Friend. How may we be of assistance?"

"As you know, our outreach efforts are progressing rapidly. Those who were assisted are now taking steps to assist others. There is an air of possibility that inspires one to hope. My Friends, I hope you are pleased with the efforts thus far. I come now to request guidance for the days ahead. My interactions with these fine people have gone well. Relationships have developed nicely, and they understand the need to move forward with this work. Although they are reluctant to leave each other's company, they know that the Earth's situation demands that they do so.

I find myself in a similar situation. I have grown accustomed to their company as well, and the need to move onward has proven more difficult than anticipated. Your guidance is needed, Old Friends."

"The heart has been healed in the company of these Old Friends. So long had it been since you were united, and how quickly the time together has passed. Our hearts hold your heart, Dear Friend. It is most difficult to stand near Old Friends without experiencing the connection that is so desired. We share your grief.

Even though one knows that relationships are eternal, the absence of heartfelt connection during periods of separation is excruciating. As do you feel this for them, so too do they feel the separation from you. As do we with those who are separated momentarily from our presence. As you ache for connection with your Old Friends, so too do we ache for yours when you are attending other matters.

We understand, Old Friend, and we ask you to remember that you are not alone. The same guidance that you offer others, we offer you. You are not alone, Old Friend. Just as you reassured your Friends, we do the same for you. Dear Old Friend, we are but a breath away.

Anytime that you desire our company please do not hesitate to reach out to us. We consider such initiations as a Gift of immeasurable proportions.

Old Friend, we offer you condolences for your present losses, and we applaud the efforts that you and your associates are making. You serve well, Dear Friend. Please trust you, as do we.

In peace be!"

26

"**S**ister, am I calling too early?"

"Not at all, Barb. What is going on in that magnificent mind of yours? Your energy is so large, it feels like it is right outside my door."

"It is right outside your door! I'm here! Can I come in?" I rushed to the front door and found my Dear Friend standing on the porch in her walking clothes. She brought a smile to my face.

"Have you been out haunting the trails already?" Barb confessed she had been out since pre-dawn. "You know how I am! My best inner work comes when I'm walking." My Friend's passion for walking was well known. Many of her friends often wanted to join her, but when they found out how early she began her jaunts, they lost their zeal for the activity.

I welcomed her to the house and we automatically headed for the breakfast nook. Simple and homey, it was the space where many important conversations were enjoyed. I suspected such a conversation was in the making. She took responsibility for pouring the coffee while I popped a couple of day old croissants in the toaster oven. In minutes they were as scrumptious as the day before. "I'm so glad you stopped by, Barb. It's such a blessing that we live so close to one another."

"I feel the same way," she replied. "Sister, I am so grateful for our relationship. When the notion arose to stop by, I didn't hesitate. It is wonderful to have a friendship that is so easy and so rich. My, gosh! What incredible lives we are living!" We both mused about that for a moment, each recognizing the beauty of circumstances. "Has it always been this way, Sister?" Barb's reflection was sincere. Their lives were extraordinary, or so it seemed to her, and at this point, she couldn't remember when it had begun.

"Our present lives do seem all consuming," my thoughts were not completely clear about this topic, "but I suppose most people feel the same about their lives as well." My reaction seemed to puzzle Barb who was still trying to sort through her thoughts.

"You know," she reflected upon a previous time, "it never occurred to me that someday in the future, I would be having a quote-quote spiritual experience. I never imagined having a relationship with an invisible being. Nor did it occur to me that my friends would be sharing this unusual experience with me, and accepting it as if it was the way life was. I think this is really remarkable. Actually, it's dumbfounding. And I am so, so grateful! Grateful that it's happening, and grateful that I am not alone in this crazy and wonderful experience we are sharing."

"You're in touch with your gratefulness this morning," I noted.

"Yes, I am," acknowledged Barb.

"So, tell me! What happened on your walk this morning that demands immediate attention? You are about to burst, you know! It's obvious. So out with it!" Barb chuckled at herself and admitted she was at the popping point.

A passage from
Speaking The Truth
(Chapter Twenty)

"The invitation is extended and the Gift of Knowing awaits you. Is that not an exquisite thought? Revel in this just for a moment and realize what is being offered. You know with great acuity that there is 'more' in existence, yet you cannot explain how you know this. You hold the answers within you...you are in possession of the Gift of Knowing. Will you accept the Gift?"

"Sister, we need to create our list of candidates for our future group. It's essential! We both know people who are interested in climate issues, so let's put them on the list. And we have mutual friends who are into the healing arts, who will be wonderful advisors when we address the energy transfusions for the Earth. With these two groups alone I think we will find enough folks interested to start another group. In fact, I suspect our list of possibilities is much longer than either of us imagined. When I finally started thinking about this, the names came flowing forward.

I'm more concerned now about managing several groups at once than I am about filling up one group. My attitude about this totally shifted. Sister, people are going to be interested in this and we need to be ready to think expansively." Barb's energy was electrifying.

"Okay! I like your energy and I'm onboard. So, we can check that topic off the To Do List. Now, what's next on your agenda?" I could tell that she had an idea that was burning inside of her. My energized Friend took a deep breath.

"We can do more, Sister. Obviously, we are all called to promote and participate in the groups, but we can do more. I've been thinking about this a lot. Actually, I'm not sure how much of these are my original thoughts or if I'm being assisted with these ideas, but the point is, I have some good ones and they need to be considered."

"Tell me more, Barb! This is making me very curious!"

"Well, I've been reviewing our experiences with our Old Friend and attempting to assess the most important aspects of our time with him. Obviously, this wasn't easy to discern because everything about his presence is profoundly important. But what really assisted me the most in understanding how we can help the Earth have been the exercises that we participate in. Every time we practice sending energy to the Earth, I feel more confident in my ability to do this, and I have more trust in the validity of these energy transfusions. At first, I wasn't sure about all of this; it seemed a bit weird. Now you know I revel in the unusual, but I do have my limits, and the idea of sending energy to the Earth was a bit much for me. Can you believe that? How many years have I been a proponent of energy work, and still, I was reluctant to accept the possibility of us being able to help the Earth through the same means from which I have received assistance. Anyway, it didn't take but a few sessions for me to accept the truth about our potential for healing the Earth.

So, the point of this long story is this: I think we should record healing meditations for the Earth and develop a website where folks can go and listen to them for free. You and I are both skillful at doing guided imagery, Sister. This wouldn't take a lot of time, and talk about outreach! We could effectively reach people around the globe.

In fact, it would really be nice to have each person in our present group contribute at least one meditation. That way we would have a nice variety for folks to listen to. Actually, we can expand upon this idea by including videos. I'm sure our Friends will also have more ideas to add, but this is a beginning. So, tell me Sister, what do you think?" Barb knew her idea was noteworthy, but she still wanted feedback.

"Barb, I think this is an exceptional idea. And you're right; the potential for outreach is stunning. I love this idea! And if my intuition serves me, I think you have more to share. What else is hiding in that brilliant mind of yours?" My Friend inhaled another deep breath and I joined her in the ritual. "Tell me, Dear One!"

Barb's smile lit up the room. *Surely this is my imagination, but someday, I hope to capture the light that I perceive around her when she smiles. I really don't think it's my imagination, I truly believe her energy radiates in such a fashion that the area about her actually becomes brighter.* "Okay!" she announced boldly. "The next idea is a website. We need some means of functioning at a worldwide level and that means effectively utilizing technology. Although we will need assistance with this, it's available. We just need to go for it.

And one of the reasons for a website will be the distribution of information and materials. I believe we are going to be doing a lot more than just hosting groups, Sister. More is coming! You know this better than I do. So, I just want to say I'm onboard with the new opportunities that are coming our way and I'm ready to play my role in whatever unfolds.

Whew!" she exclaimed. "I think that's the end of my list of ideas at this point, but be forewarned, more is coming!"

"Sounds like we need to be prepared for even more activity than we've been enjoying the last several weeks. Dear One, may I ask you a question?" Barb indicated that she was open to any and all questions. "These are wonderful ideas that you are perfectly capable of initiating. But you insinuated that you were not completely sure if they were your ideas. Do you feel as if you have been assisted?" My Friend carefully considered the question. I suspected she was as curious about the answer as was I.

"Sister, I honestly don't know. I agree with you, these ideas are within me and would have come to the forefront of my mind at some point, but I do wonder if a loving assistant nudged in this direction. The information seemed to come to me all at once, as if it was a download of knowledge, which I must admit felt extremely rapid even for my rapid firing mind. I don't know what the truth is, but I like the idea that someone is helping us with this project. Of course, we know that 'someone' is helping us, but when and where and how still remains a mystery. And I also wonder just how many are involved in helping us. I cannot imagine that our beloved teacher is the only one who watches over us." Barb sighed and leaned back into her chair.

"Life is so extraordinary! I just don't remember when all this started, but I do know that I don't want it ever to end. I can hardly wait to see what unfolds next!"

"Me too, Barb! Whatever is coming is coming, so we might as well face it with open hearts and hopeful attitudes. I'm so grateful you stopped by this morning. You've made my day!"

A passage from
Speaking The Truth
(Chapter Twenty-One)

"Today is a day of new beginnings, and as such, we begin by accepting our Gift of Knowing. In so doing, we take the initial step in reclaiming who we really are. Let us begin with an exercise!

Opportunities For Expansion – Reclamation Of Self

Breathe deeply...
> *And repeat as many times as necessary to quiet your beautiful mind.*
Be with the silence...
> *Allow the silence to embrace you...*
> *Rest in the fullness of this embrace...*
> *And simply be...there is nothing to do...simply be...*
Breathe deeply...
> *Drift into the void of nothingness...*
> *And be with the silence...the beautiful silence.*
Sit with the silence...
> *Join with the silence...*
> *Be the silence...*

Breathe deeply...
  Open to the silence...
  Listen...breathe...listen...breathe...
  And blend with the silence...
  You are One...
  Breathing in union...listening in union...
  Remembering in union...remembering as One...
Breathe deeply...
  You are One with the silence...
  You are the silence...
  You are One with All in the silence...
Breathe deeply...
  As One, welcome you to the silence...
  As One, accept you into the silence...
  As One, remember All in the silence...
Breathe deeply...
  Allow your memories to surface...
  Allow your knowing to come forward...
  Simply receive what is given...and remember...
Breathe deeply...
  *Accept the memory...the knowing received...and
  breathe it in...*
  *Breathe your Gift of Knowing into the depths of
  your consciousness...*
  And remember...
Breathe deeply...
  Remember the retrieved knowing...
  Remember the process...
  And be in gratitude...
Breathe deeply...
  And remember!

*Come back, Dear Reader, and be in the moment.
Hopefully, this simple exercise enabled you to move into
your most cherished place of knowing...the Sacred Space
that allows you to unite with the Silence, culminating in
the realization of Oneness that brings all truths forward
into conscious awareness.*

*Each visit into the Silence facilitates the retrieval of
old memories. Old memories learned anew actualize and
validate the sense of 'knowing' we repeatedly experience*

that reminds us there is 'more.' Because we cannot always remember exactly what the 'more is, we doubt our knowing and question if it is imagination, fantasy, or reality. And then we hear the small still voice from within calling to us and we begin the process of retrieving our Gift of Knowing all over again.

The process is real, ongoing, and never-ending because it is necessary. Life is eternal, existence is eternal, thus the means for connection and reconnection, remembering and remembering anew, must operate within the eternal framework. Suffice it to say, we believe that there is more, because we know there is more. Each new life experience brings us more opportunities to learn new information, which will in turn be added to the mass of information previously gained from earlier lifetimes, and when we venture into the next life experience, we will 'know' with all that we are that there is 'more,' even though we have no valid explanation for our knowing.

Then at some point in the new lifetime, we will feel the ache to know more, and in an effort to quiet the persistent and insistent discomfort, we will eventually pursue the Silence, not knowing why or what we are seeking, but simply knowing that it must be done. And in those quiet moments when we reunite with the Silence, we will once again be gifted with memories from the past that validate and confirm our deep, heartfelt awareness and belief that there is more."

27

At day's end, I retired to my favorite space in the house. I was filled with gratitude. It had been a lovely day. Barb's early morning arrival started the day in the most uplifting way, and the rest of the day followed in similar fashion. Each client seen was enjoyed and the work had gone well. I was grateful for my life, for my work, for my relationships, and for all the wonderful mysteries that continued to unfold before me day by day.

As did my day begin with Barb's question regarding the unfolding mysteries of our shared lives, so too did the end of the day bring forward more wonderment about our extraordinary lives.

Approaching my favorite chair with the nearby favorite pen and journal, I thought to myself that it would be wise to record the discussion that my Friend and I had shared many hours before. I hoped that I would be able to recall the conversation. The day had been long and other conversations had been equally tantalizing, so the reality that my memory might fail me was a strong possibility. I chose to hope for the best.

My favorite chair was the most comfortable chair in the world. I was sure of it! No other chair could possibly be this inviting. It lured me to close my eyes. I thought better of this, but the chair was persistent. It called to me, and I could not help but respond.

I awoke to the doorbell sounding from the opposite side of the house. I was surprised. Not sure of the time, I rallied the energy to lift myself out of the seductive chair. I wondered how long I had been napping. As I entered into the living room, I was surprised to see light coming through the windows. *Goodness, did I sleep through the night?* The doorbell rang again. I peeked through the side window to find my early-rising Friend patiently waiting on the porch.

"My word, Barb! Is it morning?" My Friend was horrified.

"Oh, my gosh! I've awakened you! I am so sorry, Sister!" Her apologies continued to flow from her mouth.

"Nonsense!" came my inadequate reply. "You are always welcome here. I'm just totally discombobulated. What time is it, Barb?" She informed me it was a little after seven, and then tagged on several more apologies.

"How can that be?" My astonishment was obvious. "I must look like a wreck!" And then I noticed the bag in Barb's hand. "Have you been by the bakery?"

She jiggled the bag in front of me, "Your favorite, Sister!"

"Oh, thank goodness! Will you please take care of things in the kitchen, while I attempt to make myself presentable." She reassured me that I looked fine, but urged me to freshen up while she put the coffee on.

I made my way back to the bedroom, still in amazement that the night was gone. The bed was never slept in, I was still in the same clothes I had on yesterday, and I was completely unaware of what had happened to the evening. A quick trip to the bathroom revealed no answers. I brushed my teeth, combed my hair, and put on enough makeup to fool myself into thinking I was refreshed and then returned to the bedroom. Clothes were hastily changed, which made me feel a bit brighter and then I turned to face the chair. *What did you do to me last night?*

My journal was opened, which made me wonder if I had actually accomplished something before falling asleep in the chair. I grabbed it to take a quick look and was shocked. My journal, which was just recently started, was nearly filled. Only a few pages remained empty. Pages and pages were written illuminating the situation of Earth's crisis, and the necessary steps that were needed to help her recover, and on, and on, and on. I couldn't believe it. The handwriting was mine. I could not deny that. My mind was whirling. I turned, with journal still in hand, and walked back to the kitchen. Barb was sitting at the table, coffee cup raised to her lips. When she saw me, she abruptly put the cup down.

"What has happened, Sister? What's wrong?" I was speechless. I sat down and placed the journal in the center of the table. Pointing to it, I asked her to scan the last few pages. She did as asked.

"Sister, this is beautifully written. It tells the truth about the Earth's precarious situation. It's wonderful! When did you do this?" My eyes continued to stare at the journal in her hands. The comments Barb spoke were heard, but did not register.

My Sister of Choice closed the journal and carefully placed it back on the table. She then rose, grabbed the coffee pot, filled my cup, and refilled her own. Then she carefully unfolded the bag of hidden treats. Of course, she had selected the favorite treat—the almond croissant. She placed one on each of our plates, hoping that the aroma of the freshly baked goods would reach into my mind and bring me back to the present. She returned to her chair and waited.

"Well, that was a smart move, Friend." My eyes met hers. "You have successfully captured my attention. Shall we indulge?" We each took our first bite and embraced the moment. The smell, the taste, the texture—sheer perfection! And, of course, the best part of all was the powdered sugar mask that covered our faces. Giggles ensued!

"Thank you, Barb, for being such a loving Friend. Your kindness is appreciated." She brushed my remarks aside, reassuring me that her response to my moment in need was no different from all the times I had done the same for her.

"As you have so often said, that's what friends are for. I'm glad you're back. Now, can you elaborate upon your journal entries?"

"Your question is not easy to answer, Dear. You see, I have absolutely no memory of doing this. I presume it happened during the night, but how? I remember sitting down in the chair trying very hard not to nod off, and then, the next thing I remember is awakening to the ringing of the doorbell. This is so weird! The evidence is before me. The handwriting is mine as we both can attest to, and still, how did this come about? I am stunned! Excited! And ever so curious!

This is one of those times when I want specifics. How did this happen? How long did it take? And why do I not have any memory of it? Of course, I am honored to be a part of this, but I would like to have awareness of my participation." My Friend was wonderful. She allowed me to go on and on about my confusion. Her patience was stellar.

"Okay, Dear One, you've been amazingly patient, and I am very appreciative of your willingness to listen, but now, it's your turn. What do you make of all this?"

Barb leaned forward with her elbows on the table. "Sister, I think you've been blessed. You know, as well as I do, that you did participate in bringing these messages forward. That's reality! How it actually transpired is yet to be revealed, but the truth lies before you. My goodness, what a blessing this is!" I relaxed back into my chair. Her words were exactly what I needed to hear. I didn't need any specific answers. I just needed confirmation that this was real, and as she so delightfully said, the truth lies before me. A deep sigh was released.

"Thank you, Dear Friend. That was exactly what I needed to hear, and now, I am fully present. So now that you have successfully rescued me, tell me why you are here. What brought you here so early in the morning with wonderful gifts in hand? What is going on with you?" As Barb gathered her thoughts, she played with her coffee cup, carefully circling the rim with her left index finger. Eventually, she raised her eyes to make contact. A single, tiny teardrop released from the right eye. I chose to remain silent. It was my opportunity to be a good friend for her. I was very pleased when she did not apologize for the tear. She was learning to honor her emotions.

"This morning, I woke early and felt the need to greet the sun. Sometimes, this need to meet the sun feels more like a commitment than a compulsion. Certainly, I would be the first to acknowledge that my desire to be up at sunrise feels compulsive, but today, I realized there is more to it than just my selfish need to see the glory of another sunrise. Oh, my! Every moment changes and each view surpasses the one before. How I love to immerse myself in the experience!" She paused and traced the rim of the cup again.

"But there are times, like today, when I feel it is my responsibility to be there to greet the sun. To reach out and say 'Good Morning' and 'Thank You.' And sometimes, like today, I am almost certain that an interaction takes place between us. I feel, hear, sense…I'm not certain what the correct word is; but there are times, when I am almost certain that the sun has responded to my acknowledgment of its presence. I've come to believe that, like the Earth, the sun is also a Life Being who desires and needs to be held in high regard. Does this sound crazy, Sister?"

"No, it doesn't. In fact, I love the way you articulated this. Your joy of engaging with the sun does feel more like an ancient commitment rather than a selfish passion. And by the way, I never thought your lust to see the sunrise was selfish. I've always admired your willingness to rise early to greet the Master. Barb, your intuitive skills continue to broaden, so I think it is wise that you open your heart to all possibilities. As you become more in tuned with exceptional connections with others, you may find that your connections become more expansive than you previously imagined possible." I paused for a breath, and my Friend joined me.

"I suspect many folks will smirk at the idea that we've connected with Mother Earth, and yet, people have been doing that for ages, so why should we think it is unusual. It's important for us to keep things in perspective. As we gain new skills, it's exhilarating and mind-boggling, but we certainly are not the first to connect with the Earth. Our eyes, ears, and hearts are opening to what has been before us all along. We've just been too busy, too distracted to notice.

It pleases me to hear about your experience with the Sun, and I believe your encounter was real. I suspect you will be having many more engagements with this Life Being in the future. I cannot wait to hear what you learn from the experiences. Thank you for speaking the truth, Friend." Barb smiled and said the same to me.

"Thank you for dropping by at just the right moment in time. Your presence truly was comforting and helpful." My Friend rolled her eyes and chuckled quietly.

"Sister, I don't think that was a coincidence. While waiting at my favorite spot for the sun to peek over the horizon, I saw you sleeping in your chair. Your journal was open on the table with the favorite pen resting in the crease of the book. At first I wasn't sure what to make of the image, but it wouldn't go away. I didn't sense that there was a problem, but the image was so steadfast that I felt compelled to stop by. Guess we were both being taken care of this morning. We each needed a listening ear. Thank you, Dear Sister of mine!"

28

A passage from
The Time is Now
(Chapter Eight)

"In the early stages of the mission,
the volunteers and the Ones of chosen roles
prepared for the mission with conscientious deliberation.
Each pursued diligently the data necessary to perform their purpose
and each offered willingly their experience
for this cause of extreme importance.
So concerned were the residents of the Universal Family
for the newest members of the Family
that none hesitated to offer their services
and their experiences for this Mission of Rescue."

"Old Friend, may we interrupt your endeavors for a conversation of extreme importance?"

"Indeed, my Friends, Your presence is always a delight. How may I be of service?"

"Our observations of the Children of Earth bring hopefulness to all in existence. Though we are still greatly concerned about their misguided ways, we have hope that the goodness that resides within them will overcome the misunderstandings that lead them astray. So tragic it is to witness the heartbreak of those who are lost and unaware of their circumstances. Efforts made to assist them seem to worsen their situation.

Do you concur with our assessment of this precarious dilemma?"

"I do. The truths of their circumstances do not alter the truths that they choose to believe. So entrenched are they in their own preferred beliefs that they are oblivious to the realities that are unfolding around *them. And of late, those who are invested in maintaining untruths have made greater strides in convincing those who are misled to stand firm in their errant thinking.*

The issue is extremely complex. These unfortunate ones are innocent of their own misguided ways because they truly do not understand the calculated actions that have been perpetrated against them. Because of the differences between those who are misguided and those who are aware of the truth of what is transpiring about them, the Children of Earth have become severely divided. Even this terrible crisis that now confronts them does not bring them together. Instead of uniting them, they move further apart, worsening the potential for the planet's recovery.

The issue must be confronted, my Friends, or all our efforts will be for naught."

"Your understanding of this situation is in alignment with ours, Old Friend, and we agree that this situation must be confronted. Contemplation of the predicament is underway now, and decisions will soon be discerned, Old Friend. In the interim, please continue to speak the truth truthfully. The truth must be told at all times, even when fear may be the reaction. Better it is to deal with fear than with ignorance. Those who do not know the truth are capable of learning the truth. This must be our guide. To assume that one cannot change is a diminishment of that individual. All in existence have the ability to know what is in the best interest of another. Some may choose to think only of themselves, but the knowledge remains within to make appropriate decisions. Lies and untruths blur one's ability to hold another in the same regard as self. But the truth lies within to discern what is best. We must move forward, trusting that those who have been misled will find the truth that lies within.

Old Friend, as we trust you, so too must we trust all others. Hold this truth near to your heart as you proceed with your efforts to save the Earth, and the Children who reside upon her.

In peace be, Dear Friend!"

"And to you, my Friends!"

29

A passage from
Speaking The Truth
(Chapter Twenty-Two)

"Speaking The Truth invites you to speak the truth about your Gift of Knowing. Think about this for a moment and notice your reactions.

How is your mind responding to this suggestion?

How is your heart reacting to the invitation?

Are any inner debates reviewing and discussing the pros and cons of participation in disclosing the truth about your inner wisdom?

Now pause for a moment, and allow some thought regarding the introduction of the descriptor 'Inner Wisdom.' How are your mind and heart reacting to this terminology? Are you experiencing a different reaction to the idea of revealing your inner wisdom rather than speaking the truth about your Gift of Knowing?

What notions arise in your mind when you think about your Gift of Knowing? Think about this...and take notes please. And now do the same as you contemplate your inner wisdom. Does one descriptor feel more authentic than the other? If so, which one, and why? Are you more inclined to participate in speaking the truth when you consider one descriptor rather than the other? Why?

Speaking The Truth is indeed here for a reason. Not only does it serve as an invitation to openly speak the truth about your inner wisdom, your Gift of Knowing, or whatever term you prefer, but it is also here to assist you in understanding what your true feelings are regarding the idea of coming forward and speaking the truth about who you really are.

Although speaking the truth appears to be a simple life choice, upon closer scrutiny we find it a choice that demands great thought, heartfelt consideration, and courage. Some of you have already explored the truthful path in this and other lifetimes, and you are acutely aware of the consequences associated with such actions; and needless to say, one does not always receive accolades for bravely speaking openly and truthfully. Because of previous experiences, which you may or may not remember, you may naturally and instinctively be reluctant to accept the invitation extended by Speaking The Truth. Your reticence is understood and respected; however, the book before you is here for a reason and was purposefully planned, written, delivered, and presented to the people of Earth. Perhaps you erroneously selected Speaking The Truth and are really not intended to receive its messages. If that appears to be your truth, then by all means end this process and pass your book on to another who may be an intended recipient. However, before taking that action, please give your decision another moment of consideration.

You are invited to continue, not because your encounter with Speaking The Truth was in error, but because you are intended to remember who you really are and you are intended to know the truth about the 'more' that you fervently know exists.

There really are no coincidences and your introduction to Speaking The Truth is not the first one to occur. You are here for a reason, as is the book before you...ask why?"

"**W**elcome, Dear Friends! Good to see you, as always!" Barb invited everyone into the house as her Sister continued bringing in a few items to the dining room table. Once again, the trays of goodies were supplied by their guests. The rotation of responsibility was working well. Many hugs were exchanged before Barb suggested that everyone grab a plate before relocating to the living room. This thrilled Jim Anderson, who openly admitted his passion for treats. The group followed instructions well and within minutes, plates were filled and everyone had found their preferred chair. Barb glanced at the empty chair and wondered if their invisible Friend would join them this evening. She was uncertain about his plans.

"Are you wondering if our Companion is going to join us tonight?" Faye asked while casually nibbling on a carrot stick.

"Oh, dear, Faye's showing off again," teased Annie. Faye shook her finger at her Dear Friend and returned a similar comment.

"You overheard her inner conversation too, you rascal." Annie giggled and confessed she had.

Barb just watched their antics, enjoying the lightheartedness of their exchange. Her fabulous smile grabbed my attention again. *She really does radiate light!* My unspoken thoughts did not go unnoticed.

"Of course, she does, Dear," asserted Faye, and Annie nodded in agreement. Barb and I broke into laughter. So did Jim.

"Their abilities," he chuckled, "are expanding to the point that they don't even know when they're intruding upon someone's thoughts anymore." His statement was absolutely true, but there were times when the two of them just loved showing off and this was one of those times.

"By the way, Barb, do you know that your smile radiates light?" Sally's question revealed her skills as well, and more chuckles circled the room.

Jill observed and wondered if these old friends realized how fortunate they were. She assumed they did, but then her unspoken thoughts received a response.

"Jill, forgive me for intruding upon your thoughts, but your question merits an answer." Sally suggested that she vocalize her question and Jill complied.

"Before I do, may I check in with all of you? Obviously, Sally just overheard my thoughts, but did anyone else?" Faye immediately answered that she had not. Annie said that she was too distracted by all the giggling.

"Well, I have many questions," admitted Jill, "but the one Sally overheard is this one. Do you know how fortunate you are to have this ability? I marvel at your candor and the camaraderie that you share. This is really a privilege to witness." Jill's compliments gave the group pause.

Mark was the first to respond. "We are fortunate, Jill. And thank you for bringing it to our attention. I think we've all become so comfortable with this that we don't notice it as being unusual anymore. And certainly, being able to talk about it and joke about it in this group has definitely increased our comfort level with this phenomenon."

"That's true," added Dave. "Sally and I were much more careful about this before we started seeing each other so often. Obviously, we witnessed what was transpiring between the two of us, and we were very curious, but we didn't talk about it with anyone else. And there were times when we were in public that Sally would slip, and I would make some silly remark to distract people from the truth that they had just witnessed. Essentially, we were hiding this big secret, and then, this group started, and we learned we were not the only ones experiencing these unusual communication abilities. It's so much easier being open about this. And it's a lot of fun."

"I too must admit that keeping this a secret was tedious," emphasized Sally. "I'm not exactly sure what we were afraid of, but fear often tricks us into believing something that doesn't merit time or attention. I suppose the worst-case scenario would be that someone might think we were nuts. So be it!" Sally paused and then revealed another twinge of uncertainty. "Of course, that's easy for me to say now, when I'm in the safety of Dear Friends. Perhaps I would not be so candid if I were among strangers."

Faye nodded in agreement to Sally's last comment. "Jill, I'm so glad you revealed your unspoken thoughts because your question has been very beneficial. Mark and I were very quiet about this unusual development in our lives. We were excited about it, and very curious, but our excitement was stifled by the fear that someone might judge our enthusiasm. Isn't that sad? You know, I don't regard myself as someone who typically needs other people's approval, but at the same time, I don't want to inspire disapproval.

So, being in this group and having everyone's support has been wonderful. We really are most fortunate."

"Well," interjected Barbara, "I too can attest to the importance of our group regarding this particular topic. For some time now, I've noticed an increase in my intuitive abilities. As a single person this can be a lonely experience. It's like having a great toy that you are not allowed to share with anyone. Fortunately, my Sister of Choice has always been very supportive. It was so helpful to have someone to talk to about the new and exciting things that kept happening. I mean, let's face it, you aren't going to share this with just anyone. So, yes it was a lonely experience at first, but not anymore. In this group, anything can be discussed and that is a beautiful adventure to be a part of. Oh, indeed we are fortunate, and I want to inspire this type of environment for others. People shouldn't have to live with secrets. People shouldn't have to be afraid to talk about the things that are important to them. People shouldn't have to be afraid, period!

Thank you for voicing your question, Jill. This has been a very helpful conversation."

"Jill, may I ask you a question?" After observing my Friends and witnessing the exchanges that occurred from Jill's question, I could not help but wonder where she was with the responses that her question inspired.

"Please, do," came Jill's reply.

"Well, you just inspired a wonderful conversation, and I wonder if you would like to share your own experiences with us." Her husband, Stephen, repositioned himself to see what her response might be. She glanced at him with a reassuring look.

"My beloved spouse is curious as to how I will answer your question, because we are still in the cautious phase, but it is obvious that there is no need for caution here." She looked about the group and sighed. "I am so grateful to be here with you. How refreshing it is to speak freely and to simply be who you are. I believe this is the safest place I've ever been. Stephen and I both commented on this after our first meeting with you. It is a joy to be part of this group. And I must admit the idea that we are splitting up does not sit well with me. I've waited for this for so long, and I do not want to lose this closeness, this safety. It is very special." Jill needed a few moments to breathe fully. She had released years of desire in a matter of seconds. The empty space provided by the release felt odd.

"I am aware that an opening has occurred within me." She pondered possibilities and then voiced a quiet prayer. "Dear Ones, who watch over me, please help me to attract only those energies that are of an assisting nature. Fill me with joy, compassion, and loving intentions so that I may share that energy with others. And thank you for helping me to release that which was no longer needed." She paused again and inhaled another deep breath.

"Thank you for listening. And thank you for having us in your wonderful group." Expressions of gratitude were exchanged. Inwardly,

I noted that the group had already had a success, and the meeting was yet to come.

A passage from
The Time is Now
(Chapter Nine)

"When in the final stages of preparation,
All joined in unified connection and focused their intentions
on the success of their endeavors.
Never had so many given so much to help those in need.
To serve was expected and considered an honor,
but none had served in this manner before
and the willingness to brave such circumstances
stunned even those of most ancient age.
This situation of such profound and unusual circumstances
created more unknowns than ever known before.
And of all the unknowns, only this was known.
The children were in need of assistance and
the Watchers of the Universe were determined
to provide the assistance."

"My Friends, I could not help but notice that all of you have come with folders this evening. Is it time for us to focus upon our outreach efforts?" Immediately, the room filled with noises of activity. I saw this and my breath was taken away. I had erred, but the moment was not lost.

"Dear Ones, before we embark upon this cause of great importance, may I ask that we offer the Earth a moment of our time?" The group embraced the idea, which did not surprise me. We all needed to be grounded before we confronted the next phase of our mission of purpose.

"Join me, my Friends. Please take the necessary deep breaths to bring yourself in alignment with Mother Earth. She awaits us! How blessed are we that we may spend time with her." I fell silent giving my Friends time to make the necessary adjustments to prepare for the energy transfusion. When the time was right, time awakened me to take charge again. "Old

Friends, it is such an honor to be in your presence, and a privilege to serve in this way. The Earth, as we all know, has served our kind since we came into existence, and still she continues to care for us. Now, it is our time to care for her. Old Friend, we come together on your behalf and ask that you accept our gift fully. Please do not attempt to assist us during this transmission process.

My Friends, take the deep breaths that will help you to assist the Earth. Feel the rise of your healing energy within you, and know that this energy is the Gift of your beginnings. As you are endowed with this Gift, so too are all in existence, and with this Gift, we have the privilege to aid others. Now, we must come to the assistance of the Life Being who has cared for us since our beginning. Bring your energy to the surface, Dear Friends, and propel it to the center of this room so that our energies can merge with one another. See this in your mind's eye and marvel at the wonder of this precious act of generosity. Together let us lift our energy up into the sky where it can shower itself upon the Mother. Allow each tiny droplet of our energy to serve to the fullest and allow the Earth to be sustained from this assistance. We are most grateful to serve in this way. And so grateful for all that she has done for us. Please hold her in peace and allow her to flourish for another day. Rest now, Old Friend, and we will do the same. We return to our respective bodies now, but please know that you remain in our hearts, and we promise to attend you again tomorrow. In peace be."

Time passed as we all acclimated to our return. The shifting of positions began, the stretching transpired, and the peace we experienced was beyond imagination.

"That was lovely, Sister! And needed!" Barb leaned back into her chair, and announced that she was ready to begin. "Now that I'm grounded, I'm ready to tackle the first issue of outreach." Her energy was inspiring. Other members of the group also indicated that they were ready to start the meeting as well.

"Barb, since you were first to announce your readiness, would you like to take the lead?" Her response was immediate. Without a word, she began distributing the invitation list. Once the list had completed the circle, she did what was always done. She inhaled the essential deep breath.

"As you can see, Friends, my Sister and I came up with several lists. We have our easy list, which is the 'no brainer' list. We feel very optimistic about these folks and believe they will be very interested in learning more about our activities. Because we are both feeling just a bit antsy about this, we want to initiate a group that will boost our confidence. It's odd, but we both feel more confident about the people we want to invite than we do about ourselves. I'm sure this is our version of stage fright, but confessing it out loud may release some of the anxiety." Other members of the group resonated to Barb's uneasiness, but Faye offer an important reminder.

"I appreciate your nervousness, because we are certainly experiencing that as well, but I do want to remind you of something that I think the two of you have forgotten. Dear Ones, you've already started a group! We're it! And if I may boast just a little, I think we are a stellar example of your good work. So, remember this when your anxiety skyrockets."

"Goodness, Barb, we have lost sight of this. Faye, this is an important reminder. Thank you. Shall we say that we chose wisely? If memory serves me, we were very excited about initiating the first meeting, and also very optimistic."

"And a bit antsy!" added Barb. "And we felt similar anxiety when we expanded the group with the Carsons and the Barkleys, and that resulted in another positive outcome. So, we already have a track record that all of us can feel good about." Recalling their successes enlivened the group.

"We really can do this!" exclaimed Ron. "And from the length of your invitation list, I think we are going to have many possibilities for more groups. May I make a suggestion before you continue, Barb?" She invited Ron to continue. "Well, I think it might be efficient if we all exchange our invitation lists now, so we can have a sense of what we are dealing with." Ron's suggestion resulted in immediate action.

As everyone reviewed the list, eyes sparkled with excitement. "Well," Jim spoke, and then lingered in silence. "Excuse me folks, but I'm still trying to wrap my brain around this. We definitely have some duplicate invitations, which we all expected, but our list is much more extensive than I anticipated. This is really great! And I'm having some ideas about how to move forward."

"Jim, if you're ready, tell us more!" encouraged Barbara, who was delighted to have him take the lead. He rubbed his upper lip with his right index finger trying to sort through his thoughts. His wife recognized the process and winked at Barb. *He's working on it!* Annie's unspoken words were captured by several other friends in addition to Barb.

Jim smiled and chuckled. "Well, I know several of you have been speaking in silence again. So be it! I will speak aloud just for the sake of conserving this old tradition. Some day, this may be a rare experience, but for now, it is still my preferred way of communicating.

So, here are my thoughts. Each pair has a group of folks they feel really comfortable with and it is only natural that we will want to work with folks that we already know and trust. There's merit in that approach. As we've seen with this group, our years of friendship facilitated immediate closeness. And this gave us confidence to reach out to others rather quickly. That's an expeditious model, and a good one.

Now, let's consider another option. What if we choose several folks that are known to us and also invite a couple who are not? That would give us the comfort factor that we need and also stretch our outreach to another circle of folks that are still unknown to us. That might allow us to expand our outreach more quickly. As you can see from our list, we have a delightful circle of folks that we are all acquainted with, but we need to stretch ourselves. For the sake of the Earth, we cannot remain in our comfort zones. So I suggest that we pad ourselves with folks that we trust and feel strongly about, and at the same time, we reach out to others who are beyond our present circle of acquaintances." Pausing briefly, Jim tried to remember his second point. It was circling about in his head. Annie offered assistance.

"Jim, Dear, I think you also wanted to discuss the people who are attached to various organizations that may be of help in spreading the word about these groups."

"Thank you, Annie! I do have some thoughts about that as well. It seems that we have a couple of options. We can invite them to join a group now, or we can start our new groups and inform the folks of our activities. Then at some point, our groups could invite these guests to participate in a session, so they have a sense of what is being done. Some of the names certainly have the means of expanding our outreach very quickly, and they also have their own callings that they are addressing. Perhaps, we can help one another!"

Jim's suggestions were well received and more ideas were added that led the group in a good direction. Everyone agreed that they wanted to review all the lists before any invitations were announced. Decisions regarding some of the duplicate listings needed to be made first. And they also agreed that they wanted their first experience to primarily include people that they already knew. Sally and Dave openly admitted that they had mixed feelings; confident in some moments and less so in others, but they were certain that their commitment to continue was resolute.

The Barkleys were eager to get started, but acknowledged they had moments of second thoughts, which they concluded were better than thirds and fourths. Their lightheartedness about the ebbs and flows of confidence raised the spirits of others.

"Oh, thank you for your humor," commented Faye. "We must remember to laugh at ourselves! It is essential!" And everyone agreed to put that suggestion at the top of their To Do List.

"Well, I am going to urge Barb to share some of the wonderful ideas that she came up with yesterday. I think you will all be impressed with that incredible creativity of hers." Barb blushed but eagerly shared her thoughts about establishing a website where information could be dispersed. That idea and the one related to recording energy transfusion sessions met with great excitement. And everyone agreed to contribute at least one recording to the yet to be designed website.

"And," she continued, "any recordings that are made before the website is up and running can be sent out to our email contacts. That will be a quick way of creating interest in this project. In fact, now that we're on this topic, we all need to gather up our contact lists so that we can merge them into one large list for dispersing information."

"These are wonderful ideas," acknowledged Sally. "I feel so inspired. I believe I may be able to make a contribution through my photography. We have so many lovely photos of the Earth and wildlife that would be wonderful to share. And if we attached some powerful message to it, that would also be a way of spreading the word about the Earth's situation. I'll start working on that and create a few ideas for you guys to review, and if anyone wants to be a part of the just proclaimed committee, let me know." Annie immediately raised her hand, as several recent photos taken along the forest trail came to mind. This idea really pleased her. *There are ways that I can help!*

Of course, there are, Dear! Jim's reply brought a smile to his beloved's face.

"We all have something to contribute, my Friends!" My response to the Andersons' exchange was intended for everyone. "Even though we sometimes doubt our own abilities, we see the gifts of our Friends clearly. We must remember it is human nature to doubt ourselves. While we see the strengths in our Friends and loved ones, we are blind to our own. Let's remember this quirk in our nature and accept responsibility for reminding each other that we are more than we appear to be." My suggestion met with approval. "I think it is only natural that we will have doubts during this planning stage. One moment we are alive and eager and the next we are second guessing ourselves. So be it! We can manage our moments of frailty.

I also think the issue of speaking the truth is critical at this time. Obviously, it is always critical, but now, during these unusual times, it seems even more important that we model this behavior for ourselves and for others."

"I agree," expressed Sally. "For some unknown reason, we have succumbed to the idea that spouting untruths is acceptable behavior. I do not understand this, nor do I want to be a part of it. Sister, I appreciate your leadership regarding this topic. You have a way of articulating ideas that invites people to carefully consider what is being said. Somehow, that art of kindness must be reintroduced into our speech and our mannerisms. I fear the combative manner of speaking that is so prevalent today is not helping our relationships." Sally appeared to have more to say, but her energy for the topic seemed to vanish. Her friends noticed this change, but decided not to confront her. *She just needs time!* Her husband's internal voice was loud and clear.

"Thank you, friends, for that moment of respite. This is one of those times when I must speak my truth." Sally took the restorative deep breath that our group was so accustomed to doing, and then expressed the issue that was troublesome to her. "Dear Ones, I am embarrassed to admit this, but it is my truth, so I must. I find the lies, the bullying, and the arrogant posturing that seem to dominate our social structure most appalling. Rest assured, I am aware that my judgment is flashing itself, but I do not understand why this has happened.

Have I become so old that I cannot see the value of new ways?" Her question roused her friends to react.

"The answer to that question is NO!" inserted Annie. "You know, Sal, there is a part of you that worries you are becoming your mother. And you are not! And I'm not becoming my parents. Obviously, there are things about today's world that we don't enjoy as much as the youth of today do. We love our music; they love theirs. We prefer trousers without holes; they embrace jeans that are frayed and faded. Those are age differences! But what you are addressing is far more vital to the success of our societal norms. Violence is not acceptable. Whether it is physical or verbal, it is not acceptable. Maltreatment of any individual, regardless of color, ethnicity, or gender differences is not acceptable. And the instigators of such misconduct are as responsible as those who actually perpetrate the actions, and should be held equally accountable. This behavior is ill fated, and it is wrong. Everyone knows the difference between right and wrong! When did wrong become right?" Annie shook her head and started to apologize, but changed her mind. "My friends, obviously, my judgment just surfaced. I, too, am deeply concerned about what's happening, Sally. And I want to learn how to express my disappointment, my concerns, in a manner that does not mimic the behaviors that I feel strongly are inappropriate.

I would like this to become a topic that our group takes on."

"Well, I am very grateful this is being discussed," remarked Ron. "Like you, Annie, I too want to be able to articulate my feelings about the unscrupulous behavior that now seems to be the new norm of our culture. But I do not want to take on the behaviors of those whom I am not in alignment with. Perhaps this is a lesson for us. Maybe some of the folks who are so unhappy and dissatisfied with their circumstances don't know how to articulate their feelings any better than we do. So they end up behaving in ways that aren't congruent with their self-image, because it is the only way they can get attention for their concerns. And if that's the case, then we really need to review our own judgments. I know this is a very complex issue. There are those who are suffering and who need help. And there are those who are using these unfortunate situations to cultivate unrest and division among us, when we should be doing everything possible to create unity and to resolve problems that have gone unnoticed for too long.

I want to be someone who can help bridge differences and create positive change. This work goes hand-in-hand with healing the Earth. As our teacher often stated, if we are going to save the Earth, we, meaning all of us, must change." I watched my Friends sharing their viewpoints and realized how important it was for us to be having this conversation. It appeared that everyone had been thinking about this topic from various perspectives.

"Friends, may I interject a question? Is it true that all of you have been mulling over this idea about speaking the truth for some time now?"

"Yes," replied Barb. "Ever since our Old Friend brought the topic up to us. His repeated messages about speaking the truth still echo inside of me and it has given me pause. I'm glad we are talking about this now; it feels good to hear other people's concerns and frustrations. I, for one, find that I am reluctant to express myself at times, because I don't want my emotions or my words to overflow in a way that isn't polite or constructive. And by the way, I just used a word that I personally would like to bring back into our society. I would like people to be polite to one another again. That may sound crazy, but I think it's time for all of us to seriously review our personal manners. I think it would be very helpful. And I am making a promise to all of you and to myself to do that." The Circle of Friends were all in agreement.

"I am very excited about this, Friends. It seems to me that we have all been reluctant to face this topic because we didn't know how to express ourselves in a manner that we regarded as appropriate. So essentially, we've stifled ourselves. Like you, Ron, I wonder how many other people have done this in the past and have now reached a boiling point. So their words and emotions, which definitely need to be discussed, have come out in ways that have caused fears and disdain in others, further worsening their circumstances.

Folks, I have a suggestion. I want to tag onto Barb's idea. I believe we can enhance this self-exploration process by reviewing our individual manners as she suggested, and then, when we come together to discuss these issues, we must agree to talk about our concerns based upon our own individual behaviors. When we focus upon someone else's behavior, then that person is the issue, which takes us away from focusing upon our own. This model will expedite our process and also help us to articulate these issues more clearly and kindly.

I am so glad we are going to tackle this together. I can tell you now that I will need honest feedback and gentle challenges. I trust all of you to help me through this." My appeal for assistance stirred similar comments from the group. We were so blessed to have one another. My heart filled with hope. Together, we could help each other change, which would in turn help the Earth.

A passage from
Speaking The Truth
(Chapter Twenty-Three)

"Speaking The Truth is indeed an invitation to those, such as you, who are here for a reason. As you read these words, you know the truth of this statement, even if you do not remember the specifics of your purpose. Too often individuals become overly concerned about the details of their reason for being and lose sight of the inevitable truth that purpose develops and unfolds as intended and needed. Rest comfortably, Dear Reader, your reason for being is unfolding purposefully and your conscious awareness of this truth will become increasingly more obvious as you relax into the transitional moment.

Many of you have come into your present life experience for a specific meaningful reason and you are the ones for whom Speaking The Truth has been especially prepared. As ones who are essential to the Mission of Mercy and its purposeful intentions, you will face the challenges of speaking the truth.

Just as you are here for a reason, so too is this book, and rest assured, there is no coincidence that your paths have crossed. This encounter introduces you to a book whose purpose is to bring the truth forward to you, and others similar to you, who are called upon to speak the truth truthfully. The synchronicity of this reunion is really quite marvelous and deserves applause...or at least conscious recognition. Are you aware that your presence at this moment in time, in this particular place, is for a reason and the reason is significant? Think about this... make the effort, please...and speak the truth truthfully. Allow your imagination and your heart to engage with this question. It is posed for a reason and you are here at this point in time to receive the inquiry.

Once again you are confronted with reality...your Gift of Knowing. The inner wisdom that resides within you is... it simply is. Will you allow your gift to come forward *and will you accept the reality that you are more than you appear to be and your reason for being here at this exact moment and place is noteworthy? This occurrence is not mere happenstance. Please open your heart to the beautiful reality you are living and 'be' in the moment. This message demands repeating...at this precious point in time, you are here for a reason and your reason for being is truly significant. Is this not a wonderful reality?*

Hopefully, you will welcome this special truth into your heart fully and completely, for acceptance will aid your transitional process.

Shall we speak of the transition that you are now entering? Suffice it to say, the time is now, and this simple, but profound truth is as relevant and important as the repetitive message reminding you of your purposeful being. As your awakening process continues to gain momentum, you may expect great changes, some of which will unfold slowly and methodically while others will transpire so rapidly you will wonder what is happening to your life...and why...and then you will hear the voice within persistently and insistently reminding you again, 'You are here for a reason.'

There is a reason for the reminders. Each is as purposeful as the intentional message itself. You are here for a reason. The reminders are here for a reason. Speaking The Truth is here for a reason.

None of this is a coincidence; it is all happening for a reason and it is happening now because we have reached a point in time that is of such extreme significance we cannot pretend indifference. Now is the time of relevance. Let no one dissuade you of this truth, for it is critical for the future of humankind."

"My Friends, our To Do Lists have grown long. Let me check in with everyone. Is it time for us to close this evening, or is there energy to continue?"

Annie quickly waved her hand with the usual exuberance that was her norm. "I have two thoughts that are both founded in my waning energy." This comment tickled her friends who witnessed, or so they thought, her usual high energy. She took their teasing with good spirits, but reiterated that she was tired. "I know my appearance belies my truth, but I truly am feeling tired and I do want to have energy to send to the Earth before we close the session, which by the way is one of my requests. Let's remember to do an energy transfusion and I will be happy to lead that, if that's okay with everyone.

So back to my point, I suggest that we all try to bring a contribution of some type to our next meeting. Sal, I will find an appropriate photo and a message of beauty and relevance to accompany the photo. And I will also take care of our personal email contacts and have that ready for the main file that we put together."

Everyone agreed to collect their contacts and forward them to Jill, who volunteered to create a master file for the group. She also said that she would gather a few words of wisdom from a favorite book and send them to Sally and Annie for their project. Other commitments were also made in alignment with Annie's suggestion. And everyone vowed to grapple with the huge topic of reviewing Self. Barb started chuckling, and soon the room was filled with laughter.

"So glad we have something to occupy our time!" announced Mark. Similar comments were made before the group settled down again. And then, without any direction, deep breaths circled the room and Annie took the lead.

"Oh, Dear Friends, thank you for accompanying me on this wonderful journey to assist our Beloved Earth. Please do what is necessary for you to reach that sweet place of peace and serenity." She followed with silence and her own deep breathing exercises. Every person in the group took responsibility for their own experience, trusting that they did indeed know how to facilitate this act of generosity.

"My Friends, how blessed are we to have the opportunity to meet with the Earth once again. So grateful are we for everything she has done on our behalf. Dear Mother, so kind and generous you have been. Please allow us now to offer you an act of kindness that is long overdue. Together we come on your behalf. Within each of us is the Source energy that exists with all in the Universe. With this energy we intend to bring you renewed spirits and wellness. Please accept our offer and please do not feel the need to return this favor. Our Gift is for you, Old Friend.

And now, my Dear Friends, make yourselves ready for the transfer of energy. In your mind's eye, I ask all of you to envision the gardens at the city park. Refresh your memory of that beautiful setting and allow that to be our point of entry tonight. With a deep breath, release your particle of pure healing energy to the center of our circle so it may unite with all others. There in the center of our Circle of Old Friends, our energies merge into One, and from there we raise the energy into the sky. Let the ball of energy move over to the gardens, and there let it hover momentarily in the sky for all to see. And with the next breath release the energy to shower the gardens, entering there into the Mother so that she may disperse the energy as is needed.

Thank you, Mother Earth for receiving our Gift, and may you rest comfortably tonight.

Now, Friends, release yourself from the garden and return back to your respective bodies. And rest. Rest here in the company of Dear Old Friends.

Thank you all for this experience of unity and generosity.

In peace be!"

I stood on the porch watching my Friends as they headed home for the evening. Filled with gratitude, I waved goodbye as they turned the corner into the night.

❧ 30 ❧

"*The time has come, Dear Readers, for the truth to be spoken. As you have read so many times already within the pages of this book, speaking the truth is essential to the well being of all who reside upon the planet Earth. This truth, heralded by so many cultures, has its origins in ancient wisdom that is far older than any today can imagine. What has existed throughout all existence for all existence continues to be the preferred way of existence.*

Dear Readers, it will not surprise you to know this manner of being came to your kind from another kind who learned this way of being from others, who learned it from others, who also learned it from others so very long ago that the original birth of speaking the truth is no longer remembered. What is known is the efficacy of this practice.

We impress upon you the truth of this statement. Speaking the truth is essential to the well being of all in existence. The consequence of diverting from speaking the truth leads one into situations that are undesirable and not easily rectified. Those who have chosen to stray from this practice have regretted their decision.

We hope that the peoples of Earth will carefully consider the options. Returning to a world where speaking the truth is honored and respected enhances your ability to create peace on Earth. Continue to support and foster untruths and ill manners and your circumstances will become increasingly more perilous.

As is learned in this series of books, negative energy generated by the human species is the primary cause of the Earth's declining health. If you continue your perpetration of misconduct, including your lies, abuses, and scandalous affronts to the health of all species upon the planet, then you will incur the consequences of your behaviors. The consequences will be spoken truthfully. Your beautiful residence, the Life Being Earth, will cease to provide you with the provisions that you take for granted. This will not be an act of the maliciousness that you have so cruelly perpetrated upon her. It will be the result of her escaping into dormancy for the sake of survival. This reaction is simply how a Life Being of her kind retains her eternal being. Though she does not wish this to happen, it will, unless the peoples of Earth choose to behave appropriately.

Speaking the truth is appropriate behavior. Acts of kindness, love, and generosity fall into the same category. As you can see, very little is required of you. You are asked to be the people of goodness that you truly are. You are asked to care for one another and for all other species as well. You are asked to think of others before you think of yourself. These are reasonable requests and reasonable behaviors to expect from another and from oneself. In turn, you must give up your greed, your meanness and cruelty, and your arrogant ways. You must come to accept that you are equal with all others in existence. You are no better than any other and you are no less. You are what all are. You are equal. You are same. You are One with all others in existence.

With this in mind, we ask you, Dear Readers, to continue with this book of new beginning. As you seek your humanity, let us hope you will discover the goodness that resides within."

~ 31 ~

A passage from
Speaking The Truth
(Chapter Twenty-Four)

"Speaking The Truth is presented at this time, for you are ready to receive its messages of truth. Your Gift of Knowing validates this truth and confirms what is being purported. Presently, your developmental level demands growth, and for this reason, you and Speaking The Truth were brought together. You require expansion and Speaking The Truth is intended to assist you with your evolutionary process. Is it not convenient that you found each other? Once again, we are reminded there are no coincidences. In actuality, the messages of assistance provided throughout this literary opportunity were prepared long ago in anticipation of this moment in time when you would be ready for these gentle reminders. Your presence is evidence that you are ready.

Shall we commence our collaborative efforts by discussing the title of this book? Speaking The Truth is a not so subtle, gentle reminder. Perhaps you have already noticed how frequently it was repeated in this and previous chapters, and if so, hopefully you realize it happened for a reason. Indeed, Speaking The Truth is a title with purposeful intentions and far reaching possibilities that will most likely affect each reader differently and potentially result in life-altering ramifications.

Immediately, a question comes to mind...can a book title wield such influence? What is your answer? How are you affected each time you encounter the title implying that you must speak the truth? Please pause for a moment and give this question careful consideration before you speak the truth truthfully.

Now...continue if you will. How does the title of this book affect you? Does it spark interest or indifference? Are you inspired to explore more about your truthful nature or are you intimidated by the prospect? Does the inferred message cause you to review and/or question your present behaviors, and if so, in what ways? Do you feel challenged by the title to speak the truth truthfully and does it make you wonder if you are actually doing so presently?

Hopefully, you will find Speaking The Truth a companionable assistant—one that lovingly holds you as you pursue preferred endeavors that will successfully deepen your conscious awareness of the truthful ways in which you live your present life. Speaking The Truth is truly an invitation that welcomes you to the journey of Self. It is an opportunity to get to know you and your truthful Self fully, completely, and wholly. As a participant in the Mission of Mercy, this is a critical and essential part of your evolutionary path.

As many of you already recognize, the purpose of this literary experience is multi-layered, multi-faceted, and multi-dimensional. While some of you are acutely aware of your role in the Mission of Mercy, others are still awakening to that truth. Regardless of your present status, whether you are an initiate or a seasoned member of the Mission, you are here for a reason and your presence is deeply appreciated.

Although the Mission of Mercy is a project of very long-standing, few of you are yet acquainted with its intentions. Actually, this statement is not presented truthfully. In truth, all of you know about the Mission of Mercy, but your memories of this 'knowing' may not have fully reached conscious awareness. Your participation in speaking the truth will advance your awakening process, allowing you to retrieve these memories, which will clarify your purpose for being, including your role in the project that was initiated longer ago than you can presently imagine.

Rest assured, Dear Reader, your active participation in speaking the truth will significantly alter the potential of humankind's future. Each of you has a unique role to perform and each role is as important as the other, thus it is essential that all participants in the Mission of Mercy learn to support and assist one another...and this we will do in many different and varied ways, one of which will be actively and forthrightly partaking in speaking the truth.

Speaking the truth is a concept that may challenge your sensibilities. You may wonder why an entire book is dedicated to the topic and you may question if it is warranted. Then again, you may find the topic is causing you significant discomfort.

Although few of you regard yourselves as individuals who do not speak the truth, upon greater self-examination, one begins to wonder. Please process your truth in the privacy of your own heart, for this is not an exercise for public review. Through careful self-study, you may learn many truths about you that are surprising and gratifying.

For instance, anticipating this self-exposure of your truthful nature will reveal what a remarkable being you really are. Anticipate that you will find you are a gifted, delightful, and loving individual, who is worthy of your respect and admiration.

With deeper examination, also anticipate that you will discover you have potential for great change that will accentuate and enhance the wonderful person you already are. Indeed, Dear Reader, by exploring your truthful nature, you may find that you are more than you appear to be, and you may actually accept the remarkable being you truly are.

As you delve deeply into your inner concept of self, tread lightly, please. Remember, you suffer from the human affliction of self-judgment and there is no room for such unkindness in this courageous and honorable endeavor.

When reviewing your personal records—the heartfelt information that only you are privilege to have—you may experience hesitation, reticence, and vulnerability. Take a deep breath and just know you are not alone. When working at this advanced level of self-revelation, you are indeed in good company and you will be aided if and when you are in need. So take another deep breath and jump in and do the good work that you are so capable of doing. Remember, you are not alone on this solo journey. Even though you pursue the work individually and privately, the search for truth regarding your truthful nature is one that is held in the highest regard by those who faithfully guard your quest.

You are embarking upon one of the most challenging and cherished adventures of your evolutionary experience. You seek the truth about your truthful manner, and in so doing, you gain more truths about your True Self. The journey is yours to design and define, and it will be honored. Although the journey is yours alone to navigate, you will never be alone. Rest assured, Dear Friend, you will never be alone.

There is no need for concern, worry, or fear. You are safe. You are unconditionally accepted and this is true now, during, and upon completion of your journey. Please accept this message of unconditional acceptance, for it makes the experience gentler, easier, and faster. The time is now and you are ready."

32

After waving goodnight to my Friends, I retreated back to the bedroom and my Sacred Space. The day had seemed long and I was eager to journal about the experience of the previous night. I was determined to gain clarity about the intense and expansive journal entry from the evening before. I quickly changed into more comfy clothes and then positioned myself into the favorite chair of the house. The moment was magical. *I love this chair!* Nestling deeply into its soft cushions, I was ready to address the issue. With favorite pen in hand and the opened journal on my lap, I asked the question that had been racing about in my mind throughout the entire day.

Who are you? Then I sat very quietly waiting for a response. I wondered how long one should wait, and whether there was a particular way one was to broach such a topic. And then, I checked the clock. Much to my surprise only a minute or two had passed. I would have sworn it was an hour. *Patience now! You've waited all day; you can wait a bit longer.* I did, and still no response was heard. With a deep breath, I began anew.

Dear Unknown Assistant, the words that you shared last night were remarkable. I am amazed by the process and embarrassed that I have no memory of what transpired. I see the words before me and recognize my handwriting, but these are not my words. I wish they were, but such ability is not in my possession. I assume the words were provided through some type of communication, but as I said, I have no recollection of this.

I am honored to be of service, but this experience is puzzling. Is it possible that we might discuss the process, the purpose, and my role in this very unusual experience? Once again, I took a deep breath and hoped for an answer. This time I remained poised and ready to receive a message if one was forthcoming. I closed my eyes hoping that this might facilitate a response, but again nothing transpired but the passing of time. And then I just started writing.

Why does this bother me? Do I really need to know who is assisting me? Will that make a difference? Just look at the words you received last night. Are they not evidence that something important is happening? Can you not accept the beauty of this unusual experience even if you do not understand how it transpired? How sad that would be!

"Indeed, how sad that would be! What is up with you?" I asked aloud. "Since when are you one who must have proof before you will believe. For goodness' sake, you openly accepted an invisible man into your life, and because you did, your life has totally changed. Must you have a name to associate with these writings before you will give them credence? Nonsense!" I declared boldly. "Okay, I am officially over myself! I cannot explain what is happening to me, but the evidence is here in my journal. And the text is profoundly beautiful and meaningful. I wish that I could produce such beauty, but it is not within me. But I am honored to be the recipient of these messages and I offer my assistance. I will gladly bring the messages forward and distribute them as you desire. I will await your instructions." I had spoken my truth, and was glad that I had done so. And my words were sincere. I really did want to assist the author of these astounding messages.

"Old Friends, I am tired now and in need of a good night's sleep. In peace be!" I waited a moment longer hoping for a reply, but still I heard only silence. I was satisfied with that. Tomorrow is another day.

A passage from
Speaking The Truth
(Chapter Twenty-Five)

"The time is now. This is a statement of truth and so much more. Each of you recognizes this internal message as one that is surfacing and literally 'calling' to you. For each, the calling will of course be different; however, in case it needs to be said again, you are being called and the time is now. Is it not wonderful to be called? The message—the time is now—is one that has been presented and heard throughout the ages, and yet, it is announced again with the same significance and urgency as in endless times before. This message has not run its course, and in truth, becomes more relevant with time. You are a testament to this, for the inner clock within you

ticks louder with each passing moment as the repeated message reverberates as if an alarm is resounding. Indeed the message harkens to you, mimicking an alarm clock as it reaches through the waves of sleep, striving to awaken you. Yes, Dear Friend, the alarm is sounding and calling you to awaken, gently and not so gently, reminding you 'the time is now.'

Hopefully our present discourse awakens you to the issue...you are being called to awaken! The sense of urgency that you feel within you is real. Your inner knowing is calling out to you, attempting to awaken you to your reality. This is not a ruse, nor is it fantasy; it is a message from you to you. How convenient! You devised this plan...this wake up call...and you even set the alarm for repetitious alerts. Maybe you are one that cherishes the snooze button and prefers to ignore the reality of your situation, but like it or not, the time to awaken is now! No more need be said.

Now, assuming that you accept the truth about your wakeup call, let us continue. Why did you orchestrate such an event? Surely it was more than just a playful joke to cause disruption in your present existence. Undoubtedly there was a reason for your efforts, and if this is true, are you not curious as to why you would go to such great lengths to get your attention? Presumably, you are one who is mindfully heart driven or you would not have created such a remarkable means of alerting you to the poignant moment...and rest assured, this is the moment of relevance. Something...some deed, some act, some event, some 'thing'... was of such great significance to you that you deliberately devised a plan to alert yourself to its imminent arrival, so at the allotted time you would awaken and commence preparations for the yet unknown unfolding. Needless to say, you are a being of creative genius and you may wish to respond to your own creative process. Awaken, Dear Friend, you are calling!

Speaking The Truth is the result of a similar creative, awakening process, and was brought forward at the allotted time due to a persistent calling. Is it not fitting that this book, which was developed in response to a calling, was designed to come forward at this particular time so that it could assist you with your awakening process? Sweet beauty!

In accordance with the purpose of Speaking The Truth, you are duly reminded that the time is now, and as such, you are also reminded that you are a being of extraordinary creative abilities that await your attention.

You are here for a reason...and the time is now!"

33

Barb waited quietly for the sun to come up over the hill. Without doubt, this was the most important part of her day. Patience was not an issue when waiting for the sun's arrival, and she was never disappointed. Her mind was filled with ideas. She was happier than she had ever been and very excited about recent events that were broadening her desires to know more about the More that existed. Although she was surrounded by goodness, there was a restlessness that puzzled her. She had everything anyone could ever hope for. Her work was deeply satisfying and kept her very active and happy, and she was blessed with wonderful friends. There was little else that she could imagine wanting, and still, there was something else going on internally that demanded her attention.

For some time, Barbara had been considering a change in her life. It didn't make sense to her because she was very happy in her present circumstances. Nevertheless, she often dreamed of a place that she believed was calling her. This puzzled her in the waking hours of the day, but at night, when the hour was late and the world was quiet, she could hear the waves of the ocean. She thought this odd, very peculiar, since she wasn't near any oceanic waters, but Barb found that she loved the ocean sounds, whether they were robust and turbulent or peaceful and gentle. She looked forward to their company every night.

Although the idea of leaving her friends made absolutely no sense to her, she recognized that she needed to talk about her internal struggle.

"Ah! There you are, Old Friend! What a pleasure it is to be in your company this morning!" She took in the glorious view with a huge deep breath and simply reveled in the moment. *What wisdom do you have for me this day, Dear Friend? Tell me everything about the existence that you know! Oh, how much you must know...*Lost in the moment, Barb briefly closed her eyes to hear the sounds of the morning. Much to her surprise, she heard the sound of waves crashing against the seashore and the quiet sounds of retreat as the waters returned to the sea. She opened her eyes again in anticipation of finding herself on a beach, but alas, she was still on the trail where she was before.

Amazing! I really felt as if I had been transported. "Dear Old Friend, did you just make that happen? Or was it another?" She shrugged her shoulders. "Master Sun, it was a pleasure to be with you, as always. Have a nice day!"

Barb turned away from the horizon and decided to return to her home. Ordinarily, she would walk a few miles further, but today, she felt the need to journal. This idea of moving closer to an ocean was growing stronger and she could no longer ignore the compulsion to do so.

When she was just blocks away from her house, the phone in her vest pocket began to ring. She knew immediately who was calling. "Sister, what are you up to?"

"Well, I'm wondering when you are going to stop by. How far out are you?" They both laughed when Barb announced she was just five minutes away. "Guess you were sending me vibes or vice versa. Come on by. The coffee us brewing!"

Within minutes they were settled around the kitchen table with beverage and healthy treats. "Sorry about the health food, Dear, but I decided to be an adult today."

"Once a week won't hurt us," replied Barb with a giggle. "Actually, Sister, this really looks yummy."

"So, how was Master Sun? Did you two have a powwow this morning?" We giggled about that too, but Barb knew her Sister was probing for information. Fortunately, her mouth was full which gave her moment to think about her response.

"Now, don't just tiptoe around this, Barb. You know it's time you started talking about the ache that's burning inside of you."

"How do you know these things? I haven't talked about this with anyone yet. How do you know this?" Her look was incredulous, but it didn't need to be. Barb knew her Sister was highly intuitive. They both were! And it still astounded both of them.

"I'm not sure I know anything, Barb, other than you've been of another mind lately. And quiet honestly, I don't know how you've managed to hold this energy at bay. Even though we've been incredibly busy with our new adventure, you've also been dealing with another huge transition in your life. I've tried to be patient, Dear, but as you know, patience and I are often at odds. So, this morning it occurred to me that this might be the time to broach the topic with you. Is this a good time, Sister? Of course, you can say no, and I will totally understand and respect your decision, but if not now, when?"

Barb burst out laughing. "You have the most delightful way of being pushy." I nodded in agreement and we giggled some more.

"Okay, I'll be serious now. I am very interested in what's going on with you, and whenever you would like to talk about it, I'm available." The timing of this invitation was perfect. Of course, that was no coincidence.

"I am so grateful that we share this remarkable psychic connection. Just a short while ago, I was wondering when I was going to broach this topic with you. Then, I headed home to journal about what's going on, and that's when your call came through. It is amazing how connected we are."

"I'm so grateful!" Our words of gratitude were spoken simultaneously. We both smiled and enjoyed another bite of cereal.

A passage from
Speaking The Truth
(Chapter Twenty-Six)

"Accepting that you are here for a reason is a choice. Accept it now or accept it later, but remember the time is now, so perhaps wisdom dictates that you accept it now. Is it not perplexing that one would doubt this possibility? If someone approached you and adamantly announced that you have no reason for being, would you not be offended? Would you not take issue with such nonsense? If the latter is true, then why do you struggle with accepting that you are indeed here for a reason? Accept the truth. Accept your reality, and remember the time is now.

Perhaps you wonder why so much emphasis is given to this issue and what it has to do with Speaking The Truth. Accepting that you are here for a reason is speaking the truth. Accepting that the urgency of the moment is real is also speaking the truth. When you are able to accept your truth...your reality...you will then be able to speak your truth to self and others. Initially, it may feel odd, even unsafe, to reveal your truth to others. You may worry about their reactions and wonder if their opinions of you will change after you disclose your new self to them. In truth, the possibility that you will experience many doubts, questions, and misgivings about revealing your reason for being is highly likely. Once again, you will find yourself in very good company...each who reaches this level of participation experiences unrest before peace of mind is achieved.

Speaking The Truth is here to remind you of another truth that will be of extreme assistance during your unveiling process. You must trust your heart, not your mind. Please remember this, Dear Friend, for your heart is and always will be your guide. It is your heart that understands the calling is real, while your mind wrangles with the idea. The heart knows you are here for a reason. It does not question or doubt, it simply knows the truth and awaits the mind to quiet itself; and as it waits, the heart recognizes that time is of the essence and it aches for the mind to relinquish its worrisome ways.

The heart is ready to proceed with your reason for being; it knows the time is now, but the mind is reasonably certain the heart is in error and counters with endless reasons for distrusting your alleged reason for being. The struggle within will continue until you are able to speak the truth to the one who matters most...You!

Initially, you will focus upon others and it will be a genuine tussle as you address your fears about their reactions to the new you, but ultimately, this outward unrest is just a distraction from the real discord that lies within. As you battle inwardly to accept your newfound reality, heartfelt dialogue with self must ensue regarding your fears about being a person who is here for a reason... after all, what does this really mean?

Of course, the mind will want to step in at this point with countless reasons for you to be fearful, but such assistance is not beneficial. Remember, the heart is your guide and the conversations within are between you and this sagacious leader. The heart knows you are here for a reason and it understands your confusion and

unconditionally accepts your fears without judgment.
Trust your heart to take the lead and it will safely and
swiftly navigate you through this period of unrest.

The time ahead is rich with opportunity! You are
on the brink of remembering who you really are...this
is a time for joyous optimism and hopeful anticipation.
Speaking The Truth is here to remind you once again
that your reason for being is significant and when you
can speak the truth about this reality, you will be living
your truth."

"Barb, may I ask you a question?"

"If I said no, would that stop you?"

We both laughed about that and then I jokingly responded. "Probably not, but I would prefer to have your permission. And yes, Dear Friend, I can hear 'no' if that is your preference."

She placed her hand on mine and reassured me that she was aware that I was trying to help. And permission was granted.

"Okay, so here comes the question!" I purposefully made eye contact with Barb before expressing myself. "What is keeping you from talking about this? You are typically very open and forthcoming about your thoughts and concerns, so your behavior is different than usual. Do you know what's keeping you silent?" Barb deliberated carefully before finally speaking. This was the Friend that I knew so well: a person who thought before she spoke.

"As always Sister, you have nudged me in the right direction at the right time. My initial reaction to your question was 'I don't know!' But the question itself led me to a modicum of clarity about what's going on." I knew it was time for Barb to take her deep breath. This too was typical behavior for her. I joined her in the refreshing exercise.

"Sister, I think the reason...no, let me rephrase that. One of the reasons that I've been reluctant to talk about this is you. And when I tell you what's going on, you will understand why I say that. For some time, I've been thinking about relocating. In fact, I think you questioned me about this a while back, but at the time I really didn't know what was going through my mind. My so-called journey was overtaking my life, and I didn't know what to do other than to take the next step and the next and the next. I was living moment to moment back then." Barb rolled her eyes and admitted she still was. "Life has been so full and rich that every day feels like a new beginning. It's exciting and wonderful and I am so happy! And I'm also very confused. I cannot imagine letting go of what I have here, and yet, I feel pulled to go elsewhere. It's so strange, and it's so real." My Friend released a huge sigh.

"Thank you for being pushy, Sister! It is such a relief to talk about this, and I know you have compassion for my confusion."

"Yes, I do, and even though the idea of your relocating is upsetting, I will support you. Barb, I want what is best for you. You are here for a reason, Dear Heart, and you must do what you must do." Tears streamed down our faces. Fortunately, the ever-handy tissue box was nearby. We each grabbed one and took care of our sniffles.

"The other reason I haven't brought this up, Sister, is because I don't know what I'm supposed to do, which of course, makes me feel totally foolish. All I know is that I hear the ocean all the time, and as you well know, that isn't possible from this location. But I fall asleep almost every night to the sounds of the ocean, and I often hear it when I'm on my walks. Sister, it's calling me. When we do our energy sessions, I'm there at the ocean, with my feet in the sand, merging with Mother Earth. I cannot explain this, but I think I'm supposed to be there, wherever there is." Barb leaned back in her chair, closed her eyes, and just sat in silence. I honored her need to retreat from the conversation and joined her in the silence. Time passed as it always does and eventually her eyes opened.

"May I have another bowl of cereal?"

"The next step?" I asked.

"Yes! The next step is another bowl of cereal!" She boldly and decisively grabbed the cereal box.

After a few bites, Barb was ready to reengage. "Sister, I cannot imagine moving away from here. You are my best Friend!" Tears welled up again. She put her spoon down and leaned back into the chair and just let the tears flow.

Although I was able to control my urge to console her, I was not able to stop my own tears from releasing. The thought of my best Friend living somewhere other than a few blocks away just didn't sit well with me. We were both a mess. *How blessed we are with this friendship!*

"Yes, we are!" Through her sniffles she managed to respond to my unspoken thoughts. "And I just cannot imagine why we would be separated. We have work to do together. Why would our journeys take us in different directions?" More tears came from both of us. Eventually the well was dry and we were able to resume our conversation.

"Barb, Dear Best Friend, I don't have any answers at this point. It is puzzling, or so it seems, for two people who are totally incapable of being impartial at the moment. But this is happening for a reason and it demands that we practice patience. Please don't roll your eyes at me. It is essential that we keep our fear emotions at bay. There is no need for us to go down dreary paths anticipating worst-case scenarios. We must be open-minded, and more importantly, we must open our hearts to what is coming. I trust that something really wonderful is in store for you and for me. And regardless of what unfolds, we will face it together!" I reached across the table to join hands with Barbara. It was comforting for both of us.

"Thank you, Sister. Those are wise words, which I will hold onto. You were right about the worst-case scenario option. I have been scaring myself with ridiculous thoughts about leaving here and never seeing anyone again. What nonsense! That simply will not happen."

"No, it won't! Neither of us would tolerate it, so we can erase that option from the mind's video log. Barb, do you have any idea of where this unknown place might be? Do you have previous experiences visiting ocean settings?" Barb shrugged her shoulders.

"That's what is so weird about this. Well, there are a lot of things about my so-called journey that are weird, but I have absolutely no idea where this yearning is taking me. Which ocean? Which continent? This is a very big planet with many possibilities; I don't know where to start searching for answers. I'm open to exploring various settings, but where does one begin?" We sat quietly for a moment, and I wondered when the answer would strike my Friend. My intuition led me to remain silent. It didn't take long for the answer to surface.

"Oh, I get it!" she mused. "This is one of those times when I must seek within. Hmm! Of course, it really is time for me to curl up with my journal. Thank you, Dear Sister, for being my Best Friend. Thank you for being here. And thank you for walking this path with me!"

"You are so welcome, and I am equally grateful for all the same reasons. Now, off you go! Have a great day! And connect soon!"

A passage from
Speaking The Truth
(Chapter Twenty-Seven)

"Let us continue. Are you ready, Dear Reader, to accept the truth that you are here for a reason and are you ready to speak the truth regarding this awareness? As you can see, Speaking The Truth builds upon itself. With awareness comes acceptance and with acceptance comes action.

Perhaps you doubt your inner knowing and question whether you are really and truly growing in awareness, or if in fact, you are merely opening to the idea of having a purposeful existence because of the repeated messages received regarding this topic. Speaking The Truth is indeed here to deliver a message of purposeful intentions, and so the messages are presented repetitively for the intended recipient, but are you the intended recipient? Are you really here for a reason? If you feel like a skeptic, do not apologize...express gratitude! You are not here to be led down a path of misdirection. By all means, question what you read, deliberate each new notion that you encounter, and follow your heart's leadership.

Please do not shy away from any questions regarding your reason for being, for no one other than you is privileged to discern the answers to your inquiries. Although Speaking The Truth proclaims that it is a book with a purpose, which indeed it is, you must discern if it was brought to you for a reason or if the encounter was simply an error. Only you can determine this. As you deliberate your many doubts and questions, let your heart be your guide...each question warrants heartfelt consideration, and in so doing, your awareness, your inner knowing, will expand within you illuminating the clarity you seek."

The hour was still early and I realized that Barb was not the only one who needed time with her journal. I retreated to my sacred place, lit the votive candle in its gracious cobalt blue holder that rested in front of the blue Earth globe that Barb had gifted to each of us in the group. It was a lovely gesture, filled with beautiful intentions honoring friendship and purpose. The candlelight reflecting from the globe was a sight to behold. I wondered if this was how the Earth looked from outer space. *Did she glow like this?* The thought captured my imagination. It was time to offer an energy transfusion to the Earth.

"Oh, Dear Friend, how beautiful you are. May I join you for a moment? My heart is full this day, and I wonder what will come in the future. As you know many of us are working on your behalf. I regret that my understanding of your situation was so long in coming, but I am aware now, and I choose to participate in this wonderful endeavor of restoring your energy back to full health. I am most pleased to be a part of this task force.

My Friend, I know that you are aware of the presence of every one of us, and I also know that you have the means of communicating with us. So, today, I ask you to take a question under consideration for me. I do not need an immediate answer, but if there is an answer that could be offered, I would appreciate it at some time that is convenient for you.

The issue is about relocation for my Friend, Barbara, and for myself as well. She believes she is intended to move elsewhere and desires guidance. I, too, have had similar thoughts of late, and also would benefit from your guidance. Is there some place, Dear Friend, where our presence might be more helpful to you? I know you are busy, but if you have a preference, I would be most grateful to know what it is.

And now, my Friend, I will prepare myself to send you energy. With a few deep breaths, my energy will be ready to share with you. Please accept this donation, for it gives me great pleasure to be of assistance." And with that said, the transfusion was achieved, and the heartfelt task was done. "Thank you, Dear Friend! So grateful to be in your presence."

After the energy session was completed, I addressed my journal. As often is the case, I spoke to the journal as if it were a Being of Importance. "Dear Journal of Mine, the conversation of relocation is finally out in the open. Barbara is confused, of course, but she is strong willed and devoted. She will find her way and act accordingly. Of this, I am certain.

I did not share with her my confusion regarding the possibility that I too might be moving elsewhere. It didn't seem appropriate at the time. She needs time to work through her own confusion before hearing about my transition. It is odd that we are both feeling pulled to relocate. I do not yet understand the purpose of this, for we clearly have been brought together for a reason. We are a team in many different ways and certainly our work regarding saving the Earth has solidified our collaborative abilities."

Specifically addressing those who often assist me, I continued to pen my communication. "Dear Ones, I assume you are listening to me as I go on and on in my journal. And I trust you will offer suggestions when the time is appropriate, but time's a wasting, as the old phrase goes. I know that patience is a virtue, but Dear Friends, relocating requires time, adjustments, finances, and hard work. Some guidance would be very useful." I started to pause to create space for an answer, but found myself taking over the one-sided conversation once again.

"Friends, unlike Barb, I do have connections with a place that has been held in my heart for years. Oddly enough, it is a seacoast community with wonderful places to walk and beaches to enjoy. When Barb shared her image of merging with the Earth while barefoot on the beach, my thoughts took me to my favorite location. And her passion for the ocean is shared deeply. Is this a coincidence? Are you validating my ideas about relocating to the City by the Sea through the camaraderie of this wonderful friendship that Barb and I share? Or are you reminding me of my lust for the oceanic waters so that I can reassure her that her choices are viable? Whatever is going on, Dear Friends, your input would be most helpful." I placed the pen down, and released a big sigh that reminded me of the huge sigh that Barb had released earlier. *What a Dear Friend she is! I am so grateful that we've had this time together.* For reasons unknown to me I picked up the pen again. Although I thought my time with the journal was done for the morning, I was mistaken. As if of its own accord, the pen gripped by my hand began to convey the message of another.

"Old Friend, so good it is to be in your presence once again. Your desire to know more about what is coming is understood. Always, have you been One who prefers to be prepared for a transition before the transition unfolds. So too are you in this life experience.

We are very grateful that you are willing to uproot yourself for the sake of that which you do not fully remember. Our plans are coming to fruition, Dear Friend. Many across the globe are coming together on behalf of the Earth. As you well know, this is critically important for her to regain her vibrancy once again. Others from places far and near are also assisting. The momentum is accelerating and we must take advantage of the good will that so many are offering. More hopeful are we than ever before. The Earth can be saved if necessary changes are made and sustained. My Friend, your assistance is needed. Although the notion of relocating is not easily grasped, it is one that must be considered thoroughly. Your dearest friends reside in your present location, but new friends await you in locations that are yet to be revealed. There is much to do, Old Friend, on the Earth's behalf. She requires those who are willing to spread the news about her situation and who are willing to provide guidance to those who will in turn act on the Earth's behalf. Many are willing to assist, but of these many, few currently are aware that the solution to the Earth's health issue lies within. As you know so well, this situation is easily managed. Just as you and the other members of the group quickly learned the truth, so too will others. And just as you and your friends benefitted from the assistance of a helper, so too will these new students of the healing arts. These new friends, yet to be, must be educated about the healing abilities that lie within every person on Earth, and they must be taught the simple act of healing another. Because of your own experiences, you now fully understand the truth of this process. You are One who is an able teacher, Old Friend, and your services are required. Easier is it for one to travel to others than it is for others to travel to the one. Everywhere you go, new students of the healing arts will emerge and new teachers will as well. Most will remain in their own locations, but there will be others who feel the ache to move onward. Through this means, the energy of the Earth will change, and as she recovers from her illness, so too will humankind recover from their present crisis of ill will. Now is the time for the people of Earth to regain their humanity.

Old Friend, new ways are unfolding and you are to be part of that process. Rest easy, knowing that your services are needed. For now, you are where you are intended to be, but changes are coming. Know that you will be provided ample time for preparations to be made. Always, we are most grateful to be in your presence.

In peace be, Dear Friend!"

"Thank you! Your message is helpful and of course, I want to know more, but your words sustain me. I am very grateful for your time, your assistance, and your ever-present presence." A deep sigh was heard. Was it another's or mine? I did not know, and it didn't matter. I was at peace. More questions would come, more solutions would be sought, but for this moment in time, I was at peace with myself and the world about me.

A passage from
Speaking The Truth
(Chapter Twenty-Seven)

"As your awareness grows, so too will your need to know 'more.' Excitement will mount as your curiosity reaches to new heights, and with each new acquisition of additional information, the ache to know 'more' will reach a feverous pitch, propelling you forward to seek, explore, and examine more of the infinite possibilities that await you. The process is never-ending, the adventure is ongoing, and the more delicious particles of infinite awareness that you gather into your heart, the more you want to consume. Each scrumptious growth experience nourishes your evolving awareness, while planting seeds for the next cycle of development. Acceptance emerges as each new reality of growth inspires an ever-increasing urgency to advance...to seek, to discover, to assimilate and to begin anew.

Awareness naturally evolves, acceptance develops after assimilation of the newly gained experiences, and action necessarily results in response to the unfolding process. Internally driven, purposefully motivated, and intentionally deliberate, the three A's, awareness, acceptance, and action, perpetuate the evolutionary process forward.

In similar fashion, Speaking The Truth serves to advance each individual reader forward in his or her adjustment and acclimation to the reality of their purposeful existence. Awareness of this simple yet profound truth exists within you at some level; however, acceptance of this truth elevates awareness to a new level of existence, indicating an active response to the newly forming awareness and setting in motion the ongoing, never-ending, self-perpetuating need to evolve. Speaking The Truth is intended to assist with the evolutionary process by repeatedly challenging you, the reader, to awaken to your purposeful existence.

In fulfillment of its purpose, Speaking The Truth now offers another demonstration of its reason for being. Dear Reader, please listen with the ears of your heart as you slowly and purposefully read and absorb this message.

You are here for a reason!
You are needed, you are necessary, and
the time is now for you to advance forward
in regaining your purposeful identity.

Seek Within!

Re-discover who you really are and
speak the truth of that which you find.

The Time is Now!"

A few blocks away, Barb was also engaged with her journal. Not knowing what she would discover, she opened her heart to learning more about herself and her so-called journey. Her Earth altar was nearby and like her Sister of Choice, she too was mesmerized by the light reflecting from the globe. She forced herself to lower her gaze. *You are here to write, remember? Your eyes are required to be on the page, please. Why are you so rattled by this, Barb? What are you afraid of?* "Enough questions!" She announced aloud. "Just be quiet and see what happens!" Barb followed her own instructions and was finally able to quiet the mind. With pen in hand, she was poised to begin, but found she had nothing to say. Her hands remained in a position of readiness, but nothing came to her. *What is wrong with me? Why am I making this so difficult?* And then the voice of an Old Friend was heard.

"May I join you, my Old Friend?" Barb quickly looked about the room, but saw no one.

"Are you here, my Friend?" Again, she scanned the room waiting for the Old Friend to materialize, but to her surprise, it did not happen. She asked again, but no response was forthcoming. Disappointment surfaced, but she quickly released it. "I'm confused my Friend. You are of course welcome here any time, but I am at a loss. Are you here or not?"

"Please prepare to hear me differently this time, Old Friend. With your pen in hand, let us communicate."

Barb did as instructed. Repositioning herself in the preferred chair and with the pen in hand, she announced that she was ready, and then the communication began. *"Old Friend, it is a pleasure to connect with you in this way. Although you have had this experience before, it is time to become proficient in receiving messages in this way. You will be receiving many more messages, Old Friend, and this will be one of the ways in which you will assist the Earth and serve the peoples of Earth. Your intuitive skills prepare you for this type of communication. I am most grateful to be part of your transition. I hope you are amenable to my presence."*

"Indeed, I am!" Barb responded by means of the pen. "In fact, I am honored to have you as a teacher again. And I look forward to many more opportunities to be in your presence and to serve in this way. What is your plan?"

Through the written hand came the reply, *"Our plan, Old Friend, is to assist you in remembering the skills of old. You are One who is efficient at receiving and recording the messages from those who are here to assist the people of Earth. This is not your first time as a receiver and presenter of messages. You are, in truth, remarkably skilled and simply need practice to regain that which is already in your possession. In days ahead, many will approach you and offer to be of assistance. These are Old Friends with whom you have worked before, and through these connections your abilities of old will be refined once again.*

Please accept your other Friends, as you do me. Once you are in their company, you will sense familiarity. Many times before have we all worked together. Consider this to be a reunion of many, many old friends, for essentially that is exactly what will be transpiring. Soon, you will recognize the energy of each individual and you will also witness a change in your handwriting. You will be amused, and of course, you will desire to know More about everyone who approaches you. Old Friend, please trust that each is a Dear Old Friend, and they come to be of service. Little time is there for reminiscing, unfortunately. Please focus your attention upon the learning experiences that are offered rather than the curiosity that often distracts you." Barb could not help herself. Even with this new means of communicating, she found it necessary to tease the beloved teacher. Her right eyebrow raised for the occasion.

"Are you insinuating that my curiosity can be problematic and potentially disruptive?"

The Old Friend managed her playfulness graciously, *"Yes, Dear Friend, that is exactly what is being insinuated. You are a very astute learner."* Laughter filled the room. The lighthearted banter eased her mind.

"Will this be a daily activity?" she asked.

"Your companions are eager to assist you and they tend to be insistent and persistent. They will prefer regular connection, but you will need to develop a schedule that complements your busy life. Old Friend, what is coming is purposeful. You will learn more of this in the near future. Because all involved made commitments to one another long ago, each is eager to fulfill the commitments made. They will be tireless in their efforts to assist you. All are most grateful for the opportunity to serve with you again."

"I am humbled by this opportunity and embarrassed that I cannot remember the agreements made. And I am most grateful to be a part of this collective and eager to learn from all of you." Barb leaned back into her comfy chair and sighed. Her curiosity was large and she appreciated the wonderful guidance received from her teacher. She was aware that her curious nature was a gift that often got her into trouble. Her smile lit up the room. She knew that More was coming and she knew that she could handle it.

34

A passage from
Speaking The Truth
(Chapter Twenty-Eight)

"You are charged, Dear Readers, to speak the truth. Ponder this, and as you do, perhaps you may wish to challenge the audacity of such impudence. After all, who dares you to speak the truth? Who possesses such privilege? Once again, questions arise that beg to be answered and as many, many times before you are guided to seek within.

Speaking The Truth is just a book. You may feel as if this 'book' orders you about...dictating commands to speak the truth and challenging you to accept that you are here for a reason. Presumably it even wields its authority by intimating a sense of urgency through repeated announcements emphasizing, 'The Time is Now!'

Indeed, you may choose to believe Speaking The Truth has such power, but why would you believe such a fantasy? Are you one who would actually fall for such a ruse? Think better of yourself, please!

If you are experiencing unrest by reading Speaking The Truth, ask why. Rather than assuming the book is at fault, perhaps a better approach might be to question why it is creating disruption in your life. Rather than blaming this literary piece for its forward manner, why not explore the impact the messages are having upon you. By mere utterance of its name, Speaking The Truth causes one to question his or her own truthful ways and challenges one's integrity and sense of self. The preferred image that each of us clings to is confronted by this thought-provoking title, and each time Speaking The Truth is mentioned, it gives us pause and invites us to review our present reality and perception of self. With each new invitation, an opportunity to explore one's evolving identity more deeply presents itself. Hopefully, Dear Reader, you will accept these invitations, for each is an exquisite gift of self-creation. By accepting these opportunities for self-examination and further exploration, you proactively define and re-define your remarkable self, thus becoming more in alignment with who you really desire to be. Speaking The Truth is not intended to derail or demoralize you; it is intended to open your heart to the glory of who you really are. Please read the previous sentence again because it warrants another look."

As I relaxed in the living room, waiting for my Friends to arrive, I wondered what would transpire this evening. Our assignments from the last meeting warranted more than one meeting, but the group consistently managed to address details rapidly. So who knew what would unfold tonight? My thoughts visited many places. First, the memory of my favorite walk along the cliffs of the seacoast town that I so admired came rushing forward. Then the thought of saying goodbyes to local friends flashed before me, followed by the unthinkable reality of searching for another place to live. Exhilaration and fatigue brought the mind's video to a screeching halt. Fortunately, footsteps heard from the porch announced the arrival of at least one guest, possibly more. I opened the door and found a package instead. I waved to the deliveryman already back in his truck. Written in very large letters on the outside of the box was "Deliver before 6:00 pm!"

"Hmm! What could this be?" Maneuvering about to retrieve the box, I saw Barb rushing down the street. She was waving both hands trying to get my attention. I walked to the end of the sidewalk to meet her.

"Oh, thank goodness, it arrived in time!" she hollered from about twenty feet away. I naturally wondered what she was up to this time. "I'm not late, am I?" Barb looked at her watch to reassure herself.

"You're early, as usual! Come on in and tell me what surprises are in this box?" Her excitement was typical Barb. Clearly her creative juices were overflowing again.

"You're going to love this!" she confidently replied. "At least, I think you will! Hope you will! Here, let me help with that; it's a bit heavy." We carried the box into the kitchen and placed it on the counter and Barb immediately started to open it. "I was hoping to get here in time to arrange these beauties around the living room. You'll understand when you see them."

"Well, I can't wait. That box feels like it's full of rocks. Can't wait to see what actually is hiding in there!" Just as I spoke, my Friend pulled out the first object that was carefully padded with tissue paper. She pulled the paper away and there it was...a ROCK! But not just any rock. The rock had obviously been carefully selected. It was rather flat, dark in color, and perfectly smooth, but there was more. In the center of the rock, Barb had carefully painted 'Save The Earth!"

"Barb, this is brilliant! Tell me about this! What are your plans for these beauties?" My reaction undoubtedly pleased her and her enthusiasm grew.

"Well, ultimately, the decision lies in the beholder, but I thought this particular size had great potential for the entryway into one's yard or house. For instance, yours could be placed by the front gate or on the front porch, or wherever you choose. Basically, this is yard art with an important STATEMENT! I made one for each household, and hopefully, these messages will inspire other folks to create their own Love Notes to the Earth." She continued to unwrap the rocks as we chatted. One was painted Love The Earth; another, The Earth Rocks; and another, The Earth Matters; and another, Thank you, Mother Earth. Each was beautifully done.

"Barb, this is so thoughtful. Our Friends will really appreciate these gifts." Just then, the gang came in. Hugs were exchanged, good cheer was expressed, and everyone fell in love with the Love Rocks.

As was usual, everyone filled their plates with goodies and relocated into the living room. The conversation continued to focus upon Barb's latest creative project.

"What inspired this idea?" asked Annie who was an avid lover of projects.

"Actually, it came from our assignment. The repeated message about speaking the truth seemed to be an avenue for artistic expression. Obviously, there are countless ways of delivering messages; bumper stickers, clothing, posters, coffee cups, etc. But I preferred the idea of utilizing the Earth's stones to make a statement. This is something that anyone can do. It's a fun project for children, and adults who still feel like children. I'm just curious about where a small act of acknowledgment to the Earth may lead. Who knows? I just want to see what kind of reactions we get from putting our stones in places where they can be noticed. The question is: will they be noticed?

For me personally, I enjoy seeing my stone every time I go out to check the mail. It reminds me to be grateful. And I'm working on a set of stones now for my entryway from the garage. Three separate stones that read Love The Earth. I have found this project very healing. And also fascinating! This is such a small act of kindness, but it's relevant. It made me aware of how important little acts of goodness can be. A smile. A hello. A wave of the hand. These small acts can brighten someone's day. Likewise, acknowledging a tree, or some other plant or a flower is a sign of good will towards the Earth. She hears our compliments and she appreciates being noticed. It's so little to do, for someone without whom we could not exist.

Thinking about our assignment on speaking the truth has made me more cognizant of those around me, including all the other life beings with whom we co-exist. I don't want to be neglectful of or disrespectful towards anyone. Speaking the truth means more than just articulating the truth. For me it also means behaving with integrity: i.e., doing the right thing! If we are going to speak the truth about the Earth, then we also have to behave in accordance with our words.

And this is true regarding every other virtue that we believe we possess. It's time for us to shape up and become the people that we believe we are. Good people do not treat others unkindly. Good people do not regard decency as an inconvenience that can be discarded. Good people understand the difference between right and wrong and they don't speak untruths to justify their misbehaviors." Barb took a deep breath and wondered if she had spoken too forthrightly.

Negative thoughts started rushing through her mind, but a quick intervention by Dave brought the onslaught to a halt. "Don't doubt yourself, Barbara! Don't even think about having any regrets about what you just said."

"Absolutely not!" agreed Sally. "Let me thank you, Dear, for those powerful statements. It was inspiring! And you brought another perspective of speaking the truth that is very helpful. In essence you are saying that we must practice what we preach! Remember that old phrase. Well, once again it comes in handy.

Tell us, Barb, what happened when you paused? Do you have any idea what triggered the barrage of doubts? I ask because this happens to all of us and your experience may offer clues to our own reactions." Barb understood the merit of these opportunities and gave her response considerable thought.

"Sally that's a wonderful question, and I think there are multiple components that facilitated the shift in mood. I first reacted to the silence, which for me felt like an eternity, but I suspect it was actually a negligible amount of time." Her friends reassured her that very little time had passed. "Well, that confirms my suspicion about misperceiving time. I think when we feel embarrassment or shame that we actually lose our sense of time. On one hand, time seems agonizingly elongated when in reality; it is not. And on the other hand, the brain, which seems to be stunned by the event, is actually over-reacting. In response to the physiological reaction of shame and embarrassment, the brain discharges a rapid firing of thoughts to counteract the impact of the emotional reactions. Unfortunately, the thoughts founded in negativity worsen the effects of the initial emotional response. Because I have a history of negative self-talk, this unhealthy reaction is typical for me. And I dare say this is true for a lot of people." Numerous comments affirmed her last statement.

"Another facet of the negative self-talk was the judgment that instantaneously rose up within me. I believed my comments and my delivery of the comments were harsh. And regrets about that immediately took hold, which led to the feelings of shame and embarrassment." Barb paused for a deep breath. The inner work she was doing was very intense.

"My Friends, your feedback about this would be very helpful. Was my voice or my demeanor harsh? I don't think this is something that I can honestly review, so any feedback you can provide me will be appreciated." The minute Barb asked for feedback her heart sank and the fear surfaced again.

"Okay, Friends, just so you know the truth about me, I just had another negative reaction. So, let me fess up. I am sincere about needing feedback, but I am also afraid to hear it. Dear Ones, I need your help and I trust you, so even though I'm confessing my fears, please be truthful with me. I cannot improve if you are not honest with me."

"Goodness, Barb, you are a model for all of us," exclaimed Annie. "This takes a lot of courage, Dear, and I want you to know that we are all grateful. This is an incredible learning experience. What's happening here is helping all of us, and we will be able to help others because of the work you are now doing. We love you, Dear Heart!" Tears welled up in Barb's eyes and others' as well, but the work continued.

"Well," said Mark, "I'll be glad to give you some feedback, Barb. And I want you to listen carefully, because what I'm about to say is important. So please take one of those deep breaths that you are famous for, and listen up. Your comments were stellar! You weren't pretending to be anyone other than yourself, and that made the conversation real. It didn't feel like a lecture or a presentation; it was just one person talking with other people. Your concern about sounding harsh didn't ring true for me. You were passionate about what you were saying, but your delivery was not harsh. If anything, Barb, there are times when I actually have a hard time hearing you because you tend to speak very softly. I agree with Sally. Your comments were inspirational. And I'm so sorry for those negative voices. I have them, too. They are no fun! Thank you for the strength you've demonstrated tonight."

"I have a thought that is related to Barb's reactions that is very important for all of us who were observing her." I knew my Friend would be particularly concerned about my feedback and wanted to move her focus in another direction. "One of the gifts of Barb's personality is that she is vibrant. Her smile, as we all know, lights up a room. Well, what I witnessed was the change of expression in her face after she briefly paused. It was like the energy inside of her just faded away. When that happened, I knew she had taken a downswing. That reminds me of how important it is to be visually vigilant. Often, we do not maintain visual contact when we are listening to someone, and when that happens we interrupt the fullness of the communication. Fortunately, Dave was on top of this. He knew immediately when Barb shifted and he intervened. That was excellent work, Dave. Thank you for being so present." Dave nodded his acceptance of the compliment.

"Now, Barb, I must check in with you and see how you are reacting to my feedback. Are you hearing anything I said from a negative perspective?"

"No, I'm not: however, it does make me wonder if I need to change something."

"Okay, I thought this might happen, so let me reassure you that you do not need to change anything about who you are. Your demeanor, Barb, speaks the truth about your feelings and your thoughts. Because you are so honest, Dave was able to help you immediately. Don't stop being you, Barb, because you are a winner!" This comment aroused cheers and applause.

"Before we move on, may I make a suggestion?" Everyone was responsive; this was such a good group of people. "Actually, I have two suggestions. First, we've started off with some rather intense work. Barb, you certainly took the brunt of that, but the rest of us also dealt with the intensity of her good work. So, I want all of you to sit quietly for a moment and assess your own needs. How are you doing? Is there anything that you still want to say about this work? Are any of you in distress of any kind that we might need to remedy?" The questions aroused a great deal of consideration. If one were watching carefully, one would have noticed if another was in need. But because of the personal nature of the questions, no one was really observing the outer cues that their friends might be exhibiting. After some time, the group members checked in and all seemed to be well. I decided to ask one more question.

"Okay, Dear Ones, here's another opportunity for growth!" I tried to make light of the situation, but indeed it was an opportunity to enhance our facilitation skills. "Did you happen to notice what was going on with any of your fellow group members during that self-assessment period?" Several groans and self-critical comments circled the group.

"Not to worry Friends! As I said, this is a learning opportunity for facilitating groups. Obviously, the inner work that I just asked you to do was deeply personal. It was an inward exercise and as a result you obeyed the instructions given and paid attention to your own needs. This is exactly what we want to have happen as facilitators. However, as the facilitator you must remember to observe what is going on with the participants of your group. You will be playing the role that Dave just demonstrated.

Because our group has reached a level of trust and cooperation, we are all participants and facilitators during our sessions. For a brief moment, I lost sight of the fact that I was the facilitator of this last exercise. Fortunately, reality returned quickly, and from that point on, I monitored what was going on. My momentary loss of responsibility warranted discussion."

"That's a good reminder," acknowledged Faye. "And another beautiful example of speaking the truth. Thank you for revealing that moment with us. As you spoke of it, I could imagine what it felt like when you remembered that you had momentarily forgotten your task. I felt the sense of guilt moving through me. Whether that was your feeling or mine, I'm not certain, but I know that would have been my reaction. Thank you for demonstrating this learning opportunity; it was very helpful."

"Thank you for that feedback, Faye. Okay folks, the other suggestion I was going to make is in the dining room. Before we start another round of conversation, I urge all of you to reload your plates and glasses." Standing up was refreshing. Although the night was still young, it seemed like the session had been going on for hours. I wondered where our conversation would lead us next. As everyone started reentering the circle, I noticed the Earth candle was not lit. Our first conversation that began in the dining room led us straight into a deep conversation. I had forgotten to honor the Earth.

"Oh, my goodness!" declared Barb. "I forgot to light the altar candle. Excuse me while I fetch a match." She returned in a flash, lit the candle and gave me a wink. "Perhaps it would be appropriate if we started the second phase of our gathering with an energy session for the Earth. Who would like to practice this evening?"

"*May I take the lead, my Friends?*" The arrival of the beloved teacher was a surprise. Even though the additional chair was always available, no one really anticipated his presence at the meeting.

"What a wonderful surprise this is, Old Friend. We are most happy to see you. And of course, you may take the lead." His smile filled the room. Everyone was deeply grateful for his presence.

"*Beloved Friends, so grateful am I to be with you once again. Please join me now as we prepare ourselves to assist the Earth in her time of need. Breathe deeply, recognizing that the powerful healing energy within you is real. Within each of you this energy resides and waits to be of service. No other purpose does it serve than to be available for one who is in need. The healing energy with which all are endowed is the energy of life. As does this energy exist in all, so too does it exist within you. How blessed are we!*

Old Friend, envision the powerful healing energy within you and request its service. So happy is this energy when it can serve another. Know that your willingness to assist the Earth also assists the healing energy within, for each time it is accessed, more powerful it becomes. Breathe deeply, Dear Friends, and make your intentions to the Earth clear. Let her know that we are here to assist her with our particles of pure Source energy.

Inhale again, and when you are ready, release the particle of energy from your form and send it to any location on the Earth that you desire. Your energy is powerful. Release it to the Earth, so she may utilize this powerful gift that will assist her in recovering her full vibrancy. Visualize this, my Friends, and implement your intentions.

Breathe deeply again and feel the Earth's gratitude. Know that you have served her well, and know that she is deeply grateful.

Rest now, Old Friend, and we will do the same.

Return to your respective bodies, and be in peace!"

The activity in the room was evidence of everyone's return. Eyes were focused upon the teacher, who returned the smiles that were embracing him.

"Old Friend, do you have time to visit? We would love your company." My question was selfish. I so hoped he would stay a while.

"My time with you must be brief, for I have other matters that must be attended. But I could not resist stopping by and expressing my gratitude for your advancements. You work hard and you progress rapidly. I hope you are pleased with your progress, for those who watch over you are most definitely pleased. My Friends, you serve well. Thank you for your efforts made and thank you for watching over each other. You are in my hearts at all times. In peace be, Dear Friends."

And then he was gone.

"Okay, folks," Jim was the first to speak up after the beloved teacher's departure. "I need to speak my truth, but honestly, it's embarrassing to do so." Annie watched her husband struggling and wanted to help, but this was an important step for him. She remained silent, and vigilant.

"Truth is…this is difficult to deal with. On the one hand, I am truly grateful that he stopped by. It was so good to see him and to be with him. On the other hand, his visit was so brief that it leaves you feeling… oh, I'm not sure what I'm trying to say." Jim shrugged his shoulders in frustration. He looked toward Annie hoping that she would help and she did.

"I'm sad too, Jimmy. His brief appearance brings up all the heartache again. We became so attached to him during our gatherings and so enjoyed his company, and now, we miss his presence. We miss him! Knowing that he still exists is comforting, but not having time with him is a huge loss." Annie turned to her husband and apologized for not being able to articulate the pain any better than he had. She faced her friends and added, "We just miss him and we wish that he could continue to be with us the way he was before."

"I think you both expressed your feelings with love and sincerity," acknowledged Faye. "And it helped me to understand my own feelings. Like you, I too find these brief appearances a mixture of joy and deep disappointment. And part of me doesn't want to be subjected to this.

But, I also do not want to lose the opportunity of having even a moment with him, because of my fear of feeling the pain of his leaving again. Friends, I think we need to find a way of dealing with this that is healthy and realistic."

"Excellent idea, Faye! Do you have any ideas about that?" Sally invited everyone to respond to the question.

"What comes to mind," I said pensively, "is a message that our Friend has repeated to us numerous times before. All of you will remember how often he reminded us to trust ourselves. This is one of those times when we need to heed this advice.

Is it safe to say that all of us are grieving the loss of his companionship?" Comments indicating this was true circled the room.

"It's hard for Ron and me even though we barely know him," Carolyn interjected. "We had such hopes of spending more time with him, learning from him, and just being with his peaceful and joyful energy. His presence is remarkable and it makes you want more. So, yes, we are very disappointed, and also, it is painful enduring the repeated goodbyes.

Your idea of trusting ourselves is an important one, Sister! We really do have to trust that we can handle these assumed losses. Part of me feels like I need to redefine my understanding of losses."

"I feel the same way, Carolyn." Faye continued with her train of thoughts. "Our Friend has brought us a new perspective of what reality truly is, and I think we need to find a way of adapting to this new information. Obviously, he still exists! And he has repeatedly reminded us that he is near and available. So how do we focus on the truth of this reality without being overwhelmed by his apparent absence? It's only natural that we miss his presence, but somehow we must still be able to rejoice in his unseen presence. Essentially, we need to grieve the loss of the daily interaction that we so enjoyed while remembering that he is available if we need him.

And perhaps we also need to discern what 'needing him' really means."

"This is wonderful!" remarked Mark. "We are having a very meaningful discussion and I think it is important for our own development, but also a very important conversation to be shared with new group members. If we can learn to experience his absence without being stricken by the loss, then maybe the reality that he still exists will more readily come to mind. The flip side of that is by reveling in his eternal existence, maybe we can become more at ease with his absence.

My point is that we must trust ourselves to be able to manage the moments of sadness. It makes no sense to berate oneself for missing an Old Friend. If we could just embrace the moment of sadness without judgment, wouldn't that be a grand improvement?

When I was very young, I witnessed my mother crying because she was missing her mother, who had just recently passed. Her behavior was new to me. Until that moment I don't think I had ever see her cry. It was odd. She explained that her tears were a way of honoring her relationship with her mother, and that it was nothing for me to worry about. She emphasized that it was a good thing. That interaction has always stuck with me. My mother did me a great favor that day. I think that lesson is one that we might wish to incorporate into this situation.

Like all of you, I really miss our Old Friend. There are times when I just want to call him up to discuss some topic of the moment. Isn't that a sweet image? How precious our time with him was! I choose to believe that there will be more wonderful times in the future. I trust that there will be more encounters with him!" Mark's comments were very helpful. I observed my Friends' reactions and knew they were assimilating his experience. The story he shared beautifully illustrated what we were dealing with, and how we could reframe our personal reactions to Our Friend's new schedule.

Barb, who had remained quiet during the talk finally opened up. "This discussion is very important. It never occurred to me that one could healthily miss one's Friends. I just thought separation would be an agonizing experience. But I'm realizing now that separation can be managed. In our world, we have technology to help us with connection regardless of the distances that may separate us. And now, we all know that even those who have passed actually still exist in another form. Of course, we miss the one that was lost, but the fact that our loved ones still exist is a realty that must not be forgotten. And it must be shared with everyone! Too much sadness exists because of the misunderstanding of the death process.

Friends, I am very grateful for this conversation. I am also grateful that Our Friend appeared today, because his visit was the impetus for this important discussion."

"No coincidence," declared Sally and Dave simultaneously. Giggles were muffled but heard nonetheless.

"You two did that on purpose!" Carolyn's accusation brought about more laughter, which was good for the group.

A passage from
Speaking The Truth
(Chapter Twenty-Eight)

"Proceed with loving-kindness, Dear Reader, for this is a journey of creating self in your own image. Address whatever concerns arise without judgment, self-recrimination, or harsh commentary. There is no place for such unkindness in the creative process. Remember, you are a delightful work in progress and you deserve respect and caring attention from you...this is your charge.

Our present chapter offers many thought provoking moments. It began by inciting the reader to speak the truth and then it challenged the authority of such a command. After all, you are in charge of your life choices; you direct your path, no one else.

In gaining awareness of this existential truth, you reclaim an aspect of your identity that sometimes is momentarily lost because of various life circumstances. By prodding you to speak your truth, Speaking The Truth attempts to remind you of your true identity...your true self. It suggests that you are here for a reason, which you are. It implies that it is time for you to awaken to a purposeful reality, which is also true, but it also leaves you with a mystery...a confounding conundrum. Who proposes these ideas of purpose, these notions of urgency? Who tells you what you are to do? Surely a book has no authority to do so, yet Speaking The Truth is here for a reason. Why?

As stated earlier, you are a delightful work in progress. You are in actuality a miracle in the making...a miracle of your own making, and Speaking The Truth is here to assist you in your miraculous transformation. It is your charge to become who you are truly intended to be and the act of speaking the truth is a dynamic part of that transformational process. Speaking the truth actualizes your being; it is an expression of your true self, and each time you grace this opportunity, you emerge more fully whole than you were before. By speaking the truth, you honor self and others and you reveal more of your true self to your self, from which you glean the beauty of your own existence.

You are charged, Dear Reader, to speak the truth. Please hear this message as it is intended. It is not a command or an order attempting to override your own authority; it is a plea for you to awaken to your becoming. You are so much more than you presently realize and speaking the truth will assist you in recognizing, understanding, and actualizing the magnificence of your true self.

Speaking The Truth is not a book of recent origin. It was developed long ago with a very specific reason as its function. Although it may be difficult for you to accept this truth, Speaking The Truth was created deliberately and purposefully to assist you with your burgeoning development, and now you are at last ready for the next phase of your evolutionary process. You are ready! The time is now!

Ah, yes, there is one more point to be made before we continue. There is the matter of who...who developed Speaking The Truth and how did this mysterious 'who' know that you would be in need of such a book?

Who, from long ago, would possibly have known that you would need assistance at this particular time and this particular place and who would have had the foresight to create a book specifically to meet your needs?

Who would have done this for you?"

"Well, my Friends, this evening has been filled with conversations that were unexpected and necessary. And there remains much more for us to do. I have a suggestion, which is open to discussion. The evening has already been long, but there is one task that I think really needs consideration before we end. I would like us to make decisions about our invitation lists for new group members. Do you have enough energy for that now?" Everyone agreed that the task should be addressed, and that the meeting should close after the task was achieved.

In very little time, the names were divvied up, allowing for the next stage to unfold. The group members agreed to begin connecting with potential new members with a goal of completing the process within one week.

"This is so exciting," exclaimed Jill. Turning to her husband, she proclaimed, "We're going to have our own group, Stephen!" Their excitement was obvious, as was true for other group members.

"This is a big step!" asserted Ron. "And yet, it just feels like the next thing to do. No big deal! I wonder if I will still have this matter-of-fact attitude tomorrow."

"Hopefully, we all will, Ron. Your description really is accurate. This is just the next step that needs to be taken. And we can do this!" I observed the optimism that was shared and reveled in it. Such Dear, Dear Friends are these good people.

"And they will meet other good people who will become Dear Friends as well, and soon the day will come when all people on this planet will regard all others as Friends. What a glorious day that will be. There will be peace on Earth." I heard the voice of our Dear Friend internally. His words were inspirational and matter-of-fact at the same time. He believed in us. He believed in all of the people of Earth. *Thank you, Old Friend, for still having trust in us!*

Within minutes my house was returned to its normal state. Furniture back in place, the dining room table cleared and spotless, and the kitchen was sparkling. My Friends lingered briefly on the porch sharing hugs and expressing their goodbyes. It occurred to me that one more act was necessary. "Dear Ones, please join hands just for a moment before you leave. Let us breathe together and express our gratitude for the richness of our relationships. So blessed are we!

And let us also hold Mother Earth in our hearts. Old Friend, we are so grateful for all that you do for us. Please hold on, Dear Friend, we are changing. We're growing up and we are going to correct our misbehaviors. We promise this to you! In peace be, Dear Friend!"

And with that said, the last hugs were exchanged and my Friends headed for their respective homes. As always, I waited for the last wave of the evening. *In peace be, my Friends!*

35

"Carolyn, are you awake?" Ron spoke softly hoping his wife was awake, but not wanting to disturb her if she wasn't.

"Yes, Dear, I am. Are you still feeling unemotional and practical about the next step we are taking today?"

"No, I'm not! You knew this would happen, didn't you?" Carolyn sat up in bed so that she could face her beloved. Then she leaned over to give him a good morning kiss.

"How long have you been awake?" she asked. He confessed that his sleep had been restless since about four in the morning.

"I've been dozing, waking up, and dozing again. Each time I wake up, it feels driven by anxiety. This is silly. There's no reason for having this reaction. We know what we have to do, and we're perfectly capable of contacting the folks on our list. It's going to be a great experience. I'm really looking forward to this. At least, I thought I was. How about you, Hon?"

She replied with a deep breath and then chuckled at herself "Jeepers! Taking deep breaths has become the norm, hasn't it? I guess if we are going to have an addiction, this is a good one." They both giggled about that. "My sleep was filled with dreams, which were all processing my own anxiety about addressing this next task. I think it is normal, Ron. You know our present group organizers were very nervous when we first joined them. Remember how gracious they were…so very careful about being inclusive and hospitable. They were so welcoming and we immediately fell in love with all of them. They were nervous about inviting us to their group but they did it, and they are wonderful role models for us." She gave her husband a big grin, and reassured him that they were up to the task.

"Okay, let's get out of this bed and get started. We both have work to do, and we have phone calls to make during our breaks. So come on. We need to get moving!" Carolyn's energy was the driving force in their relationship. She could work endlessly and still have energy to tackle another task. Ron jumped out of bed to demonstrate his commitment.

A few blocks away, Sally and Dave were already in the garden communing with Mother Earth and reviewing the list of names that required their attention. They agreed to invite two of the couples over for dinner. These were people they had known a long time and who shared similar ideas. They thought this would be a good way to get things rolling. The other three couples they would meet separately.

"I'm excited about this, Sal! We're doing the right thing. The action we're taking may not seem like much, but it's important. People need to know the truth about the Earth and about the healing energy that exists within us. I trust that people will come to the Earth's aid when they know about this. Why wouldn't they? How could anyone decline this opportunity to save another Life Being?"

"I don't think they will decline, Dave. I agree with you, once people know that they can actually do something for the Earth, they will gladly participate. And it feels good to be part of this process. Dave, we are making a difference. I'm so grateful that we've been given this opportunity." The two old friends sat quietly observing the various birds enjoying their backyard.

"It's so wonderful to share this space with our Friends," noted Sally. "Just look at them, Dave. They love gathering here in the garden. They don't seem to mind their differences. They all just get along with one another. They have much to teach us, don't they, Dear?" Her husband nodded in agreement.

"Sally, do you think Barb and her Sister of Choice have discussed their situation yet?"

"I'm not certain, Dear, but if they haven't, it's soon in coming. Why do you ask, Dear?" Sally turned to her husband and waited for a response.

"I just want them to know that we will support whatever decisions are made."

"Are you suggesting that we should broach the topic with them?"

Dave shrugged his shoulders, "No, not at all. I don't want to intrude upon their privacy. But I just want to be available if they needed anything."

"Jimmy, you've done it again," yelled Annie. He was out of hearing range. She reached deeply into her cargo pocket and grabbed the whistle that was necessary for situations like this. The shrill tone echoed throughout the canopy of the forest. Jimmy immediately turned around and scolded himself.

"Goodness, what's wrong with me? I can be so thoughtless." He hurried in Annie's direction red with embarrassment. "So, sorry Dear, I just get lost in my excursions. Thanks for whistling! So grateful you have that; it comes in handy!"

"Not to worry, Dear, I'm fine walking by myself, except when I'm not. I love the alone time and the quiet, until it is no longer needed, and then I long for company. Hope I haven't disrupted your adventure."

"Not at all, Dear! Like you, I enjoy the alone time to do my peeking and seeking, and then I start missing your presence. I prefer to be with you, Annie!"

"Thank you, Jimmy! I prefer you, too. So, show me what you've discovered." He led his beloved to a rabbit's nest carefully situated under a fallen tree.

"Isn't that brilliant? What a perfect location! She must be an incredibly wise rabbit!"

"Aren't they all, Jimmy?" She said incredulously. "After all, rabbits are exceptional in every way, so it only makes sense that they would be extraordinarily bright. How else could such little creatures survive?" Just as she posed the question, a rabbit dashed across the path.

"Ah, she's distracting us from this area." Jim suggested that they oblige the bunny's wishes by moving away from the nest. They continued down the path.

"So, tell me Annie, are we still planning on having our new prospects over at the same time?" Their plans had changed numerous times, since the initial decision was made. At this point neither one of them was exactly clear what the plan was.

"Let's revisit the topic, Dear." She looked at her husband and asked him how he was feeling about the new adventure, now that the task was actually upon them. Annie acknowledged that she had mixed feelings.

"Me too!" he admitted. "Personally, I would rather have a smaller encounter. Let's invite our friends first. That feels more manageable to me. And then, we will have a better idea of how to approach the remaining candidates." Jim's idea suited Annie. She would make the calls when they returned home and he would plan the menu.

"Mark, do you have a minute?" Faye spoke through the closed door hoping that her husband was in a stopping place. She heard him call out to her and hurried through the door. Her excitement was evident. Mark invited her to sit down, but she was too jazzed to do so.

"I have good news! We have a date with two of the couples, and the third will let us know by this evening. I've also reached out to the other folks to set up a separate time with them. I'm feeling very optimistic."

"That is good news! Thank you for reaching out to folks, Faye, and giving me the time to address my work. This doesn't seem fair, but I'm very grateful!"

"It truly isn't a problem, Mark. I don't have any doubt about our partnership in this endeavor. I'm really looking forward to facilitating this new group. It will be odd, not having our usual clan with us, but we can do this. We must do this! Mark, I'm finally realizing how important outreach really is. We need to spread the information, as fast as we can. Of course, we must be thorough with each group we initiate, but our goal must always move toward expansion.

You know I was resistant at first about splitting up our group. It's a wonderful group and we do such good work together. I didn't want to let go of that, but we have to. And we have to model this for these new folks. If we don't keep expanding, then the truth about the Earth and about our ability to heal her will simply stagnate within our small circle of friends. What a tragedy that would be!"

"That's true, Faye. We must always keep this in mind and we must remind each other and our associates about this. Our purpose is to spread this vitally important information, not to sit on it. Faye, we can also utilize the Internet to spread the word more rapidly. I'll do the research on that and keep you posted. We can actually facilitate a group with participants from all parts of the globe. Wouldn't that be a hoot?"

"I am so curious about this, Mark. Where is it going to lead us?" Faye practiced the deep breath exercise as she pondered the possibilities. "Thank goodness, we're together, Love. I wouldn't want to be doing this alone."

"My sentiments exactly!" he responded.

"Jill, I just wanted to let you know that the couples on my list have responded positively to our invitation. Both preferred a Saturday afternoon gig rather than a dinner event. Just wanted to let you know. Check in when you can. Love, Stephen." The text came as no surprise. When Stephen was immersed in his work, texting was the easiest and fastest means of connecting.

"Yes," declared Jill with enthusiasm. *This is working! Yay!* Stephen's message was most encouraging. Her spirits had waned this morning, when she attempted to connect with the people on her list. One call went straight into voicemail with a recorded message saying that the couple were on vacation and would not be returning any calls until they returned. Another call led to a busy signal with no option for leaving a message. Jill found herself getting frustrated, which actually was a cover up for her true feeling, which was disappointment. She decided she was in need of an attitude adjustment and knew that a walk was the best remedy for such a situation.

She walked briskly at first, trying to wear herself out. Over the years, Jill had learned that she was more open to processing ideas when she was somewhat fatigued. Her strong will was tenacious, particularly when it was upset or confounded by some tedious incident, but after a brisk walk, fatigue would overcome the armored self and her Self became more open to other possibilities. *What is going on, Jill? You just made a couple of calls that didn't bring the immediate results that you wanted. Is that any reason to slide into a snit?* She continued to walk as she pondered her questions. "What is going on with me?" she spoke aloud. "I don't see any reason to get bent out of shape about this, Jill, so what's really going on?" She walked further, trying to take in the beauty around her as she did. *Mother Earth, you really are a magnificent Life Being. How did you create all these different species? You're a miracle!* Connecting with nature softened Jill's mood. Without even noticing it, her frustration was quieted and her disappointment had disappeared. She stopped at a fallen tree whose exposed root system measured over eight feet in diameter. It was astounding. Her imagination went wild, as she envisioned this massive root skeleton exhibited in a lovely park for all to see. Jill saw art in everything. She longed to have a warehouse where she could store found objects that could eventually be made into some delightful piece of art. But sometimes she had to reel herself in, because she lost sight that the object in question was serving its purpose exactly where she had found it. And that was the case with this fallen tree with its spectacular spread of roots. "Excuse my manners, Old Tree! You are so beautiful! Even now in your current state, you continue to serve the forest, nourishing it with your remains, which will provide sustenance to the forest bed for years to come. And everyone who passes by will have the same privilege that I just enjoyed, viewing your sculpture of a life well lived. What stories your exposed interconnected roots could tell. What adventures you must have had. How beautiful you are! Thank you, Dear Tree, for all you have done and continue to do. I am so grateful our paths have crossed." Jill continued to admire the tree, no longer encumbered by her earlier frustrations. She started to move on, but instead asked the tree if she could rest upon her trunk. Intuitively, she believed permission had been granted. Sitting on the huge trunk, she could feel the energy that still ran through it. What we regard as death was not true for this tree. The tree still lives, and as Jill had noted, the tree still serves. She lovingly patted the tree that had captured her imagination and her heart.

"Old Tree, I was in a state before we encountered one another. But now, sitting here with you, I have clarity. You see," she continued, "my Friends and I are working on a project to save the Earth. And I really want to do my share, but this morning the action that I attempted to take didn't produce any positive results. First, I was disappointed, then I got frustrated, and that led to grumpiness. It's a silly pattern, but effective sometimes. What really happened had nothing to do with disappointment or frustration. That was just a distraction so I didn't have to face the real truth. Old Tree, I was afraid! I was afraid that I wouldn't be able to follow through with this effort to save the Earth. I was afraid that I would fail her." Jill took a deep breath and the tree seemed to join with her. "Fear is an unpleasant character, a trickster. You know what, Old Tree? Your company soothes me, and strengthens me. I'm not going to succumb to the likes of fear. I won't have it! I'm here for a reason, Old Friend. And I'm going to live fully, which includes helping to save the Earth. We can, you know. Just as you are helping the Earth now in your present state, so too, can we be of service to her. Yes, we can! I can!" Jill placed both of her palms on the tree and sent her love and energy. "Thank you for being here. You've really helped me today! I'll come visit with you again soon."

Jill headed toward the trailhead. When she reached the car, phone service became available. There were two messages in her voicemail. The first was from the couple who were on vacation. They were very interested in meeting, and hoped to be home by the weekend. The other call was from the person with no message service. She replied to the caller ID number and invited me to call back. I did so immediately. The conversation went well and a date for a meeting was scheduled. The mission to save the Earth was on track.

A passage from
Speaking The Truth
(Chapter Twenty-Nine)

"Shall we continue? After all, you are a work in progress and this insinuates that there remains work to be done. Again, we will approach the task through inquiry. We begin with a simple question...how do you feel?

Throughout the pages of this book, you have been challenged in numerous ways. You are charged to speak the truth. You are advised that you are here for a reason. You are alerted to a sense of urgency intimating that immediate action is advisable and you are repeatedly told that seeking within is an alternative of merit. How do you feel about this?

Let us begin with the expressed purpose of Speaking The Truth. How does it make you feel each time you read the title of this book? Please give this question careful consideration and speak your truth truthfully. How do you feel about the persistent reminder emphasized by the book title? Does it cause you to question your truthful ways? Are you surprised by your reactions or your lack of reactions? Are you reacting in ways that are congruent or incongruent with your sense of self? What memories and feelings surface as a result of these repetitive reminders and challenges to speak the truth? Again, the question is presented: how do you feel?

Dear Reader, be kind to yourself. Perhaps it is presumptuous to anticipate that you are experiencing some degree of discomfort from your encounter with *Speaking The Truth*; however, if you truly are a work in progress, the possibility is high that you will indeed experience significant growing pains. Thus, you are gently reminded to be kind to yourself. Evolution naturally summons expansion, and expansion insistently demands self-examination and reflection that inevitably results in information, which when revealed often gives the seeker pause. You are encouraged to pause as often as needed during your seeking expedition, for it is a means of self-care that you deserve and that enables a safer, kinder, and gentler experience. For those of you who attach negative connotations to the idea of pausing, you may wish to revise your definition to one that is more accepting of the truth; i.e. pausing is the transitional period before great transformation.

If you decide to delve deeply into the truths of *Speaking The Truth*, you are charged to do so wisely. In other words, you are asked to take the journey seriously, and in so doing, you must accept responsibility for your self-care. With each new path explored, you must do so carefully, kindly, and without self-reproach. And you must pause frequently for rest, thoughtful assimilation, and compassionate acceptance of your new discoveries. Restoration and rejuvenation are advisable before another path of revelation is embarked upon.

In order to explore the depths of your issues regarding speaking the truth, you must prepare for the journey of a lifetime, because it will be such a journey. You will review the present and the past, childhood through adult experiences, interactions and events, and each investigation will disclose more information about you that will aid you in your quest to become the true self that you are intended to be. Remember you are here to discover your glorious truth, and in so doing, you will find aspects of your present self that you will wish to *refine, finesse, and actualize...and this you will do with loving kindness and extreme gentleness, for your goal is to respond to the question regarding how you feel with the answer, 'I feel fine!'"*

36

"**B**arb! Have I called too early?" The hour was very early, but I wanted to catch my Sister of Choice before she started her walk.

"Your timing is perfect! I'm tying my shoelaces as we speak. What's up with you, Sister?"

"Well, I was wondering if I might join you on your walk today. I don't want to intrude upon your alone time, but if you were open to company, I would love to tag along." Barb's reaction was warmhearted and welcoming. We agreed to connect at the usual meeting place. I grabbed my favorite walking stick and headed out the door. Within minutes, we were giggling like kids and walking arm in arm on the way to the trailhead.

"How are you today?" I asked. "Tell me everything!" Barb laughed and then pointed the authoritative index finger at me.

"No, no, no!" she teased. "You called me! And today, you're going first!" We laughed some more, and in a moment of jocularity, I feigned adulthood and announced that I would accept responsibility for advancing us forward. In appreciation of my outstanding performance, she applauded and cheered me on.

I, of course, began with a very large and loud deep breath. "Dear Heart, there is something that I must discuss with you." Instantly, the mood turned serious. "Barb, I'm grateful that you were available this morning, because there is something on my mind, and in my heart, that I need to share with you." My Friend became very attentive. "You see I have for some time been contemplating the idea of relocating. I haven't discussed this with anyone yet, because the idea was very tentative. Like you, Barb, I feel called to another place. And also like you, I am struggling with the idea of leaving my Family of Friends, my home, my work, etc. This is a huge decision, and one that requires the support of Friends." I chuckled at myself in disbelief of my actions.

"Isn't this interesting?" I continued. "Just look at me, Barb. I'm the image of confusion. In one sentence I express the importance of needing Friends to support me through this process, and in another, I acknowledge how I've been withholding this information from you and other Friends. Isn't this ridiculous?"

"No, it isn't ridiculous at all. I fully comprehend where you are coming from. I must admit that I'm surprised you haven't told me, but I do understand your reservations. This is a big deal! And it's complicated!" Barb started to say something else and then stopped herself. "Sister, my mind is spinning with questions and ideas, and they can all wait. Please just keep talking, and I will respond when you have finished. I am so grateful that you are talking about this."

We grasped hands briefly. The gesture of support was well taken and deeply appreciated. We both simultaneously took a deep breath and I began again. "Truthfully, one of the reasons, I've been reluctant to speak of this is because I do not want to worry my Friends, or cause anyone any heartache. And I know you understand that because you experienced similar feelings before you shared your story with me. Let's face it! We both love our Friends dearly and we appreciate the impact our leaving will have one them. This is not a statement of self-importance. It simply is the truth regarding our relationships. We do not want to hurt our Friends.

I'm also aware that my uncertainty about this has played a major role in my silence. I've been trying to sort through it for quite some time, and I'm still confused. But I'm less afraid of the idea than I was before."

"Afraid?" mused Barb. "Sister, can you say more about that?'"

"Oh, goodness, yes! When this idea first came up, I was shocked. My life is here! And it's a very good life. I love my work. I love my Friends. I love my home. I love my life!

Sister, I could not believe that I was being called to go somewhere else. It didn't make sense to me, and I still battle with it at times, but less so now. I'm still concerned about the logistics of moving, but I've finally opened my heart to the possibilities of what lies ahead.

Bottom line, Friend, I'm a work in progress." A big breath just naturally transpired as I completed my thoughts. It was a relief to share my story with my Sister of Choice. Although she was an incredible intuitive, I was reasonably sure that she was unaware of my situation. It was my time to become the listener. She would need to process this news. And I looked forward to hearing her perspective.

"Good grief!" she exclaimed. "Do you believe this? I am just stunned!" Her reaction was so like her. Exuberant! Curious! Effusive! "Sister, how long have you been dealing with this?"

"Hmm!" My mind tried to recollect when this first began. It seemed like forever and at the same time, just yesterday. The fact that this possibility was on my mind every day made it feel ever-present and recent, but in truth, it was much longer than I remembered. *That's an interesting comment,* I thought to myself, and then the reality slapped me in the face. "This is fascinating, Barb! I think an insight just came into awareness. I was struggling to remember when all this began, and then in a flash, I realized that this transition has been going on since I came into this lifetime." The reality gave me chills. Barb and I shivered at the same time. "I think the inner conversation began over a year ago, Sister. As I said, in the beginning I was very resistant, but over time I became more and more curious and interested; and lately, the idea has been very persistent. I suspect the seed of memory was planted early enough so that I would have plenty of time to get over my fears and reach a point of acceptance."

"And are you at a place of acceptance now?" inquired Barb.

"Well, I think it's fair to say that I am more inclined to take action now than I was before. Many details will need to be addressed, but I have the courage to do that at this point. We are here for a reason, Sister, and we must follow the guidance that directs us. Even if it is unnerving, unsettling, and uprooting! The time is now." We walked in silence for a while, each mulling over the possibilities that might await us.

A passage from
Speaking The Truth
(Chapter Twenty-Nine)

"When Speaking The Truth *was originally developed, it was done knowing that at this time in your life there would be challenges that required your attention. The experience of 'living life' necessarily demands that you have life experiences, which result in ramifications that influence the life experience forever after...or at least until the influences are sufficiently addressed.* Speaking

The Truth provides you with the opportunity to do just that. By reviewing your truthful ways, you will indeed overcome the painful influences still lingering within you, while discovering all the wonderful aspects of your truthful ways that may have faded from your memory. You will invariably find more about you than you presently remember or imagine, and what you discover will delightfully please you.

Now let us return to the original question of this chapter. What is your experience each time you encounter the title of this book? Where does it take you and what questions are aroused by the repetitive reminders to speak the truth?

Begin the journey. As questions surface, write each one down, for these inquiries will direct your research. Pursue each question with diligence and respect, and honor what is discovered. Yes indeed, honor whatever is discovered as an experience of development that brought new information about self and others. Whether the experience was positive or not is irrelevant. Your ability to accept the experience as instrumental in your developmental process is the point of significance. Rather than heralding positives and judging perceived negatives, challenge yourself to review all experiences as gifts that propelled you forward, which will lead you to the greater challenge of accepting all these experiences reviewed as relevant, significant, essential, and beneficial to your expanding nature.

Make your list of questions in response to Speaking The Truth. Proceed carefully, gently, and lovingly. Open your heart to the answers that come forward. Pause frequently, allowing time for rest and recovery during your self-exploration endeavors. Practice accepting what is learned, and extend acceptance to self at all times.

Speaking the truth is a journey of self-actualization. Speaking The Truth is provided to assist you with your journey. As an assistant, it is here for your discretionary use, nothing more. You are the leader of your journey. At all times, you command your development, your transformation, and your actualization into the Self you desire to be. Ponder this please. Many have written of this before; the words that come forward now are not new or better than any other spoken throughout the ages, but at this particular moment in time, you are in need of an encouraging reminder. You are indeed the leader of your journey. You are in charge of your own creative process and you are given free will to explore as you prefer, when you prefer, and how you prefer. You are in charge of your evolutionary development.

Perhaps this is a reality that gives you pause... please do so, for the pauses are yours to discern as well. If this reality takes your breath away, then by all means pause for as long as you deem necessary to absorb and assimilate this ancient, yet newfound truth. You are the creator of the creative process that was gifted you.

Sit with this truth...be with it...and when you are ready, speak the truth about this newly accepted reality that exists within you. And then in the quiet aftermath of expressing this truth, ask yourself, 'How do I feel?' Pause please, and give the question respectful consideration."

Barb was the first to break the silence. "Sister, may I disturb you?" I reassured my Sister of Choice that her presence was never a disturbance. "Thank you, that warms my heart." The ever-pending deep breath was accessed. I knew the question on her mind was finally going to be asked. "You know, Dear Sister, my curiosity cannot control itself indefinitely." We both giggled at the thought. And I invited her to continue. "So tell me," she began. "Do you know where you will be relocating to and when?" Even though I was expecting the question, it took my breath away.

I tried to answer my Friend's question, but hesitated. I tried again, and felt incapable of answering her perfectly reasonable request. *What is going on with me?* Embarrassment washed over me. *Do not make her wait; this is not kind.*

"Dear Friend, I need your help. I want to answer your question, yet something seems to be getting in my way. So for the moment, I must ask for your patience. Your question deserves an answer, Barb, and I do not want to make you feel uncomfortable while I'm searching for an answer.

May we just walk in silence for a brief period of time?" Her response was gracious and loving. *How blessed I am to have this wonderful friend!*

"So am I," responded my Sister of Choice. "Let's just enjoy the walk together."

And this we did. The time alone with my thoughts brought me clarity. I was being called to speak the truth, which was confusing to me, since I didn't really know what the truth was. *Am I being called to move to the City by the Sea, or is this just a fantasy that I'm trying to orchestrate?* I wasn't sure. "How do I speak the truth, when I do not know what the truth is?" My thoughts spoken aloud surprised both my companion and me. "Oh goodness, Barb, please excuse me. My thoughts just leaked out."

"Not to worry, Sister! I understand your confusion. If you asked me the same question, I would be at a loss as well. These are confusing times, but I wonder if they need be. Sometimes, it seems as if I'm creating confusion so that I don't have to make a decision." Her words spoke to me and challenged me.

"Barb, I think that I'm doing the same thing, and your comment has come at just the right time. No coincidence! So here's my truth as of this moment. I believe that I am being called to a place that I have lovingly called the City by the Sea for decades. I fell in love with this seacoast community long ago and never got over it. My first visit created a lasting impression upon me. The connection felt was inexplicable. The setting was so familiar to me, even though I had never been there before. Over time, I came to believe the initial visit was not my first experience to the wonderful City by the Sea. Although I never had clear memories of another lifetime, the vague flashes of information that came to mind convinced me that my love for this setting was founded in another life experience. I've always loved that place, and have often thought of relocating there. But is that what I'm intended to do? I still don't have the answer, but what I do have clarity about at this very moment is that I need to go back and visit that community again. I believe the answer I am seeking will be revealed to me when I walk the beautiful cliff walk overlooking the endless sea." I turned to Barb and gave her a huge hug. Her presence and her exquisite attention had propelled me forward.

"Thank you, Dear Friend. Because of this time together, I feel prepared to take action. I am so grateful for your help." Barb tried to brush my compliment aside. Instead of challenging this old habit, I decided to speak my truth more thoroughly.

"Barb, you do not know the power that lies within you. Your mere presence changes the energy of those with whom you come in contact. I've observed this during our group sessions and I've personally experienced it many times when we've been together. I know this may be difficult for you to hear, but please try to take this in. It's important, my Dear Friend. You have a gift that is really rather remarkable, and this gift is within you for a reason. And you are here for a reason. I know we are going to have many more conversations about what is unfolding for each of us, but for right now, in this very moment, I want you to know that your presence here today mattered. Somehow, you enabled me to have a breakthrough. I don't exactly know how this happened, but when I get home, I'm going to book a flight to the City by the Sea. And it's because of your presence that this has come about. Dear Friend, we must discover who we really are and why we are here. Thank you so much for being in my life!"

A passage from
Speaking The Truth
(Chapter Thirty)

"*Dear Reader, you are charged to speak the truth. Do so joyfully, lovingly, carefully, and wisely. Speaking The Truth is presented to you so that you may open your heart to the reality that you are One of Goodness. This small book is intended to remind each of you that your goodness does indeed exist and this will become abundantly evident as you participate in this literary experience. By engaging with Speaking The Truth, it is highly probable you will experience an in-depth, heartrending review of your present mannerisms, which may lead you to discover behaviors that require modifications. So be it! This is a time for growth and whatever reveals itself will aid you in advancing your evolutionary experience.*

Rest assured, your encounter with this book is not a coincidence. You are here for a reason, as is Speaking The Truth, and the two of you came together at this time to experience an event of a lifetime. Each of you is here to fulfill an aspect of your purposeful existence. You are here to experience an evolutionary leap, and Speaking The Truth is here to propel you forward.

How, you may wonder, can a book have such influence? As your relationship with one another grows, the answer to that question will be self-evident. Each time you are blatantly charged to speak the truth or subtly reminded of the task, the goodness that resides within you will race to the surface and make itself palpably obvious as you grapple to understand the truth about your truthful nature.

Initially, you may be one who adamantly believes you always speak the truth, and hopefully your perception is accurate; however, many of you, through your encounter with Speaking The Truth, may come to recognize a truth about yourself that you never suspected or even imagined. As you objectively examine your present circumstances, you will inevitably remember incidents that challenge your perceptions of self, and one such recollection will lead to another and then to another, resulting in disbelief, dissatisfaction, and disappointment. Please do not be dismayed, but instead hold fast to the truthful reality that you are a person of goodness. Rest assured Dear Reader, if you were not one of goodness, you would not even regard your newfound information worthy of consideration.

Speaking The Truth is indeed here for a reason. It is intended to awaken you to the truly remarkable being that you really are. It is here to remind you that you are a work in progress, who is continuously growing, changing, morphing, and becoming more than you were the moment before. Speaking The Truth is here to help you expand your definition of self by increasing your awareness and understanding of who you really are, thereby assisting you in becoming who you truly wish to be.

With hope that you will excel to your fullest potential, Speaking The Truth challenges you to refine your truthful intentions, and in so doing, you will gain greater clarity about your present abilities and disabilities regarding this vitally important aspect of your unique and wondrous evolutionary event called life. Revel in your abilities, have compassion for your disabilities, trust yourself, and move forward. You are here for a reason, Dear Reader, including fully comprehending your True Self, which cannot be achieved without careful study of your truthful nature. You are a glorious being just waiting to be discovered. By examining your truthful ways, the potential for True Self actualization is not only possible, it is highly probable."

The doorbell summoned me from the kitchen. Glancing at the clock, as I headed to the front door, I assumed the early arrival was my Sister of Choice. She stood there with a beautiful bouquet of flowers and tears streaming down her cheeks. I pulled her into the house and we hugged as if years, not hours, had passed.

"I will miss you so much," she whispered.

"We don't know what's going to happen, Sister, so let's not think the worst. And let's enjoy every moment that we have together now." She agreed. The tears started to dry as we moved towards the kitchen in search of a vase.

"Did you get your flight booked?" she asked. I nodded and told her that I would email the information to her. She offered to give me a ride to the airport, which I gladly accepted.

"We have much more to discuss, Dear One. Moves don't happen over night, and we still have responsibilities here that we must fulfill."

"Yes, we do! And by the way, my folks have already replied to our invitation and are eager to meet with us. We just need to confirm date and time." We both cheered! We were both back in the present and ready to greet our friends, who were crossing the front porch as we spoke. Barb opened the door just as the doorbell rang.

The entire gang arrived at the same time, as usual. No treats were brought because this was intended to be a brief check-in meeting. We exchanged greetings and hugs on the way to the living room, which was ready for occupancy. Barb lit the Earth candle for the evening, and we all settled into our usual positions. Then eyes closed, and we simultaneously fell silent.

Eventually, Sally softly suggested that I facilitate an energy session for the Earth. And the inspired deep breath was enjoyed by all.

"My Dear Friends, it is so good to be in your presence. Tonight I wish to begin our session in a different manner. I ask that you continue to enjoy and deepen the peaceful state that you have already initiated. Simply do what you do so well. Move to that Sacred Space that awaits you, and be with the energy of All That Is. Let us relax in that place now. Breathe deeply and find that which awaits you there." I practiced as I facilitated and tried to gauge my needs with the needs of the others. At a point when it seemed appropriate, I suggested an exercise to enhance our connection. "Dear Friends, how blessed we are to share these wonderful friendships. While we sit together in this Circle of Friendship, let us practice commanding our energy. I will begin this exercise by sending some of my energy to the person to my right, and Sally, I ask you to do the same, and Dave you do the same, and everyone here send energy to the person who is sitting to the right of you. Let's practice this, my Friends. Activate your intentions and send your energy to the person to your right. And at the same time, allow yourself to receive the energy coming from the person sitting to your left. Breathe in this new energy and send your energy to the other. Allow yourself to experience this. Feel the energy welling up inside of you, and be grateful for the gift from your Friend. Marvel at this experience." Enjoying this moment, I paused, giving my Friends time to indulge in the new exercise.

"And now, Dear Ones, with our renewed energy generating within us, envision a place that is particularly precious to you. See that setting in your mind's eye, and imagine yourself there in that location. And once you feel solidly there, release your robust energy and offer it to the Earth. Be there with your favorite place as it receives your gift of life. Feel the joy of this moment and express gratitude for the opportunity to participate in this act of love and connection." Once again, I waited for what seemed the appropriate time to continue our experience.

"And now, Dear Friends, offer your farewells to this favorite location and gently return to your respective bodies. Return safely and settle back here in this setting that awaits you. Ground yourself back into the present.

My Friends, thank you for your generosity and your commitment to the Earth. I am so grateful our paths have crossed. In peace be." Time passed and eventually movement could be heard, the sign that brought us back to reality.

"What a delightful experience!" Several others echoed Dave's compliment. "We've not done that exercise before," he noted. "I thoroughly enjoyed it. I found it interesting and effective. Sally, I definitely felt the energy you were sending me. What a hoot! I'm curious, did anyone else have a similar reaction?"

"Oh yes!" Annie's response was energized as always. "It was a remarkable experience. Did you just think that up on the spur of the moment, or have you done it before in other groups?" I confessed that it was not a spontaneous action and shared that it was an exercise that I found very informative and useful.

Faye leaned forward in her chair and also expressed her fascination with the exercise. "It certainly was effective. I'm stunned by the sense of invigoration that I felt. This was an extremely important experience. Thank you, Dear, for introducing that into our session. You do a lovely job facilitating these energy transfusions. You must really love your work!" I acknowledged that I did, and added that it was deeply satisfying.

"We must do that again," asserted Jill. "That was really powerful, and I want to learn how to facilitate that exercise before we start our new group." Everyone agreed with her suggestion.

"Well, my Friends, I will be happy to facilitate that exercise again, and now, since Jill brought up the issue of our new groups, who wants to lead with an update?"

The check-ins went by very quickly. Everyone had positive responses to their invitations and dates scheduled for initial meetings. The energy of the group was very high.

"My Friends, this is such good news. We have taken action and we are moving forward!" Everyone cheered. Although we were reluctant to part, we all agreed that we should. Our hugs were longer than usual. We didn't want to say goodbye. I took the lead. "My Dear Friends, we will see each other again very soon. Rest in knowing that we are connected through our hearts and we are but a breath away. Goodnight, my Friends!"

As always, I remained on the porch waiting for the last wave to be seen. It was a good meeting that would lead to many more in the future.

"I know you're here, my Friend! I hope you and your companions are pleased. The next step has been taken. We are advancing forward!"

A passage from
Speaking The Truth
(Chapter Thirty-One)

"*You are charged, Dear Reader, to speak the truth and you are approached because you are one who is capable of meeting the task. If you accept the invitation to explore your truthful nature, you will indeed be one of the leaders that assists with the transformation that awaits the good people of Earth.*

Please understand the purpose of this invitation. It is a request for your assistance. You are approached because you are One of Goodness and one of extreme capability, and because of these attributes you were selected to address one of humankind's most delicate complexities. The good people of Earth are on the brink of great change. Even though few are aware of this situation, it is unfolding nonetheless, and those such as you, who are called to assist, are desperately needed and essential for a successful transition. By accepting the invitation extended through Speaking The Truth, you take the lead in a comprehensive study that will aid in understanding humankind's complicated state of mind. As stated numerous times before, it is no coincidence that you and this book crossed paths. It was indeed intended, because your participation is critically important. You are one who has reached a level of maturity, sincerity, and wisdom that enables you to effectively participate in a project targeting humankind's truthful nature. You are exquisitely ready for this endeavor; however, your participation will most likely have ramifications, which will momentarily cause disruption in your life, but ultimately will foster relief, release, and freedom from the multitudes of misunderstandings that burden the populace of Earth."

~ 37 ~

The time has come, Dear Reader, for you to learn more about who you really are. You've heard many of these messages before. You are more than you appear to be! You are here for a reason! And there are, of course, many more messages that speak of your truth. The point of all these messages is the same. Each one attempts to awaken you, to impress upon you that your presence in existence is significant. Think about this, Dear Friend, and please accept this truth about yourself.

Another message that you've encountered repeatedly states, "The Time is Now!" That one really captures one's attention. First, you are told that you are more than you appear to be, and then you are told that you are here for a reason, and if that isn't stressful enough, you are then faced with the emphatic statement that the time is now! Time for what?

Dear Reader, I hope that you are one who feels excitement, curiosity, and anticipation when you encounter these messages of truth, rather than frustration. If the last is your present reaction, please just take a deep breath. Nothing is being asked of you at this time other than a moment more of your attention.

Why do you think so much is written about these messages? Countless resources repeat these declarations of the significance of your existence. Why would anybody create such an elaborate scheme to get your attention? Why indeed?

A passage from
Speaking The Truth
(Chapter Thirty-One)

"*Presently there are many misunderstandings existing on the human plane, which have resulted in great heartache and losses all across the globe. Many of these unfortunate misunderstandings are so old that those of today have no awareness of the original events or possess any factual information about these aged events, yet the stories of the past extend from one generation to another, perpetuating the unfounded and often inadequately conveyed stories that have become ill-fated truths. So remarkably sad this is for the dear people of Earth; never were you intended to live with such regrettable circumstances. The Hearts of the Universe ache for you and extend fellowship by offering you access to a text that was purposefully prepared on your behalf. Speaking The Truth was composed with heartfelt sincerity to assist you with the far-reaching and extensive ramifications of ancient misunderstandings.*

Unknown to the indigenous inhabitants of the time, a most unusual evolutionary event transpired that profoundly altered the development of the human species. Because many, if not all, of these inhabitants originated from a fear-based perspective, the developmental processes of humankind's ancestors naturally evolved to prepare them to anticipate and expect the advent of more fearful situations, which significantly influenced the neurological and physiological development of the evolving human species. What developed in innocence evolved to have a lasting detrimental impact on all the peoples of your planet. Members of the Universal Family weep for the Children of Earth."

A passage from
The Time is Now
(Chapter Ten)

*"As the Ones of Ancient Age grew
in their awareness of the complexities of the galactic event,
more in knowingness were they of the disaster about to occur.
And in this knowingness,
All agreed an action required being taken.
So odd was this circumstance that
the Ones of Ancient Age were in amazement.*

How could this have happened?
Why did it happen?
Who could have been responsible for such a happening?
The questions posed more questions,
which posed more,
and from all these questions,
only one answer appeared true.
Natural circumstances."

Dear Reader, what would it be like to simply accept that you are indeed here for a reason? How would your life change if you chose to make that decision? Ponder this for a moment or two or more. It is a significant decision to pursue, so you may choose to give it a considerable amount of thought. And while you contemplate this decision, watch where your thoughts take you. Do they move in a direction of hopeful optimism or do they lead you to scenarios of doubts, suspicion, and/or fears. Wherever your thoughts take you, simply make a notation of it for further consideration. In the meantime, you probably have other matters that need your attention. Do what is needed. Attend your day as you must and return later in the day to review the notes that you just took.

A passage from
Speaking The Truth
(Chapter Thirty-One)

"Speaking The Truth was designed to assist with the evolutionary mishap that transpired on the planet Earth so very long ago. When the situation actually began, and how, is actually no longer relevant; however, recognition that a problem does indeed exist is pertinent to rectifying the unfortunate dilemma."

A passage from
The Time is Now
(Chapter Eleven)

"No blame there is to lay on any one.
No responsibility does any one bear for this.
No reason other than natural circumstances
could be determined."

You may be wondering, Dear Reader, why our story appears to have changed its focus. Well, appearances as we all know, can sometimes be deceiving. In truth the focus has not changed. *Seeking Our Humanity* is still focused upon its reason for being. The mission of this book is to assist the people of Earth by providing information regarding the truth of our existence. This includes truthful information about our relationships with the Life Being Earth, as well as the truth about our relationships with one another.

In keeping with that mission, Dear Reader, you are personally invited to become a participant in the project to save the Earth. Your assistance in this act of generosity is needed. Hopefully, you are already participating in activities on her behalf; if not, we hope this series of books (*Seeking Our Humanity* trilogy and *The Answer* trilogy) have encouraged you to do so. Our planet is in great need of assistance. It is because of this reality that the effort to personally connect with you is being made. Throughout this series, opportunities for aiding the Earth have been suggested and demonstrated with the help of our amiable characters. Though presented in fictional format, the truths revealed throughout this story are real. The Life Being Earth is in a crisis situation. This is her reality and ours, and evidence of this truth is abundant for everyone to see. One does not need to fall victim to misinformation or become involved in debates that prolong the suffering of our planet. Look about you, Dear Reader. Climate changes are evidence. Raging fires destroying millions of acres are evidence. Garbage islands in the Earth's oceans are evidence. Pollution of the atmosphere is evidence. Deforestation, and all its tragic ramifications, is evidence.

Decisions regarding the wellness of the planet cannot be left in the hands of those who benefit from her destruction. Those who believe that our current mistreatment of the Earth can continue without severe consequences are foolhardy, and their irresponsible acts cannot be tolerated any longer. Their intentions, founded in greed and selfishness, are unconscionable. Any action taken that jeopardizes the planet also jeopardizes the people residing upon the planet. Those who believe that they can survive the aftermath of her declining health are mistaken. Dear Reader, the people of Earth must stand up for the Earth. Many practical and sustainable methods are being created and implemented to assist the Earth. These good intentions are noteworthy and must continue to make advancement, but those solutions are not enough.

As you learned from reading *Seeking Our Humanity*, the people of Earth must change their negative behaviors. And this can be done by an act of choice. We can choose to become the people we are intended to be. We can choose to be people of goodness, who honor, respect, and care for one another. This is who we really are! For reasons we no longer remember, we lost sight of our humanity. Dear Reader, please listen with the ears of your heart: we momentarily lost sight of our humanity, but we have not lost our humanity. The spark that birthed goodness within us still lives. This, too, is a truth that we must remember and accept. Goodness fosters acceptance of all others, and all kinds, and this ability still lives within us. The people of Earth are people of goodness. Remember this, Dear Reader, and accept that this is who you really are.

Soon, with your help, others will also remember who they really are, and once again, we will recognize that we are all Brothers and Sisters, who came from the original Source energy and who still are of the same energy. We are all One, and soon—one by one—this truth will be remembered, and as our woundedness heals, so will the wounds of the Earth.

A passage from
Speaking The Truth
(Chapter Thirty-One)

"In an effort to allay any more misunderstandings, Speaking The Truth is brought forward to assist you in addressing your uniquely personal aspect of the problem humankind is presently facing. Although this is definitely a planetary predicament, each of you will inevitably be responsible for managing your own facet of the issue. Because each individual's personal development is distinctively and exceptionally singular, any successful corrective procedures ultimately require the person's cooperation and commitment. Fortunately, the possibilities for positive outcomes are high."

A passage from
The Time is Now
(Chapter Twelve)

*"And in knowing of the natural circumstances
of the tragic situation,
All experienced deep compassion for the Ones
afflicted by the circumstances."*

"Speaking The Truth is intended to assist all the good peoples of Earth with the challenges that lie before you. Each of you must pursue command over your present complicated state of mind, and this book was purposely designed to help you with one profoundly significant aspect of the human mind that demands attention. In truth, all aspects of the human mind demand attention; however, by learning to command the mind as it specifically relates to speaking the truth, your ability

to command other aspects of your beautiful mind will progress more rapidly.

With great consideration and heartfelt concern, Speaking The Truth was developed on your behalf. Each of you who presently reads these pages is acutely aware that the mind is an incredible asset, and at times, it is an equally remarkable handicap. The sweet beauty of the human mind is its versatility. Once it accepts the need for change, it is adaptable; however, convincing the mind that it is in need of an adjustment can often be a bit of challenge. Speaking The Truth can effectively assist the mind in recognizing its need for improvement. By facing one of humankind's vulnerabilities, the ability to speak the truth, not only will you advance in your own development, but your mind will also gain greater understanding of its present precarious nature as it relates to receiving, interpreting, and conveying the truth.

Initially, facing the truth about your truthful ways may be quite challenging, for you may encounter a very fearful mind that is reluctant to address this issue. If this happens, simply quiet your mind and proceed with compassionate understanding. It is inevitable that exploration of one's truthful ways will uncover incidents that reveal less than truthful tendencies, and this will challenge one's identity; however, by reviewing these events, one can reclaim personal dignity and move forward.

This is the opportunity that Speaking The Truth affords each of you who accepts the challenge of speaking the truth. By objectively examining how, when, and if you speak the truth, the benefits gained will be life-altering, for once you are aware of your strengths and inadequacies, you will be motivated to change, and your motivation will enable you to command your mind's cooperation. Although the mind often seems to have a mind of its own, in actuality, the mind is simply waiting for your leadership. Will you accept the responsibility of commanding your mind by providing it with discipline?

Committing to speak the truth truthfully demands persistence, patience, discipline, and compassion, which are attributes that will assist you in commanding your mind with loving-kindness; and when consistently managed, the beautiful, but often-wayward mind will learn to respond in like manner.

Dear Reader, by now you are acutely aware of the need for speaking the truth, but are you aware of the influence your efforts will have on your planet? Imagine the changes you are now making by refining your abilities to speak truthfully...and visualize how these changes will alter your encounters with other people. And then imagine how your renewed way of being will potentially change how others are choosing to be as well. This is but a beginning...imagine the chain reaction of one person effectively changing self, thereby, positively affecting others and on, and on, and on. Imagine this, and believe the possibility for far-reaching change is realistic, because it is.

And while you are imagining such wonders, envision one more marvelous prospect. Just imagine how life on this beautiful planet might be if everyone spoke the truth at all times. There would be no need for distrust. Misunderstandings would be resolved easily, for there would be no doubts about the other person's veracity. Think of this and expand the notion to friends, family, business, politics, religions, race, personal preferences, and more. How different the world might be, if everyone spoke the truth truthfully and consistently.

As you can see, the potential for global changes begins with just one. You are one, Dear Reader, with the power to create great change by simply recognizing your own truthful nature. By examining all the wonderful ways in which you spread the truth about you and by accepting responsibility for sustaining a practice of speaking truthfully, you are one who can affect great change, which will influence others to do the same. Your outreach is unlimited...and your participation is needed.

You are 'one' who can successfully alter the course of your own existence if you choose to do so. Will you? Consider this carefully please, for you are contemplating the future of your present way of being. Reflect upon your thoughts, ideas, and concerns about taking this action, because it is, after all, life changing. It is not a

decision to be taken lightly, for in truth, this is a matter
of discernment, which must be examined within and by
the heart. Listen carefully with the ears of your heart as
you ponder this next step in your evolutionary walk."

Dear Reader, as you walked the path with our fictional characters, perhaps you recognized yourself in many of the scenarios that were presented. At first, you may have been taken aback by the kindness demonstrated among this group of friends. You may have thought they were too nice, and not representative of the real world. Unfortunately, your perceptions are more accurate than not; however, as you probably already realized, the story was presented in this way for a reason. What would the world be like if we all treated one another in this manner? Isn't it sad that a story might be judged negatively because its characters were too nice?

Hopefully, the mannerisms of this wonderful cast became commonplace for you. Hopefully, they eventually opened your heart to new possibilities in engaging with others, and also in making decisions about behaving responsibly towards others, including the Earth. The conflicts each one experienced as they faced their respective vulnerabilities were not fictional. Those examples were as real as any that might be encountered in one's present life. Wasn't it wonderful that these individuals could address their issues without judgment from another? Wasn't it wonderful to experience the support that they received from those around them? They were not alone. Even during those times when they felt they were alone, they learned that they were not. If this is a truth that you have not yet faced, Dear Reader, it will behoove you to do so soon. It is so much easier living in awareness that you are not alone. The truth exists whether you believe it or not, but accepting it will bring you great peace and satisfaction.

Dear Reader, the invitation to participate in an act of generosity still stands. The Earth needs your help. Humankind needs your help. As you seek to discover who you really are, you will uncover many answers, for we are all here for more than one reason. Please consider the possibility that one of your reasons for being is to be an instrument of good will for self, for others, for the Earth, and for the future of all humankind. Perhaps that sounds lofty and unmanageable, but it isn't. You are more than you appear to be, Dear Reader. Your willingness to be a person of goodness will help change the energy of an entire civilization of people. As you change, so too will another. So little is this to ask, and so influential your assistance will be.

You are more than you appear to be! Remember this for yourself! And know it is true for others as well. We have the ability to change ourselves, and we have the ability to heal the Earth. Trust yourself, Dear Reader. The action of one person matters. Your decision to participate in saving the Earth is the next step in your evolutionary leap that will alter the course of humankind.

A passage from
Speaking The Truth
(Chapter Thirty-Two)

"And so, we have come full circle. Speaking The Truth was developed to assist the good peoples of Earth with your evolutionary continuance; and now you, Dear Reader, are invited to continue the process. Through this literary encounter, the developers of this small book have spoken truthfully regarding the importance of speaking the truth in hopes that you and your brothers and sisters will recognize how essential this act of goodness is to the welfare of your planet and all its inhabitants.

By accepting responsibility for speaking the truth, you accept the task of reviewing your present behaviors. Please do so with joyful optimism, rather than apprehension. You are, after all, a remarkable work in progress, who deserves respect and admiration. Honor yourself please, as you command this precious personal project. By accepting authority of evaluating your truthful ways, you are privileged to discern how you wish to improve your present state of being. Do so lovingly, compassionately, and kindly.

Speaking The Truth is intended to nudge you forward on this leg of your journey because you are ready to advance into the next phase of your development.

You, Dear Reader, are a being of exquisite beauty with marvelous potential and unlimited possibilities. In each phase of your development, you possess the privilege of self-refinement. You discern what to address, when, and how, and then you have the honor of assessing your progress and making any alterations you wish before moving on to the next action of your desired restructuring. You are in charge of your creative process at all times.

Speaking The Truth was created for a reason. You are here for a reason. Is it not interesting that the two of you came together at this particular time? Obviously, this is no coincidence. Those who developed Speaking The Truth were, and remain, highly devoted to the well being of humankind. Hopefully humankind also shares this regard for their fellow beings.

In an attempt to promote good will and demonstrate their sincerity to their Friends of Earth, the creators of Speaking The Truth designed this literary tool to be a means of connection and communication through which messages of truth could be presented. The truth regarding the need for speaking the truth has been delivered.

The act of speaking the truth is the pathway to global change. No other act of goodness can be more influential than this simple, but profound, way of being. Speaking the truth is more than a mere acknowledgement of preference; it is a life choice that must be skillfully adopted and practiced. By consistently speaking the truth, trust is established, and when trust exists, acceptance follows. For far too long, the peoples of Earth have neither trusted nor accepted others of perceived differences, and because of this, great misunderstandings have transpired and festered for millennia. This cannot continue. There is no longer time for these misunderstandings. The cruelty that rises from the distrust that plagues your planet must be addressed, and the only way this objective can be gained is by speaking the truth to one another at all times. This is not the time to pretend to speak the truth nor is it the time to confuse partial truths as acceptable truths. The time is now, Dear Friends. Speaking the truth must become your way of being...your continuance depends upon it. Speaking The Truth brings you this message of truth bluntly and truthfully.

In recent days you have continued to engage with this small book that charges you to speak the truth. Hopefully, the benefits of doing so are already evident and inspire you to continue. Old Friend, your assistance is needed. If you participate in this Project of Heartfelt Truthfulness, your actions will influence all that you encounter, and because of your role as a Speaker of the Truth, the energy of your wonderful planet will change for the better. Truth is an accelerating energy that facilitates trust within, and extends outward to others. With trust, relationships can heal, mend, and begin anew. Old misunderstandings can be laid to rest as the need for grudges, revenge, and endless dissatisfaction finally abates. Just as anger and its ramifications perpetuate more of the same, so too can speaking the truth enable heartfelt connection and acceptance as a steadfast and lasting way of being.

Speaking The Truth does indeed challenge each of you to examine your present relationship with speaking the truth. Do you not owe this to yourself? Are you not one who desires to evolve more fully and who wishes to have a positive influence during this remarkable experience called life? The time is now. The means to effectively create change within you and about you is yours to command...it is your privilege, your Gift of Free Will. Will you not accept the challenge, Dear Reader, and become the marvelous person you are already evolving to be? This challenge merely encourages you to accelerate your evolutionary process. You are already a gift to humankind, and your potential for helping humankind is unlimited. This is literally the opportunity of a lifetime. Please accept it for self and for the sake of humanity.

All is well, Dear Readers. In peace be."

More to Come!

An Expression of Gratitude

Dear Reader,

Your participation in reading this series of books gives us hope. Although you will never know how many individuals have participated in the creation of the Seeking Our Humanity trilogy, it is accurate to say that many more than you can possibly imagine have played a role in its development. Every person, who has ever lived on the Life Being Earth, has indeed participated. We have all lived on this beautiful planet numerous times before and most of us have participated in actions that were not in her best interest. We have worried about her throughout the ages, but our worriment did not result in any positive changes being made on her behalf. Our concerns grew as her decline became more and more evident. Attempts were made to advise the inhabitants of her situation, but our efforts were unsuccessful. Repeated efforts resulted in little to no improvements.

We are most sorry that our attempts to aid the Earth and the people of Earth have not come to fruition. We believed that our descendants would eventually discard our negligent behaviors and become more attentive to and appreciative of the Life Being that has provided us with residence and abundance throughout the expansive lifetime of the human species. Unfortunately, that did not happen, and now, we, all of humankind must accept responsibility for righting the terrible wrong that we have perpetrated upon another Life Being. In more recent times, awareness of the Earth's situation has become so blatantly obvious that denial is no longer an option. What is, is, and what must be done, must be done now!

Old Friends, we are all responsible. Those of the present, those of the recent past, and those who came long before any of today can remember are all responsible for the Earth's declining health. We must face the truth that our actions are the cause of her poor health, and we must take appropriate steps to assist her recovery process. There is no longer time for debates about this reality, and no time will be wasted addressing those who are in denial or those who are intentionally destroying the planet for their selfish economic gains. Those who refuse to participate are offered an open invitation to join the cause to save the Earth. They are needed and we hope that they will change their minds and their actions. However, action on behalf of the Earth will not be delayed by the misguided ways of those who show no compassion, respect, or concern for the planet.

The Mission to Save the Earth is upon us. For those of you who have already read the first two books of the Seeking Our Humanity series, you are aware of its purpose and its intentions. There are many ways of helping the Earth, and many are already pursuing activities to assist her. Thank goodness for those who are already participating.

Dear Readers, there is more that can be and must be done. Again, if you have already read these books, you are acutely aware of this. We must seek our humanity! And we must change! We must improve our manners for the sake of ourselves and for all of humanity. We must improve our behaviors for the sake of the Earth. Our Home is in jeopardy because we have not taken care of her. Nor are we taking care of our Brothers and Sisters with whom we co-exist upon this planet. And let us not forget all the other remarkable Beings who also live on the Earth. It is time for the people of Earth to realize and accept that we are not the only essential Beings on this Life Being that has taken care of us since we came into existence.

It is time for us to grow up and to become the good people we are intended to be. We are all in need of improvement. And obviously, we need guidance in regards to relational issues. There is much for us to do, Dear Readers, and as you now know, we are capable of addressing the tasks that must be done. We can improve ourselves. We can become kinder people, who actually practice taking care of one another. And we can also take care of our wonderful Home, the Earth, who so desperately needs our assistance. We can save the Earth! As you have learned from reading these books, we have the means to save the planet! We must trust this truth and we must practice our reality. We are capable of saving the Earth!

Will you participate? Dear Reader, please say yes! In the final book of the Seeking Our Humanity trilogy, more information regarding our individual and collective roles in saving the Earth will be shared. Our efforts are essential to her recovery and our tasks are so easily managed.

We can do this, Dear Reader! Please join the Mission to Save the Earth. Share everything you have already learned with others. Practice sending energy to the Earth daily, and invite others to join with you when you can. Join a group that is already in progress or start your own group. What is asked of us is so little. We have the ability to heal the Earth. We *must accept this. We must actively practice sending her healing energy on a regular basis. And we must change our ways. We must become Beings of Loving Kindness. Please consider the previous statement as an invitation. Please join others who are already moving in this direction. Please become a Person of Loving Kindness.*

In peace be, Dear Reader!

Those Who Came Before

Printed in the United States
By Bookmasters